KENSINGTON BOOKS are published by

Kensington Publishing Corp.
119 West 40th Street
New York, NY 10018

First Printing: September 2020
ISBN-13: 978-1-4967-2355-0
ISBN-10: 1-4967-2355-4

ISBN-13: 978-1-4967-2356-7 (eBook)
ISBN-10: 1-4967-2356-2 (eBook)

10 9 8 7 6 5 4 3 2 1

Printed in the United States of America

GOURD TO
DEATH

Also by Kirsten Weiss

Pies Before Guys

Pie Hard

Bleeding Tarts

The Quiche and the Dead

GOURD TO DEATH

Kirsten Weiss

KENSINGTON BOOK
KENSINGTON PUBLISHING
www.kensingtonbooks.com

*Thank you to Mandy Morton-Gregory
for coming up with* Gourd to Death *as a title!*

Chapter One

All it takes is one bad impulse.

In my defense, I'd had a late night of sexy aliens and pitched battles. So my impulse control was low this morning.

But.

Going along to get it over with was still a bad impulse. I was ditching work on what could be the busiest day of the year. My staff needed me. Pie Town needed me.

The thuds of hammers and clangs of metal on metal drifted through the predawn fog. It shrouded Main Street, hiding the workers setting up festival stalls.

Yawning, I jammed my hands into the pockets of my winter-weight *Pie or Die* hoodie and hesitated guiltily in the doorway of my pie shop. The scent of baking pumpkin escaped Pie Town's open door and wafted into the chill October air.

"I can only take ten minutes," I said through another jaw-cracking yawn. Pie Town was still a start-up, and I loved it like a helicopter mom. But I couldn't ruin Charlene's fun. "Then I need to get back to the prep work."

My elderly piecrust specialist, Charlene McCree, pulled the ends of her snowy hair from her jacket collar. "You work twelve-hour days, Val. No one's going to hold it against you if you take a peek. You won't get much chance when the festival's in full swing. Relax."

In a blur of purple knit jacket, she surged past me and onto the brick sidewalk. We'd both been up until midnight watching a *Stargate* marathon, and it was now five A.M. Charlene claimed old people didn't need much sleep. I felt like deep-fried death.

"Last year," she said, "the winning pumpkin was over two thousand pounds. This year's would have been bigger if those arms dealers hadn't chiseled in on the action."

Hiding a smile, I let Pie Town's glass door swing shut behind us. Charlene might be the best piecrust maker on the NorCal coast, but I'd learned the hard way not to encourage her. "You know San Adrian isn't infested with gun runners."

But Saint Adrian was the patron saint of weapons dealers. The town's true crime, however, was starting a pumpkin festival to rival San Nicholas's. Farmers now had to choose between San Adrian and us. Our tiny beach town was feeling the pinch.

"You don't understand pumpkin festivals," she said darkly.

I yawned again and flipped up my hood, orange and black for Halloween.

Ray, a gamer who usually staked out one of Pie Town's corner tables, waved from beneath a festival booth's green awning. "Hey, Val! Hi, Charlene."

We ambled to his booth, one of dozens lining the middle of the street.

"Nice socks," he said.

Charlene pointed the toe of one of her high-tops, modeling the striped purple and black socks. They nipped at the hems of her matching purple leggings. "Thanks. I got 'em on sale."

I eyed the comic art hanging against the green canvas walls. "You drew these?" I asked, impressed.

Ray's round face flushed. His freckles darkened. "Well—"

His girlfriend, Henrietta, popped up from behind a stack of boxes. "They're all his. Isn't he amazing?" She tugged down her shapeless army-green sweatshirt. It matched the color of the knit cap flattening her sandy hair. "I told him he should work as an artist for a gaming company, but he's set on being an engineer."

Charlene squinted at a cartoon woman in a chain-mail bikini. "Looks uncomfortable. If I was going into battle, I'd want a lot more covered than those two—"

"It all looks great," I interrupted. Age had dulled Charlene's verbal restraint. If my friend had ever had any.

"And don't worry," Ray said. "I'll be sure to send customers into Pie Town."

Charlene laughed hollowly. "I don't think that will be a problem. This is my fiftieth pumpkin festival. They're wolves, I tell you. Wolves!"

Henrietta's eyes twinkled. "Werewolves?"

"Don't encourage her." I groaned, knowing it was too late. Charlene was convinced a local pastor was a werewolf. She also believed Bigfoot roamed the woods, ghost jaguars stalked the streets, and UFOs buzzed the California coast.

"I was speaking metaphorically," Charlene said, surprising me. "I meant the festivalgoers act like wolves. Though if I were you, I'd keep an eye on Pastor Hiller around the full moon. Not that he can help himself, poor man. Once you've been bitten, it's all over."

And there it was. "It was great seeing you two," I said. "We're going to check out those giant pumpkins, and then I'm going back to work." We'd left my staff slaving in the kitchen while Charlene and I scoped out the massive gourds. I wasn't sure how much pie we'd sell today, during the prefestival, but I didn't want to take any risks.

"Speak for yourself," Charlene said. "I've already completed my piecrust quota. See ya, Ray. Bye, Henrietta."

We ambled two booths down, and I stopped in front of another green awning. A sign hanging from the top read HEIDI'S HEALTH AND FITNESS. Directly beneath it: SUGAR KILLS.

I sighed. "Seriously? At a pumpkin festival?" The gym had moved in next to Pie Town earlier this year. Its owner and I had a loathe-hate relationship.

Heidi turned to me, and her blond brows drew downward. "Sugar kills every day of the year."

"So does life," Charlene said.

Heidi tossed her ponytail. "Your life might be longer and more fulfilling if it included better diet and exercise."

"I'm fit as a fiddle." Charlene thumped her chest and coughed alarmingly. "I eat what I want, and I stop when I'm full. And I have a drink every night for my heart. It's the French way."

Heidi's lip curled. "We're offering blood pressure and other fitness testing. You should stop by." She eyed me critically. "Especially you."

My eyes narrowed. I was *not* overweight.

She smoothed the front of her sleek and sporty Heidi's Health and Fitness microfiber jacket. "You're going to have some competition at the pie-making contest."

"I'm not competing, I'm a judge." Not that judging didn't have its own pressures. My boyfriend, Gordon Carmichael, had entered the pie contest. He was a good cook, and it was a blind tasting, but still. And then there was old Mrs. Thistleblossom. She won every year, and I was supercurious about her pumpkin pie. What was her secret? I'd never met the woman, but I'd heard she was over a hundred.

"I don't think it's fair for a professional baker to be in the contest," Heidi said.

I pulled my mouth into a tight smile. "Which is why I'm not in it. I'm a judge."

"Well, *I* am entering a sugar-free pumpkin pie," Heidi said. "It's low-fat and low calorie."

What was the point? But I decided to be the better woman and refrained from comment.

Charlene had no such compunction. "And low taste?" She squinted at my hips. "Though some of us *could* stand to lose a little weight."

"There's nothing wrong with my weight," I said to Charlene. And to Heidi, "And don't tell me anything more. This is a blind tasting."

"Most of the calories are in the crust anyway," Heidi said, "so it will be crust-free."

"What!" Charlene flared. "Then it will definitely be taste-free."

"But now," I ground out, "I can't judge your pie, because it won't be a blind tasting." And I was going to have to report this to the head judge. San Nicholas took its pie contest deadly serious.

"Your style of pies is on its way out," Heidi said. "Tastes are changing. Most Californians find all that sweet food gross."

"Enjoy the festival," I caroled and walked on, hoping Charlene would follow. My pies on the way out. *As if!* Had she even met a Silicon Valley engineer?

In the stall beside Heidi's, a handsome, harried-looking man unpacked boxes of reading glasses. White earbud cords dangled from his ears and faded to invisibility against his white lab coat.

Charlene nodded to the man in the optometry stall. "Morning, Tristan."

He looked up and tugged an earbud free. "Oh. Hi!"

"What are you listening to?" Charlene asked.

He blushed. "*Oklahoma!*" he said in a sultry Southern drawl. I might be a one-man gal, but I could listen to him talk all day.

Charlene chuckled benignly. "You and your show tunes."

"Have you seen Kara—I mean, Dr. Levant?" he asked.

We shook our heads.

"Why?" Charlene asked.

"She was going to help me set up for the prefestival." He motioned around the half-built stall. "I guess she got hung up at the haunted house."

"What's she doing there?" Charlene asked.

"Her husband, Elon, is volunteering there today."

"If we see her," I said, "we'll let her know you're looking for her."

Charlene and I continued on.

"I hear Heidi broke up with that fellow who left you at the altar," she said in a casual tone.

"Mark didn't leave me— Wait, really?" I *had* been dumped, though not at the altar. We'd been months away from the wedding. But Mark had done me a favor. Now I had a new and improved boyfriend, Detective Gordon Carmichael of the SNPD. My chest tingled at the thought.

I glanced over my shoulder. The booths and Pie Town had vanished into the mist, and I shivered. "We need to hurry," I said. "I really should get back soon."

"Those pies will bake without you. Your first pumpkin festival is a special event. There's something magical about a giant pumpkin. Maybe it's because they're not supposed to be that big. But when you see them, anything seems possible. You can believe a pumpkin might actually turn into a coach."

I grimaced. "Or the Pie Town staff might riot."

"Never."

Charlene was right. The people who worked at Pie Town were easygoing and professional. That was exactly why I didn't want to take advantage.

"I don't know what you're worried about," she continued. "With the street closed off to cars for the decorating today, business is going to be slow."

I jammed my hands into the pockets of my hoodie. "I hope not." The festival didn't officially begin until tomorrow. But for years, Friday had been its unofficial start. It gave stores and vendors an early jump on sales while the street was closed to traffic.

The stalls petered out. We strolled down the deserted road, our footsteps echoing. The dark shapes of low, nineteenth-century brick buildings wavered in the fog.

I squinted into the dense mist. "How far is it?" The fog this morning was deliciously thick and spooky, like something out of a Sam Spade novel.

"Why? Are you tired? Maybe Heidi was right about you needing more exercise."

"I get plenty of exercise." Sort of.

"Hold on." Charlene vanished into the mist.

I waited, inhaling the crisp, October air. It smelled faintly of salt, and I smiled. Though I'd come to San Nicholas for all the wrong reasons, I couldn't imagine living anywhere else.

Charlene returned with a newspaper and inhaled gustily. "The ink is still warm." She rustled the paper. "The festival's on the front page. Pie Town might get a mention."

We walked on. Strands of damp hay lay scattered on the pavement.

"We must be getting close," I said.

Bloblike shapes rose before us. A gust of wind parted the fog, strands spiraling like phantoms across the street.

Farm trucks with monster pumpkins in their beds blocked our way.

"Whoa," I said, stunned.

Pale and misshapen, the pumpkins lay on their flattest sides. They were big enough for me to crawl inside.

These could make a lot of pumpkin pies, if they were sweet enough. "What varieties are those?"

Charlene made a face. "They're cultivated from Mammoth pumpkins. I don't think you'd want to eat them."

I nodded. My personal favorite for pumpkin pies were Jarrahdales, but Blue Hubbards were good too, and Cinderellas . . . The latter not only tasted delicious, but they looked like something out of a fairy tale.

I studied the forklift that would be used for the weighing.

"Uh-oh." Charlene pointed at a monster pumpkin lying on the road in front of the forklift. A crack shaped like a lightning bolt shot down its side. Orange pumpkin guts oozed from the ruined shell. "They say it's not a party unless something gets broken, but someone's just lost the contest."

I frowned, edging closer. "Do you think the owner knows? How did it fall onto the ground?" These monsters couldn't exactly roll.

Charlene hissed, fists clenching. "Sabotage. It must have been one of those rats from San Adrian. Or maybe another pumpkin farmer. I told you people turn into wolves. You think this pumpkin festival is all fun and games. But it's serious business. And—"

I gasped, stopping short, and grasped the sleeve of her soft jacket. "Charlene." Hand shaking, I pointed to the broken pumpkin.

Two white tennis shoes stuck out from beneath the monstrous gourd.

Chapter Two

I gaped at the pumpkin. At the silent, still form beneath. My brain whirled, nausea making its way up my throat. My college first-aid class hadn't covered this.

Chill mist spattered my face, shocking me into speech. "Is he . . . ?"

Knees cracking, Charlene squatted beside the pumpkin. "I found a hand. And a wrist. And no pulse. She's cold."

I swayed. "It's a woman? Are you sure?" I fumbled in my hoodie's pocket for my phone.

"It's a woman's hand and a woman's watch."

I called 9-1-1.

"Nine-one-one, what is your emergency?" a female dispatcher asked, and my shoulders loosened. I recognized the voice.

"Helen? It's Val. I'm on Main Street near the giant pumpkins. Someone's hurt or dead."

"Dead," Charlene shouted, still crouching.

"Is this a Halloween prank?" Helen asked.

"I wish it were." My voice cracked. "There's a woman under one of the giant pumpkins."

"How—? It's all right, the police and fire are on their way. You stay there."

I pocketed the phone. "I can't believe this," I whispered, horrified.

"San Adrian's gone too far this time," Charlene said. "Help me up."

I grasped her gnarled hand and pulled her to standing.

"Any idea who she is?" Charlene asked.

"How could I? All that's sticking out is one arm and her shoes." I frowned. Why did those shoes look familiar? Professional white sneakers, like a baker would wear, with extra support and softness for people who stand all day. And the shoelaces . . .

I bent closer, squinting. Multicolored eyeglasses decorated the laces. I sucked in a breath. "It's the eye doctor, Dr. Levant. She must have come to help Tristan with their stall this morning and . . ."

"And what? A two-thousand-pound pumpkin rolled off its truck and squashed her? No pun intended."

I straightened, staring at the white shoes. "This doesn't make sense. How did she get under that pumpkin? I mean, they're not exactly mobile." The killer pumpkin had a flat base, like the other monster gourds.

"The only way to move those bad boys is with a forklift," Charlene agreed. She nodded toward the nearby equipment, and the thick canvas straps hanging from the lift.

"But forklifts are slow and noisy," I said slowly. "Who would stand around and wait for a pumpkin to be dropped on them?"

Sirens wailed, faint and muffled by the mist.

Charlene jammed her hands into the pockets of her knit jacket. "Maybe she was unconscious when the pumpkin dropped?"

"Or dead." Bile burned my throat, and I swallowed

hard. I really hoped she'd been dead when that thing had landed on her.

"Think Tristan did it?" she asked.

My insides quivered. I glanced into the fog swirling on Main Street. "He was nearby, setting up that booth. Tristan probably knew she'd be here. They were business partners. Still, he took an awful chance. Anyone could have seen them."

"Could they have?" Charlene turned. The stall builders hadn't reached this section of Main Street yet, and the fog was thick and obscuring.

"Maybe not," I admitted.

"Look for clues," she said.

"We shouldn't disturb the . . . crime scene."

Charlene was bent, running her fingers through the loose hay on the ground.

So much for not leaving DNA evidence. I walked around the forklift. The key was still in the ignition. That explained how someone had moved the pumpkin. Hopefully Gordon would be able to get fingerprints.

"See a purse?" Charlene called.

"No," I said. "Do you?"

A gray sedan, light flashing on its roof, glided to a stop beside us. Six-feet-two inches of muscular, square-jawed detective slowly unfolded himself from the car.

In spite of everything, my heart lifted. The sudden joie de vivre was totally inappropriate for a crime scene, but the detective and I *were* dating.

"Val." Gordon strode to me and grasped my shoulders. His gaze bored into mine, and my breath caught. "Are you okay?"

I nodded, unable to speak. There was something steadying about his solid presence, even if it was a little rumpled at this early hour. I smoothed the lapel of his blue suit jacket.

"Helen told me it was you on the phone, but I didn't want to believe it." He took in the pumpkin, the shoes. Swiftly, he released me and knelt beside the pumpkin, checking the woman's pulse. He shook his head. "You were right. She's gone. Did you touch anything?"

"I took her pulse," Charlene said.

"I didn't touch anything," I said. "What are you doing here?"

"I'm the town's only detective, remember? Of course, dispatch called me. Plus, Helen knows we're dating." He stood. "What brought you two down here?"

I dug my fisted hands into my hoodie pockets, my shoulders folding inward for warmth. "We were here early, baking, and we thought it would be a good chance to check out the giant pumpkins—"

"*I* thought it would be," Charlene said.

"—while it was quiet," I finished.

"Did you see anyone else?" he asked.

I shook my head. "Not here, but Dr. Cannon is setting up the optometry booth next to Heidi's Health and Fitness."

"Dr. Cannon?" he asked.

"Her shoelaces," I said. "I think the person under the pumpkin is Dr. Levant, the eye doctor."

"She and Cannon are partners." Charlene flipped up the collar of her purple jacket. "I mean, they *were* partners."

"Let's not jump ahead of ourselves," he said. "A pair of shoelaces isn't exactly an identification, though those do look like doctor's shoes."

A slick-looking black-and-white SUV roared to a halt beside the sedan. A uniformed officer leapt from the car and ran to the rear passenger side, opening the door for Chief Shaw.

Gordon's handsome face tightened. "Why don't you two go back to Pie Town?" he said. "I'll come by to take your statements later."

"Belay that order." Tall, ferret-faced, and slender, Chief Shaw stepped from the car.

I blinked. I'd never seen the chief in a tracksuit before.

He gripped a newspaper in his hands and scowled.

Gordon's jaw clenched. "Sir?"

Shaw braced his hands on his narrow hips. "Helen called. She said there was a body at the pumpkin festival. What have we got?"

"A woman beneath one of the giant pumpkins," Gordon said. "Her body appears to have been placed there deliberately."

"Homicide?"

"A suspicious death," Gordon corrected.

The chief arched a thin, dark brow. "Not so particular about your terms for the press, are you, GC?"

Gordon's brow wrinkled. "Sir?"

"Any idea who the victim is, *hero?*"

"What?" Gordon asked.

I looked at Charlene. She shrugged. *I* thought Gordon was heroic, but that sort of went with the boyfriend territory.

Chief Shaw walked around the pumpkin and stopped to gape at the woman's feet. "Good God, I'd know those laces anywhere. That's Elon's wife, Dr. Levant."

"Possibly, sir. We need the crime scene techs to remove the pumpkin, and then we can be sure—"

"Poor Elon. I've got to . . ." The chief shook himself. "You're off the case, GC."

Gordon's nostrils flared. "Sir, I believe I can—"

"And I believe you've got a conflict of interest."

"Val and Charlene found the body together," Gordon said. "They've got nothing to do with—"

The chief slapped the newspaper onto Gordon's chest. "You and the doctor were competitors." He glared at me.

Charlene whistled.

She held her own newspaper open and read aloud. "'Of special interest to San Nicholas locals is this year's pumpkin pie bake-off. Local hero Detective Gordon Carmichael will be facing off against newcomer ophthalmologist Kara Levant. But the local favorite still remains beloved San Nicholas centenarian, Mrs. Amelia Thistleblossom.' Hmph!"

My stomach shriveled roughly to the size of an olallieberry. But not even Shaw could think Gordon would kill someone over a bake-off. He was just steamed about the article calling Gordon a local hero.

Chief Shaw's chin quivered. "What do you have to say for yourself, GC?"

I winced. Gordon *hated* being called GC, because at the station it stood for Grumpy Cop. There was a certain lovable truth to the moniker, at least when it came to police work.

Gordon's expression hardened. "I wasn't aware of the other contestants—"

"Not about the other contestants! About this shameless self-aggrandizement. Hero of San Nicholas?"

"I did not speak with that reporter, sir. I'd no idea—"

"You're off the case."

Gordon's hands clenched. "Yes, sir," he ground out.

No, no, no. Shaw couldn't take Gordon off the case for something so trivial.

"And you two." The chief pointed the rolled newspaper at Charlene and me. "Get out of my crime scene."

Charlene took one step to the left and ducked her head behind her newspaper.

Chief Shaw glared at Gordon. "Some surfers are on that tech millionaire's beach again, GC. Go and deal with it."

"Yes, sir." Gordon strode to his sedan. He turned and caught my eye, and something softened in his gaze. Gordon slid into the car, and he did not slam the door. He made a slow turn, cruising sedately down the street.

I watched his taillights vanish into the fog.

"This is ridiculous," I hissed to Charlene.

"What are you two gawking at?" Chief Shaw shouted. "Shoo! Get out of here!"

Charlene raised her head above the paper and her blue eyes crackled. "Shoo? Did you *shoo* me, young man? I'm a senior citizen!"

He stepped backward and bumped into the giant pumpkin.

"Hey! Get off my pumpkin! What did you do?" A middle-aged man with a face like Father Christmas and a voice like a cement mixer strode angrily toward us. He rolled up the cuffs of his plaid shirt. His dark, curling hair was streaked with gray.

My stomach bottomed. I knew that man. He was my assistant manager, Petronella's father, Petros Scala. This being a small town, Gordon was related to the Scala family.

"What's going on here?" Petros asked.

"This is a crime scene," Shaw said. "Stop where you are."

"A crime . . ." The farmer's gaze traversed the pumpkin, and his mouth sagged. "My pumpkin!"

Shaw puffed out his chest and smoothed the front of his tracksuit jacket. "That's your pumpkin?"

"Of course, it's my pumpkin," Petros snapped. "Why isn't it in its truck bed, Shaw?"

"That's what we'd like to know," Charlene said.

"That's enough from you two." Shaw whirled to face us. "Get out of here."

The newcomer's face flushed red. "And it's cracked! It's ruined! Those rats!"

"What rats?" Shaw asked.

"San Adrian," he said. "They told me I'd regret it if I didn't bring my pumpkin to their festival. But how could I? I live here, and I had a real shot at winning . . ." He trailed off, finally noticing the body beneath. The blood drained from his face.

"San Nicholas's first chance in a decade for its own prizewinner." Shaw rubbed his angular chin.

I raised my hand. "Uh, do you really think San Adrian would kill a woman just to get back at you for not entering their stupid contest?"

"It's not stupid," Charlene said. "It's killing our festival."

"You don't understand pumpkin festivals," Shaw said. "They make people nuts."

I really wished people would stop telling me I didn't understand pumpkin festivals. What was there to understand?

Two more police cars rolled to a halt beside Shaw's.

"Is she . . . ?" Petros swallowed. "Oh my God. There's got to be something we can do."

Shaw clapped his hand on the farmer's shoulder and squeezed. "Your pumpkin's a murder weapon, Petros. A little less indignation and a little more information is in order."

The farmer shot us a pleading look. "Will you tell Petronella—"

"What are you two still doing here?" Shaw roared at us. "Get gone before I arrest you!"

"With pleasure." Charlene raised her chin and stalked into the swirling fog.

I scurried after her, down Main Street. Murder. Gordon

in trouble. Petros's pumpkin as a murder weapon. This was awful.

"We're in big trouble if Shaw takes over the case," Charlene said. "And you know he's going to. He and Dr. Levant's husband are golfing buddies. You know how he protects his friends."

Actually, I didn't. But I also knew Shaw wasn't the best investigator. "You don't think he'll protect Mr. Levant? This is murder."

"I think he'll see what he wants to see," Charlene said. "And that this will be too high profile for Shaw to resist."

"Dr. Levant is high profile?"

"No, but murder by pumpkin will be national news." Charlene's lips whitened. "It's sacrilege."

I understood what she meant. There was something contemptuous in crushing a person beneath a pumpkin. The act had been . . . wicked, depraved, profane. The nausea returned to clutch at my throat. Who could have done this?

"It's the age-old battle between politics and compe-tence," she continued. "Gordon doesn't stand a chance. With him gone, this murder investigation will be the loser."

She was right, of course. But I was less worried about Gordon not running the case than him becoming a suspect. He was related to the Scalas, and Chief Shaw seemed to have a grudge.

"You do know why your detective left the San Francisco PD?" she asked.

"To be closer to his aging parents."

"Because he stinks at playing the political game. Here in San Nicholas, Gordon's always been able to move inves-tigations forward behind the scenes. But what if he can't this time?"

He had to. There was a killer loose in San Nicholas. "I'm calling Gordon," I said.

He picked up on the first ring. "Val."

"Gordon, are you all right? I can't believe this."

"I was the first investigating officer on the scene. But instead of solving a murder, I'm about to explain to a spoiled tech billionaire for the eighth time that he bought a home with public access to the beach, and the public includes surfers."

I scrubbed a hand across my face. "Oh, Gordon . . ." I didn't know what to say.

He blew out his breath. "It's good to hear your voice. And I'm fine."

Liar. "There's something you should know," I said. "The pumpkin, it belonged to your uncle."

Gordon swore long and colorfully. "Shaw's going to have a field day."

"The crack disqualifies Petros from the contest," I said. "That's an incentive *not* to use his own pumpkin as a murder weapon."

He muttered another curse. His voice was muffled but faint. "Put that surfboard down!"

"Gordon?"

"Sorry," he said, "can I call you later?"

"Of co—"

He hung up.

"Everything all right?" Charlene jammed the newspaper beneath one arm.

"I don't think so," I said. "But Shaw can't really believe this pumpkin business was all a way to sabotage the San Nicholas festival, or that Gordon might kill someone over a pie contest."

"Can't he?" Charlene's voice deepened. "Can't he? San Nicholas has two things over the new San Adrian festival."

She ticked them off on her fingers. "Point one: history. Point two: a bigger prize for the winning pumpkin."

"What is the prize?"

"Forty thousand dollars."

Whoa. That was serious money and enough to inspire murder. Though I didn't believe a crazed pumpkin farmer was behind the murder, my stomach butter-churned. "This is awful. Gordon's off the case. Shaw's either going to go in the wrong direction and blame San Adrian, or he'll arrest Petros, because it was his pumpkin." That would destroy Petronella. Arresting Gordon would destroy me, but I couldn't believe Shaw was serious about the pie contest as a motive. "We've got to do something."

"Ha. You know what we've got to do."

I sighed. *Yeah.* I had to prep for the pumpkin festival, judge a bake-off, manage Pie Town through the busiest weekend of the year . . . and solve a murder.

Chapter Three

Charlene paced Pie Town's gleaming kitchen, pleasantly warm from the giant pie oven. "And then he had the nerve to tell me to shoo!"

My goth assistant manager, Petronella, turned a shade paler. "You're sure it was my father's pumpkin?" She reached behind her and untied her apron strings. "Val, can I—?"

"Of course," I said. "Go. Your dad was talking to Chief Shaw by the giant pumpkins when we left." I knew the helpless worry for a parent all too well.

Whipping off her gloves and hairnet, her black, spiky hair standing on end, Petronella hurried from the kitchen.

My assistant, Abril, paused beside the dough flattener. She clutched a round of dough in her hands, her brown eyes serious. "You don't think Mr. Scala is in trouble, do you?" Her thick, inky hair strained her hairnet. She looked a little like a mushroom, willowy at the base with a puff of white on top.

"I think whoever wrecked his prize pumpkin is in for it," Charlene said. "That was his baby. You know how nutty those pumpkin growers get."

"Chief Shaw seemed to be treating him as a witness," I said cautiously, "not a suspect." *So far*.

Abril's slim shoulders relaxed. "That's a relief."

We returned to the business of baking, and Charlene vanished into the flour-work room.

At six, I lugged the coffee urn to the counter and turned the sign in the window to OPEN. Watching the glass door for Petronella, I set a tray of day-old, half-price hand pies on the counter.

I did a final check of the dining area. The glass counter, where pies would go, was crystal clear. The pink tables and booths were spotless, the black-and-white floor blemish-free.

Everything was perfect, but I couldn't shake my worry. I knotted my hands in my pink apron. *Was* Mr. Scala in trouble with Shaw? I glanced up at the pink neon sign with its big smiley face beside the clock. TURN YOUR FROWN UPSIDE DOWN AT PIE TOWN. My logo didn't have its usual, cheering effect. I hurried into the warm kitchen, scented with baking pies.

At a central, butcher-block table, Abril arranged dough leaves and pumpkins on top of a pumpkin pie.

I paused to watch. She was better at pie decorating than me, and I was glad to let her do it. This was prefestival crunch time. Pie Town needed to shine, and our decorated pies were powerhouse sellers.

The bell over the front door jingled, and I peeked through the order window.

Senior citizens strolled into the dining area. Drawing back, I shook my head at Abril, and she grimaced. No Petronella.

The swinging kitchen door creaked open. One of our elderly regulars, Tally-Wally, poked his drink-reddened nose through. "Hey, Val. You've got a visitor."

"Thanks."

He nodded and vanished into the dining area.

I peeled off my gloves. Wiping my damp hands in my apron, I strode from the kitchen.

Chief Shaw stood beside the counter. He frowned down at the half-price hand pies, and my insides lurched.

I could guess what he wanted, and I forced a smile. "Chief Shaw, hi. How can I help you?"

Heads swiveled along the counter. The kaffeeklatsch at the center tables went quiet.

"A word alone," Shaw said, "if you don't mind?"

"Sure." I glanced at our goggling regulars. "We can talk in the back."

I led him behind the counter and to my spartan office. Metal desk. Metal shelves lined with boxes of supplies. An outdated desktop computer. All my decorating instincts had gone into the kitchen and dining areas.

The VA calendar fluttered as he shut the door.

"Are you ready for the fund-raiser?" the chief asked.

I blinked, wrong-footed by the unexpected question. Maybe he was a better investigator than I'd thought. But I nodded. During the festival tomorrow, local cops would act as waitstaff at Pie Town. All their tips would go to the Police Athletic League, a children's charity. It would be easy for the cops; people ordered at the counter, so all they had to do was bring pies to the tables. The coffee was usually self-serve, but I suspected the cops would give top-ups to work the tip angle. It had been Gordon's idea, and I loved him more for it.

"Good." The chief pulled his phone from the inside pocket of his tracksuit and tapped the screen. "I'm speaking with Val Harris. It is six-thirty A.M. on Friday, the thirteenth of October. I'm recording this conversation," he said to me as an aside. "Tell me about finding the body."

I explained about our walk down Main Street and the gruesome discovery.

"And you say you abandoned your kitchen just to look at pumpkins?" His hawkish eyes narrowed.

I stepped backward, my hip bumping the metal desk. "It was only supposed to be a quick peek."

"Of course, this isn't the first body you've found."

"Well. No. But—"

"Nor is it the first time I've had to remove Detective Carmichael from a case."

I didn't respond. Gordon didn't need me arguing on his behalf.

"I'd say it was quite a coincidence," he continued. "You find bodies and Detective Carmichael miraculously catches their killers." His eyes narrowed. "But I don't believe in coincidence. Do you believe in coincidence, Ms. Harris?"

"Well, I mean, no, probably not, but it really was—"

"Collusion?"

I gulped. "What?"

"You setting 'em up, and Carmichael knocking them down?"

"Setting what up?" What was he saying? That I was murdering people so Gordon could solve the crimes?

He tapped his phone and slipped it into his jacket's inside pocket. "I'll talk to Mrs. McCree now. Send her in. And I want you, the both of you, to stay out of my case, or I'll arrest you for interfering."

Stunned, I tottered from the office and into the kitchen.

At the butcher-block work island, Abril looked up from ladling apple filling into pie pastry. "Is everything okay?"

"He wants to ask Charlene some questions." My voice cracked like an egg, and I hurried into the flour-work room.

The air conditioner hummed, ensuring the butter stayed at the right temperature for optimal dough. I shivered in my *Pie or Die* T-shirt.

Charlene set a ball of dough on a metal rack. "That's the last of 'em." She turned to me. "What's wrong?"

I glanced at the slowly closing metal door. "I think Chief Shaw just accused me of being a serial killer."

She laughed. "Tell me another one."

The door clanged shut, and I started.

"I'm serious," I said. "He implied—" But that was too crazy. Had I heard right? I *must* have misunderstood. "I'm not sure what he was saying."

"Chief Shaw probably didn't know either."

"And he wants to talk to you now."

"Oh, does he?" She untied her apron from around her purple knit tunic and flung it onto the long table in the center of the room. Flour poofed into the air.

Charlene sailed past me and into the kitchen.

"He's in my office," I called after her.

"Huh!" She slammed out the kitchen's swinging door.

Abril stared, frozen. "He thinks you're a serial killer?"

Maybe I shouldn't have said that until *after* the door had shut. "Well, I'm not."

"I know you're not."

"I must have misunderstood. I mean, he was just trying to shake me." But why? I was a witness, not a suspect. Just because I'd found . . .

Hmm. I *had* stumbled across quite a few bodies in the last year.

I had to call Gordon, and I fumbled in my apron pocket for my phone. But what if that was what Shaw wanted?

What if he'd bugged our phones?

What if I'd tipped over the butter-knife edge into paranoia?

I hesitated, phone in hand.

The phone vibrated, and I started.

It was a text from my brother, Doran: ON MY WAY. DON'T PANIC.

In spite of the day's horror, my heart warmed. Doran was the half brother I hadn't known I'd had until last summer. He'd moved here to try his hand at graphic design in nearby Silicon Valley. But how had he found out about the murder so quickly? Or that I'd been involved?

It was a little weird.

"What is it?" Abril asked, anxiety threading her voice. "Is something else wrong?"

"No, it's Doran. He's coming to Pie Town."

She smiled. Abril and Doran had recently started dating. I hoped he didn't screw it up. Good pie makers were hard to find.

"Did you tell him about the murder?" I asked.

"No." She adjusted the net over her coal-black hair. "Why?"

"Nothing, I guess." Uneasy, I slid a pie into the oven's rotating racks.

Thirty minutes later, Charlene stormed into the kitchen. Her white ringlets trembled with indignation. "Shaw's an idiot. He accused me, *me,* of being behind murders in San Nicholas going back to Prohibition. I wasn't even alive then!"

"If he's focused on us," I said, "he's never going to figure out who really killed—was it Dr. Levant?"

"It was," she said heavily.

Abril gasped. "She's my little brother's eye doctor."

"Shaw was none too happy when he realized he'd let

that slip," Charlene said. "And with your detective off the case, you know what this means."

I nodded, glum. The Baker Street Bakers really were back in business.

Charlene and I had inherited an armchair detecting club. And since Charlene was involved, we spent less time in armchairs and more on actual footwork. But I thought we were getting pretty good at it. We'd helped solve several murder cases. Gordon was even pushing me to get a private investigator's license and make it legal. But there was no way I could study for a license. I was too busy building the best pie shop on the NorCal coast.

"Let's get started." Charlene bustled from the kitchen.

"Wait, I can't—" I said to the swinging door, and rubbed my arms. "Don't worry," I told Abril. "I'm not leaving you alone again today." Especially since Petronella still hadn't returned. I hoped she was okay.

I hurried into the dining area. The Friday morning kaffeeklatsch had dragged the center tables together. The ladies sat gossiping, their aging faces beaming with good humor. My other elderly regulars lined the counter. An elfin, white-haired lady in a flowered gray dress sat alone in a corner booth nursing a cup of coffee. She adjusted her spectacles and squinted into the cup, her nose wrinkling.

I hadn't seen her in Pie Town before. Was she all right alone? I shook myself. *Don't assume senior citizens are charity cases.* My piecrust specialist had disabused me of that notion quickly enough.

From behind the counter, Charlene glowered at her archnemesis, Marla Van Helsing.

Marla, dressed like a *Dynasty* villain in a red silk blouse and black slacks, smiled. She turned up the collar of her black sequined jacket. "I hear you've found another body,

Charlene." The elderly platinum blonde curled her lips and waved a negligent hand. Diamonds flashed, glittering beneath the pendant lamps. "You're like a rat to garbage when it comes to corpses."

Charlene glanced toward the front windows. "What are you doing out of your coffin, Marla? It's past sunrise."

"Just checking out my so-called competition for the pumpkin race."

Uh-oh. I hadn't known Charlene planned to enter the pumpkin race. This could be trouble.

"So, it's true?" Tally-Wally braced a long arm on the counter and rubbed his drink-reddened nose.

"Yes," Charlene said. "Marla is a vampire."

"I am not!"

I squinted. In her red and black outfit, Marla did look like a sequined Countess Dracula.

"I meant," he said, "was Dr. Levant really killed?"

"It looks that way," I said. "Did you know her?"

Tally-Wally pulled a pair of reading glasses from the pocket of his stained jacket. "She did my glasses."

"And my cataracts," his best friend, Graham, said from beside him. Graham was as round as Tally-Wally was tall. He crumpled his checked cap in his fist. "Terrible. Must have been the spouse."

"Or the business partner," Tally-Wally said. "I never liked that Cannon fellow."

"The killer could have been anyone who knew Dr. Levant," Marla said. "She was not an easy woman."

"Don't be catty," Charlene said. "Just because she refused to get you those fancy, colored contact lenses—"

Marla's grip tightened on her mug. "I needed them for my show." Marla ran a lifestyle channel on YouTube. It was a bone of contention, since all Charlene had was Twitter.

Marla fluffed her hair and sighed. "But she said my eyes were too delicate."

"Too—"

"Charlene," I said warningly, and she subsided, grumbling.

"I suppose your ridiculous detecting club will be snooping again," Marla said.

"We've solved plenty of cases," Charlene snapped.

Marla rolled her eyes. "Ah, yes. The Case of the Missing Moose Head? The Case of the Missing Surfboard?"

"Murders too," Charlene said. "And I'm going to win that pumpkin race."

"Doubtful. My entry is solar powered."

Charlene paled. "They're supposed to be gravity powered."

"Not this year," Marla said. "This is Silicon Valley, haven't you heard? You did read the new rules, didn't you? Oh, I forgot, you're going blind as a bat in your old age."

Charlene's nostrils flared. "Better blind as a bat than a vampire bat."

Petronella strode into the restaurant, her motorcycle boots loud on the checkerboard floor. "Sorry I took so long."

"It's fine," I said. "Is everything okay?"

"My dad's convinced San Adrian's responsible for destroying his pumpkin," Petronella said.

Customers gasped. "No!"

"Not his pumpkin!"

"San Nicholas finally had a chance to win our own prize." Graham's bushy gray brows drew downward. "I knew it would come to this."

"I warned everyone," Marla said. "San Nicholas has been resting on its laurels for too long. And now that we've stepped up our game, San Adrian is taking steps."

"What'd they do to the pumpkin?" Graham asked. "Poison?"

"They dropped it on top of Dr. Levant," Petronella said. "The fall cracked its shell."

Silence fell.

"Well," Tally-Wally said, "that'll do the trick."

I cleared my throat. "Isn't it more likely Dr. Levant was the intended victim, and the pumpkin an unintended casualty?"

There was another long silence. Customers cocked their heads and considered.

Marla blew on her coffee. "Really, Val, you don't understand a thing about pumpkin festivals."

Chapter Four

I walked to the front of the dining area and gazed through the glass at the foggy street.

In the street, Ray handed a piece of comic art to a customer from his green booth. He caught my eye and waved.

I waved back half-heartedly.

In the optometry booth, Tristan Cannon stood motionless, arms limp at his sides. The poor man looked stunned. Had he been questioned by Shaw yet?

My skin prickled, as if someone was watching me. I turned.

The elderly, pixielike woman in the booth quickly looked away.

Hmm. I'd introduce myself to her later. Right now, it looked like Dr. Cannon had the greater need.

"Petronella," I said, "do you mind—"

"Go ahead," she said from the counter.

"What?" Charlene asked. "What's going on?"

"Tristan needs help." I walked out the door and immediately regretted leaving my hoodie behind in the cold and damp.

Charlene grabbed her jacket off the peg and followed, the bell above the door jingling.

"The Baker Street Bakers are on the case." Marla's voice floated, sardonic, through the slowly closing door.

"Marla's solar-powered pumpkin will never work," Charlene muttered. "They've always been gravity only. We just run them down a hill. It's tradition." She glanced at Ray, adjusting a drawing in his booth. Her eyes narrowed with cunning.

"Thanks for coming along," I said.

"What? Oh, well, if someone's going to save Tristan, it should be me. I know him better."

Heidi scowled at us from her stall.

Ignoring the gym owner, we strode to the optometry stand.

"Tristan, I'm so sorry for your loss." Charlene reached across the narrow table to take his hands.

He swayed slightly. His eyes were hazel, his gaze as misty as the coastal morning. "Thank you, Charlene," he said in his light, Southern accent. He swallowed. "I don't— This is so . . ." Beneath his white doctor's coat, his broad shoulders folded inward. "What do you do in a situation like this?"

"The best you can," I said gently. "It's all anyone can do. How can we help?"

He rubbed his forehead, his pleasant, regular features crumpling in distress. "I've no idea. Kara and I were supposed to set up and work the booth today. Now . . ." He straightened. "I think I have to keep going. I don't have any appointments at the office, and I'd just be . . ."

"Sitting around thinking about what you've lost," Charlene finished for him. "Better to work and get your mind off the murder. What time was Dr. Levant supposed to be here this morning?"

Subtle. I shot her a look.

"At five," he said, "like me. I was surprised when she was late, but I assumed something had come up."

"Like what?" I asked.

He gnawed his bottom lip.

"Did she have any enemies?" Charlene asked.

"Enemies? No, of course . . ." Briefly, he shut his eyes. "Oh, damn. I should have told that policeman."

"Chief Shaw?" The muscles between my shoulders loosened. Someone had already interviewed Tristan. So, maybe-possibly—we weren't interfering in Shaw's investigation?

"Shaw?" Tristan's pale brow furrowed. "I think that's what his name was."

"Tell him what?" Charlene asked.

"We had to fire someone last week," he said. "It got a little ugly."

"Who?" I asked.

"Our receptionist, Alfreda. Alfreda Kuulik. But I can't believe she would have done something like this. I don't want to get her in trouble for nothing."

"Are you sure it's nothing?" Charlene asked.

"No," he said. "I guess not. I have to report it. I should have told that policeman at once, but the news of Kara's death . . ."

"You must have been horribly shocked," I said. "No wonder you didn't think of Alfreda right away. Why was she fired?"

He shifted a stack of brochures on the table. "Ah, I probably shouldn't say. Labor laws, liability, you know."

Phooey.

"Anyone else have an ax to grind with your partner?" Charlene asked.

"I don't think so."

"What about Kara's husband?" I asked.

His eyes widened. "Elon?"

"Did they get along?" I folded my arms over my apron and suppressed a shiver.

"They seemed to. He was very supportive. The poor fellow must be devastated."

Charlene's eyes narrowed.

"Have you got lunch today?" I asked. "Can I bring you anything? Coffee now? A turkey pot pie later?"

"Thanks, Val," he said, blinking rapidly, "but I couldn't."

"Take the pie," Charlene said. "She doesn't make that offer lightly, and you know you love them."

"Then, thank you. I don't have lunch organized. I assumed I'd be able to switch off with Kara and grab something." The muscles jumped in his neck. "Kara . . ."

"I've got you covered," I said, teeth chattering. "If you think of anything else, let me know."

"Thank you."

Charlene and I hurried toward Pie Town.

"What do you think?" she asked.

"I think he was somewhere on Main Street when Kara was killed," I said, "and he was her business partner."

"And that makes him a suspect."

"Yes," I said heavily. I liked Dr. Cannon. He'd always been friendly, and he provided free services to people who couldn't pay.

"I'll be a minute. You go on." Charlene beelined for Ray's stall.

Farther down the row of booths, a flash of orange caught my eye. As if my feet had a mind of their own, I found myself in front of an artist's stall. Colorful paintings blazed in a modern, American-primitive style. Rolling hills and harvest moons and fields of pumpkins, pumpkins, pumpkins.

The artist, a woman with a kerchief over her hair, hooked a painting of hot-air balloons onto a metal rack.

I leaned closer, admiring a farm scene with a black cat sitting on a pumpkin. My heart twinged with desire and regret. The painting was 500 dollars and out of this year's budget. But wow.

"I thought you were in a hurry to get back to Pie Town?" Charlene said in my ear, and I jumped.

"You're right," I said. "I got distracted."

She rested one hand casually on her hip. "Well, you'd better get undistracted. You're in Thistleblossom's cross-hairs now."

"What?"

"She was in Pie Town. Didn't you notice?"

"Wait. That woman in the corner booth?"

Charlene's expression darkened. "You know how she's made it over a hundred, don't you?"

"Clean living?"

"Because the devil can't die."

"What's that supposed to mean?" I asked, exasperated. Charlene's favorite explanations always veered toward the supernatural.

"It means she's one hundred percent mean." Charlene waggled her fingers. "She scares the whole town."

"Oh, come on. That newspaper article said she was beloved."

"Only because the editor's terrified of the woman. Why do you think she was sitting alone? Anyone old enough to really know her avoids her."

My hands fell to my sides. What a lonely existence. "That's terrible."

We turned toward Pie Town.

"That's self-preservation," Charlene said. "She wins

that pie contest every year because she's got the judges running scared. But now you're a judge, and she hasn't got anything on you. She's in Pie Town looking for weaknesses to exploit."

I shook my head.

She tugged down the cuff of her purple jacket. "Not every grumpy old person has a heart of gold, you know."

"It's a pie-making contest," I said. "The winner gets a ribbon and a mention in the local paper. It's for fun."

"I hate to say it," Charlene said, opening Pie Town's glass door, "but Marla was right. You don't understand pumpkin festivals. They're cutthroat." She rubbed her neck.

Mrs. Thistleblossom still sat alone in the corner booth.

I smiled at Charlene, smoothed the front of my apron, and approached her. "Mrs. Thistleblossom?"

She started. "Oh!" she said in a quavery voice. "Yes?"

"Hi, I'm Val Harris." I extended my hand.

She looked like I'd offered her arsenic.

"It's nice to finally meet you," I said, stuffing my hand back into my apron pocket. "I've heard your pumpkin pie is the one to beat. I'm looking forward to tasting it."

She grimaced, exposing yellowed teeth. "Why, thank you, my dear. You have such a lovely pie shop." Her voice deepened. "It would be a shame if something happened to it."

"Hap—" I blinked. "What would happen to it?"

"Nothing, nothing. This terrible news got me thinking—you've heard about Dr. Levant's murder?" Her face contorted. "A murder that shall not go unavenged."

"Y-yes. Did you know Dr. Levant?"

"She was my eye doctor. And it's no mystery why you're asking. We all know about your little detecting society. You should tread carefully, young Val."

Little detecting society? When she said it, it just sounded creepy.

"Now to business." She folded her gloved hands atop a patent leather purse. "I'd like to order one of your pumpkin pies, the one with the little maple leaves and pumpkins on the top crust?"

"You don't need to order it. I'd be happy to give you one."

Cries of outrage drifted from the counter.

"Because you're a contest entrant," I clarified. Maybe Charlene was getting to me, but I didn't want to be accused of taking bribes disguised as pie purchases. I'd had to reveal my connection to Gordon to the judges as a potential conflict of interest. They'd assured me since he was a law-abiding cop, they trusted he wouldn't give me any tip-offs about which pie was his. And he hadn't.

"Did I say one?" Her spectacles glittered. "I meant, I'd like one hundred."

"Oh," I said, taken aback.

"Attempted bribery!" Charlene howled. "Everyone saw it."

But all my customers' backs were mysteriously turned away, their shoulders hunched.

Mrs. Thistleblossom's eyes narrowed behind their spectacles. She deliberately tapped her handbag. "If you're turning down my generous offer, I will be very disappointed."

My piecrust maker stepped closer to the booth. "Get used to the feeling, you old—"

"Charlene!" I turned to the diminutive woman. "Would you like another cup of coffee?"

"Why, yes." Mrs. Thistleblossom extended the cup.

"Then you'll have to get it yourself," Charlene said, "because we're self-serve."

I took the cup. "But I'm happy to get a cup for a fellow baker." I stalked to the coffee urn and filled the mug.

"Excellent," Mrs. Thistleblossom purred. "That will give you time to reconsider my offer."

Marla shifted on her barstool. "That was your second mistake," she murmured into her mug.

"What was the first?" I asked, then thought better of it. "Never mind." *Do not engage.*

I brought Mrs. Thistleblossom her cup. "I'm afraid I can't sell you the pies before the contest. But I can give you the number of another bakery that delivers."

"How disappointing." She smiled coldly. Her lenses glinted, two flat and shining disks.

An odd chill rippled through me. In that moment, there was something uncanny about the old lady. Then the moment passed, and she was just a little old lady in a print dress.

I'd been spending too much time with Charlene. Now I was starting to see the supernatural everywhere.

The bell over the front door jingled.

I backed from the table. "It was great meeting you, Mrs.—"

"Val!" a feminine voice screeched.

Someone tackled me, and I tumbled sideways.

Chapter Five

I gasped, the breath squeezed from my lungs. Clutching the back of a pink booth, I struggled to stay upright.

"Cut it out." My brother, Doran, pried a tiny Asian woman from around my waist.

The woman gripped my shoulders and beamed up at me. "Val! It's me."

Confused, I tried to place her. She wore professional dress. Brown wool slacks. Tan sweater. Matching blazer. Plaid scarf.

Nope, I had no idea who she was.

I wheezed. "Ah . . ."

My brother scraped the shock of blue-black hair out of his eyes. "Val, this is, um, my mom, Mrs. Harris." He stared meaningfully at me. "You know, I *told you* she was coming?"

"But you can call me Takako," she said.

Doran folded his arms over his black motorcycle jacket. He shot his mother an exasperated look.

"Your mom?" I gaped, blindsided. He hadn't told me she was coming to visit.

"And your stepmom." She wiped her eyes. "I'm sorry. I told myself I wouldn't get emotional."

I remembered my manners. "It's nice to finally meet you Mrs.—uh, Takako." Why hadn't he told me she was coming?

She sniffed. "I know what you're thinking."

"You do?" I really hoped she didn't.

"But I am not here to try and take your mother's place or make things weird. I just needed to . . . meet you." She pressed both hands into a prayer position and touched them to her mouth. "You look so much like your father."

Doran and I groaned. Our father was good-looking, but he was also just one step ahead of the law. This wasn't a compliment.

"Ah, family," Mrs. Thistleblossom muttered. "So important. So painful to lose."

Okay that was . . . *Was* she trying to spook me?

"Ignore the old grouch." Charlene elbowed her way into our little group. "So, you're the wicked stepmother, eh?"

The smile Takako returned looked forced. "I suppose I am. I would have come sooner, but Doran was keeping Val a secret."

"Sorry," Charlene said gruffly. "Bad joke." She studied Takako and her son. Doran was taller and slimmer than Takako, but there was no mistaking the resemblance. "I'm Charlene."

They shook hands.

"Please, sit down." I ushered them to a booth on the opposite side of the restaurant from Mrs. Thistleblossom. The old lady was starting to give me the heebie-jeebies. "Can I get you some coffee? Pie?"

"I'll take a refill." Charlene extended her mug to me.

"Coffee," Takako said. "Black."

"I'll be right back." I hustled to the counter.

Tally-Wally whistled. "A long-lost brother, and now a long-lost mother."

"Stepmother," I said.

Doran appeared at my side. "Sorry about this, Val. I tried, but I couldn't stop her."

"You didn't have to stop her." Movements jerky, I filled a mug from the urn. "But why didn't you give me a heads-up? I could have prepared something for her or arranged time off. I've got Mondays free, but the pumpkin festival officially starts tomorrow, and—"

"Come on. You don't do time off. And you don't have to do anything special for her. The pumpkin festival can be her entertainment."

"Oh," I said, relieved. "So, she's only here for the weekend?"

His blue-eyed gaze slipped sideways. "I'm not sure. She's staying at that luxury hotel down the road."

Marla's lips curved. "No one leaves that hotel willingly. Or until they run out of money, which doesn't take long. I've heard the standard rooms are over five hundred dollars a night. What does your mother do?"

"She's made good investments," Doran said.

I grabbed the coffees and thrust one into Doran's hand. "Here."

We returned to the table.

"Val's going to be a judge," Charlene was saying, "since professionals can't participate in the pumpkin pie bake-off."

"I suppose that's fair," Takako said. "I'm sure Val's pumpkin pie would be the best."

My skin prickled, and I looked over my shoulder.

Mrs. Thistleblossom's face wrinkled in a scowl. She made a strange, quick gesture.

My grip tightened on the mug. Slowly, I lowered it to the table.

"Thanks, Val." Takako took the mug and patted her flat stomach. "I plan to eat as much of your pie as possible tomorrow at the festival."

I joined them in the booth. We chatted about things to do around San Nicholas, and when the mugs were empty, Takako stood. "And now I should let you get back to work."

I hugged her briefly. "Thanks for coming. It really is great to meet you."

"We're family." Her smile had a firm set to it. "Of course, I came."

But were we really family? Doran was. And she was his mother. I wasn't sure how these things worked. Maybe the details didn't matter? Uneasily, I backed toward the cash register. "Okay, well, see you tomorrow."

I fled to the kitchen. The ovens were off. The counters were clean. Hunter, our teenage busser/dishwasher, was loading plates into the dishwasher. Everything was under control. Now how was I supposed to take my mind off today's dose of crazy?

Petronella leaned against a metal countertop and grinned. "So, you've got a stepmother."

"Don't you start." I tightened the apron around my waist. "And she seemed nice."

"They all seem nice," my assistant manager said, "until they're not."

Abril's dark brow furrowed. "Where's Doran?"

I smothered a grimace. Why hadn't the dummy stopped by the kitchen? "I think he took his mother back to her hotel."

Her face fell. "Oh."

"It sounds like her visit was a surprise," I said. "He looked a little frazzled."

"That makes sense," Abril said uncertainly. She slid a

pie from the oven onto a wide, wooden panel and set it on a metal rack.

"And it's too soon for you to meet his mother." Petronella grinned and as quickly sobered.

"How's your dad doing?" I asked.

"He's not happy." Petronella rubbed the top of her hairnet. "Small farming's tough, and so is Dad. He'll get through it. But I don't trust Chief Shaw."

I opened my mouth to assure her, but I didn't feel particularly assured myself. "Your father wasn't responsible for what happened. His pumpkin didn't roll off the truck and crush someone." There was no way any of the pumpkins could have. They were all flat at the bottom, their shapes deformed by their enormous weight. "It was deliberately moved."

"Does Shaw understand that?" she asked.

"Maybe . . ." *Not.* I pointed over my shoulder to the swinging door. "Would you two mind if I did a little office work?"

"I don't think things are going to pick up today," Petronella said.

I didn't either. Prefestival day had been slow for a Friday. I hoped it wasn't a bad omen about the real festival, this weekend.

"We've got this," Petronella said.

I hesitated. But if things did get busy, I'd only be in my office. "Thanks." I hurried to my barren office. Sitting in the creaky executive chair, I Web surfed.

Dr. Levant's optometry office had a Facebook page. But there was nothing personal or murderous there. It was all vision tips and community events. The pumpkin festival featured prominently.

Next, I checked social media pages for Dr. Levant and Dr. Cannon. Tristan Cannon's page wasn't illuminating either, though he was thinking of adopting a puppy. I paused over the puppy pictures, then forced myself to move on. My tiny house did not have enough room for a dog.

Dr. Levant's husband, Elon, wasn't on social media at all. But their ex-employee, Alfreda Kuulik, was. After she'd been fired, she'd left a string of nastygrams on Twitter about Dr. Levant. Oh yeah, she was a suspect.

I expanded my Web search. Since becoming a Baker Street Baker, I'd become more savvy about online investigations. There's a Web site that searches the deep Web for court records and all sorts of stuff. But it too was a bust.

I leaned back in my chair and rested my heels on the metal desk. The chair creaked, zipping backward and thunking against the wall.

Scowling and rubbing the back of my head, I dug my cell phone from my apron pocket with one hand. I called the head judge for the bake-off.

"Hi, Denise," I said, "this is Val Harris."

"Oh, hi! What's going on? You're not backing out of the judging, are you?"

"No, no. I just wanted to report a contact with one of the entrants, Heidi Gladstone. She mentioned she was entering a . . ." Oh, shoot. If I gave her the details, would it make it impossible for Denise to judge the pie too? "She mentioned a detail about her pie which would make it recognizable."

She snorted. "I can guess her big reveal. Don't worry. It's not as if a low-calorie pie had much chance of winning, is it?"

"You never know," I said, taken aback by her casual attitude. "But maybe I shouldn't judge that pie."

"If you're able to identify the pie, judge it, and put a mark on your card so I'll know. And thanks for letting me know. You wouldn't believe how much agony goes into this contest."

"What do you mean? Do you need help with something?" I smacked my forehead and hoped she said *no*. I didn't have time for extra volunteer work.

Denise hesitated. "I don't suppose you've met Mrs. Thistleblossom?" she said in a low voice.

"Actually, she came into Pie Town today." I laughed uncertainly. "I think she might have tried to bribe me. She offered to buy a hundred pies."

There was a long silence.

"I told her I couldn't accept any purchases from her until after the contest." I studied my tennis shoes. "That's okay, isn't it?"

"Yes . . . yes, that's fine." Her gulp was audible. "Has she, er, said anything else?"

"No. Why?"

"No reason," Denise said quickly. "I'm sure nothing will happen."

I cocked my head toward the office door. Outside, the murmur of voices rose. "Nothing will—?"

"Gotta go. Bye!" She hung up.

I stared at the phone. *Weird*.

Pocketing my phone, I strode into the dining area and stopped short.

Marla stood on a chair, her platinum hair skimming a pendant lamp. The sequins on her black jacket glittered. A cluster of elderly regulars gathered around her.

"Revenge!" Graham shook his fist. "It's time we take 'em out."

"Yeah!" The gray-haired crowd roared.

I sidled to Charlene. "What's going on?"

"Ray caught a spy from San Adrian taking pictures of the festival decorations." She angled her head toward the window. Across the street, a man on a ladder pinned a giant black spiderweb to a building cornice. "On top of the murder and the wrecked pumpkin, catching a spy has tipped them over the edge."

"They sabotaged our best pumpkin," someone shouted.

"Guys," I said, "a woman was killed. It's not likely someone from San Adrian murdered Dr. Levant to ruin our festival."

"I don't disagree," Graham said. "But they took advantage of the murder by dropping that pumpkin on her and now stealing ideas from our festival while the cops are busy collecting evidence."

Marla's chair rocked beneath her, and she hastily stepped onto the floor. "That pumpkin was an insult to Dr. Levant and everyone in this town who cared about her."

I tried again. "But we don't know—"

"War is hell." Tally-Wally rubbed his reddened nose. "So, I don't say this lightly, but it's payback time."

"What about a zombie apocalypse prank?" a woman who worked as the church organist suggested. "We could dress as zombies and scare people at their festival."

"That would make their festival *more* interesting," Marla said. "If you really want to unnerve people . . ." She looked around, making sure everyone was listening. "A creepy clown."

The crowd muttered, shifting.

"A clown?" Graham asked. "Isn't that a bridge too far?"

Marla raised her chin. "It's better than they deserve."

I gave up on rationality and nudged Charlene. "I'm surprised you're not getting in on this action."

"Revenge was that bloodsucker Marla's idea," Charlene muttered. "Don't listen to the vampire," she said more loudly.

"Will you stop calling me that?" Marla tugged on her black jacket.

"Who's going to volunteer to be the clown?" Charlene asked. "He might get attacked or arrested."

"Only if he gets caught," Marla said.

I returned to the kitchen and left them to scheme. Creepy clowns and pumpkin plots paled in comparison to murder. If it got their minds off the real horror of Dr. Levant's death, I didn't see the harm.

But that night, I couldn't stop seeing that small hand sticking out from beneath the pumpkin. I lay awake in my tiny house and listened to branches scrape across my roof. Animals snuffled and shuffled outside, and I finally fell into an uneasy sleep.

Chapter Six

It was dark when I awoke at my usual ungodly baker's hour. Yawning, I grabbed a Pie Town T-shirt, slipped into a pair of jeans, and brushed my hair into a ponytail. I made myself peanut butter toast, jammed it in my mouth, shrugged into a Pie Town hoodie and staggered out the door.

The light above the tiny house's door flipped on, illuminating the picnic table and my delivery van.

I stumbled to a halt. The toast dropped from my mouth.

Someone had tagged the Pie Town van in shaky black text that read: FULL OF BALONEY.

I picked up the toast, which had naturally fallen peanut butter-side down, and walked around the pink van. There was more. The words COFFIN VARNISH scarred the rear doors. And on the other side, VAL HARRIS IS A FLAT TIRE.

Flat tire? What did that even mean? I checked the tires. Nope. Not flat. And coffin varnish? I vaguely remembered that had been an insult in the dark ages of the early twentieth century.

This was the weirdest graffiti ever, and in other circumstances, I might have laughed. But this was the official

Pie Town delivery van. I couldn't drive around town with this stupid graffiti. How much was getting it repainted going to cost?

I stomped around and cursed, because it made me feel better and no one could see.

Beside the picnic table, I stilled, my skin crawling. Was whoever had painted my van watching?

The automatic light over my door switched off, bathing me in darkness.

I ran back to my shipping container/tiny home. The light over the door snapped on again.

Heart pounding, I scanned my yard from the tiny home steps. The shadows seemed to shift, and I blinked rapidly. I *must* be imagining that watchful feeling. But my house was out of the way, at the end of its own winding dirt road. This wasn't a crime of opportunity. Someone had driven here and targeted me with oddball graffiti.

I ran back inside, grabbed a flashlight, and returned to the van. If the paint was wet, this had been done recently.

Swallowing, I touched the graffiti.

Dry.

Relieved, I pulled my hand away. Black smeared my fingertips.

Huh?

I rubbed my fingers together. The stuff felt chalky. I ran my finger through the graffiti, drawing a pale line.

I hurried inside and retrieved a rag from beneath the kitchen sink. The clock on the miniature stove blinked, baleful. I was going to be late.

But I trotted to the van and scrubbed. The graffiti came off, and a rush of relief flowed through my veins. A good car wash would probably remove any remaining traces.

I stepped from the van and studied its pink sides. No permanent harm had been done. Had the graffiti been a practical joke? But by whom?

It didn't seem like the gamers' style.

Charlene's? But if she'd done it, she'd have stuck around to crow over my reaction.

Locking my house, I jumped into the van and bumped down the dirt road, descending into a bank of fog.

Soon, I was pulling into the misty brick alley behind Pie Town. A light shone through one of the small, high windows in the kitchen, and I grimaced. I hated being the last person to get to my own business.

I hauled open the heavy, metal door and strode into the kitchen. "Sorry I'm late," I shouted over the roar of the mixer.

Petronella looked up from a counter full of apples in various states. With her gloved hands, she adjusted the net containing her spiky black hair. "What happened?"

Abril switched off the heavy mixer. Her brown eyes widened with concern. "You're late. Is everything okay?"

My face warmed. It was the first official day of the pumpkin festival. Tardiness was a high crime, or at least a misdemeanor. "Someone graffitied the van. Fortunately, they used chalk."

"What a lame prank," Petronella said. "Who would go all the way to your house to chalk a van?"

"Maybe Charlene's up to her tricks." Abril angled her head toward the flour-work room. Odd mechanical noises emerged from behind the closed, metal door.

"Yeah." My brow furrowed. The language on my van *had* recalled flappers and ragtime. But I couldn't see Charlene doing something so pointless. Not on the first day of the festival.

I knocked on the metal door. "Is everything okay in there?"

The whirring fell silent. "I'm fine," Charlene called. "Busy. Aren't you?"

"Yes, but did anything odd happen last night?" I pulled open the door.

"You'll ruin the temperature control," she shouted.

I released the handle as if scalded.

"And what do you mean by anything *odd* happening?" she called through the door. "What do you think I get up to after I go to bed?"

"Nothing, but—"

"Nothing? There could be something. I'm not a monk, you know."

Ugh. "Never mind."

I snapped on a hairnet, tied on an apron, and ran a round of dough through the flattener. Roughly, I slipped it into a pie tin and turned it, pinching the dough around its edges. A murder had been committed yesterday. Was there a connection between that and the graffiti? It didn't seem likely I'd become a target because I'd found the body. Two different criminal minds were likely at work—one deadly, one dippy.

At six, I hauled the coffee urn to the dining area and turned the sign in the glass front door to OPEN. I set the day-old hand pies on the counter.

Aged regulars trickled into Pie Town for self-serve coffee, cheap snacks, and gossip.

As much as I wanted to hear what they thought about Dr. Levant's murder, I had about a dillion autumn pies to bake. I'd decided to go heavy on the pumpkin, for obvious reasons. But there were other fall favorites, such as apple-cranberry, mincemeat, sweet potato, and pecan. The festival menu also included Wisconsin harvest pie, tart cherry, a maple-pumpkin with salted pecan brittle, and pumpkin chiffon.

Insides jittering, I hurriedly filled piecrusts. This would be one of our biggest days of the year. There was no margin for error.

Gordon and three uniformed cops presented themselves

for duty at nine. The tables were already nearly full of early festival arrivals grabbing coffee.

Tally-Wally sat beside the urn. He explained how the self-serve basket worked, ensuring there were no java scofflaws.

Outside, the fog had begun to lift. It blanketed the rooftops and revealed giant black spiderwebs strung across Main Street.

I explained our system of numbered tent cards to the cops. The cops would take the orders for people standing in line and speed things along. I just hoped we were busy enough to justify the system.

"A word, Val?" Gordon nodded to the hallway. Even Gordon was in uniform blues today. He looked even hotter in them than in his usual detective's power suit.

"Sure." Who can resist a man in uniform?

Gordon followed me into the hallway and stopped me with a hand to my arm. I turned, and he was close, so close I could smell his bay rum cologne. He lowered his head, his emerald eyes intent.

My heart beat more rapidly. "Maybe we should go into the office," I said in a low voice. His colleagues might see.

"You're right," he said. "And we need Charlene."

Charlene? "Um, what exactly did you have in mind?"

Gordon's handsome brow furrowed. "What did you?" His expression cleared, and he laughed shortly. "Oh. Not that."

Kissing me quickly, he zipped into the kitchen, the door swinging in his wake, and returned with my piecrust specialist. Charlene looked like an autumn leaf in her orange tunic and brown leggings.

So much for a romantic interlude. I followed them into my utilitarian office.

Gordon shut the door behind us, and the VA calendar on

its back fluttered. "Thanks for sending me those crime scene photos, Charlene."

"You took crime-scene photos?" I sat against the metal desk and folded my arms. "When?"

She shrugged. "When you weren't looking."

"I need your help," he said. "I can't get anywhere near this case—not officially."

Charlene leaned against the closed door, rumpling the VA calendar. "It goes without saying, the Baker Street Bakers are at your disposal."

"Great." He looked around the office. "Have you got a whiteboard?"

"Why would we have a whiteboard?" Charlene asked.

"It's fine." He grabbed paper from the printer tray and rummaged in my desk.

"Can I help you?" I asked, bemused.

"Got it." Extracting a roll of tape, he taped five sheets to the wall behind my desk. "I know you haven't had time to take those PI courses, so I'm going to give you a crash course."

"PI courses?" Charlene asked, looking intrigued.

He wrote across the five sheets of paper and tapped the first page that said EVERYTHING. "One, you need to document everything in your murder book."

"We do keep case files," Charlene said. "We're not total noobs."

"Everything." He underlined the word and pointed to the next sheet: TIMELINE. "Next, we need to nail down the timeline. When exactly did Dr. Levant die? Where were all the suspects at the time?"

"Her partner, Tristan Cannon, was setting up their festival booth that morning," I said. "But we don't know when Dr. Levant died or when exactly he arrived."

"Let's not get ahead of ourselves," he said.

Charlene straightened off the door. "But you asked about the suspects."

"Before we decide who the suspects are, we need to talk to potential witnesses." He numbered that three on the paper. "And that includes talking to everyone who was on the street at the time the body was discovered."

"Everybody?" I squeaked. That seemed like a lot of work. And speaking of work . . . I surreptitiously checked my watch. I needed to get back to the kitchen.

Charlene yawned. "Boring."

"This is how an investigation is conducted," he said.

"That's how the police conduct an investigation," she said, "not us."

"We need to follow every lead." He turned to the wall and marked that number four. "And treat everything you discover as evidence." He wrote EVIDENCE on the final sheet of paper.

I folded my arms. One of the benefits of having your own business is there's no one above you to tell you what to do. I wanted to help Gordon. Being taken off the case was obviously bothering him. But, well, Charlene and I had been in charge of the Baker Street Bakers too. . . .

Charlene squinted at the wall. "Everything, timeline, evidence . . . ETE? What kind of acronym is that? You work for the government. You people are supposed to be coming up with acronyms all day long."

"It's not an acronym," Gordon said.

"It should be," she said. "If you want us to remember anything, you need an acronym like SNOT or WHAM or BANG or something. Whiteboards. Huh! I've got to get back to my crusts." She strode from the room. The door banged shut behind her.

"We'll help in any way we can," I said. "Like we always do." I could think of him as a client.

"She's right. This is wrong." He scraped his hands through his hair. "What am I doing?"

"Educating us. It's interesting." Okay, that was a lie. "We can stand to be more organized in our amateur investigating. It's just that . . . organization and Charlene aren't really the peanut butter and chocolate of the investigation world."

He scrubbed his hands across his face. "Crazy. I'm going crazy. That's all. And why wouldn't I be? I'm San Nicholas's only detective, and yet I'm the only detective in Silicon Valley who never detects."

"That's not true. You've solved all sorts of crimes."

He glared. "Yesterday I stopped a surfer stampede."

"A what?"

"They were trying to knock down the new gates a spoiled techie put up. They were blocking public access to the beach."

"That's . . . that must have been interesting."

"It was a job for a beat cop." He blew out his breath. "And not your problem."

I rested my hand on his arm. "Gordon, if it's your problem, it's mine too. Consider yourself our number one client."

"Client?"

"Charlene and I will let you know everything we discover. But I'm going to be working this festival all weekend. And my stepmother turned up, so I'll probably be spending time with her on Monday if she's still around."

"Your stepmother?"

"She surprised me yesterday." I laughed weakly. "But she seems nice."

"How are you doing with it?"

"It's family, I guess. The more the merrier, right?"

He pulled me against his chest. "Thanks for putting up with my temporary insanity." He drew me into a bone-melting kiss, his hands exploring the hollows of my back.

We broke apart, breathing heavily.

"Oh," I said, my lips burning.

He grinned. "And thanks for doing this. Helping the Athletic League, I mean."

I forced my breathing to steady. "Did I mention you'll have to wear an apron?"

He quirked a brow. "You think that bothers me?"

I laced my fingers behind his neck and leaned against him. "No. I'm sure your manhood will remain intact. Plus, they've got pockets for your tips."

"Always thinking."

"I may have another non-murdery case for you." I ran my hands down the front of his pressed shirt. "Someone put graffiti on my van last night while I was sleeping. It all came off, but it's kind of weird."

"It came off? Did you take any photos?"

"Uh, no. I was so freaked out about having to take the van to the festival with that stuff on it, I forgot."

"What did it say?"

I told him.

He laughed. "Charlene?"

My glance flicked to the dented office door. "I don't think so. It made me late, and she wouldn't do that on the first day of the pumpkin festival."

"No, she wouldn't." His brow furrowed. "I don't like that someone made the trek all the way to your house. You're pretty isolated on that bluff. But it sounds like a prank. It could have been kids trying to get to that cemetery."

"What cemetery?"

"The one behind your house."

I stared. "What cemetery behind my house?"

"You know, behind your place, down the hill. It dates from the eighteen-hundreds. Now it's so covered in brambles and poison oak, most people don't bother with it."

"You're pulling my leg," I said flatly. It had to be a Halloween joke. "Did Charlene put you up to this?"

"You didn't know?"

"No!" He really wasn't kidding. "I never go down that hill. I don't want to get poison oak." And why the devil hadn't Charlene mentioned a graveyard when she'd rented me the house?

"It's just an old cemetery."

"Right." I stepped away from him and pulled some aprons from a box. "Your uniforms. Excuse me. I've got to have a chat with my landlady."

I stormed into the kitchen and yanked open the door to the flour-work room. "A cemetery? Behind my house?"

A ghost of cold air flowed into the kitchen.

Charlene patted dough into a round and dropped it onto a metal tray. "Oh, yeah. It's real historic." Stooping, she brushed flour from her brown-and-orange striped socks.

"Why didn't you tell me?"

"What does it matter?" she asked, arch. "You don't believe in ghosts, remember?"

"That's not—" I sputtered. "You should have disclosed!"

"California law only requires disclosures of deaths on the property within the last three years. Those corpses are over a century old, and they're not on my property."

"Oooh!" But there was no point being mad. The only real surprise was freewheeling Charlene hadn't held a ghost hunt in my backyard. But not even Charlene fooled around with poison oak.

Abril poked her head into the flour-work room, her white net puffed high with her thick hair. "They're coming," she squeaked. "It's a mob. I've never seen so many—"

"We'll talk about this later," I said to Charlene. "Abril, breathe."

She bent, taking deep, gusty breaths.

Charlene shrugged.

I hurried into the kitchen. A roar of voices flowed through the order window, and I looked out.

A maelstrom of pumpkin-starved festivalgoers flooded into the dining area.

If it hadn't been for the cops, there might have been a riot. But our new system for taking orders in line seemed to work. I wasn't sure if the customers were charmed or cowed by the aproned police officers. But there was no shoving or sniping.

I worked harder than I've ever worked—we all did. Even Charlene stayed beyond her usual piecrust-making hours to run the cash register.

Around three o'clock, Charlene whistled through the order window into the kitchen. "Val, you got a visitor."

The kitchen's swinging door bumped and swayed but didn't open.

I jammed a plate of pumpkin chiffon pie through the window. "Who is it?"

Charlene set the pie on the counter. A cop grabbed it, whisking it to a table.

"Open the door," Charlene said.

Shaking my head, I bustled to the kitchen door.

It bumped open, and a pumpkin zipped between my legs. I yelped.

Gears whirring, the pumpkin jounced onto the black fatigue mats. It twirled in a tight circle.

"Remote controlled!" Charlene cackled through the order window. "I'm sure to win the pumpkin race this year."

I peered at the spinning pumpkin. Someone had mounted it on what looked like miniature tank treads. "Did you make this?"

"Ray built it. He owed me one."

The pumpkin circled Abril, and she squeaked, jumping.

It raced to my feet. The contraption's metal arm extended an order slip.

I plucked the slip from its mechanical claw. Charlene's uneven script scrawled across the yellow paper: *Your stepmother is here.* "Thanks."

"De nada." Charlene pulled her head from the order window. "Oh, they changed the race time. I'm going to be a little late to your pumpkin judging."

Rats. That meant I wouldn't be able to see the races either. I would have liked to cheer on Charlene.

Peeling off my plastic gloves, I hopped over the pumpkin and hurried through the swinging door to the dining area.

Takako had jammed herself into a corner between a pink booth and the counter.

I glanced nervously at the sign that proclaimed MAXIMUM CAPACITY: 100. But I knew the cops would be watching that sign too and making sure we didn't violate any fire codes.

"Takako!" I wiped my hands on my apron and searched the crowd for Gordon. He wasn't there. "It's nice to see you again. Do you want to come into the kitchen?"

She drew her hands from the pockets of her San Nicholas Pumpkin Festival jacket and hugged me. "I can? I'm allowed?"

"As long as you don't mind wearing a hairnet. And don't mind the robot pumpkin."

Takako stepped away and bumped into a hipster with a beard a lumberjack would have envied. "I had to wear a net in the fish cannery, and I think your pumpkin is escaping."

The pumpkin motored through the crowd, eliciting shrieks, laughs, and jumps.

I tugged down my apron. "Charlene, control that thing."

Obediently, the pumpkin pivoted. It motored under the Dutch door and stopped beneath Charlene's chair, behind the register.

Charlene leaned from her seat. "You worked in a fish cannery, Takako?"

"In Alaska," she said. "But only for one summer."

"So did I." Charlene retrieved Robo-squash and set it on the counter. "I can't stand salmon anymore."

"Neither can I!"

"Or sea monsters," Charlene said. "Damned Tizheruks. One snatched Sam right off the dock in Ekuk."

Takako's brow crinkled. "Tiz . . . ?"

"Why don't you come on back?" I nodded toward the gently swinging door. "We can talk while I plate pies."

Takako followed me into the kitchen.

I grabbed a hairnet from a box atop the old-fashioned pie safe and handed it to her.

Takako snapped the net over her wavy black hair.

"This is my assistant," I said, "Abril. Abril, this is Doran's mom, Takako."

Abril smiled shyly and cut slices of apple-cranberry pie. "Hello."

While Takako and Abril got acquainted, I grabbed a ticket from the wheel in the window.

The pumpkin chiffon was popular. I plated another slice and slid it through the window.

Takako leaned against a metal counter. "Your business is booming, Val. Your mother would be proud."

An ache pinched my heart. "I'm sorry she never got a chance to see Pie Town." We'd plotted and planned it out before she'd died. Her insurance money had even gone into the start-up. A part of her was here, in spirit.

Charlene, followed by her rolling pumpkin, ambled into the kitchen. "Still working, I see." She fiddled with a black control box. The pumpkin ground to a halt beside the haint-blue pie safe.

I slid a slice of harvest pie onto a plate and set it in the window. "What else would I be doing today?"

"You haven't taken a break all day." Charlene's forehead scrunched. She maneuvered the robot arm upward.

Abril shot Charlene an indecipherable look.

"I don't mind skipping breaks during the pumpkin festival," I said. "I had a mini turkey pot pie for lunch."

"Eating on your feet while you work isn't a break," Takako scolded.

"That's what I said," Charlene said. Her robot knocked the box of hairnets to the floor. Moving creakily, she retrieved the box. "Petronella, Abril, and the coppers have got it handled. I'm old. I need a break. So do you."

Abril nodded. "Have your lunch break, Val. Get out and enjoy the festival."

"But I don't—"

"It's settled." Charlene pushed me toward the alley door.

Giving up, I stripped off gloves, hairnet, and apron. "Fine," I said, "but only if we go to the haunted house." I loved haunted houses, and it would have made me sick to miss this one. Plus, Dr. Levant's husband, Elon, had worked there. I doubted he'd be there the day after his wife's murder. But maybe one of his colleagues could tell us where he'd been the morning his wife had been killed.

"There's a haunted house?" Takako asked.

"In the old jail," Charlene said. "The church does it up every year for charity."

The robot bumped after her.

"You can't bring that to the haunted house," I said.

"Why not?" Charlene asked. "I can afford the ticket. And I need to test it under adverse conditions."

"You know," Takako said, "I've never been inside a haunted house. Not a fake one I mean."

"You've been in a real haunted house?" Charlene asked.

"That's what the locals claimed," my stepmother said.

I grabbed my orange-and-black hoodie from a hook on the door and followed them outside. The foggy air was a pleasant slap to the face. I inhaled deeply, scenting salt from the nearby Pacific.

Charlene and Takako ambled down the alley, the pumpkin racer zipping ahead.

Since this was more harvest festival than spooktacular, the decorations were mostly pumpkins, pumpkins, and more pumpkins. Pumpkins stacked beside doorsteps. Pumpkins on hay bales. Minipumpkins in shop windows. At least there was no question of mismatched colors.

Off Main Street, the town had set up wooden photo cutouts designed from vintage Halloween postcards. Grinning tourists stuck their heads through the holes, transforming into old-fashioned witches and devils for the camera. A tractor towed a wagon full of hay bales and tourists down one street.

We passed a bouncy castle full of shrieking children. Teens putted in a minigolf graveyard. Toddlers hugged goats in a petting zoo. The goats *mehhed*, weary expressions in their big brown eyes.

Private homes had gotten into the spirit too. Pumpkins

lined porch railings, and witches on broomsticks crashed into trees.

We stood in line for tickets at the old jail, a square, concrete building. Above its green doors a placard read: JAIL, BUILT 1911. The haunted house was actually in the more sizable red barn at the rear.

I looked at the clock on my phone.

"Stop checking the time and enjoy the moment." Charlene maneuvered the pumpkin around a stroller. The toddler hung over its side, watching the pumpkin fly past. "It'll be over all too soon."

I blew out my breath. *Easy for her to say.* I was responsible for Pie Town and payrolls.

"How's Frederick doing?" I asked Charlene, changing the subject.

"Frederick?" Takako asked. "Have you got a gentleman friend?"

"My cat," Charlene said. "And he's hiding at home. He hates pumpkin." She smiled. "But I might have a gentleman friend."

Was she getting serious with Ewan? The two were perfect for each other. He even owned a fake ghost town. I opened my mouth to ask, and the racer made a sharp turn beneath my feet. I stumbled, scowling.

"Whoops," she said. "Sorry."

The line moved quickly, and soon I was handing over cash for tickets for the three of us. I had to buy a child's ticket for the pumpkin.

A tall, middle-aged man with thinning brown hair stepped from the jail. He smiled wearily at the ticket seller. "I'll take over now, Gladys."

"Elon?" Charlene grasped his hand. "What are you

doing here today? I was sorry to hear about your wife. What a terrible loss."

"Thank you, Charlene." Lines fanned from the corners of Elon's eyes, owlish behind tortoiseshell glasses. He nodded, his aesthetic face somber, his tarnished eyes haunted. "Hello, Val, and is that pumpkin moving?"

"My entry in the race," Charlene said.

"And this is my, er, this is Takako Harris," I said. "Please accept my condolences on your loss. Kara was a wonderful doctor."

He studied his tennis shoes. "Thank you."

"What can we do to help?" Charlene asked.

"Nothing." He looked past my shoulder, his gaze unfocused. "Kara was such a planner, she had everything organized, even for her death. Now, I've got nothing to do, except think. And I don't want to think, not today." He swallowed convulsively. "They said I should stay home. But I'd already taken today off to volunteer, and I didn't want to sit home alone. And now I'm talking too much. That's what comes from being a salesman, I guess." He touched his eyeglasses. "I talk."

My chest pinched with sympathy. I wasn't sure what to say that wasn't a platitude.

"Such a stupid prank," he continued. "Kara's death was meaningless."

"Prank?" I asked.

He blinked and focused on me. "The pumpkin. She must have been trying to stop some foolish sabotage."

"You think she was killed because of the pumpkin," I said slowly.

"What else could it be? She didn't have enemies."

"Everybody has enemies," Charlene said.

"Not Kara," he said. "Her biggest rival was Laurelynn Lelli, and that was nothing."

"Laurelynn?" I asked. She was wholesaling our mini pumpkin pies this month at her organic pumpkin patch.

"They went to high school together," he said. "She owns the pumpkin farm on Lincoln Way. They were always bickering about something. It was silly."

"Anything lately?" *Crumb.* I really didn't want one of my wholesalers to be a killer. I was just getting that side of the business started.

He shrugged. "Who knows what it was about this time?"

This time? I glanced at the line behind us. It stretched to the street.

Charlene squeezed his hand. "You're a good man. You'll get through this."

A cast-iron weight settled in my chest. How do you get through your wife being smashed by an oversized pumpkin?

"At least Chief Shaw is taking over the investigation," Elon said. "It will get the attention it deserves."

Charlene's mouth puckered.

"I'm sure he will," I said.

"Whatever you do," he continued, "don't go back."

I looked at him blankly.

"When you're in the haunted house," he explained. "Keep moving forward, and you won't get lost or ruin it for others."

"Oh," I said. "Right."

We muttered more condolences and walked into the darkened barn.

"That poor man," Takako said.

A sheet-covered ghost popped from behind a tombstone, and I jumped.

Charlene chuckled. "He got you good." The whir of her racer was lost in the shrieks ahead of us.

Takako slid her hands into her pumpkin festival jacket pockets. "I read about his wife's death in the paper this morning."

"Oh?" I asked.

We moved into a mad scientist's laboratory.

I scanned the tables for places someone could hide. A motionless Frankenstein's monster lay upon an angled operating table. "What did the article say?" I asked.

The racer circled a long table with beakers bubbling on it. Someone squawked behind the table.

A zombie hopped up. "What the—?"

"Just testing," Charlene said to the zombie. "Sorry, Takako, you were saying?"

"The article wasn't very illuminating," Takako said. "It said the body was found beneath one of the giant pumpkins, and that her death is being considered suspicious."

No kidding.

We twisted and turned through the rooms-a haunted fairground, a haunted asylum, a classic haunted mansion. Through some trick, the barn seemed bigger on the inside than on the outside.

Takako, Charlene, and the pumpkin fell behind, and I found myself alone on a haunted pirate ship.

I waited for them beside a ship's wheel, draped with fake spiderwebs. Charlene had been right to drag me from Pie Town. I would have hated to miss this. Of course, if I hadn't come, I'd never have known—

Something creaked behind the mast.

I whirled, expecting a demented pirate.

The ship's deck was empty.

Feminine screams echoed from the room next door.

I backed up, bumping into the ship's wheel, and jumped again.

Brilliant. Scares were a feature of haunted houses, not a bug. I exhaled a shaky breath. And where were Charlene and Takako?

There was a faint popping sound. In the dim room, I turned, orienting on the noise.

A tennis ball bounced across the wooden floor. It slowed, rolling to a stop in front of my sneakers.

Oh, that wasn't creeptastic. Not one bit.

"Charlene?" I called. "Takako?" Enough of this. I'd just go back and find them. I moved toward the entrance to the pirate room.

A sheet-clad ghost leapt from behind a pyramid of grog barrels. The spirit brandished a two-by-four. Nails sprouted from its business end.

"Okay, okay." I backed toward the exit. *Sheesh*. The church took the keep-moving-forward rule seriously. "I get the point. Heh, heh. Point. Nails. Get it?"

The ghost wafted closer and raised the board, menacing.

My muscles tensed. "I'm going." I turned and hurried forward. Stupid haunted house. Stupid rules. And what did ghosts have to do with pirates?

The skin between my shoulder blades heated. Sensing movement behind me, I pivoted.

A blur of white. The ghost leapt, board swinging.

Chapter Seven

I'd like to claim my catlike reflexes saved me. But I did not dive elegantly to safety.

Awkwardly, I half jumped backward. My heel caught on a coil of thick rope and I tumbled to the straw-dusted floor.

The board whizzed past my head. It thunked against the ship's wheel, nails sparking off the brass.

I shrieked. But it was one shriek lost in a chorus of feminine screams echoing through the barn. My stomach bottomed. In a haunted house, no one can hear you scream.

I rolled blindly. My feet tangled with the ghost's, and my attacker collapsed in a pile of bedsheets. My assailant sprang to its feet. Sheet flapping, it darted from the pirate ship and into the next room.

I scrambled to standing, tripped again over the stupid rope, staggered after my attacker. Pushing past gaggles of squealing girls, I raced into a weird, fog-filled maze. A werewolf sprang from behind a cardboard tree. Unthinking, I punched, catching myself just in time and jerking back and grazing its snout.

"Hey!"

"Sorry." I ran outside the barn and into the watery sunlight.

A white sheet flapped around the corner of the jail.

I charged past clusters of giggling tourists, past the line to get into the haunted house. Rounding the corner, I ran into the pumpkin parade. The 2,100-pound winner drifted past the old jail on a flatbed truck. A young woman in a tiara sat atop the gourd carrying a sign listing its winning poundage.

I hesitated. My attacker may have dropped his weapon, but confronting him might not be the smartest plan.

I dodged into the high school's marching band anyway. Its tunes clashed with the faint thrum of music from the stage at the south end of Main Street.

A trumpeter trod on my foot. He glared, his cheeks puffing.

"Sorry." I pushed past him and onto the sidewalk.

Something white flapped ahead. I plunged into the crowd.

The sheet lay draped over a juniper in front of a familiar purple house. Fog hung low above the flat roof.

I tugged the sheet free, scattering hard, blue juniper berries onto the sidewalk.

Because Charlene would have my head if I didn't, I climbed the steps to the purple front porch and knocked.

The front door cracked open. A bloodshot eyeball stared out. "Is it safe?" Tally-Wally asked.

"It depends on what you mean by safe."

"This blasted festival." Tally-Wally pulled the door wider and groaned. "After the first hour, I want to commit homicide. Not that I ever would," he added hastily. "Are you seeking haven from the crowds?"

"No. Did you see who left this on your juniper bush?" I extended the sheet.

He frowned down at me. "Someone left that on my juniper? Damned litterbugs."

"It was a prankster who tried to, um, scare me, but I didn't get a good look at him or her. You didn't happen to see anything, did you?"

"Nope, I was watching *The History Channel*. All they're talking about this month is ghosts and famous hauntings," he griped, "not real history."

"Okay. Thanks," I said, disappointed. But it had been a long shot. "I'll see you around."

"See you tomorrow morning." He shut the door.

I hurried back to the old jail.

Takako waited beside the ticket line, her head swiveling anxiously.

"Blood is all well and good," Charlene said to a kid in a zombie costume. "But what you need is more gore. A disconnected eyeball. Rotting flesh."

His mother hurried forward. She grasped the boy's shoulders, tugging him away and frowning at Charlene.

"Parents," Charlene said. "They ruin all the fun."

The pumpkin racer bumped my sneaker.

"Val!" Takako hurried to me and gave me a hug. "What happened? We lost you inside the haunted house."

"I don't know how we got separated," I said. "And then I saw a, er, friend."

"And she gave you a bedsheet?" Charlene arched a snowy brow and fiddled with the remote control.

"Her costume was becoming a real pain." I bundled it up and tucked it beneath my arm. "I told her I'd hold it for her at Pie Town. Did you see the winning pumpkin?"

Charlene nodded. "Petros didn't win. The crack was disqualifying."

I winced. *Ouch*. "He knew it would lose him the contest, but still, that must have smarted."

"Who's Petros?" Takako asked.

"He's my assistant manager Petronella's father," I said. "It was his pumpkin that was on top of Dr. Levant."

A high-pitched scream echoed down the street.

I started. Had my ghostly attacker returned?

The crowd scattered, shrieking.

A goat charged down the street, horns curved wickedly.

"It's a stampede!" Charlene shouted.

"It's a goat," I said.

"It's a goat stampede!"

A little girl sat crying in the middle of the road.

"She'll be trampled," Charlene bellowed. "Val, do something."

"It's a goat." I glanced around. No one else was running for the girl. Where were her parents? "Oh, for Pete's sake." I jogged into the street and grabbed up the girl, clutching her to me.

The goat focused on us. It increased speed, its hooves clattering on the pavement. It lowered its head, ramming position.

Oooh, this was going to hurt. I turned one hip toward the goat and winced, readying myself for the inevitable blow.

The pumpkin racer zipped between us and the goat. The animal skidded to a halt, its hind legs collapsing.

A woman charged into the street and wrenched the girl from my arms. "What are you doing?"

"I was . . ." I stammered. "She was in the street."

"Why did you take her into the street?"

"I didn't!"

"Stay away from my daughter." She stormed away with the child.

"I was only trying to help," I said weakly.

"Charlene, Val!" Laughing, Takako jogged to my side. "You're heroes."

"If I don't get arrested for child abduction," I muttered, face warm.

Robo-pumpkin lurched toward the goat.

Shaking its wooly head, the goat clambered to its feet. It nosed the pumpkin.

"And Val thought I was sending her into a dangerous situation. I had it all under control." Charlene smiled modestly. "Now, watch me herd the goat back to the petting zoo."

The pumpkin reversed, then bumped forward and tapped the goat.

The goat nosed it back.

Charlene fiddled with her controls. The pumpkin reversed and accelerated forward.

The goat lowered its head, and the robot pumpkin rammed its skull.

The goat shook its head, sniffed, and bit into the pumpkin.

"Noooooooooo!" Charlene howled.

The goat chewed meditatively.

"Get away from my pumpkin!" Charlene hurried forward, flapping her hands.

The goat took another bite, and Charlene snatched up the racer.

A man in overalls huffed down the road. He grabbed the goat's collar. "Sorry about that."

"He ate my racer!"

"She eats everything," he said.

"We can replace the pumpkin," I said.

Charlene shook her finger at him. "Your goat's a menace. I'll—"

I steered her toward Takako, who shook with laughter.

My stepmother wiped her eyes. "I'm sorry. Is the robot mechanism damaged?"

"I guess not," Charlene grouched.

"Ray might be in Pie Town." I glanced in that direction. "Maybe he can take a look at it."

"Later," Charlene said. "I promised Takako we'd take her by the glass studio."

My lips compressed. I needed to return to Pie Town. But I also wanted to talk to Charlene about that ghost, and the glass studio was only around the block. "Fine."

We walked past the Lutheran church where I'd once planned to get married. I stifled a sigh—not about the broken engagement. Not really. But it was a beautiful church, tall, wooden, and white, painted with blue trim.

Since Pastor Hiller wasn't howling in the fog, we turned right toward Main Street. Hay bales and pumpkins sat stacked around the iron lampposts, their flower baskets filled with autumnal blooms. Not a single shop window was pumpkin-free.

Behind a white lattice fence, a man in overalls and a straw hat carved pumpkins into elaborate faces. At a nearby table, children painted faces on pumpkins.

We paused in front of a set of shop windows filled with glass pumpkins and autumnal paperweights. A video in the window showed the glassmaker at work, creating a sapphire pumpkin.

Takako leaned closer to the window and gasped. "They're beautiful."

"They'll be cheaper after the festival," Charlene said. "You should stick around."

The scent of baking pies wafted down the street. "And I need to get back to Pie Town. Takako, will you excuse me?"

"Of course. I'll see you soon."

"Thanks." I gave Charlene a look that I hoped said *follow me*, and trotted back to my pie shop.

Another surge of customers had wedged themselves inside Pie Town. Their amiable chatter echoed off the linoleum floors and Formica tables.

Uniformed police officers skimmed through the crowd, delivering pies and collecting tips. I hoped they were making some good money for their Athletic League.

Dropping the sheet on my office desk, I tied on an apron and got to work, glancing at the door for Charlene.

She didn't return.

At six, I turned the sign in the front window to CLOSED.

Officer Billings clapped my shoulder. "Nice job, Val. I think we made over a thousand bucks today for the League. We'll see you tomorrow for an encore." He and his fellow cops ambled out the door.

I surveyed the empty restaurant. Nothing looked busted, and we'd sold out. I couldn't imagine a better day. But what had happened to Charlene?

My staff and I cleaned the restaurant and kitchen. Finally, Petronella, Abril, and Hunter left, and I finished up the floor, which was always the last thing to be cleaned.

The front door rattled beneath someone's fist.

I started, dropping my mop.

On the other side of the glass, Charlene pointed at the lock.

I let her inside. "Where were you?"

"We took a pumpkin glassblowing class. Look!" She pulled a tiny cerulean pumpkin from the pocket of her knit jacket. "I made this one." A curling, black vine coiled from the pumpkin's top.

"That's gorgeous." Now *I* wanted to make a glass pumpkin. I shook myself. *Later.*

"Well, Countess Báthory was doing it—"

"Countess . . . you mean Marla?"

"Who else would I mean? I had to stick around and make sure she didn't drain your stepmother's blood."

"I thought you two were going to put this rivalry behind you?" Charlene and Marla Van Horn had been one-upping each other since they were teenyboppers.

"We will. When I win."

"How do you win a rivalry?" I asked.

"It's like pornography," she said. "I'll know it when I see it." She pocketed the glass pumpkin and pulled out her remote control. "And to start, I'll win the pumpkin race tomorrow."

There was a crash from the kitchen. The door bumped open and the half-eaten pumpkin robot rolled beneath the Dutch door.

I blew out my breath. "Come with me."

Charlene and Robo-pumpkin followed me into the office.

I plucked the sheet off my battered metal desk. "A ghost attacked me in the haunted house."

"Attacked you?" She squinted. "Don't you mean scared you?"

"I mean attacked. He swung a two-by-four at me and then ran away. He or she left the sheet in Tally-Wally's front yard."

"So, that's where you went. Did Tally-Wally see anything?"

"No."

We examined the sheet but didn't find any clues. It was just a white sheet.

"Eight hundred thread count," I said. "It seems a bit spendy to turn into a ghost costume."

"It's the sort of thing a man would do." Charlene dropped the sheet on my desk. "But most men wouldn't bother with such expensive sheets in the first place."

"That's a little sexist."

Her white brows caterpillared downward. "What's your point?"

"I've forgotten."

"Why would someone attack you?" Charlene asked.

"Could someone we talked to about the murder have gotten nervous? It would narrow down the suspects, since we've only spoken to Dr. Levant's husband and her medical partner."

Charlene winced.

"What?" I asked. "Did you talk to someone else?"

"No, but Marla's been blabbing all over town about the Baker Street Bakers investigating the murder. It was all I could do to put your wicked stepmother off the scent."

"Charlene . . ." I said warningly.

"Fine. Takako's awesome as applesauce." She pointed at me. "But she can't join the Baker Street Bakers. We've been lax with the rules in the past, but I draw the line at visiting steprelatives."

No argument there. I didn't want Takako anywhere near this investigation. "Fine. What exactly has Marla been saying?"

"The Baker Street Bakers are on the case, that sort of thing."

"That doesn't sound so bad."

"She uses a *tone*. The point is, word's gotten out we're asking questions."

My insides sank like a deflating soufflé. Had Chief Shaw heard? We'd skated too close to interfering in an investigation before. I *tried* to stay on the right side of the law, but Charlene was less persnickety. And if Shaw got wind of what we were doing, he'd use it to drop the hammer on Gordon again.

I untied my apron. "This could be a problem."

She nodded. "You need to warn your detective."

Chapter Eight

Gordon paced his condo, his muscular body tense and hard. Like Gordon, the condo was contemporary and minimalist. He crossed his arms over his ivory fisherman's sweater. "Did you call the police? Because I know you didn't call me."

Sucking in my cheeks, I tossed the plastic bag containing the ghost's sheet onto the leather couch. Unlike anything I owned, the couch was quality. It matched the cappuccino-colored floor. "He was long gone. There didn't seem much point."

He paused beside a gray, mid-century-modern chair. "At the very least, when you report it to the police, there'll be a record of the attack at the haunted house."

Sure. And also a notation that I was a hysterical female who'd misinterpreted a pre-Halloween prank. "I'll call Chief Shaw," I muttered and glanced at the gray-curtained window. I might as well go straight to the top and get the humiliation over with.

He nodded. "Thanks. Now, what Baker Street Bakering would inspire someone to attack you? Assuming this wasn't a random prank."

I tried not to stare at the fireplace, covered in narrow pieces of dark brown stone. In front of it stood a free-standing whiteboard covered with a blanket. The mystery of what was behind the blanket was too much for any Baker Street Baker to resist. I edged closer.

"I hate to join Team Charlene," I said, "but I think it might have been Marla."

"Marla Van Horn? Charlene's friend? Why would she attack you?"

"She wouldn't. Marla's been talking about our amateur sleuthing into Dr. Levant's murder. The wrong person may have overheard. Gordon, Shaw may have heard."

"Shaw wouldn't attack you."

"No, but he might cause more problems for you." I took another casual step toward the covered whiteboard.

"Don't worry about me," he said. "And I'll have a word with Marla."

I laughed hollowly. "Don't tell her she's putting us crossways of interfering in an investigation. That will just egg her on."

A smile softened his features. "I'll never get used to these small-town intrigues."

"Get used to it? You grew up here."

"And left as soon as I got the chance. I thought San Nicholas was boring. What an idiot I was."

I canted my head. "So, what's under the blanket?"

"Murder board."

I waited expectantly.

He sighed. "Fine." Gordon pulled the blanket from the whiteboard, and it folded to the floor.

A headshot of Dr. Levant in her white ophthalmologist's coat had been taped to the center of the board. Down one side, Gordon had affixed a column of blurry photos from the murder scene.

It would be hypocritical for me to worry about Gordon investigating the murder he'd been told to stay out of. But his movements were quick and hurried, his muscles rigid, his voice sharper than usual. I'd never seen him this tense. But his uncle was a suspect; of course he was tense. So, I worried but said nothing.

Instead, I squinted at the crime-scene shots. "Charlene's photos?"

"Yeah. Shaw won't let me near the official police photographs."

I walked to a map stuck to another corner. Magnetized pins marked the site where the body had been discovered, as well as Dr. Levant's home and office, and other spots. "What are these?"

He stepped close enough for me to feel the heat coming off his body, and the pit of my stomach tingled.

"Homes of the other suspects," he said, "except for her business partner, Tristan Cannon, who was setting up on Main Street, and her husband. Elon was at the haunted house. Everyone else claims they were at home." He tapped a magnet pin on Main Street, just north of Pie Town. "No one's got alibis."

"Other suspects," I said casually. "Like Alfreda Kuulik?"

"The receptionist who was fired? Yes."

"Or Laurelynn Lelli?" I winced, because I hated ratting out someone selling my pies.

"Dr. Levant's very own Marla? Yes." He tapped a magnet.

Phooey—he already knew everything. I wasn't helping at all.

He shot me a wry look. "And before you say it, Dr.

Levant's cousin, Denise Tatari, is a suspect too." He touched another round, colored magnet.

"Her cousin?" The head pie judge was Dr. Levant's cousin? I tried to remember what I'd said to Denise yesterday, but I knew condolences hadn't been involved. She must have thought I was a jerk. But she hadn't seemed in shock or mourning when I'd called. Was it possible she hadn't known yet her cousin had died?

"The husband's the most likely suspect," he rumbled. "But according to Elon, Kara stipulated in her will that her portion of their grandparents' inheritance should go to her cousin."

"Not to Elon?"

"No. The grandparents' estate isn't a huge inheritance, but we can't ignore Denise as a suspect. And of course, Elon gets the rest."

"Is that why Shaw hasn't brought Elon in for questioning yet?"

"Maybe." He turned to the board and planted his broad hands on his hips.

"I need to get photos of the suspects on the board," he muttered.

I coughed politely. "I suppose you'll be sleuthing during the pie contest tomorrow?"

Gordon looked over his shoulder and quirked a brow. "Won't you be?"

"With Denise as a judge, it does seem like an opportunity too good to waste," I said. "Though I wonder if she'll go ahead with the judging under the circumstances."

He looped an arm around my waist and pulled me close.

"At least I'll be able to keep an eye on you," he said.

My stomach rumbled, and my face warmed.

He laughed. "I did promise dinner, didn't I?" Gordon

looked toward the sleek kitchen. It bled into the living room, the two spaces separated only by the leather couch.

"You know," I said, "I haven't had pizza in a dog's age."

His handsome face relaxed. "Pizza it is. I'll make the call."

While he phoned, I studied the murder board. It was loads more professional than the one Ray had once created using a dungeon map from a role-playing game.

Gordon stole up behind me and wrapped his arms around my waist. "Not the romantic evening you'd envisioned," he said, wry.

I leaned against him, his warm breath tickling my neck. "I don't need flowers and ocean views every night." Especially since my tiny house overlooked the Pacific. "But don't think you can take me for granted. Certain standards must be maintained."

"I'll keep that in mind." He trailed a hand down my arm. "Is something bothering you?"

"Aside from finding a murder victim?"

"I guess that was a stupid question."

"No, it's not." Especially when I was really concerned about him. But when you don't want to tell *the* truth, tell *a* truth. "It's Doran's mother."

"Doran's—your stepmother?"

"I just can't figure out *why* she's here."

"Presumably because of you and Doran."

"Well, yeah," I said, "but that can't be the only reason."

"Why not?"

"Something just seems . . . off."

"Ah." He turned me to face him. "You're thinking she's got an ulterior motive, that she and your father are two of a kind."

"She's not, though. And she's nothing like my mother either."

His dark brow arched like a cresting wave. "Should she be?"

"No," I said, "of course not. Forget it. I'm babbling. There's just been a lot going on."

"Do you want me to do some checking?"

"No. You've got enough to deal with. Takako's not at the heart of any conspiracy. That would put Doran in it too, and why am I even talking about conspiracies? She's my . . . She's Doran's mom."

The pizza arrived. We sat at his coffee table noshing pepperoni pizza, drinking Zinfandel, and discussing the murder board. I reveled in the coziness. Gordon was sharing his life and his investigation. We were a team, and the thought sent a twinge of guilt through me. Charlene and I were a team too. I'd need to report what I'd learned.

We finished the pizza and put the plates in the dishwasher. I yawned.

"Early night?" He lightly stroked my forearm. "You must be exhausted."

"Yeah, and I want to check on Charlene." It had been a long day. Though mentally Charlene might be seventy-something going on thirteen, physically, she was seventy-plus. Besides, we had a case to discuss.

"Is she okay?"

"She's Charlene." I stood on my toes and kissed him.

Gordon walked me to my pink van. He leaned through my open window, and his emerald eyes glinted. "Do me a favor?"

"Depends on the favor."

"Never tail a suspect in this van."

I laughed. "Deal." Though Charlene's yellow Jeep wasn't any less conspicuous.

Slowly, I drove from his condo. The night was thick with fog, and my hands clenched on the wheel. I sat forward, my chest straining against the seat belt, as if the extra inches would improve my vision. If a car was stopped ahead of me, I wouldn't see it until I was on top of it.

A spot between my shoulder blades prickled. I shook myself. There was no way anyone could follow me in this pea soup. I was only nervous driving in such thick fog.

Gritting my teeth, I pulled onto the One. Cars would be moving more quickly here, in spite of the low visibility. I edged up to the speed limit, so I didn't get rear-ended.

A semi flashed past on the left, its wake buffeting the van.

I continued on, muscles tight.

Finally, I turned east onto a surface street and drove farther inland, into Charlene's neighborhood. The fog lightened here, and I relaxed against my seat.

I pulled to a stop in front of her picket fence. Pumpkins on curling green vines glimmered with moisture in the glow of a nearby street lamp.

I stepped from the van.

Somewhere in the darkness, a car's motor cut.

I looked up and down the street. Lights from nearby homes cut rectangles in the mist.

No one stalked menacingly up the street. No one loomed from behind the nearby juniper bush. No one lay in wait behind the nearby Lexus.

I am not being followed.

But I hustled up the stone path to Charlene's front porch. Lights streamed from the front windows, illuminating the hanging ferns. I knocked, scuffing my knuckles on the white, wood door.

After a moment, Takako answered the knock.

"Val!" She dragged me inside and clutched me in a python hug.

"Takako," I said, breathless. I pried myself free and bumped into a doily-covered end table.

"What are you doing here?" Takako asked.

"Val's checking to see if I died," Charlene grumped from her new leather couch. "She's convinced I'm at death's door and occasionally comes 'round to check if I'm decomposing."

Right. And that had nothing to do with the heart attack Charlene had faked last month.

Takako's face wrinkled. "I'm sure Val doesn't think that at all."

"She shouldn't." Charlene lifted a glass from the couch's cupholder and took a long slurp. "Val's the one headed for heart failure. And stop letting all the warm air out," Charlene said. "I'm not paying to heat the entire street."

Frederick raised his head from the back of the brown leather couch and growled.

Hastily, I shut the front door. "That's not why I came by. I thought you might want to watch some *Stargate*."

"What's *Stargate*?" Takako asked.

Charlene gaped. "What's *Stargate*? What's *Stargate*? Only one of the longest-running science-fiction TV shows of the twentieth century. Wormholes! Sexy aliens! Speaking of which, didn't you have a date with that detective of yours, Val?"

"Gordon's not an alien."

"I know that," she said. "What happened?"

"My date turned out not be a date after all." I glanced at the curtained front window.

"I know what'll make you feel better," Charlene said. "How about a glass of my special root beer?"

"I'm driving." And her "special" root beer was loaded with Kahlúa.

"Why do you keep looking out the window?" Charlene asked.

"Rampant paranoia." I dropped the curtain. "On the way here, I imagined someone was following me."

Charlene lurched from the couch. "Is he outside?"

"I don't know." I shifted my weight. "Like I said, I was probably imagining it."

"Do you usually imagine things?" Takako asked.

"Well, no." Usually my bad feelings paid off.

It's a gift.

Charlene reached behind a couch cushion and pulled out her shotgun.

"Whoa!" I ducked, heart thumping, and raised my hands in a defensive gesture. "I don't think that's necessary."

Charlene strode to the window and pulled back a faded curtain. "I can't see anything in all this fog."

A light snicked off, plunging the living room into darkness.

"It's all right," Takako whispered, coming to stand beside us. "That was me."

"Good thinking," Charlene said. "Now, whoever's out there won't be able to see in."

I turned to my stepmother. "Takak-Oh!" I yelped.

My stepmother had raised a curved blade near my throat. The size and shape of a T. rex's claw, its metal glinted in the faint streetlight struggling past the curtains.

Takako scanned the front garden through narrowed eyes.

I edged the claw away with one finger. "Is that thing legal?"

"No," she said. "But if I ever need to use it, I'll worry about legal later."

Charlene nodded approvingly. "Easier to carry than a shotgun."

"Is that a Mossberg?" Takako nodded toward the gun.

"Yep." Charlene racked a shell, and the gun made an ominous clacking sound. "The 500 Tactical."

"I hear those are good for home defense," Takako said, "though I prefer the Benelli M4."

"The Italians know firearms," Charlene agreed, "but isn't the Benelli heavy?"

"I don't plan on hiking with it."

The two women laughed.

I wiped damp palms on my jeans. Holy guacamole, Charlene and Takako were bonding.

"All right," Charlene said. "Takako, you're with me."

"With you where?" I bleated.

"We'll go around the back of the house and see if we surprise anyone," Charlene explained.

"Wait," I said. "No—"

"Val," Charlene said, "you stay here. Turn the light back on and keep 'em focused on you. If anything happens, guard Frederick."

"Guard—"

The two women scuttled into the kitchen, leaving the door swinging behind them. I heard another door open and softly shut.

Swearing, I flipped on the living room light. I stepped toward the front door and banged my thigh into another low table. "Ow!"

From the couch, Frederick meowed a warning.

"Thanks for nothing."

I cursed some more and paced in front of the window. I didn't think Charlene would actually shoot anyone. Would she?

After an eternity, footsteps sounded on the front porch,

and I jerked open the door. Charlene and Takako trooped into the living room. Their hair glittered with droplets of fog.

"No one," Charlene said.

"I told you I'd imagined it."

"But we did hear a car driving off," Takako said.

"It was probably Thistleblossom," Charlene said.

"Who's Thistleblossom?" My stepmother tucked her curved knife somewhere inside the folds of her *Pie or Die* hoodie. Takako was loyal to extended family; I'd give her that.

Charlene dropped onto her new couch. "The old bat who wins the pumpkin pie contest every year. She tried to intimidate Val earlier."

Takako's nostrils flared. "Did she now?"

"It's no big thing," I said. "It's a blind taste test, so I don't know how she could influence the judging anyway."

Takako's mouth puckered. "There are all sorts of ways. You'd be surprised what I've seen."

"What have you seen?" Charlene cocked her head.

"The world of academia can be cutthroat. Reviews that have been tampered with, bribery, blackmail. If there's a way to cheat, people will find it."

"You are preaching to the choir," Charlene said. "Anyway, Takako and I have agreed we'll follow you home."

"You don't have to," I said. "The fog is terrible."

Charlene growled. "You think I don't know how to drive in fog?"

I wasn't sure she knew how to drive in daylight. "No, that's not—"

"Great, then I can see where you live." Takako reached for a parka hanging from a wall peg. "Let's go."

The two women followed my van to my tiny home on the bluff.

Beside the picnic table, Takako stepped from Charlene's yellow Jeep. She looked around, frowning. "Where is it?"

"It's the tiny house." I motioned toward the converted shipping container. "Do you want to come inside?"

"Maybe it's best Val gets her rest," Charlene said. "She's got a big day tomorrow."

"Oh," I said, relieved. "Right. Pie judging."

Takako hugged me. "Then a rain check? I'd love to see your, er, home later."

"Definitely. Rain check." I glanced at the eucalyptus trees bordering the property, sloping down to the hidden cemetery. Were Gordon and Charlene pranking me or not?

I backed away and my thigh bumped the picnic table. Grimacing, I rubbed the spot on my jeans—the same place I'd knocked against Charlene's end tables. My recent clumsiness had to be a message from my subconscious. Unfortunately, I'd no idea how to interpret it.

They waited until I was inside my house before driving off.

I listened to the Jeep grumble down the hill, its engine fading to silence. Then I lay in bed and listened to other night sounds—the patter of paws across my metal roof, the scrape of a branch.

I fell asleep. Crumbling tombstones and drifting white figures haunted my dreams.

Chapter Nine

Repressing a shiver, I burrowed deeper into my Pie Town hoodie. The pumpkin pie contest had taken over the stage at the south end of Main Street, near our white adobe firehouse. Pumpkins and pedestrians thronged Main Street. Awnings and food trucks drifted in and out of my vision, obscured by the drifting mist. Though it was nearly noon, the fog refused to lift, and I hunched lower in the metal chair. I didn't trust Charlene and Takako's new friendship. What was my piecrust maker up to?

A breeze spattered my face with droplets of moisture. The orange tablecloth fluttered on the long table. I slapped my palm onto the scorecard before it could fly away.

We'd been asked to judge the pies on ten criteria, ranging from the aroma to whether the crust was properly flaky. I studied the scorecard. I baked pies for a living, and even I wasn't this picky.

People crowded a table to the side of the stage for free samples. Entering this contest required some serious baking—a dozen pies per entrant. That way, the audience could participate in the tasting. The audience didn't get to vote, but the lure of free pumpkin pie was a huge draw.

Heidi strode up the steps and stopped in front of my

seat. "So. You're still judging." The gym owner's mouth flattened.

I folded my arms. "Why wouldn't I . . . ? Hold on. You told me about your crust to get me disqualified?" Sheesh, this bake-off was cutthroat.

"It isn't fair that you're judging me, given our relationship."

"I'm not judging you—I told the head judge about our contact."

She stuffed her hands into the pockets of her green Heidi's Health and Fitness jacket. "And?"

"And you should talk to Denise if you've got a problem with me," I said, weaseling out.

"I don't see much point to that, do you?"

"Why not?"

The head judge, Denise Tatari, cleared her throat.

Heidi shot me a final glare and hopped off the stage, her ponytail bobbing. I really hated having a nemesis. On the flip side, that made me Heidi's nemesis, and b*eing* a nemesis carried a heady, seductive power. I could almost understand Charlene's attraction to her ongoing battle with Marla.

Denise was a middle-aged woman in businesslike black slacks and knit top. Her black jacket sported an eyeglasses logo. Tasteful highlights streaked her mid-length brown hair. She tapped the microphone. "Welcome—"

The microphone screeched, and we all cringed.

Denise fiddled with the controls and blew on the mic. "Welcome to the San Nicholas Annual Pumpkin Pie Bake-off." Her voice, echoing down the street, carried a marked lack of enthusiasm. But in fairness, she'd just lost her cousin beneath a giant pumpkin.

"To keep things simple," she continued, "we asked our

entrants to bake classic pumpkin pies. But as I'm sure you noticed in your own tasting, there can be a lot of variation between even the classics."

Murmurs and cheerful laughter erupted from the crowd.

I scanned the rows of chairs. Charlene hadn't shown yet, and the pumpkin races should have finished by now. I hoped she and her pumpkin robot had placed.

Denise explained how the pies would be ranked, and she handed the microphone to Graham.

He waddled to the center of the stage and adjusted the cabbie's hat over his balding head. "Before we get started, let's introduce our judges!"

He moved to stand slightly beside Denise, who'd taken her seat at the end of the long table. "You've already met our head judge, Denise Tatari. Denise is the founder of a local ophthalmology software company. She's also our most exciting San Nicholas resident. I saw those Facebook photos." He waggled his plump finger at the judge. "Bungee jumping in Fiji? At your age?"

She smiled.

Graham strolled down the length of the table, introducing judges, until he got to me. "Val Harris is the owner of Pie Town, right here on Main Street. So, if you haven't gotten your fill of pie yet, be sure to stop by. But what many people don't know about Val is, she's also a member of the highly secretive Baker Street Bakers. The Bakers are an amateur sleuthing society responsible for solving several local crimes."

From the base of the stage, where the other amateur bakers sat, Gordon grinned.

I flushed. It was fine for our friends to know, but the Baker Street Bakers wasn't something I'd wanted to advertise to the world.

Mrs. Thistleblossom scowled and made an odd gesture toward me, as if casting a curse. Her gaze bored into mine.

I shivered again and not from the cold. *Curses?* Where had that idea come from? Maybe I was spending too much time with Charlene.

Takako waved from the front row, and I waggled my fingers in her direction.

"Let's give all the judges a big round of applause," Graham finished. He set the mic in front of Denise. It thunked loudly on the table, and she hastily turned it off.

In front of each of us were two pies cut into slender slices. Numbers had been taped to the bottom of each tin.

I tasted the first pie. The bottom crust was a little mushy, but the flavor was intense. I scored the pie and passed it to my fellow judge, then tried the next pie in front of me.

It was crustless—Heidi's no doubt. The flavor was milder than I liked, but it wasn't bad. I wasn't sure how to judge the crust though, since there wasn't any. I ended up leaving that square blank, made a notation for Denise, and passed the pie to the next judge.

Two more pies were set in front of me. Slowly, we worked our way through the judging. My favorite was pie number six. It had obviously had some sort of whiskey added to the mix. I savored the pie on my tongue and closed my eyes. Was it a cinnamon whiskey? The pie had a kick, but not so much as to overwhelm the pumpkin flavor, and the crust was perfection. Even Charlene would have approved. I checked the watch on my phone. Where was she?

I did a double take.

Takako had left the crowd.

I shifted in my folding chair. Maybe she'd gotten bored

and gone to check out the food trucks. Watching people judge pie can't be very exciting unless you're a contestant.

Graham, carrying two round, plastic bakery boxes, approached Denise. He bent to mutter something in her ear.

Denise's expression hardened, her lips forming a taut line. She gave her head a small shake.

I watched, perplexed. What was going on?

The two held a whispered discussion. Graham handed her a pumpkin pie in a round, plastic bakery box, and a second, empty box.

Denise rose and walked to my end of the table. She removed one of the pies from in front of me. It had scored high as well, hitting all the "classic" pumpkin pie notes.

"Excuse me." Denise returned to her seat.

She took a bite of the pie she'd taken from me, then sampled a bite of the pie from the bakery box and grimaced. Denise tapped the bemused-looking judge beside her. They held another whispered conference, and she gave him both pies. He tasted them and shook his head, then passed the pies to the judge beside him.

Joy, the owner of a comic book store and a fellow judge, nudged my arm. Her ponytail of blue-black hair cascaded down the back of her brown coat. "What's going on?" In her monotone voice, she flattened the question into a demand.

"No idea," I whispered. "But the pie in the plastic box looks professional." I glanced at the audience. Takako had returned to her seat, a grim look on her face.

The judge beside Joy handed her both pies. "There's strong evidence this pie was bought commercially." He pointed to pie number three. "Someone bought this pie as a comparison." He held up the pie in the plastic box. "It looks and tastes identical to me."

We tried the two pies. They were, indeed, the same,

right down to the fluted pattern in the edge of the crusts. We huddled and agreed that pie number three should be disqualified, but I felt a hot flush. The Germans have a great word for feeling embarrassed on someone else's behalf: *fremdschämen*. Even though I didn't know who the culprit was, I felt that now. Who would cheat like that? The prize was only a ribbon.

"We won't announce there was a cheater," Denise said. "Not to the public. I'll talk to the entrant personally."

Denise gathered the scorecards, and Graham tallied the numbers.

Ten minutes later, he stepped to the front of the stage and tapped on the mic. "And the winner is pie number six, baked by local detective Gordon Carmichael!"

I clapped wildly. I'd known Gordon could cook, but it was the first time I'd tried one of his baked goods. He'd been hiding his talents.

Mrs. Thistleblossom's jaw sagged. She paled, then colored.

Gordon shook hands with the other contestants. Heidi smiled graciously and wrung his hand between two of hers. When his back turned, Heidi stomped away, nose in the air. He glanced over his shoulder toward the gym owner, and his forehead creased. Then he bounded up the steps.

Graham handed him a blue ribbon. "Now, the judges thought they detected whiskey in your pie. Were they correct?"

"Yes," Gordon said. "But the alcohol burns off during the baking."

Congratulations were conferred, hands were shook, and the crowd broke up.

I made my way across the stage. "Denise," I said in a

low voice, "I didn't get a chance to say anything earlier, but I'm so sorry about your cousin."

The judge looked down at the scorecards in her hands. "Thank you. It's been . . . it's been a shock. We grew up together. We were like sisters. I keep reaching for my phone to call her, and then I remember I can't."

"Please, let me know what I can do to help," I said, an ache growing in my throat. I still reached for my phone to call my mother.

Denise shook her head, her mid-length hair falling into place about her shoulders. "There's nothing. I mean, I don't know, but—" She sucked in her cheeks. "Actually, there is something."

"Oh?"

"My company is sponsoring the corn maze down the road."

"I love corn mazes." I had a weakness for mazes of any sort, even labyrinths, which weren't true mazes, since there was only one way in and out.

"Then you should definitely come. We've got a pumpkin cannon and some other activities as well."

"A cannon that shoots pumpkins. Seriously?"

One corner of her mouth lifted. "It's a thing. The maze is open all month. But this Thursday, all the proceeds are being donated to Kara's favorite charity. It provides vision treatment for low-income families. Would you come Thursday? And bring friends."

"Yes, of course." It was the least I could do. I nodded toward the eyeglasses logo on her black jacket. "Is that your firm?"

She tugged down her jacket, flattening the logo. "My baby. It may not be the height of fashion, but I can't resist wearing my company jacket every chance I get."

I smiled, pointing to the Pie Town logo on my hoodie. "Trust me, I know how that is."

"You should join the Women's Professional Networking Association. You're a small business owner, like me. You'd fit right in to our local chapter."

Ugh. Meetings. "I don't know," I waffled. "I'm so busy."

"I get it. I once felt the same. But I found that they were really supportive. They didn't just help me find business, they also cheered me on. They understand what small business owners go through. The long hours. The excitement. The stress."

"Wow. You really get me."

She laughed. "Are bakers' hours as bad as they say?"

"Nah. They're worse."

She patted my arm. "Then think about it. They're a group of smart, hardworking, interesting women. Our next meeting's on Friday. Come as my guest."

"I will. Thanks."

I turned, and Gordon was there.

"If I kiss you," he said, "will you be accused of favoritism?"

"Probably." I tugged lightly on his fisherman's sweater. Standing on tiptoes, I brushed a kiss across his cheek. "Congratulations. Your pie was spectacular."

He pulled me closer, and I could feel the hard lines of his muscles against me. My heart thudded unevenly. "Maybe I'll give you the recipe," he said.

"You'd do that for me?" I teased, breathless.

"Val!" Takako barreled up the stage, Charlene in tow.

My piecrust maker scowled in her brown-and-white striped leggings and a burnt-orange knit jacket. A pumpkin beanie rested on her curling white hair.

"Congratulations," Takako said to Gordon. "I sampled your pie. It really was the best."

"This is my, uh, stepmother," I said, stumbling over the word. "Takako Harris."

He shook her hand.

Takako pointed to her orange-and-black Pie Town hoodie. "I'm telling everyone about Pie Town."

"Thanks. How was the pumpkin race?" I asked Charlene.

My piecrust specialist scowled. "I lost!"

"Oh, no," I said. We were never going to hear the end of this.

"Ray swore we would win." Charlene fumed. "Stupid robot. It was never the same after the goat attack."

"Goat?" Gordon asked.

"After the ghost attack," Charlene said.

"Ghost?" Takako asked.

"You were able to replace the pumpkin," I said, "weren't you?" We hadn't told Takako about the ghost in the haunted house. I didn't want to worry her.

"Of course, I replaced the pumpkin," Charlene said. "It wouldn't have qualified with only a half-eaten pumpkin."

"Did Marla win?"

"Her? No. Her solar-powered pumpkin didn't budge. Not enough sun today. The fog is good for vampires, bad for solar cells."

"Then who won?" I asked.

"That diabolical Brinks kid."

"Diabolical?" Brinks was the universe's vengeance on all the childhood pranks Charlene had ever played. The kid had TP'd her house, egged her picket fence, and made fun of her cat.

In fairness, I made fun of Frederick too, just not within earshot of Charlene.

"And guess who let that goat loose from the petting zoo?" Charlene asked. "Brinks."

"He couldn't possibly have known the goat would go for your pumpkin," I said. "The streets are littered with pumpkins."

Charlene folded her arms. "Oh, you think so? Because it gets worse. I have it on good authority the Brinks kid didn't even make his own racer. His *father* built it."

Uh-huh. "Didn't Ray make your—?"

"I hear you had some excitement here," Charlene said quickly.

"Mrs. Thistleblossom." Takako made a rueful face. "Charlene had her number, all right."

I pulled away from Gordon. "Had her number? What do you mean?"

She glanced sidelong at Charlene. "We followed her this morning to a bakery on the Peninsula."

"I drove," Charlene said.

Gordon shook his head. "I shouldn't be hearing this."

Whoa. Mrs. Thistleblossom was the cheater?

"There's my uncle Petros," Gordon said. "I promised to buy him a pumpkin beer. His archrival won the giant pumpkin contest and won't shut up about it."

"Go. Buy beer," I said. "I'll see you around."

He hopped from the stage.

I turned to my stepmother. "You two—?"

"Caught Thistleblossom red-handed," Charlene said.

"So, you narced on her?" I asked, disbelieving. I looked to my stepmother. "Is that where you went during the judging?"

"No, I went to the ladies' room," Takako said.

Charlene's head reared up. "Narc? No way. Snitches get stitches."

A family in pumpkin beanies like Charlene's edged past the stage.

"We thought we were following her to something more

nefarious this morning," Takako said. "We thought she was buying more spray chalk."

"You think Thistleblossom tagged my van?" The graffiti's archaic language fit, but she seemed a little old for pranks.

"I don't know which judge figured out she was cheating," Charlene said, "but we didn't tattle."

"I'm a little hurt you would think we would do that to her," Takako said. "Mrs. Thistleblossom is over a hundred."

"Only the good die young," Charlene grumbled.

"Did Mrs. Thistleblossom see you following her?" I asked.

Charlene rubbed her chin. "She might have."

"She was cursing and shaking her fist," Takako said. "I'm pretty sure she saw us."

"Does she know you didn't rat her out to the judges?" I asked.

The two older women looked at each other, at me.

I scraped a hand through my hair. Oh boy. What were the odds of this ending well?

Chapter Ten

"So, let me get this straight," I said. "Mrs. Thistle-blossom saw you two spying on her at the bakery. She knows we're friends. And the first time I judge the contest, she gets booted for cheating."

Charlene flattened her pumpkin beanie with both hands. "You're right. You're screwed."

"I'm sure she'll understand you had nothing to do with it." Takako tugged at the collar of her orange-and-black hoodie. "We'll talk to her for you."

"I don't think that's such a good idea," Charlene said. "Let's give Thistleblossom time to cool off."

In other words, avoid the problem. "Thanks." And why were Takako and Charlene going off on spy missions without me? My stomach burned with an unfamiliar sensation.

I made my way to the stage steps. My hands were oddly damp on the cool metal railing. Mrs. Thistleblossom might look like a crone out of the Brothers Grimm, but she wasn't going to put a curse on me. Right?

A woman in a green, medieval-looking gown walked up the steps. She carried scrolls beneath one arm. I guessed she was the storyteller, armed with pumpkin-themed fairy tales.

Charlene grabbed my arm. "That's Alfreda Kuulik."

I took another look at the storyteller, adjusting the folds of her skirt. "She doesn't look anything like Alfreda."

"Not her! *Her!*" Charlene pointed.

The ophthalmologist's receptionist stood in front of a stall selling tea. She was a tall, big-boned brunette. Her straight hair stopped at her jaw, emphasizing its squarish shape.

"We should talk to her," I said.

"Talk to her?" Takako asked. "An interview? You *are* investigating the murder."

"Val is." Charlene leaned forward on the toes of her high-tops and made a "get-over-here" gesture at Ray.

The red-headed engineer blanched. He ducked behind a taco truck.

"I've got a bone to pick with you, engineer." Charlene trotted down the wobbly steps. They rattled metallically beneath her sneakers. "Get back here!"

I frowned after her, but the four horsemen of the apocalypse were not thundering down Main Street. Charlene was turning down a chance to interview a witness? She could yell at Ray any old day, but suspects were hard to come by. My piecrust maker must really be mad about losing that race.

"Let's hurry before we lose your suspect." Takako nudged my arm.

"Oh, right."

We trotted down the stage steps and made our way to the tea booth.

Eyes closed, Alfreda sniffed an open Mason jar filled with brown leaves the color of her long coat. Bits of orange flecked the tea.

"Alfreda?" I asked.

She turned, her cornflower eyes widening, then narrowing. "Sorry. I know I know you, but I can't remember . . ."

"I'm Val Harris, from Pie Town. I came in for an eye exam a few months ago. I'm not surprised you don't remember me. This is my, um, this is Takako Harris."

Takako, dwarfed by the taller woman, pumped her hand. "How nice to meet a friend of Val's. I'm so sorry to hear about Dr. Levant. I understand you were her receptionist."

Had I told Takako about Alfreda's relationship to Dr. Levant, or that she'd been fired? I didn't think so. That left Charlene as the leaker, or else Takako had done her own investigating.

Alfreda's square jaw tightened. "I was the office manager." Carefully, she recapped the jar. "It so happened that my desk was at reception."

"That must have kept you busy," I said. "What a shock for you now that she's gone. How are you holding up?"

"I have bigger problems to worry about," Alfreda said coolly. She set the jar on the table, and the tea seller passed the tea to another potential customer. "I no longer work for Kara. Though I'm sure Dr. Cannon is taking it hard."

"Why?" Takako asked. "Were they close? Were they having an affair? Did her husband know?" She colored and pinched her lips shut.

I froze. *Takako!* As Gordon frequently reminded me, I was not a professional investigator. But even I knew better than this.

Alfreda's fair brow wrinkled. "Um, no, I mean, I don't think so. I don't think they were— What exactly are you asking?"

"I think the town is trying to figure out who would have done such a thing," I said, hoping she'd offer some ideas.

"Small towns are far too nosy for their own good," Alfreda said. "People should leave it to the police."

"Have the police spoken with you?" I asked.

"Did they take you to the police station?" Takako asked. "They didn't accuse you of killing her, did they?"

I smothered a groan. Alfreda would never talk now.

Alfreda's high cheekbones pinked. "No, of course not!"

"Of course not," I echoed, laughing uneasily. "Not when there are so many other, more likely suspects." *And please tell me who they might be.*

Alfreda folded her arms over her long, brown coat. "It was nice seeing you again, Val," she said in a voice that made it plain it hadn't been nice at all. She nodded to my stepmother and moved to leave.

"I'm hiring!" I said, desperate.

Alfreda turned. "For what?"

"Cashier. You should come in for an interview."

Her smile was brief. "I'm not sure that's a good fit for me." She disappeared into the crowd.

Takako groaned. "I can't believe I did that."

"Interrogate a murder suspect?"

"Interrogate her so badly." She clutched her hair at the roots. "I'm an anthropologist. I *know* how to conduct an interview, and I just spewed accusations. I was clumsy and inattentive and . . . Val, I'm sorry. Everything I do to help . . . Did I ruin your investigation?"

"No." My annoyance evaporated in the face of her obvious regret. And who was I to criticize? I was no more than a nosy amateur. "It's fine. What did you think of Alfreda?"

We walked through the crowd.

"She makes a good murder suspect," Takako said slowly. "Did you notice how big and strong she is? It would have made maneuvering that giant pumpkin easier."

"Hmm. I wonder how much strength was needed to get it into the forklift's straps." I'm not sure I could have figured out how to even use a forklift.

"I hope you weren't serious about hiring her," Takako said.

"Not after those posts she wrote about her old employer. But it seemed like a way to keep her talking and maybe bring her back for more."

"At least *you* were thinking. Please don't tell Doran about this. I'll never hear the end of it."

"Mum's the word."

We returned to Pie Town. The dining area heaved, every pink booth filled. The line at the register edged out the front door.

Uniformed cops moved through the crowd delivering pie. This was an all-hands-on-deck situation, and guilt bit me hard. I should have been here instead of faffing around the festival.

I hugged Takako. "I have to get to work."

"I know." She reached up and patted my cheek. "You're a hard worker. Good luck today." Takako zipped up her Pie Town hoodie, and we said our good-byes.

Grimacing, I hurried into the kitchen.

Petronella bustled past in her usual black goth jeans and long-sleeved tee. She slid a turkey pot pie and side salad into the order window.

"Have you seen Charlene?" I snapped on my hairnet.

"No. Not since you left for the contest." She grinned. "I hear my cousin won."

"Gordon deserved to win." I slipped a Pie Town apron over my head and tied it behind my back. "And it was a blind tasting," I said, more defensively than strictly necessary.

Petronella sobered. "At least one person in our family did well this pumpkin festival."

"I'm sorry about your father's pumpkin." I pulled an order ticket from the wheel for two slices of pumpkin pie. "All that work, wrecked in a morning."

"And in such an awful way. He was really embarrassed about going on and on about the pumpkin when there was a dead woman under it. But I think the pumpkin was all he could focus on. And on top of everything, he thinks it made him look guilty in front of Shaw."

I glanced sidelong at her. "Shaw can't believe your father or Gordon had anything to do with the murder." I plated the pumpkin pies and slid them through the window with the ticket.

Petronella's mouth pressed into a tight line. She grabbed a ticket from the wheel.

I adjusted my apron. "Wait! Shaw doesn't think that, does he?"

"Who knows?" she asked, her voice brittle. Petronella plated a slice of pecan pie. "He keeps coming back to my parents' house with more questions. I heard he's been talking to the winner, Farmer John, too." She smiled bitterly. "That's the only bright spot for my father. Farmer John might get busted for sabotaging his pumpkin. He and my dad don't get along."

I grabbed another order ticket. "But Farmer John wouldn't have killed a woman because of a pumpkin competition with your dad. That would be insane."

"No, but for forty thousand dollars, he might have seen the body and dropped my dad's pumpkin on it."

"Maybe." I plated a slice of pumpkin chiffon and a slice of maple-pumpkin pie. Sliding them into the order window, I grabbed another ticket. "But it still seems a little extreme."

"You don't know Farmer John. I mean, who calls themselves Farmer John?"

"Yeah, that is a little weird." I sliced a Wisconsin harvest pie and plated two slices.

Work did not keep my mind off the murder, even if the

ticket wheel stayed nightmarishly full. No sooner did I rip a ticket from one of the clips, than the wheel spun and another ticket was added. As much as the thought of all the money we were making delighted me, it was getting stressful.

Charlene ambled into the kitchen an hour later. Removing her pumpkin beanie, she pulled out a black hairnet from the pocket of her knit jacket. She tugged it over her snowy hair. "What's Thistleblossom doing here?"

"Is she here?" *Didn't matter*. I shook my head. "Forget Mrs. Thistleblossom. Where have you been?" It didn't take *that* long to yell at Ray for losing her the pumpkin race.

"Thistleblossom's probably stuffing disposable diapers down your toilet right now."

I swallowed. Maybe I *should* check the ladies' room. "What have you been up to?"

She flicked an imaginary speck of dust from the sleeve of her orangey jacket. "Breaking into Alfreda Kuulik's apartment."

My chest hitched. "You *what?* Without me?"

"You've been busy."

"This is murder," I whisper-shouted.

She rubbed her brown-and-white striped sock with the toe of her high-top. "Besides, I knew you'd be keeping Alfreda busy. After Ray and I had our little chat, it seemed like the perfect opportunity."

"You broke—Charlene, that's illegal! And I wasn't talking to Alfreda that long. You could have been caught. Why didn't you at least call me first?" Not that I'd have been able to talk her out of it, but it would have been nice to try.

"I knew you'd keep your interrogation brief," she said, "so I moved fast."

"How could you possibly know that?"

"You'd never leave Pie Town that long in the middle of

the pumpkin festival. You're responsible." She said it like it was a bad thing.

"I left to judge the pie contest," I said.

"Which was a promotion for Pie Town."

"Well, yeah, but—"

"Face facts. You're a slave to Pie Town."

"Pie Town's a start-up. Of course, I work hard."

She rubbed her neck and avoided my gaze. "This pie shop is nearly a year old. It's not a start-up anymore."

"That's still—"

"Anyway, I didn't break in. Not technically." She unsnapped her jacket, exposing the brown tunic beneath. "Everyone knows Alfreda keeps her key under the potted jade plant."

Steamed, I returned to plating pies. "Good thing you were quick. We talked to her for five minutes, tops, not even long enough for you to ream out Ray, who by the way is one of our best customers."

My metal spatula clattered against the plate.

"But it was long enough for me to find this." Charlene reached into her pocket and slapped a photograph on the metal counter. A smiling Alfreda wearing a hard hat was surrounded by a group of men in front of a forklift. "Alfreda used to work for a construction company."

Whoa. That was real evidence. Evidence we couldn't use or share with Gordon, because it had been obtained illegally.

"Alfreda might have known how to use that forklift," she continued.

I blew out my breath and plated a caramel-apple pie. "Did you hear Farmer John won the giant pumpkin contest?"

"His pumpkin was in the parade yesterday," Charlene

said. "Everyone knows he won. And that he's in the pocket of those so-and-so's in San Adrian."

"How can he possibly be in a town's pocket?"

"He may live north of here, but he's got a pumpkin farm in San Adrian. Farmer John was a driving force behind their festival. Mark my words, he's going to win their contest too, making ours seem even more irrelevant. But steps will be taken."

Uh-oh. Maybe I should have paid more attention to the pumpkin plotters in Pie Town. "San Nicholas is loads more charming than San Adrian," I said, trying to divert her. "The committee outdid themselves this year. Country bands. Pumpkin folktales. Making all the vendors sell at least one pumpkin product. Our haunted house is in an old jail!"

"In a barn behind the old jail."

"The point is, San Nicholas has a special vibe. Our pumpkin festival will always be popular."

"We'll see."

"And what were you doing with Takako last night?"

She raised a white brow. "You don't think I'd let a stepmother come crashing into your life without figuring out why, did you?"

"You—oh." That was . . . sweet, in a Charlene sort of way. My stomach warmed, a pleasant feeling this time. "So, what did you find out?"

"Nothing. But I will. What did you learn from Alfreda?" Charlene asked.

"Our talk with Alfreda was a bust."

"Nothing? You got nothing?"

I held the pie plate between us like a shield. "We—I blew it." Shame on me for wanting to throw Takako under the bus. The buck stopped at the bakery. "Alfreda stormed off, righteously indignant."

"Ah, well," she said philosophically. "It's no secret you're no great shakes as an interrogator."

"What? I can interrogate people." I slid a cherry pie through the window. "I just had an off morning."

She patted my arm. "Sure you did."

"Judging the pies was stressful!" I knew Charlene was only trying to get my goat, and she was succeeding.

"We'll revisit Alfreda Kuulik together, and you can show me how it's done."

"I will," I said. I could salvage the interview.

Somehow.

Chapter Eleven

Monday, my day off, I should have been sleeping in.

But that morning, I got up at my usual early hour and drove to Pie Town. I parked in the alley, murky in the pre-dawn light, and walked around the corner to Main Street.

Men with push brooms swept hay and broken pumpkin shells from the damp street. The vendor stands had been taken down overnight. All that remained were stray hay bales, the denuded bandstand, and giant spiderwebs. The mayor had vowed to keep the webbing up through Halloween.

My footsteps echoed on the sidewalk. I inhaled, catching the faint tang of salt in the October air. The world was still and quiet, and patches of fog spiraled down the street. I loved this hour, but I shivered in the lonely gloom.

At the north end of Main Street, where the pumpkin weigh-in had taken place, I paused. Any evidence from Dr. Levant's murder had to be long gone. But I scanned for clues anyway, hood pulled over my head, my hands in the pockets of my Pie Town hoodie.

Graham, in overalls that strained across his round belly, swept hay. The forklift and flatbeds and pumpkins were gone, along with any suggestion a woman had died here.

The elderly man leaned on his broom and adjusted his cabbie's hat. "What are you doing here at this hour? Shouldn't you be sleeping in today?"

"It's my first pumpkin festival," I said. "I wanted to see how it ended."

"If you listen to those San Adrian folks, it doesn't. It just continues next weekend in their town." He shook his broom at me. "Have you seen their flyers?"

I sighed. I got that San Nicholas didn't like their new competition, but maybe it was time to let it go? "No. Do you know what the festival numbers were this year compared to last?"

"Exactly the same, and that's not a good sign." He scowled. "The population in this area is growing. Our festival should have grown too."

"Maybe slow growth isn't so bad," I said tentatively. "If it weren't for the cops working Pie Town for tips, we would have been overwhelmed."

"It isn't slow growth, it's no growth. I'll bet the murder scared off the kids."

Or their parents.

He grimaced. "Well, we'll find out in December. With our name, San Nicholas has got a lock on the Christmas festival."

My ex-fiancé had brought me to the San Nicholas Christmas Festival last December. The vendor stalls had been modeled after Munich's Christmas market. Santa's Village–themed fun for the young and young at heart, plus twinkle lights. Lots and lots of twinkle lights. I'd already started planning a Christmas pie menu for December.

"You okay?" Graham asked. "You've got a funny look on your face."

"Sorry. I was daydreaming." I gazed at the straw-littered

pavement, and my shoulders hunched. "It's hard to believe someone was killed here three days ago."

"Dr. Levant wasn't killed here. She was killed in front of the haunted house and her body brought here."

I goggled at him. The haunted house? Where Elon had been working? He had to be Shaw's prime suspect. Means, motive, and opportunity. "What? Are you sure? How do you know?"

He tapped his cabbie's hat. "I deduced. The cops are swarming the old jail this morning, and there's no ambulance there, which means there's no second body."

"Thanks." I hurried to the historic jail. Yellow police tape marked off the street in front of the square, adobe building.

Crime scene techs in white suits squatted in front of hay bales and knelt beside a patch of driveway. One scraped at something with what looked like a plastic knife.

Cold wriggling in my gut, I stopped behind the tape and scanned the scene.

Chief Shaw strutted back and forth shouting orders. "Under every piece of straw!" He clutched a plastic bag with something metal and rusted inside—a wrench?

Noticing me, his brows slashed downward. "Ms. Harris."

"Hello, Chief Shaw. I was, um, taking a walk."

"And decided to be a nosy neighbor."

"Has something happened?" So, yes, I *was* being a nosy neighbor.

"Nothing new."

Graham had been right. This *did* have to do with Kara Levant's murder. "Is this where Dr. Levant was killed?"

"Why would you think that?" he asked sharply.

I motioned to the suited techies. "You said this wasn't about anything new. And the only old crime that would call for this level of analysis was Dr. Levant's murder. Is that a wrench you're holding?"

He hid it behind his back and thrust out his chest. "I warned you about interfering. Detective Carmichael has given you and your little crime-solving club wide latitude. But don't think I share his attitude. And *I* am in charge of this investigation."

I backed away. "Right. Right. Sorry. I heard the fund-raiser for the Police Athletic League went well."

His expression flickered. "Over five thousand dollars. People were very generous."

"Maybe we can do it again during the Christmas festival?"

He aimed his finger at me. "Changing the subject?"

"Trying to."

"Don't think you can bribe me with social goodwill. And stay away from my crime scene!"

"I won't. I mean, I will." Scuttling away, I hurried into the alley.

I unlocked Pie Town's metal kitchen door and darted inside. Gray morning light filtered through the skylights and layered the kitchen in cobwebby shadows. I shut the door behind me. The lock clanged, comforting.

Not that I was nervous or anything.

Suddenly, I remembered a moment when I'd thought I'd been alone in Pie Town and had been horribly wrong. Heart rabbiting, I flipped on the lights. The kitchen gleamed, knives stuck to their wall magnets, utensils twinkling in their containers. The room smelled faintly of cleaning supplies.

Quietly, I pushed open the swinging door and peered into the empty dining area. I walked inside. The pink booths and barstools were empty. No criminals waltzed across the black-and-white floor.

No one was here.

My neck muscles relaxed.

I ran my hand along the back of a pink booth. Sometimes I still had to pinch myself to believe I'd done it, that this tiny kingdom of pie was all mine. Yes, I worked hard. I'd do whatever it took to keep my dream—and my mother's—alive. My eyes grew hot. Did my mom know I'd done it? Was she somewhere, watching?

I sniffed and shook myself. She knew. I might not believe in ghosts, but I believed in her.

Something creaked behind me.

I spun to face the counter.

No one was there.

Of course, no one was there. It was only the sound of the old building settling.

Maybe Charlene was right. Maybe I *was* working too hard. Maybe it was making me paranoid, prone to flights of fancy.

So what if I lived beside a cemetery? So what if Mrs. Thistleblossom had been making weird, spell-casting gestures in my direction? I wasn't Charlene. And I didn't believe in the paranormal.

I paced to my austere office and edged the door open. The room was dark and quiet, and I switched on the lights. The cheap fluorescents hummed, illuminating the battered metal desk, my dingy desktop computer, the utilitarian metal shelves lined with supplies.

I jerked open the door of the walk-in supply closet. No one lurked inside.

I'd once slept in this closet, before Charlene had come through with her tiny house. In the choice between paying rent and paying staff, the staff had won. The staff and Pie Town would always come first.

I sat in my "lightly used" executive chair and booted up

my computer. We couldn't share Charlene's stolen photo
of Dr. Levant's ex-office manager. They'd know she'd
broken into Alfreda's apartment. But Alfreda was job
hunting now, and her résumé might be online. That could
prove she'd once worked at a construction firm, so we
wouldn't need Charlene's contraband.

I clicked over to a professional job-hunting site and
searched for Alfreda Kuulik. Pay dirt. She'd updated her
résumé recently, and it included her time working as a receptionist for the construction firm called Builder Gorilla.
Forklift driver wasn't listed as one of her talents though.

I searched for the construction company. They had a
simple Web site, but it told me enough. Builder Gorilla
was a small operation. In my experience, at small companies, everyone ended up doing pretty much everything.
But that didn't mean Alfreda had pitched in driving forklifts, only that she'd had access to them at one time.

Was Denise's software company on the site too? I did a
quick search, and discovered it was. I scanned the page.

ABOUT US

OphthaSoft Solutions provides the leading cloud-
based software for your eye-care practice, simplify-
ing your work so you can spend time on what you're
passionate about—care for your patients.

We are a community-based close corporation of
eye-care professionals. OphthaSoft understands your
needs. Contact us today for a free demo.

Not helpful.

Graham had mentioned he'd seen photos of Denise
on social media. Fortunately, she'd set her privacy to
open, and I was able to view the photos on her page.
She'd recently gone skydiving right here in the Bay Area.

I shuddered. No way, no how. Maybe we didn't have as much in common as I'd thought.

"Hey."

I jumped, my chair rattling backward and banging against the wall. "Charlene!" I clutched my chest.

In a purple knit jacket and green tunic, she leaned into my office. Her cat, Frederick, draped around her neck in a fluff of polar white. "Jumpy, aren't you? What are you doing here on a Monday?"

"Research." I motioned toward the computer.

"Don't you have one of those at home?"

"Yes, but—"

"It's not healthy to spend so much time here," she said.

My gaze flicked to the aging ceiling tiles. Yeah, yeah, yeah. "Did you see what's going on in front of the jail?"

She nodded. "Dr. Levant must have been killed there, and her body moved to the giant pumpkins."

"But why? Why not just leave her at the jail? There weren't many people on Main Street at that hour, and it was foggy, but moving the body was still a risk. The killer might have been spotted."

"Either someone moved the body to make a statement," she said, "or they moved her because leaving the doctor there would implicate the killer."

Elon. "Shaw's going to have to bring her husband in for questioning."

"Does he?"

I pushed my hands into the pockets of my hoodie, and my chair squeaked on the cheap linoleum floor. "Elon Levant was working at the haunted house. And Dr. Cannon said he'd thought Elon was going to be at the optometry stall that morning, helping set up. Where exactly was Elon when his wife died?"

"We don't know exactly when Dr. Levant died. But Gordon might."

"I'll ask, but Shaw's keeping him out of the loop. In the meantime, we should talk to Elon," I said, reluctant.

"We need to have hard talks with all our suspects," Charlene said. "The festival's over. It's time we get down to the important business. Murder."

Keeping my staff employed and myself fed was important, but I nodded. I wasn't looking forward to paying a condolence call on the grieving widower. It could only be awkward, since I didn't really know the man. But there were alternate sources of intel.

"Do you think Laurelynn's working at her pumpkin patch today?" I asked. Dropping a pumpkin on Kara's body had to mean something. Laurelynn and Kara's old high school rivalry might have been nothing, like Elon had said. But it created a connection between the women. Laurelynn might know something about the eye doctor's death. And the meaning of the pumpkin.

"Of course, she's at her patch," Charlene said. "Where else would she be?"

I drummed my fingers on the desk. Laurelynn had been the one to suggest selling my mini pumpkin pies at her patch. I had to be careful not to screw up our business relationship with rude questions. But Gordon and Petronella's father were in Shaw's crosshairs. Laurelynn had to be interviewed.

Stomach twisting, I skidded my chair forward and stood. "Let's go."

Chapter Twelve

Traffic crawled along the road to the pumpkin patch. It might be a working Monday, but Halloween was only two weeks away. The pressure to find the perfect pumpkin was on.

"All this for a root vegetable?" I frowned at the Mazda's bumper ahead of us. "Can't they buy pumpkins at the grocery store?"

Charlene leaned on the Jeep's horn and made a rude gesture. "Taking the kids to a pumpkin patch is an annual ritual. Then you get the photos of your toddler trying to lift a pumpkin as big as he is, the picture of your toddler sitting on the pumpkin . . . It's tradition."

I grumbled some more, but I got it. San Nicholas was magic in October. Fog crept over the brown, rolling hills dotted with rows of orange. Who wouldn't want to bring kids here for a picture-perfect pre-Halloween moment?

Charlene turned at a picket fence lined with miniature pumpkins. More white pumpkins decorated the eaves of a red barn. We bumped along the dirt road to a parking lot and found a spot at the very back.

I stepped from the Jeep into a puddle and shook the muck from my shoes.

Charlene extricated herself and adjusted Frederick over one shoulder.

"We've got to play this casual," I said.

"What are you worried about? I'm always frosted."

"I think you mean *frosty*. And Gordon knows about Laurelynn's relationship to Dr. Levant. If he hasn't spoken to her yet, she's on his list."

"Gordon's not on the case."

A children's train, painted orange and black, chugged past.

"Not officially," I said, "no. But he's still a cop, and we can't look like we're interfering with an investigation."

"When do we interfere?"

Like, always. "I just think we can be subtle about this," I said, desperation mounting.

"Subtle." She adjusted the collar of her purple knit jacket. "Got it."

We found our way to a break in the low wooden fence and crossed into the pumpkin patch. Children squealed inside a Halloween-themed bouncy castle. Pumpkins lined the top of the red-painted miniature train station. Waiting children hopped up and down with excitement. Doting parents smiled, watching and snapping photos.

A small boy in overalls and a woolen jacket pulled a red wagon filled to the brim with pumpkins. His older brother selected another pumpkin for the pile, and my heart squeezed.

I loved this season because of my own childhood memories with my mother. What would it be like with a child of my own? I squashed that thought. It was way too soon to be thinking of kids.

Flowers blossomed along the paths, winding between different varieties of pumpkins. Sunflowers formed a fence around a pony ride. It might have been a chilly October, but this was still California farm country. Flowers bloomed here year-round. San Nicholas was a coastal utopia. But utopia didn't exist—not as long as people were people. Dr. Levant's murder was proof of that, and I shivered.

Charlene and I made our way to the barn. Its double doors hung open, and we walked inside the cool interior. Twinkle lights hung from the rafters. Stuffed ravens stared down at roving customers.

Winding aisles led through a selection of upscale Halloween décor. Papier-mâché black cats. Wooden silhouettes of witches. Gilt pumpkins and vintage-looking pumpkin people. And flowers—the barn was flooded with their scent, sweet and clean. Hanging moss swayed, stirred by currents of cool air from antiqued chandeliers. Maybe I should have done more to decorate Pie Town?

Laurelynn stood behind a long wooden counter. A black apron and stylish fawn-colored sweater seemed to embrace her curvy figure. She tucked a ghost-shaped cookie cutter inside a black paper bag.

"Enjoy," Laurelynn warbled. Laugh lines furrowed the corners of her eyes, the color of bark.

"Thanks!" The customer moved on, and we stepped to the register.

"Hi, Laurelynn," I said. "How's it going?"

The African-American woman pushed a wisp of curling black hair from her face and blew out her breath. "Whew! Hi, Val, Charlene. We've sold out of your pies. Are we on track for another order tomorrow?" A coil of hair escaped from her colorful headwrap.

"I'll deliver the pies myself," I said.

"Thanks!" Her round face wreathed in a relieved smile. "Now what brings you two to the patch?"

Charlene adjusted Frederick around her collar. "We wanted—"

"This is the best time of year in San Nicholas," I said quickly. "We thought it was time we enjoy the season."

"San Nicholas really is wonderful at Halloween." Laurelynn grinned.

"Aside from the murder," Charlene said. "Doesn't look like it's put much of a dent in your business though."

She sobered. "No. No, that was terrible." She raised her chin, looking past us, and plastered on a smile. "Hello! Can I help you?"

A woman carrying a black, skeletal tree wound with orange twinkle lights hefted it to the counter. "I'll take this."

We waited while Laurelynn rang up the Halloween tree.

When the customer staggered out the barn doors, Charlene braced her elbow on the counter. "You and Kara were friends from high school, weren't you?"

"Wow." Laurelynn turned away and adjusted a miniature haunted mansion. An entire Halloween village took up one end of the counter. "You have a good memory."

"I eat my vegetables." Charlene tapped her head. "Keeps you sharp."

"I'm sorry for your loss," I said. "It's hard losing a friend."

"We weren't friends," she said shortly. "We'd lost touch."

My breath quickened. Maybe Laurelynn's rivalry with the eye doctor wasn't as sweet and silly as Elon had implied.

Charlene's white brows lifted. "Lost touch in a town this size? What's the trick to that? Because there's an old *friend* I wouldn't mind losing."

"It's awful to think someone we know was killed," I

said. "And to think someone we know might have been responsible."

"Did you know Kara?" Laurelynn asked.

"Not well," I said, "but we found the body. I guess that's why her murder is top of mind."

"I heard she—" Laurelynn swallowed. "She was found during the festival setup. What were you doing out there?"

"We wanted a look at the pumpkins before everything got started," I said. "Bakers' hours. We're up before dawn most days. I've heard farmers like you keep early hours too."

"It depends."

"Your house is on the farm, isn't it?" Charlene motioned around the barn.

"At the base of the hill. The train runs past it."

So Laurelynn hadn't been far from downtown, such as it was, when Kara had died. She could have snuck into town, killed Kara Levant, and snuck back. But was there a real motive?

"Who would want to kill Dr. Levant?" I asked.

"Kara was very good at everything she did," Laurelynn said carefully.

"Too good?" Charlene asked.

"You could say that." The pumpkin farmer laughed unevenly. "Kara always made sure you knew how well she'd done, and how you didn't measure up. In high school, there wasn't a test I took where she didn't ask how I'd done and then announce she'd beaten me by a few points. Even when I got a hundred percent, she always managed to swing some extra credit and get a hundred and two." Her laugh was hollow as a desert cave.

"But that was high school," I said. "People change."

"Not in my experience." Laurelynn jammed her hands in her black apron's pockets, her nostrils flaring. "Kara knew exactly how to make you feel inadequate. I know how Elon stood it—he's a saint. But I don't know how Tristan managed. She never stopped reminding him he was only an optometrist."

"Wasn't she an optometrist?" I asked.

"She was an ophthalmologist, making her a *real* doctor. And poor Denise. She actually quit medical school because she could never measure up to her cousin. That's why she got an MBA, but as far as Kara was concerned, that was only another inadequacy. Forget that Denise has a hugely successful software start-up—it's never enough."

"A wife that demanding couldn't have been easy for Elon," Charlene said.

Laurelynn smiled tightly and shook her head. "He loved her."

"What—?" I began.

Laurelynn raised a finger and smiled past my shoulder. "Can I help you?"

I turned, stepping smartly away from the high counter.

Takako and Marla stood in line behind us. My step-mother's face lit. Beside her, in an elegant trench coat, Marla's lips curved in a smile.

"Val." Takako crushed me in a one-armed hug, jostling the small, black leather pack on her back. "Marla guessed right that you'd be here."

"That's because vampires have psychic senses," Charlene said.

Marla glared.

Takako set a box of Harvest-themed dessert plates on the counter. "I'd like to buy these, please." On the front of her San Nicholas Pumpkin Festival sweatshirt was the painting I'd admired of the farm cat and pumpkins.

While Laurelynn rang up the plates, Charlene scowled at her archfrenemy. "Snooping again?"

"How can you accuse me of snooping," Marla said, "when you're obviously investigating?"

"Investigating?" Laurelynn slid Takako's plates into a black paper bag.

"Investigating your barn for Halloween decorations," I said, laughing maniacally.

"And obviously your relationship to Kara Levant," Marla said.

Marla! If only she *would* turn into a bat and flap away.

Laurelynn's cheeks darkened. "That's what this is about?"

"No," I babbled. "I mean, of course we're worried about what's happened. The town seems to think San Adrian is behind the murder. A local kaffeeklatsch has been plotting revenge in Pie Town. I tried to tell them it's unlikely an entire town committed murder just to sabotage our pumpkin festival. But cooler heads have not prevailed. Plus, my assistant manager's father was the one whose pumpkin was wrecked—"

"Petros Scala," Marla said.

"Yes, thank you," I said, shrill. "So, can I take that Halloween village? No need to wrap it. It will be perfect in Pie Town's window. I don't know why I didn't decorate sooner. And do you want the same amount of minipies tomorrow?"

Laurelynn stared at me for a long time. She wet her lips. "Let me get back to you on the pies."

My mouth went dry. "Okay," I said. "I get it. We'll let you finish up with Takako, and then we can deal with the village."

Grasping Marla and Charlene by the elbows, I steered

them into the barn's interior. This was exactly what I *hadn't* wanted to happen.

"Is there anything you won't do to sabotage our investigation?" Charlene asked Marla.

"I was helping," Marla whispered. "Val's stepmother was hurt when she went to her tiny home, and she wasn't there."

"Why didn't she call?" I asked.

"She did," Marla said. "Check your messages."

I dug into the pocket of my Pie Town hoodie. "No, she—" Oh, crumb. Three missed calls—last night I'd turned my phone's sound off and forgotten to turn it back on.

"She thought you'd been murdered in your bed," Marla said severely. "You're all alone out there in that flimsy shipping container."

"Tiny home!" Charlene crossed her arms over her knit jacket.

"Plus," Marla said, "there's that creepy cemetery. God only knows what people get up to in there."

Even *Marla* knew about the cemetery?

"None of that explains what *you* were doing at Val's house," Charlene said.

Marla fluffed her hair. "Never mind what I was doing there. When I ran into Takako, I took it upon myself to help your stepmother find you." Her diamonds glittered beneath the barn's chandelier.

"What was in it for you?" Charlene said.

"Oh, Charlene, your little escapades are so, how do you say? Entertaining. And not just for me, for the entire town."

Dread curdled in my gut. "Oh, no. You haven't been vlogging about them again?"

"I'm a reporter. I report."

"You're not a reporter." Charlene shook a gnarled finger at her. "You're a rotten—"

"I'm back." Takako popped up at my elbow, black paper bag in one hand. "What did I miss?"

"Nothing," I said. "I'd better go buy that village."

I trudged to the counter. All I had to do was go online to see what Marla had reported. But I suspected this was one of those ignorance-is-bliss situations.

FYI, Halloween villages get pricey when you add in tiny costumed people and miniature lampposts and dying trees. I had to commandeer a red wagon to cart all the black paper bags through the pumpkin patch.

A wheel jammed beside a profusion of purple flowers blossoming beside a set of hay bales. I bent to remove a rind from the wagon's wheel guard.

"We interrupted your interrogation," Takako said. "Did you learn— Oh!" She pointed to the peewee train, and her gaze turned wistful. "When I was a child, my parents used to take me to a park with a children's train. It looked almost exactly like that one."

Marla's lips curved wickedly. "Val, why don't you ride the kiddie train with your stepmother?"

I shook my head. "You are seriously underestimating the width of my wheelhouse."

"Nah," Charlene said. "Takako's small. She'll make up for your extra padding."

I glared. "Thanks!" Honestly, I was within normal weight range, if at the high end.

"I'll take your stuff to the Jeep," she continued. "But I'm not loading those boxes."

"Sciatica acting up again?" Marla's voice dripped syrup.

"My back's fine," Charlene said serenely. "Because

unlike some people, I don't get all my exercise on a mattress."

"Let's get train tickets," I said quickly.

I hustled Takako to the white-painted station. Before I knew it, she was forking over money for two tickets.

"I hope you learned something before we turned up and ruined things," she said.

The train puffed steam at the miniature station. Parents and children boarded.

"You didn't ruin anything." I squeezed beside Takako into the tiny seat, my knees pressed to my chest.

The engineer blew his whistle. We chugged slowly from the station.

"So," Takako said. "Tell me about the investigation. I'm really intrigued by this hobby of yours. Or is it a calling? Doran's told me about some of your past successes."

We rolled around the edge of the pumpkin patch.

"I'm not sure what it is. But usually at this point, Charlene and I do an info download. We'll go over what we've learned and figure out our next steps."

We puffed past Charlene and Marla. The two elderly women waved. I was pretty sure they were laughing at me and not with me.

I hunched lower in my seat, my knees nearly touching my chin. It could be worse. Someone I knew could see me. And pretty much everyone I knew would never let me hear the end of it.

"In spite of my poor performance with Ms. Kuulik, my career's been based on first-person research," Takako said. "Anthropologists and archaeologists often work to piece together people's actions and motivations. Maybe I can help?"

"Thanks, but we're probably going to go to Pie Town next to set up the village."

"No problem. I'm happy to help decorate."

"That would be great," I said. But a part of me, the part I didn't like very much, wanted to leap from the train. Finding out I had a stepbrother had been exciting. Why hadn't I realized the natural corollary, that I had a step-mother too? And why did I feel like this new tie was cutting off my air supply?

We trundled up a low hill, past a heard of goats, and circled back toward the patch. I scowled at the goats, wondering if one had been the petting zoo escapee.

"I'm so impressed with everything you've accomplished," Takako said. "None of it could have been easy on your own."

"I wasn't entirely on my own. If it hadn't been for Charlene, I don't know if I could have made it." She was more than my landlady/piecrust maker. She was my best friend.

"I didn't know about you." Takako's voice was strained. "Frank didn't tell me about a child. He told me . . ." She swallowed. "He told me his marriage was over. If I'd known he'd abandoned you, I don't think I could have married Frank. I'm so sorry."

"Don't be," I said sourly. "Frank's good at keeping secrets."

"How . . . ? How old were you when he left?"

"Three."

Her jaw tightened. "You were so young. I should have known. I should have asked more questions, but I wanted to believe. I hope you can forgive me."

I folded my arms, bumping my elbows on my knees. "Honestly, there's nothing to forgive." It wasn't Takako's fault my father had left. And I could well believe she'd never known about our existence.

The toddler in the seat in front of us turned around and stared at me. Beneath his red knit cap, his brown eyes were wide and serious.

"I can't help but feel there's a debt that must be repaid." Takako was quiet a long moment. "I'm afraid Doran's still bitter about Frank. I'm glad to see you're not."

"I wouldn't exactly say that," I mumbled. I knew it would be better for me if I could forgive Frank for being who he was. But forgiveness doesn't come by wishing. Sometimes, you have to work for it.

The little boy kept staring. Sheesh. Didn't he have anything better to do? *Look, goats!*

Slowly, he raised his finger and deliberately stuck it in his nose.

Yeah, kid. I know how you feel.

Takako squeezed my hand. "I'm glad you're okay, Val, even if—" She bit her bottom lip. "Everything is going to work out."

I made a face at the boy, and he giggled.

"Thanks," I said. "I think so too." Why was I keeping her at a distance? Takako wasn't the enemy. She was smart and thoughtful, and she wasn't trying to take over my mother's place in my heart. What did I have to lose?

We chugged past the parking lot.

Charlene and Marla hooted. Gamely, I waved at the two women.

And Gordon Carmichael.

Chapter Thirteen

Grinning, Gordon loaded our bags into the back of Charlene's Jeep. His muscles moved fluidly beneath his blue sweater. "How was your train ride?"

"Bracing." My heart fluttered. No matter what we were doing, he had that effect on me. "What are you doing here?"

He gave me a long look. "I could ask you the same question. If Chief Shaw thinks you're interfering in his investigation, I may not be able to protect you."

I gave him a look.

"Okay," he said. "If he catches me, I could be in even deeper trouble."

"For visiting a pumpkin patch?" I asked. "It's the post-pumpkin festival place to go."

"Especially when you're investigating a murder," Marla said.

My gaze flicked to the gray sky. "That too."

He set the last black bag in the Jeep and shut the rear door. "Let me guess—the Halloween village was a bribe to get Laurelynn talking?"

"More a bribe to get her not to drop Pie Town as a wholesaler." I scrubbed my hands over my face.

"What happened?" he asked.

Marla had happened. I shot the older woman an annoyed glance. "A misunderstanding."

He frowned but didn't pursue the subject. "Learn anything you want to share?"

"It sounds like she doesn't have an alibi for Kara's murder," I said, "but I'm not certain."

"Then I'll work from there. Thanks." Gordon kissed me chastely on the forehead and strode through the hard-packed dirt lot and into the pumpkin patch.

I got in the Jeep, and we made our way to Pie Town, Takako lecturing on the symbolism of pumpkins from the back seat.

"In the medieval period," she said, "they represented the world. Today, the vines symbolize our connections to others. In certain folklore, dreaming of a pumpkin is believed to break a curse. But I don't see how any of that would have bearing on the murder."

"I'm starting to think you're right," I said. "But it is interesting."

For reasons unfathomable to mere mortals such as myself, Marla followed as we turned into Pie Town's narrow alley.

Charlene slammed on the brakes, the seat belt catching me sharply in the chest. Marla's silver Mercedes screeched to a halt.

"We've been hit!"

"The Jeep?" I twisted in my seat. I hadn't felt a bump.

Charlene pointed to Pie Town's brick wall. In yellow paint, someone had written: PUMPKIN DIE.

Anger flooded my veins. "Oh, for . . . Pete's sake!" San Nicholas had a forty-eight-hour rule regarding removal of graffiti. The law made sense, since graffiti attracts more graffiti. But how was I going to get paint off raw brick?

Takako *tsk*ed. "Kids."

I shifted the bags piled in my lap. Why tag Pie Town instead of the comic book shop or the gym next door? Maybe Mrs. Thistleblossom really *had* cursed me.

"Kids didn't do this," Charlene said. "It's Thistleblossom."

I groaned. "So much for my day off."

Takako reached through the seats and gripped my shoulder. "All we need are scrub brushes and paint stripper. A friend of mine had to do this last year. She said it wasn't that bad. I'll call her and find out what she used."

"Thanks," I said, grateful.

Behind us, Marla honked.

Muttering beneath her breath, Charlene pulled to the side of the alley and parked.

Since I was loaded with black bags, I let Charlene unlock the alley door. The four of us trooped into the kitchen.

Marla paused to wipe her finger along a metal countertop. "It's cleaner than I expected."

"If you really thought Pie Town was a dive," Charlene said, "you wouldn't park your backside on a counter stool every morning."

"The day-old pastries are half price!"

I led them into the dining area and dumped the bags in a booth beside the front windows. Sunlight streamed through the blinds and reflected off napkin holders. If I had a happy place, Pie Town was it. I sighed, my muscles slackening.

"Where's the coffee?" Marla asked.

"We're closed today," Charlene said.

Marla's forehead puckered. "So?"

"So, there's no coffee."

Marla threw her hands in the air and stormed to the

front door. After some fiddling with the lock, she strode out, her trench coat flapping in the damp breeze.

"Good riddance." Charlene shoved a bag aside and dropped into the booth.

Takako wedged her phone into her small, black leather backpack and slung it over one shoulder. "I got the name of that paint remover. There's a hardware store down the road. Would you like me to see if they carry it?"

"That would be great," I said. "Thanks."

"I'll be right back." Takako pushed open the front door, the bell above it jingling. She hurried onto the sidewalk.

"Alone at last," Charlene said. "Let's talk fast before any more helpful people return."

"What happened at the pumpkin patch wasn't Takako's fault. What did you think about Laurelynn?"

"I thought she was suspiciously helpful."

"Mmm. Interesting what she said about Dr. Levant's personality. Do you think it's true?"

Charlene cocked her head. "It fits. I didn't know the good doctor that well, but I got the impression the doctor was driven."

I tugged Styrofoam from a box and removed a haunted hotel. "Even if Dr. Levant did run people down, like Laurelynn said, is it a motive for murder?"

"If someone was pushed hard enough, maybe."

"Elon did tell us that she and Laurelynn were rivals." I pried open another box—a haunted house—and attempted to pull out the rectangular, Styrofoam packing. It didn't move, wedged firmly against the sides of the box.

"And Laurelynn said Kara and Elon had a good marriage, but everyone already knew that."

Scrunching my face, I turned the box upside down and shook it lightly. The Styrofoam didn't budge. "The spouse is usually the prime suspect. We can't count out Elon."

Charlene snatched the box from my hand. "You've got to open the bottom and push." She demonstrated, and the Styrofoam slid free.

I forced the two sides apart, revealing a ceramic haunted house with a plug attached. "Ooh! It's electric. Why is it electric?"

"Plug it in and find out. Didn't you ever have a Christmas village?"

I plugged in the hotel. There was a grinding noise, and the door opened. A witch with a cauldron emerged.

It was the sort of contraption a normal cat would have gone for. On the table, Frederick just flicked his ear and closed his eyes.

"Er, does that witch remind you of anyone?" I asked. Because I thought she looked a lot like Mrs. Thistleblossom.

"No."

"Not even a little?"

"No," she said. "Why? Who do you think that old witch looks like?"

"Mrs. Thistleblossom."

"Forget Thistleblossom. The real question is, what's Marla up to with your stepmother?"

I set the haunted house in the window and grabbed another box. "Aside from irritating you?"

"She's up to something."

"Probably." The Laurelynn-Kara rivalry had nothing on Charlene vs. Marla.

The front door swung open, jangling the bell.

I started, nearly dropping a ceramic graveyard to the checkerboard floor.

Marla strolled inside carrying a paper coffee cup. "Where's Takako?"

"What are you doing back here?" Charlene asked.

"Drinking my coffee, obviously." Marla took a cautious sip and smiled.

"And you only brought one? Thanks for thinking of others," Charlene snapped.

Marla's smile was wintery. "Oh, Charlene. If you wanted coffee, all you had to do was get it yourself."

I handed Marla the graveyard before the battle could escalate. "Find a place to put this, would you?"

"I know where she can put it," Charlene said warningly.

"And here's a costume shop for you." I handed my piecrust specialist another box.

They argued about proper village layout while I unboxed. Even though the foam protectors were molded to fit the pieces inside, mysterious crumbs of white Styrofoam scattered across the booth and checkerboard floor.

Takako returned with the paint remover. We abandoned Charlene and Marla to the village and walked to the alley. Anything was better than listening to those two squabble.

Takako and I scrubbed at the yellow paint with a stiff brush soaked in the solvent. To my relief, the paint lifted from the brick.

I stepped away from the wall and frowned. Was the handwriting similar to the graffiti left on my delivery van? Since I hadn't bothered to take a picture of the van, I couldn't be sure.

"Hold on, Takako. I want to take a picture of this."

"For the police?"

"I think we should have a record." I pulled my phone from my hoodie's pocket and snapped two pictures of the wall.

"Thanks for helping me." I retrieved my scrub brush. "I'm sure cleaning a wall wasn't what you'd planned for your vacation."

"The point of this visit wasn't the festival. It was to

meet you." She scrubbed at an *i*. "I'm only sorry I was too late to meet your mother."

"She would have liked you."

"What was she like?"

"Creative. Fun." Until life as a single mother and then cancer had beaten her down.

When we returned inside, a fight was brewing over where the creepy cabin belonged.

"You can't put a graveyard beside city hall," Marla said.

"Why not? That's where all good ideas go to die."

I tucked a dangling cord along the window ledge. "I think that's enough village building."

"But we haven't plugged in the houses," Charlene said.

I jammed empty boxes into the bags and lugged them into the hallway. "I'll need to buy a power strip," I called over my shoulder. "There are too many plugs for the outlets."

"Honestly Val," Marla drawled, "you need to plan ahead."

"No kidding," I muttered and ducked into my office. I dropped the empty boxes in the walk-in closet and returned to the dining area.

Takako looked at me expectantly. "Who will you investigate next?"

"I suppose we *could* pay a condolence call on the widower, Elon." Marla angled her head toward the kitchen. "Have you got any pies back there we could bring?"

"We?" Charlene pointed at her rival. "So that's your game. You're trying to chisel in on our investigation."

A pained expression creased Takako's face. "I've been moving too fast, haven't I?"

"What? No," I said quickly. "You haven't."

"Doran wanted to spend time with his girlfriend, Abril, and I was at loose ends—"

"You've been great," I said. "But I've got housekeeping

of my own to do today. One interrogation plus a window display is enough work on my day off," I half joked.

"And this is your only day to clean your own house." Takako grimaced. "Speaking of which, that's where I left my car. Why don't Marla and I take you home?"

"Good," Charlene said, "because I've got an errand to run."

"Oh?" Marla asked, arch. "What errand?"

"Never you mind what errand. It's an errand."

I herded the bickering septuagenarians plus Takako into the alley. Charlene and Frederick roared off in her Jeep, and I crammed into the tiny back seat of Marla's Mercedes. We drove at a sedate pace to my tiny house.

A black Lincoln SUV sat parked beside my shipping container. The fog had lifted slightly. Past the bluff, a thin line of cobalt marked the Pacific.

Balancing her leather backpack and black shopping bag, Takako wriggled from the car.

I squeezed out.

"Thank you, Marla." Takako leaned inside the Mercedes. "This was lovely."

"I'll call you tomorrow," Marla said.

"Tomorrow?" I asked, suspicious.

Takako shut the door and waved as the Mercedes drove sedately down the winding dirt road. It vanished between the eucalyptus trees.

"Now show me this tiny house of yours," Takako said.

Beneath the awning, I unlocked my door and climbed the two metal steps inside. "There's not much to see. Literally." I stepped aside, shoving aside a chair in the square dining nook with my hip.

Monday really was my day for housekeeping, but the house didn't need much. Its laminate floors glowed. Light reflected off the soft-white walls. A kitchenette anchored the center of the room.

Takako set her bag and small backpack on the kitchen counter and walked past me to the other end of the house. A bookshelf blocked off the sleeping area, where I kept a pull-out futon.

"What's this?" She touched a handle in the wall.

I tugged it open, and a desk complete with inset drawers folded from the wall. "It's small, but I do most of my work in Pie Town anyway." Suddenly, I felt nervous. I wanted Takako to love my shoebox home as much as I did.

She pulled down the cuff of her pumpkin festival sweatshirt. "It reminds me of my parents' home in Japan. They moved back there ten years ago. Their house is bigger."

"Everyone's is bigger." I laughed. "But things are so expensive here in Silicon Valley, it was all I could afford. And when there's no fog, the view goes on forever." I motioned to the sliding glass doors that took up most of one wall. The long blinds were turned so sunlight sliced across my futon.

"You were smart to buy property."

"Oh, I'm renting this from Charlene."

Her dark brows pinched. "From Charlene?"

"I got lucky. Her tenant had moved out right when I needed a place."

"It's so small though."

"Can I make you tea?"

"Yes, please."

I set her up in the dining nook and boiled water, set out tea bags. Scraping back my chair, I sat across from her. "How are you enjoying San Nicholas?"

"It's a charming town, if a bit foggy. The more important question is, how do you like it?"

"I love it. I've got great friends here. The town's cute,

the ocean's right there"—I gestured to the window—"and it's not always this foggy."

"You didn't tell me what Laurelynn said before we ruined your interview."

"You didn't ruin anything." I hesitated, but why not tell her? "She said Dr. Levant had a knack for making people feel insecure. Actually, *inadequate* was the word she used."

She smiled. "We all have insecurities, don't we? I worry that I didn't do right by Doran, though he's never said or done anything to make me feel that way."

I turned my mug on the drop-down table. "It's funny what we do to ourselves."

"What do you do to yourself?" she asked gently.

I straightened. "Oh, nothing. I mean, I'm sure I tell myself things that aren't true or helpful. We all do. But . . . I wasn't thinking of anything in particular."

"You weren't thinking of Pie Town?"

"Pie Town?" I asked, surprised. "No."

She sighed. "Do you know why I married Frank?"

"Doran never told me."

"I was obsessed with my career, and it was exciting. I loved my work. I still do. But even as the work expanded my world in so many ways, my personal life, my connections, were shrinking. And then Frank came. He was a breath of fresh air—wild, exciting, fun."

"Hmm." My mother had sent him packing because of the dark side of those qualities. The man was Mayhem, Inc.

She laughed. "Yes, he's a little *too* much fun. At the time, I didn't see his recklessness for what it was. And I didn't ask . . ." She looked to the glass door. "I let myself be carried away, and it didn't work out. When we go too far in one direction, sometimes the reaction can be just as extreme. What I really needed, what I strive for now, is balance. That's one reason why I took this time off to meet you. Do you understand?"

Something small scampered across the metal roof, and we both glanced up.

I brushed back my hair. "Balance is important."

"Yes. I couldn't help but notice today was your one day off, and you ended up at Pie Town."

"I like spending time there."

She shot me a skeptical look.

"I do," I said. "It may seem like I've got no life outside Pie Town, but you caught me during a pumpkin festival. I have friends, and a life, and the Baker Street Bakers." And if most of those—okay, all of those—were friends from Pie Town, what was the big deal?

"Having a life outside work is important. But as fascinating as a murder investigation must be, I can't imagine it's very relaxing."

I hesitated again, unsure where this conversation was going. "What's stressful is knowing there's a murderer nearby and not knowing who he or she is." Chief Shaw wasn't going to find the killer. It was up to Gordon to bring the murderer in, and he wasn't going to have to fight this battle on his own.

Chapter Fourteen

Smothering a yawn, I handed the customer her plastic number tent. Pie Town was packed this Wednesday afternoon, and I beamed at the full tables.

Takako sat in a booth and tapped at a laptop, a half-eaten slice of harvest pie and cup of coffee at her elbow. My new Halloween village glowed on the sill. Outside, fog pressed against the windows and darkened the sidewalk to a stygian gray.

A steady flow of pumpkin-obsessed tourists had blown through San Nicholas and Pie Town today. Much to Charlene and Marla's annoyance, I'd been too busy doing actual baking to do any Baker Street Bakering.

"Of course," Marla said from her perch at the far end of the counter, "I told poor Elon if he needed anything, he should call. He said he was fine, but it was clear by the state of his house he wasn't."

Charlene leaned forward at the counter's opposite end. "In other words, you got nothing."

Marla sniffed. "Kara would never have put up with such a mess."

"And how do you know what Kara and Elon's house looked like when she was alive?" Charlene asked.

"I can *imagine*."

"Oh," Charlene said, "imagining! There's a solid investigative technique."

I did some imagining of my own—a Tahitian beach, Paris, Afghanistan . . . pretty much anywhere but stuck listening to these two.

"Val, what do you think?" Charlene asked.

I thought I hadn't been sleeping well, imagining sounds from the graveyard behind my tiny house. But there hadn't been any more vandalism at my home or at Pie Town, so the drama really was all in my sleepy head. "I think—"

Petronella stuck her head through the swinging door to the kitchen. "Val, you got a minute?"

Relieved, I handed another customer a tent card. "Sorry, Charlene. Duty calls." I jammed the ticket in the wheel and turned to my assistant manager. "What's up?"

Her pale face flushed. "We're um, out of coffee."

I blinked. Out of coffee? How did that happen?

"It's my fault," she said. "I just didn't think we'd have this much dining-in business today. The urn's low, and we're just . . . out."

And she'd been understandably distracted by her father, who was still in Chief Shaw's crosshairs. I untied my apron. "I'll run to the store if you can take over here. That'll get us to closing, and then I can make a run to the Big Store." The Big Store was the massive wholesaler on the Peninsula where we got napkins, coffee, and other basics.

She emerged from the kitchen and nodded. "Deal. And sorry again."

"It's fine," I said. "I didn't expect so much traffic either." And I could use the fresh air.

"Where are you going?" Charlene called.

"Out."

"You can't leave me alone with Marla," Charlene said.

"Eat pie and make up!" I bustled into my office and slipped into my orange-and-black hoodie. Patting my jeans back pocket to verify my wallet was in it, I left, striding through the crowded dining area.

Takako raised her head and looked as if she wanted to say something.

Pretending I didn't see, I hurried onto the sidewalk.

Cold mist dampened my face as I strode past iron lamp-posts and hanging flower baskets.

I started to cross the street.

Tires whispered on the pavement, and I stepped backward.

An SUV whipped past.

Unnerved, I peered into the fog for more hazards, eyes and ears straining.

A prickle of warmth spread across my upper back.

I looked over my shoulder. The sidewalk vanished into the fog. A gust of wind stirred my hair, twisted the mist into a spiral. It wafted, phantomlike, down the street.

I shivered and jammed my hands into the pockets of my hoodie. Hurrying across the street, I bustled inside the warmth of the country store, a three-story adobe-colored building.

The door closed behind me. *Safety*. My muscles unbunched. Not that I had anything to be safe *from*.

I wound through the narrow aisles toward the coffee section. Tall shelves loomed above me, and I pulled my arms closer, feeling claustrophobic.

A familiar, Southern drawl drifted from the other side of the peanut butter shelf. ". . . need to close out. . . ." Tristan Cannon's voice dropped, and I strained to hear. ". . . out of the producers—"

Pulse speeding, I leaned closer to the shelf. Who said I couldn't combine work with snooping?

"Okay," Dr. Cannon muttered, "I'll see you—Wait. You're *where?*"

A woman with a cart pushed past. "Excuse me."

"Sorry," I said automatically, giving myself away.

"Let's not talk on the phone," Cannon said.

Wincing, I rounded the aisle.

"Val!" Tristan Cannon pulled the phone away from his sandy-blond head. An earbud dangled from one ear. "Nice to see you again," he drawled.

"Hi, Tristan. Sorry, I didn't mean to interrupt."

His pleasant features contorted into a grimace. He pocketed the phone in his long, wool coat. It looked good on his tall form. "I'm glad for the interruption, truth to tell. The last few days have been a nightmare."

"I can imagine. How are things at the office?"

"Honestly, I don't know how I'll keep things running. Alfreda's agreed to return temporarily, but we need an opthalmologist."

If he'd brought Alfreda Kuulik back, then she mustn't have done anything too terrible. So who had been the driving force behind her termination? Tristan or Kara? "The town likes and respects you. They'll understand if things are topsy-turvy at first."

He laughed shortly. "That's the nicest thing anyone's said to me in a long time."

I hesitated. "I did hear Kara could be a little critical."

"Who'd you hear—?" He shook his head. "I suppose it's no secret. She had strong opinions about the way things should be, and she was the kind of woman who spoke her mind. It could rub people the wrong way. But I prefer to look at that quality as one of her strengths."

That put me in my place, and my cheeks warmed. "I'm

glad you're keeping the office going. It can be a long drive over the hill to the bigger cities."

"I'm going to do my best. I like living and working here. Thank God for our insurance policy—right now it's the only thing keeping us in business. That, and my other investments . . ." His brows drew together, then he shot me a summer-lightning smile. "Kara said I was wasting my time, but I'm sure glad I did now. What are you doing here?"

"Coffee. Things have been crazy at Pie Town, and we're low." And I needed to buy my java and get back. "I'd really like to talk to you more later, if it's okay."

"About what?"

"About Kara."

His mouth opened, closed. "Sure," he finally said. "I don't have my calendar on me, but give me a call, and we'll set something up."

"Thanks. I will."

He walked past me, toward the front of the grocery store, and I continued to the coffee section. The store was out of the brand we normally used, and I pondered the dozens of alternatives. We wouldn't be using it long, but I didn't want to get something super expensive that everyone loved. I might get stuck with it as the regular brew.

The dilemmas of a pie shop owner are myriad.

A shiver rippled the skin at the back of my neck, and I glanced over my shoulder.

The aisle was empty.

Giving myself a shake, I grabbed a canister. I was overthinking the coffee issue, probably because I didn't want to think about other things. When Takako had tried to catch my attention earlier, I'd run like an undercooked egg. She wasn't exactly smothering me by doing her work in Pie Town. So, why did it feel that way? All the time I'd spent wishing for connection, and now someone was offering—

Metal groaned. Boxes of tea cascaded from shelves.

I stared, uncomprehending.

The shelf tilted, leaning at an impossible angle. Its base skidded sideways and it arced downward.

Chapter Fifteen

Coffee cans spiraled past in slow motion. Shielding my head, I shrieked and dropped to the floor. A crash reverberated, shaking my bones. Boxes and canisters pelted my shoulders and thudded to the linoleum.

Silence fell.

Shaken, I looked up. Above me, the metal shelf canted against the shelving opposite, forming a triangular metal tunnel. I was safe and unhurt. I released a ragged breath. I sat on the floor. Caught my breath.

The metal groaned.

Freshly motivated, I scrambled over the detritus and toward freedom.

Hands grasped my arms and pulled me from beneath the shelves. Coffee tins rolled, fanning from the scene of the disaster. They ricocheted against heels and toes and shopping cart wheels.

"Are you okay?" A young, sandy-haired checker clasped my arm and frowned.

"Yes." I nodded, breathing hard, and struggled to remember his name. "Yes, Tom. You're Tom," I said stupidly.

"And you're bleeding." Tom pointed to my head, then

jammed his hands in the pockets of his green apron and flushed.

A half-dozen customers gaped at me and the tilting shelf. Tristan Cannon wasn't in the crowd. He couldn't have gone far, so he must have heard the crash. My pulse quickened. Was he really that uninterested? Or had he pushed the shelf over himself?

"Val?" Tom asked.

"What?"

He pointed to my forehead.

"Oh." I touched a spot in front of my ear, and my fingertips came away bloody. "It's just a scratch. I wasn't hurt." I willed my heartbeat to slow.

"Why don't you sit down?" He led me to a stool beside an open door to a storage area. "I'll get the first-aid kit." The checker hurried off.

I drew my phone from the pocket of my hoodie, called Gordon.

"Val." His voice was a soothing rumble. "What are you wearing? No, wait, let me guess—"

"There was an incident at the country store. One of the shelves tipped over on me. I'm not sure it was an accident."

"Are you all right?" he asked sharply.

"Yes, I'm fine. It's just—"

"I'll be right there." He hung up.

Tom reappeared with a first-aid kit in hand. He pawed through the plastic box. "Okay, let's see. Alcohol wipes. Here." He handed me a small, square alcohol wipe.

I tore open the packet. The wipe inside was bone-dry, but I dabbed at the spot above my ear anyway.

Tom handed me a squeeze bottle of antiseptic. I applied that to the wipe and then to my skin. By the time actual bandages emerged from the box, Gordon was striding down the aisle, his emerald eyes blazing.

"Val. What happened?"

I motioned toward the fallen shelf with one hand, the wipe pressed to my cut with the other. It wouldn't stop bleeding.

"It fell over," Tom said.

"Those don't just fall," Gordon snarled. He blew out his breath. In a calmer voice, he asked, "Have you got video?"

Tom winced. "Only at the registers. But I'm not supposed to know that."

Gordon bent to me. "Let me take a look." Gently, he pried the wipe from my head. "It doesn't look bad. It's only bleeding a lot because it's a head wound."

"I'll . . ." Tom pointed with his thumb over one shoulder. "I should call the manager." He trotted away.

"I'll get the shelves fingerprinted," Gordon said in a low voice and ripped open a bandage. "But the odds are low we'll get anything useful. The whole town's been through this store."

"Then you think—?" My voice squeaked. "You think someone pushed it over?" *Someone like Tristan?*

He taped the bandage to my head, his touch unbearably gentle.

I grasped his wrist, and he stilled.

"I'm glad you're here," I said.

"I'll always come when you call."

Our gazes locked, and I knew it was true. He didn't say words like that lightly. And I couldn't imagine not being there for him. I leaned closer.

Tom peered around the corner of the aisle. "Should I phone the police?"

"Yes," Gordon said, the spell broken, and the checker vanished again.

Gordon cleared his throat. "Short of a major earthquake

or human intervention, I don't know what would make one of those tip. Did you notice anyone suspicious?"

"I was talking to Tristan Cannon before it happened."

He angled his head toward the fallen racks. "Was he underneath that too?"

"No. He left earlier, not long before it fell."

His jaw tightened. "Did you see him leave the store?"

I shook my head and winced.

"I'll talk to him." His voice brooked no argument, and that just made me want to argue. I opened my mouth to speak.

"Did you learn anything interesting from Cannon?" he continued.

I raised a brow. "Thanks for assuming I slipped an interrogation into that conversation."

"Assuming? I expect it."

I laughed in spite of myself. "I didn't learn much. He only confirmed that Kara could be tough on people."

"Was she tough on him?"

"He said no. I'm not sure I believed him."

"Did he seem resentful?"

"No." I rubbed one finger along the edge of my bandage. "He seemed worried."

"Unusually so?"

"No," I admitted. "His business partner was murdered. His practice is in jeopardy, and he's a suspect. If I were in Tristan's shoes, I'd be terrified."

"If he knows something, he needs to come forward."

"Do you think he's holding back?"

"Do you?"

"Yes." I nudged a fallen canister with my toe. "And I think I nearly got killed because of it. Either Tristan did this, or someone else did, thinking we were together."

He encircled me in his muscular arms. "I'll take you home," he said into my hair.

"Thanks, but I've got to get back to Pie Town." Regretfully, I pulled away. "I only came here for coffee."

He scooped a random canister off the floor. "Here you go."

That was one way to make a decision.

Gordon followed me to the cash register. He paid for the coffee and walked me to Pie Town's glass front door. "I'm returning to the store." He pressed his lips to mine, sending my heart into a delicious spiral. "I want to make sure no one touches that shelf before it gets printed."

"Will you let me know if you find anything?"

He smiled. "Probably not."

I laughed. "Fine. Be that way. And thanks for the coffee."

I boxed a pumpkin pie and handed it to a gray-haired customer. "Happy Almost Halloween!"

"Thank you." The woman strode to the glass door. Watery Thursday-morning sunlight drifted through Pie Town's front windows.

Charlene set down her cell phone and swiveled her barstool to face me. "You're too early for Halloween. Are you sure you didn't get a concussion from one of those cans yesterday?"

"It's *almost* Halloween," I said, unfazed. Sales had stayed high—people buying pies for Halloween parties and stopping by for a bite of pumpkin nostalgia. My stepmother was off on a day trip to Monterey. Most importantly, no one else had died. Win-win-win.

"Should have called me," she grumped. "We're partners. I could have protected you."

"It was an eavesdropping of opportunity." Thank God she hadn't been there. If she'd been hurt . . . An icicle pierced my core.

"Well, since you're not concussed, get a move on. We're going to be late meeting Denise." Charlene flipped up the collar of her red knit coat.

Draped around her shoulders, Frederick flicked his ears. A matching white hat and mittens lay on the counter in front of Charlene. She'd moved past Halloween and moved straight on to Christmas.

"We agreed to tackle Denise later this afternoon." I glanced at the tables, filled by locals stopping by for pot pies and quiches and coffee.

"That's a no-go. If we wait until after school gets out," Charlene said, "the corn maze will be packed with screaming teens."

"You can go, Val." Petronella strode through the swinging door from the kitchen. "Abril and I have got this."

"See?" Charlene said. "Your assistant manager has got this, and I have it on good authority Denise is at the maze now."

"But—" I snapped shut my mouth. If Petronella said she could manage, she could manage, even if Pie Town was packed to the gills. Besides, I wouldn't be gone long. "Okay. Thanks, Petronella."

The bell over the front door jingled. My brother, Doran, strolled into the dining area.

I smiled. "Hey, you."

He nodded. His blue eyes, brilliant against his dark skin, crinkled. "Hey, Val. Is Abril here?"

Doran might not find me as fascinating as his girlfriend, but they seemed to be back on track—if they'd ever been off. "She's in the kitchen, and don't forget your hairnet."

He made a face and strode past me into the kitchen.

"Ah," Charlene said, "young love. He can't bear a moment away from Abril. It's like you and Pie Town."

"We like it when Val's chained to the counter." Tally-Wally swiveled on his barstool to face Charlene. "It means more pie."

"Yeah, don't rock the boat." Graham tugged at the suspenders holding up his khaki pants.

"I'll get my jacket." I collected my winter hoodie, a scarf, mittens, and hat from my office and returned to the dining area.

"*Now* are you ready?" Charlene asked.

"Ready as instant soup."

We zipped down the One in Charlene's yellow Jeep. Charlene wrenched the wheel, and we lurched onto a dirt road lined with pumpkins. Signs urged us forward: CORN MAZE! PUMPKIN CANNON! SOUVENIRS!

"I'm not sure how I feel about this pumpkin cannon," I said, bumping in my seat as Charlene raced down the road. "It seems like a waste of pumpkins."

She swerved around a dirt pothole, and I clutched the grab bar.

"Flying pumpkins are good fun," she said. "Besides, San Nicholas produces more pumpkins every year than we can sell."

We skidded into the parking lot and stepped from the Jeep. Half a dozen cars filled the other spots. Fog hung low above us, twining through the tops of the cypress trees and veiling the roof of a black-painted barn lined with more pumpkins. The sign above its open doors proclaimed:

TICKETS! SOUVENIRS! Charlene adjusted Frederick around her neck, and we strolled inside.

I scanned the barn for Denise. Pumpkin festival T-shirts vied for space with orange candles and plastic skeletons. Fake spiderwebs dangled from the rafters.

At the counter, a gray-haired woman in cat-eye glasses read a paperback thriller, her face pinched with concentration.

"Afternoon, Gladys," Charlene said. "Where's Denise?"

Gladys glanced up from her book and looked toward a door in the side of the barn. A MAZE ENTRANCE sign arched above it. "She's in the center of the maze."

"What's she doing there?" Charlene asked.

"Checking people's time," the woman said in a *duh* tone. She pulled her fuzzy gray sweater tighter.

"I see Denise isn't above putting in some volunteer hours," Charlene said.

"Not when there's free publicity to be had," the ticket taker said dryly. "A reporter was in there with her earlier."

I zipped my Pie Town hoodie higher. "Makes sense. Denise *is* a sponsor."

"Are we going in or what?" Charlene asked.

"We'll take two tickets." I pulled my wallet from the rear pocket of my jeans.

Charlene raised a palm. "Hold on. I need my running shoes." She hurried out the barn's front door.

The woman took my money, and we waited.

Charlene returned, huffing.

Gladys time-stamped the two tickets. "Better get going if you want to win."

"I'm on it!" Charlene grabbed a ticket off the counter and hustled through the maze entrance.

"Thanks." I took my ticket and receipt and jogged after Charlene.

"Those are tax-deductible," the woman called after me.

I ran beneath the arch and entered a long corridor of fading cornstalks.

Charlene's red coat vanished around a bend.

"Wait up." I jogged after her.

Charlene paused at a T-intersection. "Right or left?"

"Right," I said.

Something mechanical buzzed in the distance.

She glanced at her phone. "Left, it is." Charlene turned and strode down the narrow passage.

Then why had she bothered to ask? A better question was why had I bothered to answer? Shrugging, I followed.

The corn reached high above our heads. It rustled eerily at our passage. I was glad we were doing this during the daytime, even if it was a weak, foggy daylight. At night, the creepy factor had to be off the charts.

I nodded to Charlene's red high-tops. "You didn't change your shoes."

"Why would I?"

"Because you said . . ." *Never mind.* "I've been thinking about Elon. He's the victim's husband, but I know the least about him. I'd like to get Denise's take on that relationship."

"He's a good man," Charlene said. "But that doesn't mean he's not a killer."

"Doesn't it?" I asked.

"People are flawed." She checked her phone and turned right at an intersection. "Even the good ones."

"Marla had the right idea. We should bring him a pie. And are you checking a satellite map of the maze?"

"Since when do we listen to Marla? You realize she wants to be a Baker Street Baker?"

"I know." The last time we'd "worked" with Marla on a case, she'd intentionally gotten us caught holding bags of garbage. But I couldn't ignore how she'd been dogging our investigation now. Were her antics all a weird way of saying she wanted to join the team? Marla had gone through some rough times recently—emotionally and financially. Maybe she just wanted to be part of something? "I think we should let her help." I stopped at another intersection and shifted on the dried corn leaves lining the path. They crackled beneath my feet.

"Did that shelf land on your head?"

"She has a different perspective on San Nicholas—"

"A vampire's perspective. She'll blab any clues we uncover across cyberspace."

"If she's an associate, we don't have to tell her *everything*."

Frederick snuggled his head against Charlene's neck.

"No, to bringing in Marla," Charlene said. "Did Gordon get those prints back from the lab?"

I let her change the subject, but this discussion wasn't over. Even if I didn't bring it up, Marla would. "Prints?"

"From the country store."

"The shelf was covered in prints. So far, the police haven't been able to match them to any suspects."

She snorted and turned another corner. "How did Chief Shaw take it that Gordon brought in new evidence?"

"I'm not sure." I jammed my hands in my pockets. Gordon had been terse when he'd called this morning to let me know what he hadn't found. "He said another police officer filed the report, and that someone from the SNPD might want to speak with me. So far, no one has, but it's early."

"And Shaw's an idiot." She turned again. Something

flashed in her hand, and she whipped it behind her back. "What if Tristan didn't knock over that shelf?"

I gnawed my bottom lip. "When I was walking to the store yesterday, I did think someone was following me."

"Why didn't you tell me sooner? Did you tell Gordon?"

"No. I mean, it was creepy and foggy, and I didn't see anyone."

A faint hum, like a swarm of insects, tightened my shoulders.

"What's that sound?" I asked.

"What sound?" She paused at another juncture and looked at her hand again.

"That buzzing—"

The sound faded.

"Whoever followed you to the store may have overheard your conversation with Tristan," she said.

"I don't even know if someone *was* following me. Why do you keep looking at your phone?"

She slipped her phone into the pocket of her red coat. "No, I'm not."

"You are too! Are you cheating?"

"A better question is, are *you* cheating, since you're following me?"

"Charlene—"

"I'm checking Twitter." Casually, she pulled out her phone and glanced at the screen.

"You've got an overhead picture of the corn maze on your phone, don't you?"

She lifted her chin. "If you must know, I have a drone."

"A—" I looked up. The tip of something black emerged from the low fog. "So that's what I've been hearing."

She scowled. "I'm going to have a word with Ray about the motor. It's supposed to be a stealth drone."

Did I want to know why? No, I did not. "You blackmailed poor Ray into setting this up for you?"

"It wasn't blackmail. It was good, honest guilt, expertly applied. Ray lost me that pumpkin race."

Frederick raised his head and stared at me coldly, as if in agreement.

"Charlene, how many times have I asked you not to terrify the customers?"

Her eyes narrowed to slits. "That Brinks kid will never know what hit him."

"Charlene, you need to leave that kid alone."

"I will, if he leaves me and Frederick alone. And stops scuffing my fence! A fence doesn't repaint itself, you know."

"Charlene—"

She raised the phone to my eye level. "Look, I control the drone using my phone app. Come on, we're almost at the center of the maze. What do you think the prize for best time is?"

I pushed the phone away. "We can't cheat. This is for charity."

"Huh. We're wasting daylight." She moved deeper into the maze.

Why did I bother? I trudged after her.

We made a left, another left, and a right. The rows of corn opened to a wide circle.

Denise sat on a gilt throne at its center. "Welcome, to the center of the maze!"

"Hi, Denise," I said, sheepish.

Something thumped in the distance, and I started. "What's that?"

"Oh," Denise said, rising, "they must be testing the pumpkin cannon." She tugged down the hem of her thick, quilted black jacket. The eyeglasses logo over her heart seemed to wink.

Charlene thrust her ticket at Denise. "How'd we do?"

"Wow." Denise's brows rose. "You made it in record time." She stamped the ticket. "Have you walked the maze before?"

"No, but I've got an excellent sense of direction." Charlene tapped her nose.

Denise held out her hand. "Here, Val, I'll stamp your ticket."

"It's okay." I shuffled my feet. "I don't need a prize. It's all for charity."

"Thanks," Denise said. "That's thoughtful of you."

A breeze rustled the cornstalks and tossed strands of Denise's mid-length, brown hair.

"How are you doing?" I asked quietly. It was too easy to remember what it had been like when my mother had died. But at least I'd been able to say good-bye. Denise and Elon hadn't had that chance with Kara.

Unless one of them had killed her.

Denise stared at her black hiking boots. "Oh. You mean my cousin." She raised her head. "I want to find whoever did it and make them pay. I guess I'm in the anger stage of grief. Kara and I might not have always seen eye to eye, but we were like sisters, you know?"

"Are the police any closer to finding her killer?" Charlene asked.

"They haven't shared anything with me," she said tartly, rising from the gilt throne. "I've half a mind to hire you two."

I started. "Us? You mean, the Baker Street Bakers?"

"Is that crazy?" she asked.

The pumpkin cannon whumped.

"Well—" I began.

"It's not crazy," Charlene said. "We've solved lots of cases. We'd be happy to take on yours."

"I guess I should ask how much you charge," Denise said.

"We don't," Charlene said. "If we charged, we'd need private investigator licenses."

I wasn't sure that was how the law worked. "We need to be careful not to interfere in the police investigation. But we'll help any way we can." And this opening was too good to miss, since we were nosing about already. "What can you tell us?"

Her eyes flashed. "I can tell you that Laurelynn should be the prime suspect. She and my cousin hated each other."

"Really?" I asked. "Elon said their rivalry was trivial, a joke."

"Is that what he told you?" Denise paced in front of the throne. "Elon sees the best in everyone."

"Did he see the best in Kara?" Charlene asked.

"Well, of course—they were married."

"We heard Kara could be rough on people," Charlene said. "They say she lorded it over Tristan Cannon that he was a mere optometrist."

"I don't know who *they* are, but that's no reason to commit murder." Her hands clenched and unclenched. "And it isn't true. My cousin was always supportive. When I started my company, she even helped me with the funding. I gave her a percent of the partnership as payment. You know how iffy Silicon Valley start-ups can be. Kara believed in me, or she wouldn't have helped."

"But she wasn't supportive with Laurelynn?" I asked.

"That was different. And why would she have to be supportive? She didn't owe Laurelynn anything."

"Tell us more about Elon," I said.

She crossed her arms, her cheeks pinking. "Those two

were a wonderful couple. If the police are looking at Elon, they're barking up the wrong tree. He adored her. Honestly, he's—" She snapped her mouth shut and shook her head. "I know everyone suspects the husband in situations like this. But I want the real killer caught. It's not Elon."

"Where were you the morning your cousin was killed?" I asked.

"You want my alibi?" Denise arched a brow. "I asked you to work *for* me."

"It's only so we can determine if you might have any evidence or insight into the murder," I said quickly.

She pursed her lips. "I was home, alone."

Charlene and I asked her more questions, but we didn't learn anything useful.

We exited the maze, and I checked my phone. At least Charlene's cheating meant I'd return to Pie Town at a reasonable hour.

Charlene hurried inside the barn. Five minutes later, she returned, scowling.

"What's wrong?" I asked.

"All I got was this stupid badge." She pulled an orange button from her pocket. It read, LOVE CORN MAZES.

"At least you have the satisfaction of knowing you beat the maze. Oh, wait. You don't, because you cheated."

She opened the Jeep's rear door. Using her phone's controls, she maneuvered the drone until it rested inside.

I stared at the drone. It had a jack-o'-lantern on top. "And you said *I* was getting a jump start on Halloween."

"Keep it up, and you'll have to find your own ride to Pie Town."

I mimed zipping my lips and tried not to smile.

Chapter Sixteen

Charlene and I strode through Pie Town's front door. Its bell jingled a welcome. The neon smiley face logo above the order window beamed at our return. Locals and tourists filled the tables and ate savory pies.

Charlene patted her badge. "I beat the maze."

Frederick's tail coiled around her neck.

"All on your own?" Marla swiveled on her counter stool. "Wasn't Val with you?"

"I plead the Fifth." I pushed through the Dutch door beside the register. "Petronella, what did I miss?"

The cell phone in my assistant manager's pink apron pocket buzzed. "Nothing." She pulled out her phone and frowned at the number. "Can you take the register? I'd like to get this."

"Sure." Whipping a spare apron from beneath the register, I looped it over my head.

Petronella pressed the phone to her ear. She strode into the kitchen, her motorcycle boots clomping on the black-and-white floor.

Charlene grabbed a clean coffee mug and poured coffee from the urn. "Something wrong with Petronella?" She eyed the swinging kitchen door.

"She's worried about her dad." I'd been clinging to the fragile hope Petros Scala wasn't a serious suspect. But a queasy feeling in my stomach told me not to trust Shaw.

Charlene blew on her coffee. She turned toward the corner booth, where the gamers rattled dice across the table.

Ray slouched lower in his seat, his ears reddening.

Charlene pointed at the student engineer. "A word, if you don't mind."

Leaving Ray to fend for himself, I surveyed my empire. Shiny pink tables and booths. The scent of baking pies. Cheerful chatter and the clink of silverware. On the sidewalk outside, two women stopped to admire the Halloween village in the windows. The counter seats were filled. . . .

I frowned.

Tally-Wally and Graham were still here, and my blood chilled.

Those two only stayed late if something was up, or they thought something interesting might happen. Neither boded well.

They spoke in low voices with a local farmer, Dell Martins. Dell's weather-beaten skin seemed to crackle with age. The wind had blown his white hair sideways.

I ambled along the counter. "Hi, guys. How's it going?"

They jerked apart.

Graham's eyes widened with innocence. "So, you beat the corn maze." He fiddled with his cabbie's hat, lying on the counter in front of him.

"In a manner of speaking." I slid my hands into my apron pockets. "What are you two still doing here?"

Tally-Wally rubbed his drink-reddened nose. "Is there a law against it?"

"No," I said. "I'm thrilled to have your company and your

business." Even if the latter consisted mainly of cheap coffee and half-price, day-old hand pies. "I was only curious."

"Curiosity killed the cat," the farmer snapped.

"Now, Dell," Graham said. "Val's a friend, even if she is nosy."

"I'm not—" Okay, I was nosy.

The bell over the door tinkled, and I looked up.

Mrs. Thistleblossom stumped into the dining area, her black galoshes squeaking on the linoleum. She stopped dead in the center of the checkerboard floor and glared like the fairy who'd crashed Sleeping Beauty's party.

Silence rippled outward from where she stood. Even the dice at the gamers' corner table seemed muffled.

Tally-Wally's shoulders hunched to his ears. "You've got bigger problems now."

I walked to the register and forced a smile. "Good afternoon, Mrs. Thistleblossom."

The old woman shrugged beneath her lumpy charcoal coat. Slowly, she lifted her cane. She banged it on the floor once. Twice. Thrice.

An inexplicable shiver raced up my spine. What the heck was *this* about?

Turning on her heels with a loud, rubbery squeak, she strode from the restaurant. The door drifted shut behind her.

Had that been a threat? A curse? Not that I believed in any of that stuff, but it wasn't nice to think someone wished me ill.

"Well," Marla drawled, "you don't see that every day."

"She's, um, old," I said loudly for the sake of my unnerved customers.

The senior citizens at the counter swiveled to glare.

My cheeks flamed. *She's old?* Half the people in Pie Town fell into that category.

Charlene strolled to the counter. "When I get to be Thistleblossom's age, I'll probably be cracked too."

"*When* you get to be her age?" Marla arched a platinum brow.

Charlene scowled. "What's that—?"

"More coffee?" I asked, before the ribbing could go nuclear.

"You never offer *us* coffee." Tally-Wally thrust a mug in my direction.

Petronella hurried from the kitchen, her normally pale face a shade whiter. "Val, I've got to leave."

"Is something wrong?" I asked, worried.

She swallowed. "It's my father," she said in a low voice. "He's been arrested."

"Arrested?" Marla bellowed.

Heads swiveled toward us.

"Are you sure he wasn't just brought in for questioning?" I asked quietly.

Petronella shook her head. "I'm not sure about anything."

"It'll be fine," I said. But my insides tensed. "Your dad was the victim here. His pumpkin was destroyed. More importantly, he's got no connection to Dr. Levant."

"But that's the problem." Petronella's face contorted with misery. "He did. My parents live on the same street as the Levants. Dad was growing his giant pumpkins in the front yard—he said the soil was better. Dr. Levant complained to the city about them."

"You can't grow vegetables in your own front yard?" I asked. That couldn't be right.

Petronella rubbed her slender arms and looked toward the door. "You can. And you know how San Nicholas is about pumpkins. But Dr. Levant complained it was attracting rats and was a nuisance—"

"Rats." Graham's hand clenched on his checked cap. "My neighbor's ivy attracts 'em too."

Petronella glanced his way. "Apparently, someone called in an anonymous tip. They said they'd seen my dad around the giant pumpkins the morning of . . . you know."

There was a collective inhalation at the counter.

"Anonymous?" Tally-Wally said. Thumping his gnarled fist on the counter, he turned to Graham and Mr. Martins. "Just as we suspected."

"Suspected?" I asked.

Petronella rubbed the back of her neck. "My mom's freaking out. It's probably nothing—just questions, but—"

"Of course," I said. "Go. We can manage."

"Thanks." She whipped off her apron, handed it to me, and jogged out the front door.

"Looks like the Baker Street Bakers didn't see *that* coming." Marla sipped her coffee, her diamond rings glittering beneath the pink pendant lights.

"Shut it, Vampira," Charlene said.

"It makes no sense," I said. "Why would Petros destroy his own pumpkin? It lost him the prize money."

"Maybe he realized he couldn't win," Marla said, "and decided to wreck it rather than lose."

"Petros was passionate about pumpkins," Graham said. "He'd never vandalize one of his own. Or anyone else's."

"What if he needed to kill Dr. Levant," Marla said, "and was too honorable to use someone else's contest entry?"

"You're off your gourd if you believe that," Charlene said.

My jaw tightened. If Chief Shaw had arrested Petros, then he either had information we didn't, or he was . . . being Chief Shaw. We had to save Petronella and her family. "What did you mean by 'just as we suspected'?" I asked Tally-Wally.

The oldsters at the counter looked at each other and fell silent.

"What?" I asked.

No one responded, and I looked to Charlene.

My piecrust specialist checked her gold watch. "Well, look at the time." She adjusted Frederick around her neck. "I forgot I've got to be somewhere."

"Whoops," Graham said. "Me too."

"Me three," Tally-Wally said.

The counter emptied, the bell over the door tolling a dirge as all the senior citizens exited.

What had just happened? I puzzled over the vacant barstools. They were up to something, Charlene was in on it, and she wasn't telling me.

That meant that whatever was going on was not good.

Not good at all.

Chapter Seventeen

From my spot behind the register, I glanced out Pie Town's front windows. Mercury fog pressed against the glass and turned passersby into blurred silhouettes. In the corner booth, the gamers argued a fine point of dungeon etiquette.

It was nearly four o'clock—the dead hour. Lunch was long past, dinner too close to spoil. No one stopped by on their way home from work, because work wasn't quite over yet. But where had Charlene gone? And how were Petronella and her father?

"Order up," Abril called through the kitchen window.

I whirled, grabbing the plate—a mini turkey pot pie—and the ticket beneath it. Scanning the tables, I located the corresponding number tent. I whisked the pie to a construction worker, his steel-toed boots hooked behind the legs of his chair.

"Enjoy," I said. "And be careful, it's hot."

"It had better be." The construction worker grabbed a fork and cracked open the crust. Steam spiraled upward.

The phone in my apron pocket buzzed. Was Charlene finally returning my calls? Hastily, I drew it out. My shoulders slumped. *Takako*.

I answered and tried to force enthusiasm into my voice. "Hi, Takako. How's Monterey?"

"I'm not in Monterey," she whispered.

"Did you get back to the hotel early?"

She made an odd sound, almost a sob. "I lied. I didn't go."

"You don't need to tell me where you're spending time," I said, baffled.

"This is terrible. There's been a terrible— Oh, Val!"

My voice sharpened. "Takako? What's wrong? Has something happened?"

"I'm at the dog park and—"

"Takako?" I checked the phone. We'd been disconnected. I called her back.

Voice mail.

She was probably trying to call me right now. The fact she wasn't answering likely didn't mean anything.

But what if it did?

Lead weighting my gut, I dialed again. And again, my call went to voice mail.

I untied my apron and hurried behind the counter to the order window. "Abril?"

Her head popped into view. "Yes?"

"I got a weird call from Takako at the dog park. I'm worried something's happened. It should be slow for the next thirty minutes or so, and then our evening customers will be buying whole pies to go. Can you manage the shop for a bit?"

Her brow creased. "Sure." She disappeared from the window and hurried through the swinging door.

"Thanks. I'll get back as soon as I can."

I strode into my office. It was too cold today for my usual Pie Town hoodie, and I grabbed a thick, brown microfiber jacket off the back of my executive chair. Shrugging into the jacket, I hurried from the restaurant and down the foggy street.

I flipped up my hood, with its faux-fur trim. Low shapes rose and fell in the thick mist—a mailbox, a newspaper kiosk, a public bench.

Turning off Main Street, I wound through a quasiresidential area. Twisted cypress and eucalyptus trees stretched their gnarled branches above the road.

Why hadn't Takako tried calling again?

I broke into a jog, stumbling once on the crooked sidewalk.

The chain-link fence surrounding the dog park emerged from the fog. Growls and sharp barks peppered the chill air.

"Takako?" I shouted.

"Over here!" Her voice cracked on the last word.

I found the gate and trotted into the dog park. "Takako?"

"Come quickly!"

Reorienting on her voice, I cut across the path.

Takako huddled beneath a cypress tree, her hands jammed into the pockets of a puffy black jacket. Her face was reddened and streaked with tears.

She wasn't alone.

Mrs. Thistleblossom stood beside her. In one hand, the old woman held her black umbrella. In the other, she gripped the leash of the ugliest dog I'd ever seen. It stood shin high, with crossed eyes, bald spots, and wild tufts of gray fur. Tiny fangs jutted from its jaw in random directions.

The animal lunged at me.

"Milo!" the old woman said.

He growled and subsided.

"Takako," I asked, "are you all right? What's happened?"

She gulped and pointed a shaking finger at the wide base of the cypress.

I turned.

The optometrist, Tristan Cannon, lay against the trunk. Blood streaked his skull. He stared, his jaw sagging open.

I gasped and moved toward him. "Oh my—"

Takako grabbed my arm. "He's dead."

I'd spoken with Tristan just the other day. He couldn't be dead. But he clearly was. Swallowing, I tore my gaze from the man. "Have you called the police?"

"I didn't," Mrs. Thistleblossom said.

"No," Takako said. "I didn't . . . Look." She pointed.

Near the hem of Tristan's slacks, damp from the wet grass, lay a glass paperweight. Blood stained its oval shape. Within its clear glass, black bats burst from spirals of orange, black, and purple flames.

"It's mine," Takako whispered.

My voice shook. "You didn't—"

"No." She moaned. "Charlene said everything would be cheaper after the festival, and she was right. I bought a paperweight. That paperweight."

I pulled out my phone. "Are you sure it's yours?" It did look like one of the paperweights from the local glass factory, but they made a lot of similar designs. Halloween themes and pumpkins were popular this time of year.

"It looks like mine," Takako said. "But Mrs. Thistle-blossom and I arrived here at the same time. She knows I didn't hurt anyone."

"I know you didn't hurt anyone when I was here." Mrs. Thistleblossom raised her chin.

I dialed the police. "So, you can verify Takako's story?"

"No. I have no idea what your stepmother is talking about."

"What?" Takako cried. "We practically walked here together. We discovered him together!"

"That's what *you* say. I didn't see what you were up to earlier."

"San Nicholas PD," said a familiar woman's voice. "How can I help you?"

"This is Val Harris." My words came quick and fast and terrified. "I'm at the dog park. We've found a body—Tristan Cannon. It looks like he's been killed."

The woman sucked in her breath. "Val? It's Helen. I'm sending someone right now. Don't touch anything, and stay put."

Life in a small town. I'd gotten to know the police dispatchers over pie and coffee.

I thanked her, hung up, and called Gordon.

"Val." His voice rumbled through my belly. "What's up?"

"My stepmother and Mrs. Thistleblossom found Tristan Cannon's body in the dog park."

"I did not!" Thistleblossom shouted. "She's lying."

Her dog howled.

"What was that?" he asked.

"Mrs. Thistleblossom is a hostile witness," I sputtered.

"I'll be right there," he said. "Have you called the department?"

Sirens wailed.

"Yes," I said. "They're on their way."

"So am I. You know the drill." Gordon hung up.

Right. The drill. Take pictures for Charlene and now for Gordon too. But not in front of Thistleblossom. I didn't trust her not to rat me out to Shaw.

"What's that?" I asked, pointing behind the old lady.

"What?" She turned.

Blindly, I aimed my phone in the body's general direction and snapped photos, hoping at least one would be useful. "I guess it's nothing." I pocketed the phone.

"He was still warm." Takako said unevenly. "The killer

must have been nearby. If we'd gotten here sooner, we might have stopped him."

Then if Mr. Scala was still at the police station, he was in the clear. He couldn't have attacked Dr. Cannon. "What were you doing here at all?" I asked. "I thought you'd gone to Monterey today?"

"I was following her." She pointed at Thistleblossom.

"Me?" Mrs. Thistleblossom pressed her leash hand to her chest. "How dare you!"

"You're trying to intimidate Val." My stepmother arched a brow. "I saw it through the window."

Mrs. Thistleblossom sniffed. "Intimidate? Ridiculous."

"Then what do you call that performance in Pie Town today?" Takako stepped closer to the old woman. Since they were roughly the same height, if Takako was trying to loom over her, she failed. "This isn't my first rodeo. She's trying to get in your head, Val."

Not her first rodeo? My stepmother was an anthropologist. Or an archaeologist. Maybe that career was more exciting than I'd guessed. "But . . . you should have been in Monterey."

"My hotel was too tempting. I slept in and decided to stay in San Nicholas."

I nodded. The hotel really was amazing. Too bad I'd been banned after an incident with a hijacked golf cart.

"So, I went for a walk on the hotel grounds," Takako continued, "and then I decided to come to Pie Town. That's when I saw *her*." Her voice hardened. "I wanted to know what she was up to."

The sirens grew louder over the dog's frantic barking.

"What was she up to?" I asked.

"Nothing," Takako said. "It was a little disappointing."

"This is outrageous." Mrs. Thistleblossom huffed. "You

brain this poor optometrist and try to divert attention from it with these wild tales—"

"Murder's a serious accusation," I said. "And false statements to the cops are punishable with jail time."

The dog sniffed my shoelaces. I edged away in case it got any ideas.

Mrs. Thistleblossom blew out her breath. "I'm an old woman. My eyesight isn't what it used to be. I can't possibly be expected to confirm or deny her story."

"Wait," I said. "If you were following Mrs. Thistleblossom, how did you both arrive here at the same time?"

"Exactly!" The elderly woman crossed her arms, jerking the leash. The dog's eyes bulged.

"I lost her in the fog," Takako said, "and then I heard her dog scratching around. We both saw each other at the same time. I'd been caught, so I decided to brazen it out and pretend I was here for a walk. Then the fog cleared a bit, and there *he* was." She motioned toward the corpse.

The dog gnawed on the hem of my jeans. Cars screeched to a halt in the street.

"Just tell the police the truth." I glared at Mrs. Thistleblossom and shook the dog free. "All of it."

"Why wouldn't I?"

Chief Shaw, flanked by two uniformed cops, strode toward us. "Val Harris. Why aren't I surprised?" He stopped short and studied the body. "Dammit."

"I didn't find the body," I said. "I—"

He raised a palm. "No. Say no more. Gentlemen, separate the witnesses and take their statements, please."

I gave my statement to an African-American cop I knew, Officer Sanders. He was a rhubarb-pie fan. The officer looked at me askance. "Why did your stepmother call you and not the police?"

I shifted my weight and grass squelched beneath my tennis shoes. "I'm not sure. She was pretty shaken up when I arrived. I don't think she was thinking clearly."

Gordon, in a navy fisherman's sweater, strode through the fog. "Sanders. Val. What's going on?"

Sanders clicked off the black plastic recording device at his jacket collar. "The chief is here," he said warningly.

"And so's Val," Gordon said. "What have you got?"

Sanders angled his head toward a cluster of cops beneath the dripping cypress tree. "Tristan Cannon. Looks like homicide by paperweight."

"Are we done?" I asked Officer Sanders.

"For now," he said. "If we have more questions, we'll be in touch."

Gordon drew me aside. "Tell me what you know."

"Takako thinks the paperweight that killed Dr. Cannon might be hers. It's from that glassblower on Main Street."

"How could the killer have gotten hold of it?" he asked.

Gordon believed Takako couldn't have done this. My shoulders unknotted. "No idea. I'm assuming she kept it in her hotel room. But she might be wrong. You know once that glassblower gets a design he likes, he makes multiples."

"Then all she has to do is produce her paperweight to prove it wasn't the murder weapon."

But Takako didn't get the chance.

Shaw arrested my stepmother.

Chapter Eighteen

"I can't believe you let them arrest my mother." Doran fumed, pacing Pie Town's checkerboard floor.

I clutched a sheaf of plastic menus to my chest. "Takako's not under arrest," I said. "She's free."

"Why'd they let her go?" Graham asked from the counter.

"Because she had no reason to kill anyone," I said. Besides, the police had found Takako's paperweight in her hotel room. The murder weapon wasn't hers after all. Shaw might want to prefer arresting Takako to arresting his golfing partner, but he couldn't ignore the facts.

"They raided her room." Doran's blue eyes flashed. "Shaw threatened her."

In their corner booth, the gamers pretended not to hear Doran's raised voice. The other Friday-morning regulars had no such compunction. They watched avidly.

"Shaw threatens everyone," I said. "He just didn't like that your mom called me before she called the police."

"I don't understand why either," he grumbled.

"How's she doing?" I asked meekly.

"She's recovering in her hotel."

I was a little jealous. The hotel's ban on me was totally unfair.

Okay, mostly unfair.

Marla swiveled on her barstool at the counter. "The real question, is why Val and Charlene involved your mother in the first place."

Doran crossed his arms over his black leather jacket. "Yeah. Why did you?"

"We didn't! I mean, we didn't ask her to. And she wasn't. She told me she was . . ." I trailed off. This was starting to feel like tattling.

"Was what?" Doran's dark brows curved downward.

"Takako's her own woman," Charlene said from the opposite end of the counter. It was as far as she could get from Marla. "And she's an adult who makes her own decisions. She does what she wants to do."

Draped over her shoulders, Frederick yawned.

"She didn't want to get arrested!" Doran shouted.

Marla blew on her coffee. "Well, she did find a murder victim and then delay reporting it. What do you expect?"

"Cannon was a good man." Graham shifted on his barstool. "He got me my reading glasses."

"If you trained your eyes," Tally-Wally said from beside him, "you wouldn't need glasses, like me. Look." He rolled his eyes and made exaggerated, blinking movements.

Graham harrumphed. "Balderdash! Don't think I haven't noticed you squinting at menus, which, by the way, you hold at arm's length. The reason you like this place so much is because you can use distance vision for the chalkboard." He pointed at the menu on the wall, where we listed the day's specials.

"I like the coffee," Tally-Wally said.

"No one likes the coffee," Marla said.

What was wrong with my coffee?

"Forget the coffee," Charlene said. "Another person's been murdered. Something stinks at that optometry office."

"Obviously," Marla said, "that receptionist they fired is the killer."

"Office manager," I corrected absently. Maybe I *should* get better coffee.

"I heard Cannon was hit with a paperweight from that glass shop," Tally-Wally said. "Maybe the glassblower did it."

"Where'd you hear that?" Charlene glanced at me. I'd shown her the photos I'd taken and told her about the murder weapon, but she'd never blab. He hadn't heard it from Charlene.

"Old Thistleblossom's been telling people all over town," Tally-Wally said.

"Why would a glassblower kill two optometrists?" Charlene asked.

"Maybe his vision was failing," Tally-Wally said, "and they couldn't help him. With the prospect of losing his ability to blow glass, he killed them both."

Graham swiveled on his stool and slapped one beefy hand on the counter. "Are you kidding me? Smokey wears contacts!"

"The glassblower's name is Smokey?" Doran shook his head, a shock of near-black hair falling across one eye. "Never mind."

"It was the receptionist," Marla singsonged.

"If Wrongstradamus thinks so," Charlene said, "I know Alfreda's innocent." But she frowned.

"What if Thistleblossom did it?" Graham asked.

Silence fell along the counter.

"She's a little short to be bashing tall fellows like Cannon on the head," Tally-Wally said.

"She could have thrown the paperweight," Graham said. "Maybe she got confused, thought she was throwing a ball to that ugly mutt of hers."

The bell over the front door jingled, and we all turned to look.

As if summoned, Mrs. Thistleblossom stumped into the restaurant. The scent of mildew rose like an unquiet ghost from her black coat. Her dog nipped at the cloth.

Thumping her cane, she marched to a table near the center of the room. The dog tracked muddy paw prints on the linoleum. She sat, and her dog sprang onto the chair opposite. It drooled through crooked teeth.

The plastic menus crinkled against my chest. "The coffee's . . ." I'd started to say "self-serve," but what was the point? She was over a hundred. I wasn't going to make her get her own coffee. Or complain about her dog, muddying up my chair—not with Frederick hanging off Charlene like a stole. "Would you like a cup of coffee?"

"Black," she said.

Cowed, I poured her a mug and set it on her table. "Can I get you anything else?"

"No."

I sidled back to the counter. Surreptitiously, I poured a splash of coffee into a mug and sipped it. It tasted okay to me.

Doran hissed. "My mother—"

I handed Marla the mug. "Let's talk in my office," I said, shooting a glance at Mrs. Thistleblossom. I didn't mind airing the family laundry in front of our regulars, but I didn't trust Thistleblossom. Not after she'd tried to throw Takako under the bus yesterday.

"What do you want me to do with this?" Marla set the mug on the counter. "I'm not the kitchen help."

Doran didn't budge from his spot. "I shouldn't have yelled." He blew out his breath and raked both hands through his mop of hair. "I know this isn't your fault. Mom's going to do what she's going to do. But this was exactly what I was worried about when she turned up. She doesn't believe anything bad will ever happen, even after . . ." He grimaced.

"After our father?" I asked in a low voice.

At the counter, Graham and Tally-Wally nodded sagely to each other.

"No," Doran said. "After she's nearly gotten killed in countless war zones and dicey countries for her stupid job."

"Spy?" Marla asked.

"Archaeologist," he said.

"I thought she was an anthropologist?" Charlene said.

"You wouldn't believe the crazy crap my mother's done," he said. "And because she's gotten away with it so far, she thinks nothing bad will ever happen. She's relentless."

"I get it," I said. "And I'm starting to understand how you felt when I was trying too hard, pressuring you to be my family. It's exhausting."

His head reared backward. "What's wrong with my mom?"

"Nothing," I said. "She's great. I'm just saying, new family members can be overwhelming."

"Thanks a lot."

"I didn't mean—"

"Yes, you did. You are unbelievable." He stormed from the restaurant, the bell over the door jangling in his wake.

Marla *tsk*ed, her lips twitching over her coffee mug. "That did not go well."

"She's right." Graham shook his head. "Could have been handled better, young Val."

"He was the one who said Takako was relentless," I said. They shook their heads.

My shoulders collapsed. I couldn't win. "I *like* Takako." They busied themselves with their coffee mugs.

At least Petros was off the hook. He'd been in the police department the afternoon Tristan Cannon had been murdered. Even Shaw had to see the murders of Dr. Levant and Cannon were connected.

"Bah." Mrs. Thistleblossom snorted.

Shoulders to their ears, Graham and Tally-Wally turned to face the counter.

I closed up two hours later. To my surprise, Charlene lingered, perched on her counter stool while I mopped. The Halloween village glowed cheerfully in the front windows.

"There's something I think you should know." She adjusted Frederick over the shoulder of her green knit jacket.

I stuffed the mop in the bucket and leaned on the wooden handle. "You bullied Ray into lowering the noise level on your drone? Why do you need a stealth drone anyway?"

She lowered her chin and glared from beneath her snowy brows. "You remember I was in Alfreda's house?"

"How could I forget?"

"I'm pretty sure I remember seeing a paperweight collection."

"Pretty sure?" I pursed my lips.

"Reasonably sure."

I twisted the mop in the bucket, and it squelched. "That makes it less likely Alfreda's the killer. Why would

anyone take something from their own collection, carry
it to a dog park, and use it to bash someone in the head?
That would mean it was premeditated, *and* she's monu-
mentally stupid. The paperweight points straight at her."

"Unless she'd just bought it on Main Street, saw
Cannon, followed him, and killed him."

"You mean she *happened* to buy a paperweight murder
weapon the day he was killed? Come on."

"I can't remember if she had a bat paperweight in her
collection or not. But you know how the prices for Halloween items drop after the festival. Maybe she was waiting for it to go on sale."

"Oh." That did sound sickeningly plausible. I blew out
my breath. "Okay. All we have to do is find out if Alfreda
bought that paperweight yesterday. If Alfreda's a collector,
then the people in the shop probably will remember the
purchase."

She adjusted Frederick around her neck. "The shop's
closed now."

"We'll go tomorrow morning. And tonight, how would
you like to go to a networking meeting with me?"

She wrinkled her nose. "Why would I do that?"

"Because Denise will be there?"

She crossed her arms, rumpling her green knit jacket.
"Not good enough. You don't know what these meetings
are like. They'll make you listen to presentations on pyramid schemes for selling vitamins. Then they'll invite you
to coffee, so they can talk you into becoming one of their
salesgirls for the high price of a starter kit. *Then* all you
have to do is get ten more people to sell vitamins in order
to make any money. They're like Cthulu or the Bilderberg
Group," she said. "Tentacles everywhere."

"It's the Women's Professional Networking Association. They're international."

"So are the Illuminati."

First, she'd complained I wasn't invested enough in our investigation, and now she didn't want to help. "Well, Denise invited me, and she was Kara's cousin, so I think at least one Baker Street Baker should go."

Ignoring Charlene's grumbles, I finished cleaning and grabbed my short, gray wool coat from the office. I knotted a red scarf around my neck and returned to the dining area.

"I'm locking up," I said.

"Wait!" Charlene pulled a napkin from its metal holder and reached into her pocket, drawing out a pen. She scrawled something on the napkin and folded it carefully. "Take this."

"What is it?" I started to open the napkin.

"Don't do that! You'll know when the time is right to open it. Just keep it in your pocket during the meeting."

"Whatever." Exasperated, I stuffed it in my coat pocket and ushered her through the kitchen and out the alley door.

She watched while I locked it behind me. We parted, Charlene clambering into her yellow Jeep. She arranged the cat's limp body on the dashboard. The Jeep's taillights flared, and she roared from the alley.

I walked past my delivery van, past the gym next door, and out the other end of the alley.

The meeting was in a hall above the country grocery store. I tensed walking down the store's narrow aisles, my gaze darting to the high shelving. But nothing came crashing down as I made my way to the back stairs and to the third floor.

A low murmur of women's voices flowed through open

metal double doors. I slowed and walked into the room.
Hard plastic chairs were arranged in rows in front of a
long table.

A woman with gray-streaked hair greeted me at the
door. The name tag on the lapel of her navy blazer read
HI, I'M JULIE. "Hello, is this your first time at the meeting?"

"Yes, I'm Val Harris from Pie Town."

She relieved me of ten dollars and handed me a blank
name sticker to slap on my chest.

I made my way through the crowded hall. Women stood
in clusters, chatting. Infiltrating one of the groups looked
like too much trouble. So, I migrated to a long, folding
table lined with crudités, pastries, and a tea and coffee
setup.

I poured a cup of tea from an urn that looked a lot like
Pie Town's.

"Hi," a woman said from beside me. "Are you new
here?" She was tall, redheaded, middle-aged, and dressed
in a long, flowing scarlet dress. In blue ink, her name tag
said HI, I'M MARGARITE!

"Yep," I said. "I'm Val Harris. I own Pie Town on Main
Street."

Marguerite rolled her eyes. "That place looks so tempting, but I've been trying to cut down on my sugar. I'm
Marguerite."

"We sell pot pies and quiche as well, but you're not ob-
ligated to stop in. Not everyone in San Nicholas needs to
eat at Pie Town." But they *should*. "What do you do?"

"I'm an astrologer."

I grinned. Charlene was going to be furious she missed
this.

"I take it you don't believe in astrology," she said wryly.

"No, it's not that at all. I was trying to talk a friend of
mine into coming tonight. But she said it would all be

network marketing schemes. She would have loved meeting you."

"There are some network marketers," Marguerite admitted. "But we have a pretty good mix. How did you hear about us?"

"Denise Tatari invited me."

A woman nudged past me to get to a tray of lemon bars. I stepped away from the table.

Marguerite's face fell. "The poor woman. I can't believe what happened to her cousin. I suppose that's why she's not here tonight."

"I wouldn't blame her for skipping either." *Crudzilla*. She wasn't coming. But I'd thought Denise would, since she'd invited me. "How do you know Denise?"

"Through this group. I'm an investor in her software company. One of the shareholders, I mean."

"The only thing I can afford to invest in right now is my own business."

She flushed. "Oh, my investment is small potatoes. But her company was a place to start, and I like being invested in a local business. Actually, several of the women in the group are too." She pointed. "Sandy, over there. She's a chiropractor. And Carmella, she's a caterer. You might want to meet her. Do you wholesale your pies?"

"I do." I'd been working hard building that side of the business.

"Come on then. I'll introduce you."

Marguerite led me to a middle-aged Filipino woman. "Carmella, this is Val Harris. She's a friend of Denise. Val owns Pie Town, and she wholesales."

Carmella and I discussed the finer points of catering and finger foods and exchanged cards.

The meeting started, and we found seats in rows of

metal chairs. I scanned the crowd for Denise. Marguerite had been right, dang it. Denise wasn't coming.

I sat through half a dozen lectures on various women-owned businesses. My butt was aching from the hard metal chair when we finally broke for more mingling.

No one knew much about Kara. But roughly half the women I met were investors in Denise's software company, and they all had opinions, all uniformly wonderful. Good for Denise. Bad for profiling a murder suspect.

Relieved and disappointed, I ripped off my name tag and moved toward the exit. Charlene had called it, as usual. The meeting had been a waste of time.

A blonde with frizzy hair cornered me about selling fruit and vegetables in capsule form. Her eyes gleamed with the fanaticism of Charlene contemplating a Bigfoot hunt. "The starter kit is only two hundred dollars. Even if you decide not to resell, you get everything at a discount."

I edged backward. "I'm so busy right now with Pie Town, I really can't."

"Warren Buffett says you should never depend on a single income, and he's right. Everyone needs an alternate source."

"Maybe someday." I edged away, and my hip bumped a folding chair. It squeaked on the linoleum. "I just don't have the money—"

"This is the cheapest investment you can make. It's not like investing in a software company."

"Software?" That was oddly specific. I leaned closer. "Wait, are you talking about Denise Tatari's company?"

She tossed her head. "The minimum investment there was twenty thousand dollars. I know a lot of women can swing it, but most can't. That's why programs like Multi-Vita-Energy are so wonderful. Bill Gates said that if he could do it all over again, he wouldn't go into software, he'd go into network marketing. So, what do you think?"

Jamming my hands into my coat pockets, I touched a crumpled napkin. I pulled it out and unfolded the thick tissue.

In big letters, Charlene had written one word: *NO*.

"Um, no," I said. "But thanks."

"But—"

I fled.

Chapter Nineteen

I peered through the order window into the restaurant. It was ten A.M. on a Saturday. The pie shop was predictably light on customers at this hour, relieving me of a portion of my abandonment guilt. Untying my apron, I pulled it over my head.

Charlene tapped her high-tops, one hand on the kitchen door. "That glassblower won't interview himself."

"I'm almost ready." I boxed a mini caramel-apple and pumpkin chiffon pie. Folding the pink cardboard, I taped the boxes shut.

"Sweetening him up with pie? That's thinking."

"We may as well play to our strengths." In the kitchen, I mouthed *thank you* to Petronella.

She smiled in response and slid the giant wooden paddle into the oven.

Grabbing my hoodie and thick down vest from a peg on the wall, I strode from the kitchen.

"Aren't you forgetting something?" Charlene tapped her head.

My face heated. "Oh." I whipped off my hairnet and stuffed it into my pocket.

Charlene followed me to the front door. "We need to

approach Smokey carefully. Whatever you do, don't call him a glassblower. He's a glass *artist*."

I zipped up my vest and tugged open the door. "He probably didn't ring up the sale for the paperweight himself." The few times I'd been in the shop, a woman named Chloe had worked the register. If the police had already spoken with her, we wouldn't be interfering in Shaw's investigation. Much.

We emerged on the brick sidewalk. A sky the color of slate pressed against the tops of the low buildings. I caught myself playing with my hoodie's zipper, and jammed my hands into my pockets.

"How are things with your brother?" Charlene asked.

"You know. The usual."

"He's not really angry about you getting his mother involved in a murder, you know."

"I know." He'd been worried, and I couldn't blame him.

"Though it didn't help when you told him she was more smother than stepmother."

I sighed. "I know."

We strolled past planter boxes of autumn-themed flowers beaded with moisture.

I stopped to shove a bill in the mailbox as a gunmetal gray F-150 glided past, its tires whooshing on the damp street.

"No one likes to see their mother dragged to the police station."

"And you need to be patient," she said.

We walked on and paused in front of the glassblowing shop. Its windows glittered, pumpkins and paperweights sparkling beneath elaborate blown-glass lamps. Sale tags on the pumpkins advertised ten percent off.

Climbing the concrete steps, Charlene and I strolled inside, jingling the bell over the door.

Chloe Chang looked up from a computer tablet and adjusted her glasses. Strands of silver threaded her mid-length, blue-black hair. "Can I help you?"

I set the pink boxes on the counter. "These are for you."

Her brow furrowed. "Does Pie Town deliver now? But I didn't place an order for pie."

"We've got extras," I said. "I thought I'd give them away to fellow shop owners. Caramel-apple for you and a pumpkin chiffon for, er, Smokey."

"You remembered my favorite order! Thanks."

"Is Smokey around?" Charlene asked.

Chloe shook her head, her jade earrings bouncing against her slender neck. "He's in his workshop, recovering from the festival. He said if he made one more pumpkin, he'd blow his gourd." She grinned. "I doubt he's tired of pumpkin pie though. I'll be sure to give it to him."

"I see the glass pumpkins are on sale," I said.

"Only the Halloween-colored ones." Chloe pointed to an orange, black, and white pumpkin. "Why, are you interested?"

"I don't have much room in my tiny house," I said.

"That house is plenty big." Charlene tossed her white curls.

"I hear Alfreda Kuulik is taking advantage of the sale to build her paperweight collection," I said.

"Alfreda's not a bad glass artist herself." Chloe pushed up the glasses on her nose. "She's taken classes with Smokey."

"Did she get that bat paperweight she had her eye on?" I asked. "I really liked that one. The bats looked like they were emerging from smoke."

"Yes, that one was on sale."

"Did she buy it on Thursday?" Charlene asked.

"Um." Chloe's forehead wrinkled. "Yes, I guess she did buy it two days ago. Why?"

"She must have just beat me to it," I said quickly. We had to be discreet. If Shaw learned we were asking questions, he might follow through on his threats. "I'd hoped to pick that one up as a gift. A friend of mine's goth. She loves bats."

"You didn't stand a chance." Chloe laughed sympathetically. "Alfreda's a true collector. She was waiting on the step when I opened the store Thursday morning. We only had two left. She got one, and a tourist bought the other."

I nodded. "I think that might have been Ta—my, er, stepmother, Takako."

Charlene nodded. "Have the police—"

"Enjoy the pie!" I half dragged Charlene from the shop.

"I was going to ask Chloe if the police had questioned her about Alfreda," Charlene huffed, taking a swipe at the sleeve of her knit jacket.

"Yeah, I got that. But I don't think we should ask her what the police are up to. Chief Shaw has already got a grudge against us. He might say we're interfering in an investigation. Let's tell Gordon what we've learned and move on."

"Tell me what?" he asked from behind me.

I turned, my heart fluttering in my chest. "Gordon."

He brushed a wisp of hair off my face.

I eyed him. A spot of what looked like strawberry jam dotted his chin. He was obviously off duty in jeans and a navy sweater, and that wasn't good. Had Shaw put him on leave?

"Let me guess," he said. "You couldn't resist the siren song of a glass pumpkin sale?"

"We're questioning a witness." Charlene sniffed. "As a

diver, you of all people should know there are no sirens in this area."

His emerald eyes twinkled. "I wasn't speaking literally."

"This isn't Australia, you know," she said. "That place has got a real siren infestation."

"That's surprising," he said amiably, "what with all the great white sharks Down Under."

"We've got 'em here too." She folded her arms. "But it's not the sharks scaring off the sirens."

"Alfreda bought one of the bat paperweights," I said, before Charlene could explain what eldritch horror from the deep was keeping mermaids at bay.

"Nice detecting," he said. "When?"

I rubbed the red splotch off his chin with my thumb. "Thursday morning."

Gordon whistled. "That doesn't look good."

"Strawberry?" I held up my thumb.

He flushed. "I may have picked up a mini strawberry rhubarb earlier."

It seemed a little early in the morning for him to be eating pie. "And you didn't stop in the kitchen to see me?"

"You looked busy," he said.

Hmm. I changed the subject. "Takako told me Tristan's body was still warm when they found him. That would imply he died not too long before they came across him on Thursday afternoon. Plus, it's a dog park. How long could he have been lying there before someone discovered his body? Alfreda wouldn't have carried a paperweight around all day, would she? They're heavy, and she doesn't live that far away. She's also unemployed. Why not go home and drop it off?"

"Maybe she didn't get a chance," he said. "Or maybe it's not her paperweight. That glass shop has been selling bat paperweights all week. And the police haven't searched Alfreda's house to check out her collection."

"Will they?" Charlene asked sharply.

He shook his head. "I'm not on the case."

She laughed. "Sure. And neither are we."

"Are you busy tonight, Val?" he asked.

Charlene edged a discreet distance away and pretended to study the headlines in a newspaper kiosk.

"No," I said. "Why?"

"Can I pick you up after work?"

"Let me check my calendar." I studied the unyielding fog. "Yes. I'm free." I grinned. "You know when I close."

He drew me in for another kiss, this one longer and more insistent. "I'll see you then," he murmured into my ear, and I shivered.

I watched him climb the steps to the glassblower's shop and go inside.

The kiosk's door clanged shut.

Charlene tucked a paper beneath her arm. "Doesn't he trust our intel?"

"A good detective verifies."

"Hmph." She didn't look at me. "I deduce there will be no *Stargate* tonight."

My stomach pinched. "Oh, sorry. I forgot." Charlene and I usually watched DVDs on Saturday nights. "I'll tell him we'll have to get together another time." I moved toward the concrete steps.

She made a disgusted noise. "Who am I to stand in the way of young love? Go on your date."

"Are you sure?"

She glared at me. "Do I sound unsure? I was going to have to cancel tonight anyway. Ewan and I have plans. He called last night. It was a spur-of-the-moment thing."

"Say *hi* for me," I said, my guilt easing. Ewan was her

on-again, off-again romantic interest and the owner of a local faux-ghost town. He rented it out for events. "How's he doing?"

"The Bar X hosted a wedding today. Business is booming." She nudged my side and cackled. "Get it? *Booming*. Boomtown."

We returned to Pie Town, and Charlene abandoned me for whatever it was she did on Saturday afternoons. I baked and sold pie. Lots and lots of pies.

I surveyed the crowded dining area from behind the register, and warmth flowed through my veins. Nine months ago, Pie Town had been struggling. We'd come a long way.

Petronella swept past the register and deposited a tray of pies at a table of four. My assistant manager returned and set the empty tray behind the counter. "Have you and Charlene figured anything out about you-know-what? My mom is freaked out Dad might get called in for questioning again."

"He can't be a suspect any longer. He was in the police station when Tristan was killed."

"I didn't say her freak-out was rational. But . . ." She gnawed her bottom lip.

"But what?"

"Shaw asked me where I was Thursday afternoon."

"Why would—?" *Oh, no.* I dragged my palms down the front of my pink apron. Did Shaw think Petros might have an accomplice, like his daughter? "And where were you?"

"I was with my mom, but Shaw didn't seem to think that was a very good answer."

"It was the truth," I said stoutly.

"It doesn't matter. When my dad heard about it, he went nuts. I just want this to be over."

"Gordon isn't going to let your dad get railroaded. Or you, Petronella."

"Gordon's not in charge." She jammed her fists in her apron pockets. "I hate feeling so helpless. You and Charlene usually meet up Saturday nights, right? Why don't I come over? We can hash things out."

"Charlene's got a date with Ewan tonight."

Petronella frowned. "But he's in Florida."

"Florida?" I fumbled my ticket pad. It fluttered to the checkerboard floor.

"Yeah, his daughter and I are friends. He went to Florida to visit relatives, and she's home managing the ghost town."

I bent to pick up the pad. "Huh." Had Charlene spaced? Or had she lied? I wasn't sure which worried me more. "Well, I've got a date with your cousin. I'm sure he'll have some ideas."

There was a crash from the kitchen, and we flinched.

"Hunter," Petronella muttered. "I'll go help him with whatever he broke this time." She strode through the swinging door.

If only fixing what had gone wrong in San Nicholas was that easy.

Gordon picked me up at seven in what I'd come to think of as his cop sedan. The gray car wasn't flashy, but it had serious horsepower.

I buckled my seat belt and smoothed my hands over the thighs of my jeans. I wasn't dressed for anything fancy. Where was he taking me? The British Pub? The White Lady? Their bars were casual. My brow wrinkled. Had Charlene gone on her own to the White Lady? It was her favorite watering hole.

"I thought we'd grab Chinese," he said. "There's a new place at the minimall."

"Oh." *The minimall?* I swallowed my disappointment. "Chinese food sounds great."

"Sorry," he said. "I wanted to cook, but the chief called me in on Brinks patrol."

Not the kid who'd been tormenting Charlene? "Brinks—?"

"Is a menace to society." His hands throttled the wheel. "Mrs. Malloy caught him stealing her washing—"

"Why?"

"I never found out. I ended up chasing him through three blocks of backyards and finally lost him in the creek. If there's any justice in the universe—and there isn't—he'll get poison oak."

I winced. "I thought you were off duty today?"

"I'm never off duty." He leaned closer, a faint light gleaming in the depths of his emerald eyes. "The other bad news is the Chinese restaurant is takeout only. Mind if we eat at my place?"

Hmm . . . His place had definite possibilities.

We picked up a Peking Combo Dinner, and he drove me to his modern condo. Gordon opened the boxes on the kitchen's gray, granite counter and handed me a plate.

"How are your parents?" I asked. Gordon had moved back to San Nicholas to be closer to them as they dealt with age-related illnesses.

"My father is still denying he has diabetes, and my mother is playing along. So, the same."

"That can't be easy." I hadn't met his parents yet. We were taking things slowly on a lot of levels.

"It is what it is," he said, shutting down that line of conversation. "So, what have you and Charlene learned?" He nodded to his murder board, where he'd taped the photograph I'd taken of Tristan Cannon's body. Gordon had blown it up into eight-by-ten segments. The body. The paperweight. Tristan's hands, curled and vulnerable.

I shuddered. "Not much."

Plate in hand, his tall figure wandered past to stare at the whiteboard. "Chloe sold half a dozen of those bat paperweights this week, but she didn't keep records of whom she sold them to."

Gamely, I smothered my disappointment. So, this wasn't a date, it was an investigation. On the bright side, at least Gordon trusted me enough to talk over the murder. "Did you ask Chloe about any of the suspects, specifically? It's a small town. She might remember if any came in."

He shook his head. "I asked, and none had, aside from Alfreda."

"Are the police going to search Alfreda's house?"

He paced, his footsteps silent on the stone floor. "I don't know. I've told one of the officers on the case she bought a paperweight. He'll relay the info to Shaw."

"Do you know Shaw asked Petronella where she was Thursday afternoon?"

"Petronella? Why . . . ?" His expression darkened, and he cursed. "He thinks she killed Cannon to cover for her father."

"It's ridiculous. That theory can't go anywhere."

"Especially since she was working at Pie Town."

I winced. "Actually, she was at home, with her mother."

"Why wasn't she at work?"

"Her mother was in a panic. Petros was being questioned by Shaw, and Petronella went home to be with her."

He rubbed the back of his neck. "The timing couldn't have been worse."

"Speaking of timing, do you know when exactly Tristan died?"

"He'd been dead roughly an hour," he said, "so he was

killed around three in the afternoon. And I'm only telling you that because you'd already guessed."

"Deduced."

"Sorry, deduced. You're not a half-bad detective, you know."

It was a backhanded compliment, but I wasn't complaining. Much. "As I see it, if the police search Alfreda's house and find the paperweight, Alfreda's in the clear. And if they search her house, and it's not there, is that it? She did it, and Petronella and her dad are off the hook?"

He gripped the top of the whiteboard. "Only if we can prove it was her paperweight that killed Cannon."

"Hmph."

"You don't sound satisfied."

"I don't know. If she did hit him with her paperweight and leave it at the scene, then it looks like a spontaneous attack. But that doesn't track. We're assuming Tristan knew too much or was somehow involved. That speaks to premeditation."

"Which brings us to Kara Levant's murder, which does have the feel of spontaneity."

"I can't see a killer planning to leave her beneath a giant pumpkin." But her murder didn't exactly feel spur-of-the-moment either. "Her body was moved from the jail. Do you know how she was killed?"

His mouth flattened into a line. "I can't say."

I dropped the spring roll to my plate on the coffee table. "Seriously?" *Didn't* he trust me?

"I'll get wine," he said hastily and strode into the open kitchen.

Annoyed, I walked to the murder board. Can't tell me? After everything?

I gazed at the photos. Charlene would love seeing this, and I wondered again what she was up to tonight. Because

I had the feeling she had more than drinks planned. She was up to something, and she didn't want me around.

I studied an official-looking photo of a pitchfork with some sort of tag on the handle. The murder weapon? This was farm country. Even the non-farmers tended to have old pitchforks and scythes in their garages. This pitchfork could have come from anywhere, including the barn behind the old jail.

Gordon returned with a bottle of cabernet and a hopeful expression.

I pointed to the pitchfork. "Murder weapon?"

The wine bottle dropped loosely to his side. "No comment."

"Shaw seemed to think it was a wrench that killed her."

"Do we have to play this game?"

"Yes," I said. "So, Shaw was wrong, and it was a pitchfork."

"He wasn't wrong, and it was a pitchfork. Shaw took all sorts of potential evidence from the crime scene. That's the way it works."

"Hmm. There was a key in the forklift when the body was found. Was it left there for the killer, or did the killer find it somewhere else?"

"I can't get into details."

"Come on." I stiffened. "I *gave* you those photos of Tristan's murder scene."

"For which I thank you," he said.

"You can thank me by telling me Kara's time of death."

"You're a Baker Street Baker. You must have narrowed it down by now."

"When you invited me out tonight, I thought it was for more than using me as your confidential informant."

He quirked a brow. "Well, we could always—"

"Fughhedaboutit." I jerked my chin toward the murder

board, and smiled, wry. "I guess we're officially out of the honeymoon phase of our relationship and into the boring phase."

"We're not boring. We're investigating a murder."

"Are *we?*" I asked pointedly. Because the information seemed to be flowing on one direction, and what was I? Chopped liver? "Is that why I'm here?"

"Okay," he said, "maybe this wasn't the best idea for a date. But how else are we going to get together if we don't multitask?"

"What's that supposed to mean?" I asked.

"You work twelve-hour days, six days a week. Petronella's starting to wonder why you made her an assistant manager."

"What?" I stuttered, flustered. "Did she say something to you?"

"I don't want to get in the middle of this."

"So, there is something to get in the middle of." I raked a hand through my hair. Had I accidentally offended Petronella?

He grimaced. "I'm just saying, you're busy."

"So are you. Your hours are all over the map."

"I know," he said. "There's nothing I can do about that. But you have an assistant manager—"

"Pie Town is still understaffed. We nearly went under last spring."

"And you came through it. Look, I'm not going to tell you how to manage your business. We're both busy people. Sometimes, we're going to have to get creative if we want to spend time together."

If? What was happening here? "Have you been talking to Charlene?"

"No. Why?"

Because I was starting to detect a theme. Charlene had

been nagging me about my work life too. "I need to think about this," I said slowly.

"I've upset you. I didn't mean to."

"I know. It's just . . . I'm not sure how to respond to this, and I want to think before I do. This relationship—" I swallowed. "You mean a lot to me. I don't want to screw things up. And right now, that means taking a breath."

How had Charlene seen relationship trouble was coming, and I hadn't? And why had I let Charlene, the *Sharknado* of scheming, lie to me tonight? I *knew* that could only mean trouble. "I need to find her," I said abruptly.

"Val—"

"Charlene lied about her date with Ewan. She wanted me out of her hair tonight."

"Now *I'm* worried." He grabbed his car keys off the hook by the front door. "I'll drive."

"You'll have to. My van's at Pie Town."

We hurried outside and sped in his sedan through the light fog.

On Highway One, Gordon's cell phone rang. Lifting one hip, he pulled it from the back pocket of his jeans and glanced at the screen. "It's the station. Something's up."

I tensed. "Charlene?"

He put the phone to his ear. "Carmichael . . . Yes . . . I'll be there in fifteen." Gordon hung up.

"What's wrong?" I knotted my hand in the seat belt.

"Nothing to do with Charlene—or the Levant/Cannon murders. But I've got to go. Mind if I drop you at your van?"

"No, it's fine."

He sped into the alley behind Pie Town and waited until I'd started my delivery van before roaring off.

Pensive, I drove at a more sedate pace to Charlene's house, thoughts of Gordon tangling with thoughts of Mark, my ex-fiancé. We'd been deliriously in love, and then Mark had begun pulling away, preoccupied with building his real estate business. I'd been so focused on starting up Pie Town, that I hadn't noticed the drift until after I'd bought the blasted wedding dress.

After our engagement had blown up, I'd eventually realized I couldn't put all the blame on my ex. I'd been at fault too. Was I driving a wedge between myself and Gordon? Was I *too* obsessed with Pie Town?

I turned onto Charlene's street.

Her yellow Jeep zipped in the opposite direction. A line of cars followed.

I winced, blinded by the headlights.

Tally-Wally and Graham puttered past in an ancient Oldsmobile.

After the last car in the caravan passed, I made a U-turn and followed them onto the highway.

We drove east out of San Nicholas, over the hill, and onto a wide freeway, heading south.

Charlene wasn't alone. She was with at least a dozen people. So, I probably had no reason to worry. But my stomach tightened. Why had she lied about seeing Ewan tonight?

We passed a highway sign. ENTERING SAN ADRIAN.

Nuts. I tried to swallow, my hands clenching the wheel.

They were sabotaging San Adrian's pumpkin festival.

Chapter Twenty

The caravan of vehicles parked on a quiet shopping street. Above the low brick buildings, the stars were dim, faded by nearby big-city lights rather than fog.

I let my van drift to a halt behind Graham's battered Oldsmobile.

People in dark clothing emerged from the cars. They carried manila file folders beneath their arms. Flashing traffic barriers blocked the street, lined with familiar-looking columns of green stalls. Their canvases rippled emptily in the breeze.

I stepped from my van, slamming the door harder than I'd planned, and strode to Charlene's Jeep. "What's going on?"

Charlene pawed through a cardboard box balanced on the hood of her Jeep. "You made it. How was your date?"

"Fine. What are you doing?"

"Only fine?"

"You're going to sabotage the San Adrian Pumpkin Festival, aren't you? Charlene, you can't. Whatever you're planning is probably illegal. Plus, it's only"—I checked my phone—"eleven o'clock. You'll get caught. It's too obvious. There are still people around."

A couple emerged from a Georgian restaurant and strolled past. Wow. San Adrian had a Georgian restaurant? They really were cooler than San Nicholas.

"We know what we're doing." Charlene slapped an orange ball cap onto her head. SAN ADRIAN PUMPKIN FEST was scrawled across the bill. "We've got disguises."

"Where did you get that?"

Her eyes narrowed. "We've got our sources. Here's one for you." She pulled a contraband cap from the box and handed it to me.

Four columns of empty stands lined the elegant street. Folders beneath their arms, her coconspirators disappeared amidst the green stalls.

"Charlene, what are you up to?" I peered into the back of her Jeep. The jack-o'-lantern drone grinned up at me.

"What's in the folders?" I asked.

Charlene opened the Jeep's passenger door and slid the box onto the seat. "Decorations." Tucking two thick folders beneath one arm, she shut the door and strode down the street.

"You're *adding* decorations?" I hurried after her. As pranks went, this one didn't sound destructive. It wasn't like they were sabotaging a water main or glueing doors shut. Maybe the easiest way to contain this was to go along for the ride. "All right," I said. "What's the plan?"

She handed me a folder. "That's the plan."

I opened the folder. A paper Easter bunny winked out at me. I flipped through the cardboard cutouts. Folding tissue paper eggs. Paper bunnies. Pastel butterfly garlands. "You're—"

"Easter decorations in their Halloween displays." She cackled, turning the corner.

Stacks of hay bales and pumpkins and sheaves of corn dotted the sidewalks. The setup wasn't that different from our Main Street's pumpkin festival. Just bigger and sleeker, with modern chain stores and better lighting.

I raised a brow. "Easter decorations?"

"It wasn't *my* idea." Her voice dropped. "But it should let some of the air out of their thirst for vengeance. There were a lot of worse plans I managed to veto."

"The fact that you're the voice of reason is terrifying."

Tally-Wally slapped a giant pastel egg on the window of a cake-pop shop.

"Don't get used to it," Charlene said. "It was Easter bunnies or a dance-off."

Good Lord. She wasn't joking. I swallowed. "Give me a folder," I said. "Let's get this over with."

"You'd better be. W—They spent all afternoon putting double-sided tape on the back of these decorations. That way, you can stick them on fast and run. This is a high-speed operation. We're in, we're out."

"Gotcha. In and out."

Did it make me a bad person that the raid was . . . fun? My heart raced as I slapped Easter bunnies on windows and lampposts. I turned my back to shield my face when stray pedestrians strolled past. But no one paid me any attention.

Since I was younger and speedier, I got through my folder of decorations before the others. The oldsters handed their folders to me and ambled down the street, leaving me to unfold tissue-paper eggs. I perched a 3-D Easter bunny on top of a stack of pumpkins.

Graham ambled past with an empty wheelbarrow. "Keep up the good work, Val."

"Thanks." I paused, clipping the egg open and staring after him. Charlene hadn't mentioned wheelbarrows.

Petronella's father trundled past pushing another empty wheelbarrow. "Nice egg."

I pointed. "What are you—?"

Winded, Charlene trotted up to stand beside me. "You done with those?" She set down the end of her wheelbarrow.

I fumbled with the plastic clip. "Almost. What's with the wheelbarrows?"

"These are for the pumpkins," she said. "Since most of them were grown in San Nicholas, we're taking them back."

My tissue-paper egg snapped shut. "What?"

"For the pumpkin cannon."

"But that's—"

Her grin eerily resembled her jack-o'-lantern drone's. "My idea. It won't be much of a pumpkin festival without the pumpkins, will it?"

"I thought you were trying to defuse the situation."

"We're not stealing their *giant* pumpkins. Farmers brought those from all over the country to be weighed. It wouldn't be right. Plus, we'd need forklifts. Not that those San Adrian people had any such fine thinking when they sabotaged our festival."

"They didn't sabotage our festival!"

She motioned toward the stalls. "This entire street is sabotaging our festival."

"This is stealing. It's grand-theft pumpkin."

Graham trundled past, his wheelbarrow full of contraband gourds.

"The Easter decorations won't have much impact unless we reduce the amount of their Halloween decor." Charlene grabbed a nearby pumpkin. She dropped it into her wheelbarrow. It clanged against the metal. "Taking the pumpkins is sending a signal."

"That we're criminals?"

"That we won't be trifled with."

"It's going too far," I hissed.

"Oh, are you scared?"

"I'm an adult!" I snatched the fallen paper egg from the pavement.

"Who's putting paper eggs up in a rival town's pumpkin festival."

Tally-Wally and Mr. Scala rolled past, maneuvering stolen pumpkins around a hay bale.

I grabbed the pumpkin from Charlene's wheelbarrow and returned it to the pyramid. "We've done enough."

"Killjoy." Charlene turned on her heel and stalked away.

"I am not a killjoy," I called after her. "I'm just being an adult."

I stared down the road. In a short time, the San Nicholas contingent had removed every pumpkin they could carry. The only pumpkins left were the small pyramid beside me. And they looked pretty sad now.

I returned the Easter egg to the top of the pumpkins and grabbed the empty wheelbarrow. I recognized it from Charlene's garden. She'd want it back.

A police siren burped. Blue and red lights flashed at one end of the street.

I swore and dropped the end of the wheelbarrow. Its metal stands clanged on the pavement.

Pressing against the canvas side of a nearby stall, I edged toward the other end of the street.

My pulse accelerated. A second police car parked behind the traffic barrier on the opposite end of the festival.

I was trapped.

Crumb. Crumb, crumb, crumb! I whipped off my bright orange hat and ducked between two stalls. Mouth dry, I crouched between the green canvases.

Footsteps padded toward me. I scrambled under the heavy canvas, emerging into a stall with a long table and nothing else. I crawled beneath the table and slithered under the canvas into another stand.

A flashlight whitened the fabric wall from behind.

I kept moving, winding dizzily in and out of the stalls, staying a step ahead of the cop with the flashlight. At some point, I'd run out of stalls. I was going to get caught. And arrested. Evading the police, wasn't that a crime too? Would I go to jail? What would happen to Pie Town?

"Hey, Sam," a familiar male voice said.

My shoulders hunched.

"GC." Another man chuckled. "What are you doing here?"

"I got a tip some scofflaws from San Nicholas might be raiding your pumpkin festival." Gordon's deep voice vibrated with suppressed laughter.

I buried my face in my hands.

The other man laughed louder. "Easter bunnies."

"Is that the extent of the vandalism?"

"It's all I can see right now. I wish it would put a damper on this damned festival. It's attracted every teenage punk in the county who wants to smash a pumpkin."

Gordon made a sympathetic noise. "Mind if I take a look around?"

"Be my guest. I'm already fed up."

A set of footsteps walked away.

"You can come out now, Val," Gordon said.

I edged from beneath a table and rounded the corner of the empty stall. "How did you—?"

"Charlene called." He regarded me, an amused expression on his chiseled face.

"But you were an hour away."

"Not exactly. I didn't like how we left things. So, I followed you at a distance, in case Charlene was pulling a stunt too hot for you to handle."

"I thought you had a police emergency?"

"Two minutes after I dropped you off, the dispatcher called back. It was a false alarm."

I glanced down the column of stalls. A flashlight bobbed at the far end of the street. "So, you saw us pranking the San Adrian festival and did nothing?"

"It's not my jurisdiction." His broad shoulders lifted beneath his navy sweater. "Besides, I never liked San Adrian."

"Petronella?"

My assistant manager pivoted from her spot at the kitchen's metal counter. In the dining area, Sunday-morning customers clattered and chattered.

"Um," I said, "I need to step out for a bit. You okay to manage the shop?"

"Yes," she said, emphatic.

"The lunch rush will probably start . . ."

Her brow creased with annoyance. Of course, she knew when the lunch rush would start.

"Okay then." I tugged off my apron. "I'll see you when I get back."

I stuck my head through the swinging door into the dining area, where Charlene lounged at the counter. "Want to come with me to Laurelynn's pumpkin farm?"

She slid from her barstool. "About time. We'll take—"

"The van," I said, before she could suggest the Jeep. "I need to pick up some pumpkins."

Charlene made a face but followed me into the pink delivery van, and we drove to the pumpkin farm. "You're mad about last night," she said. "I can tell by that constipated look on your face."

"I do not look—" Ugh! The truth was, I *was* peeved.

But I was mad at myself. I'd actually been having fun until the cops had shown up. "I nearly got arrested."

My delivery van bumped down the pumpkin farm's rutted road.

She folded her arms over her green knit jacket. "If you'd stuck with me, you wouldn't have been in that fix in the first place. And I wouldn't have lost a perfectly good wheelbarrow."

"If you—" I tucked a coil of hair into my chignon. "If we hadn't raided their pumpkin festival, I wouldn't have had to hide from the cops."

"If you hadn't followed us—"

"You knew I would. You even had an extra folder for me. And a hat!"

"So, you're claiming entrapment?"

"No." I sighed. "I'm responsible for my own actions. Whatever did or might have happened was my fault."

The miniature train choo-chooed past my van.

"Our problem," she mused, "is we didn't go far enough. Things are escalating. I heard San Adrian vandalized the sign at the corn maze last night."

"Was anyone caught?" I asked.

"No."

"Then you don't know who vandalized the sign. It could have been kids."

She snorted. "Kids from San *Adrian*."

"Please let it go." I edged the van into a spot at the farthest end of the lot, beneath a eucalyptus tree.

We walked through the pumpkin patch, and I marveled again at all the flowers in bloom. California is far from perfect, but it's darned near Nirvana for natural beauty.

At the rear of the barn, a large gray farm truck, mud coating its windows, sat parked, its bed loaded with pumpkins.

Laurelynn stood in front of a half-closed barn door. The

paint at the back of the barn was peeling, revealing strips of faded wood. By her feet sat crates filled with blue-gray pumpkins.

"I'm glad you want these." Laurelynn nodded toward the Blue Hubbards. "No one else does." Coils of her black hair spilled from the top of her headscarf, an orange-and-yellow geometric design.

"Then why'd you grow them?" Charlene asked.

"It was an experiment." She jammed her hands into the pockets of her black apron and glanced toward the barn door. "I read they were great in pies, but I should have known better. Most people who come here aren't looking for baking pumpkins. They want something they can carve and stick a candle inside. Kara—" She grimaced and shook her head.

"Kara?" I asked.

"Last year she said I should stick to the basics. I guess I wanted to prove her wrong."

Angry voices erupted from inside the barn. Color blossomed on Laurelynn's cheeks. She nudged the door shut with her foot.

"Well, it's Pie Town's gain." I handed her the check. "These Blue Hubbards bake string-free and silky smooth. They're perfect for my pumpkin chiffon, and for pretty much every other kind of pumpkin pie." And I really had underestimated the demand for pumpkin this week.

The faded door swung open. Mrs. Thistleblossom glared out, her ancient face puckering. "You two. I should have guessed."

Startled, I stepped backward. "Guessed what?"

"A spy!" She called over her shoulder and stepped into the yard. A breeze rippled her moldering black gown.

Denise and Elon emerged from the barn.

"Spies?" Elon's brown eyes, flecked with gold, seemed

dazed, a night bird blinded by headlights. He jammed up the sleeves of his loose, brown cardigan. The cuffs dropped again to his wrists.

My laugh was faint. "Spies? What's there to spy on?" And why were my top murder suspects consorting at the back of Laurelynn's barn? It was enough to make me join Charlene's conspiracy-theory bandwagon. "What are you doing here?"

"Mrs. Thistleblossom was telling us about last night's vandalism at the corn maze." Elon carefully avoided looking at Laurelynn. "Denise is a sponsor."

It sounded like one of those not-quite-lies, and it didn't explain what had brought them here in the first place.

Denise shoved up the cuff of her black company jacket and checked her watch. "We'll repaint the sign." The morning sun set alight the reddish highlights in her hair. "It's annoying, but not a disaster."

"The sign's not the problem." Thistleblossom leaned on her thick, black cane. "Last night, some San Nicholas hooligans vandalized San Adrian's festival."

My chest heated, the warmth spreading to my neck. "Did they?"

"They stole the pumpkins and put up inappropriate decor," Mrs. Thistleblossom continued. "The vandalism at the corn maze is tit-for-tat. You know what will happen next. The same fools who attacked the San Adrian festival will do something worse. Things are spiraling out of control. Someone needs to put a stop to these idiots."

"I wouldn't call them *idiots,*" Charlene said loftily.

I would. I never should have gone along with the raid.

"People are on edge because of the murders," I said. "Maybe a harmless prank on San Adrian is like a safety valve, a way to blow off steam."

Charlene rubbed her chin. "If you want people to calm

down, we need to solve these murders. Where were you three Thursday afternoon between three and four o'clock?"

"What do I have to do with the murders?" Mrs. Thistleblossom squawked. "And you already know where I was. Finding the poor man's body."

"Where were you, Laurelynn?" Denise asked coolly.

The pumpkin farmer shot her a startled look. "I was here. Working, like I always am."

A crow alighted on the old truck and cawed, stretching its massive wings. Mrs. Thistleblossom glanced at the bird and shook her head slightly.

"Can anyone verify that?" Charlene asked. "You could have slipped away to murder Tristan."

"Why would I want to murder Tristan?" Laurelynn snapped.

"I don't know," Charlene said. "Why would you?"

"Laurelynn wouldn't hurt a fly." Elon stepped closer to her. "This needs to stop."

Denise's nostrils flared. "What needs to stop are these murders."

"Whatever's going on clearly has to do with that optometry practice," Laurelynn said, "not me."

"We can't know that for sure," I said. "True, Tristan and Kara worked together. But they could have had connections outside work."

Elon frowned and adjusted his tortoiseshell glasses. "I know you're coming at this from a good place, Val, but these are real people we're talking about. I loved my wife, and I respected Tristan. This isn't a game for us or a puzzle for your Baker Street Bakers. It's a nightmare, and one we'd do anything to end."

He was right. This wasn't a game. Two people were dead, and I swallowed, but I fumbled onward. "Have the police questioned you about Tristan's death?"

"No," he said quietly. "They have not." He reached toward Laurelynn, then his hand dropped to his side.

Mrs. Thistleblossom lowered herself to sit atop a box of Blue Hubbards. She cocked her head, looking like a wicked fairy on its proper perch.

"The police haven't questioned me either." Denise's voice was sharp, and she rubbed her watch. "I assumed it's because they have other leads they're following."

"What if they don't?" Charlene asked.

"They'd be wasting their time with me anyway." Denise's mouth pinched. "I have an alibi. I was working at my office that afternoon. Elon, where were you when Tristan was murdered?"

His head reared back, his face contorting as if he'd been struck. "Denise?"

"Kara and I may not have always gotten along," Denise said, "but she *was* my cousin. And whoever killed her, killed Tristan."

A second crow joined the first on the truck's muddy cab. They clicked deep in their throats, a secret conversation.

Mrs. Thistleblossom shifted on the pumpkins and clicked her tongue.

The birds lifted into the air and winged toward the grass-covered hill.

"Elon?" Denise prompted.

Pressing my back against the barn, I stared after the black specks, winging over the hill. It almost seemed like the old woman had ordered the birds to leave.

Nah.

"I was at the cemetery," Elon said, "talking to the people in charge." He smiled bitterly. "I don't know why I bothered. Kara had everything planned. She's already got us both a plot, and an inscription for her headstone. Even the service is organized."

"It's almost as if she knew she was going to die," Mrs. Thistleblossom graveled.

"No." He shook his head and glanced at Laurelynn. "She was just that way—a planner."

"So, what were you doing at the cemetery?" I asked him.

"Talking to one of the representatives about Kara's service. Or being talked *to* by one of the representatives, to be more accurate. But, Denise, you know I couldn't have hurt Kara."

Denise's face crumpled. "I know." She strode into the barn.

"Denise, wait." Elon hurried after her.

Mrs. Thistleblossom lurched off the pumpkins. "Curiouser and curiouser." She stumped around the corner of the barn.

"Well, that's it then." Laurelynn shot a worried look toward the barn. "Thanks for the check." She strode inside and banged the door shut.

"I wouldn't put murder past the lot of 'em," Charlene said.

I stacked the boxes of pumpkins in two nearby wagons. "Let's get out of here." I pulled the red wagons through the pumpkin patch and to my van.

Charlene leaned against the pink van as I loaded the Blue Hubbards into the rear. "No one's got an alibi," she said, "except maybe Elon."

"What do you bet they really came here to exchange notes on the murder?"

Charlene nodded. "They're worried. But I can't figure Mrs. Thistleblossom's interest."

Aside from an infernal curiosity? "She did help discover Tristan's body." I shut the rear doors with a clang.

We climbed into the van, and I backed from the spot.

A Bel Air station wagon turned sharply in front of

us, blocking the drive. Its front passenger wheel sank into a ditch beside the fence. The Bel Air's tires spun, flinging mud.

I cleared my throat. "Did you, uh, see what Mrs. Thistleblossom did with the crows?"

"No. What?"

"She clicked at them, and they flew off."

"And?"

"It just seemed strange, that's all."

The station wagon lurched forward and settled deeper into the mud.

"So, she shooed them off."

"It's more than that."

She swiveled in her seat. "What are you saying?"

"Don't you think she's a little . . . strange?"

She smiled. "Ah. I see."

"See what?"

"You think she's a witch." She patted my knee. "It's all right. When I was a girl, I thought so too. It's a rite of passage. But Mrs. Thistleblossom's no witch. She's just old and mean."

"Does *she* know she's not a witch?"

"Of course, she knows."

I shifted in my seat. "What about that performance she put on in Pie Town with her cane?"

"She's always banging that thing around. It makes her feel powerful."

"And those weird gestures she makes with her fingers?"

"So, she's got weird fingers. What? Do you think she cast a spell for someone to graffiti Pie Town?"

"Exactly!" Tingling swept my face. "I mean, no, of course not, but—"

My protests were drowned by Charlene's hooting. She wiped her eyes. "Oh, Thistleblossom got you good."

A teenager stepped from the station wagon and glared at the sunk tire.

"Learn to drive!" Charlene shook her fist out the open window and turned to me. "We're not getting out this way. Go around the back of the patch. I know a shortcut."

Face burning, I made an eight-point turn and reoriented the van. Since when did Charlene talk *me* down from thinking something supernatural was going on?

My idea wasn't so crazy. There are plenty of people who practice witchcraft, especially in California. True, Thistleblossom didn't look like the New Age type. But there was something off about the woman.

We drove up the muddy hill, following the arc of the miniature train track. The dirt road narrowed, curving downward.

"Turn right," Charlene said, "and it will take us behind that little winery and back to the highway."

The massive gray farm truck we'd seen earlier, its windows obscured by mud, ground up the hill toward us.

I shifted gears. This track wasn't wide enough for the both of us. "I don't remember the rules. Do I have to back up or does he?"

"You do."

"Goody." I slowed to a stop and shifted into reverse.

The truck didn't alter its pace.

"Okay, okay," I muttered. "Don't be so impatient." I twisted, one arm on the back of Charlene's seat, and peered through the rear windows.

"Val, watch out!"

The van lurched. Metal screamed, and we tilted sideways.

Chapter Twenty-One

Metal rending, the farm truck pushed the van, angling us upward.

I stood on the brake. But my van was out of the truck's weight class. Helplessly, we slid up the hill and sideways.

I swore, steering wheel in a death grip. "What's that idiot doing?"

My van listed, its nose swinging upward.

Charlene and I screamed.

Another screech of metal. The van pitched.

The truck roared past and up the hill. Pumpkins jounced from its bed and rolled down the road.

I gasped, still clutching the wheel. "Are you okay?"

Face pale, she clung to the seat belt across her chest. "I'm okay. Are you okay?"

"I'm okay." I panted. "Our pumpkins!" I twisted in my seat. Bluish-gray pumpkins lay piled against the van's rear doors, but none seemed broken.

Charlene's eyes bulged. "Fred—" She reached for her knit jacket's collar and sagged. "I didn't bring him this morning. Thank God. He could have gotten whiplash."

We might have whiplash. Shifting the van's gears, I

stepped on the gas. The engine ground. The van skidded farther off the road.

"Why are you turning the van that way?" Ropy tendons bulged in Charlene's neck.

My pulse skittered. "I'm not! There must be something wrong with the wheel."

Dread puddling in my gut, I pushed open my door. Gravity swung it back toward me, and I struggled to escape the van. Finally, I managed to haul myself out and drop to the sodden ground.

A nasty gray scuff striped one side of my van, cutting through Pie Town's smiley face logo like a knife. The metal above the front-passenger wheel crumpled inward.

I walked around the van and winced. It hung catawampus over a low ridge on the road's shoulder. Only three wheels were on terra firma. The fourth, rear wheel, hung in midair over the ridge.

I stomped around and swore some more.

Charlene leaned out the open window. "What if whoever drove us off the road is still out there?"

I froze, my scalp prickling. Was pushing us off the road only stage one in a deadly plot? I fumbled in my hoodie's pocket for my phone, dialed Gordon.

Silence. No signal.

I kicked a loose stone down the hill. "Seriously?"

"What's wrong?" Charlene asked.

"I don't have a signal. Do you?"

She held her phone out the open window and waved it in a circle. "Nope. It must be blocked by that hill. Reception is sketchy on the coast."

"Tell me about it," I muttered.

We stared at each other.

"Well," I said, "we can't wait here. I'll walk back to Laurelynn's pumpkin patch. Maybe I'll have better luck with reception there." And I wanted to find out who had been driving that truck. It *had* to have been the truck behind Laurelynn's barn.

"You're going to leave me here? Alone?" Face ashen, Charlene opened her door and scrambled to the ground. She buttoned her green knit jacket to the top, brushed off her brown leggings, and we squelched down the road.

Soon, we arrived in a small vineyard, the wrinkled grape leaves painted in autumnal hues.

"I got a signal!" Panting, Charlene plopped onto a wooden bench beside a bocce ball court. "I'll call a tow truck."

"I'm going to find Laurelynn."

I walked behind the winery, along a narrow road to the pumpkin patch.

Laurelynn stood behind the counter in her red barn. She looked up from wrapping a papier-mâché pumpkin, and her eyes widened. "I thought you'd left."

Her customer, a woman with salt-and-pepper hair, edged away and put her back to the counter.

"We tried." I worked to keep my voice steady. Some of the earlier adrenaline was still jouncing around my system. "One of your farm trucks ran us off the road."

Laurelynn fumbled the decoration, catching it before it could hit the counter. "What? How do you know it was mine?"

"Because it was on your road, and it was full of pumpkins."

"In the parking lot?"

I dug my fists deeper into my hoodie pockets. If only. Then there might have been witnesses. "No, on the road that wraps behind the train track and runs down to the winery."

She stuffed the wrapped pumpkin in a black paper bag. "What were you doing there?"

"The driveway was blocked."

"By the farm truck? I thought you said it ran you off the road."

The customer's gaze ping-ponged between us.

"No," I said, frustrated. I got it, I really did. It was a weird story, and who wanted to believe their truck was stolen? But I just wanted to find out if it had been Laurelynn's truck, get help, and go. "By some teens in a station wagon. Then someone in a gray farm truck with muddy windows pushed my van off the road. It looked like the one that was behind the barn."

"I thought you said he ran you off the road," Laurelynn said, "not *pushed* you off the road."

"He did both. My van's stuck. Charlene's calling a tow truck."

"Well, I hope it isn't blocking the road. My neighbors use it too."

"The gray farm truck behind your barn . . ." I inhaled slowly, exhaled. *Never mind*. "Look, can I go back there?"

"Only if I go with you." She handed the customer the black bag and hurried from behind the counter. "And I will, if it will get you to better explain what you're talking about."

Striding to the rear of the barn, she opened a door into a storage area, and I followed. A second door, at the end of a path lined with boxes, stood open.

"I thought I closed that door," Laurelynn said.

"Denise and Elon and Mrs. Thistleblossom were in here. Where are they, by the way?" I stepped past her and outside. The gray truck was gone.

"No idea." She emerged into the hay-strewn yard. "What the . . . ? You were telling the truth. My truck's gone!" She cursed.

"Who had access to the keys?"

"I kept them . . ." She motioned behind her.

"In the storage area?"

"There's a board," she said, deflating. "I mean, who would want to steal that old truck? This is a good neighborhood."

"So, anyone who'd walked through the storage area could have grabbed them?" Like Elon. Denise. Laurelynn.

"I suppose. I just didn't think . . . But I didn't think anyone would kill my old high school rival, either. What is happening to this town?"

And where *was* that truck? I eyed the pumpkin farmer. Could she have parked it nearby and returned to the barn before me?

"I'm calling the police," Laurelynn said, turning to the barn door.

"Good idea."

I spent the next hour dealing with cops and a tow truck driver. The SNPD found Laurelynn's truck parked at the top of the road, behind a stand of eucalyptus trees. They fingerprinted the door and wheel but didn't seem hopeful.

The tow truck driver, Fred, was able to drag the Pie Town van off its perch. But my delivery vehicle wasn't going anywhere soon.

Fred cheerfully rattled off a string of mechanic's jargon that left me dazed.

He crossed his arms over his broad chest, exposing a hole in the elbow of his greasy sweater. "The good news is, I've got a part I can cannibalize to get you back on the road. The bad news is, it's going to take a few hours. I'll have to tow your van back to my shop."

I slumped against a eucalyptus tree and stared glumly at my van. "Can you give us a lift back to town?"

"No need," Charlene said. "I've got us a ride."

A black Lincoln SUV drove up the dirt road and parked. The window whirred down.

"I heard you need rescuing." Takako leaned from the SUV, the strings of her hoodie dangling. It was the same *Pies Before Guys* hoodie I wore today.

I glanced at the open doors of the van. "Do you have room for pumpkins?"

I ended up sharing the SUV's back seat with bluish pumpkins. Charlene explained what we'd learned, and the two plotted the next steps in our investigation.

"Do you think they're lying?" Takako asked.

"Assume everyone's lying." Charlene scratched her arm over the fabric of her tunic jacket. "That's my motto."

"I don't like that someone tried to hurt you and Val." Takako slowed at a stoplight, and we idled behind a silver Audi. "We need to check their alibis."

I shifted the pumpkin on my lap. "No, you don't—"

"I'd like to redeem myself," Takako said in a low, firm voice. "And I do know how to dig out the truth."

"I'm game, if you are," Charlene said.

"We could split up to save time," Takako suggested. "I can check Laurelynn's alibi, because it would be strange if the two of you returned to her pumpkin patch. It sounds like she might not be too happy to see either of you."

Charlene glanced over the seat at me. "That's not a bad idea. What do you think?"

I shoved aside a pumpkin that had been digging into my hip. "I think Doran will kill me."

"Doran?" Takako flicked a glance at me in the rearview mirror. "What does your brother have to do with this?"

"Nothing," I said quickly. "But he's a little worried about you since your arrest."

"I wasn't arrested. I was questioned. And Doran left me to start a graphic design business at the other end of the state," she said tartly. "I'm old enough to decide what I want to do."

I hunched lower in my chair, pumpkins bumping against my knees.

"Then I'll take Denise's alibi," Charlene said, "and you, Val, can tackle Elon's."

"It's lunchtime on a Sunday," I squawked. "I've got to get back to Pie Town."

"Isn't Petronella working today?" Charlene asked.

"Yes," I said, "but Sunday lunch is our busiest time."

"Fine." Charlene swatted the air. "I'll take the cemetery too. They'll think it's strange someone young like me is asking about buying a plot, but I'll make it work. We'll report back at Pie Town."

They returned me to Pie Town. I left our teenage busboy, Hunter, to unload the pumpkins from the car, and I hurried into the warm kitchen. It smelled heavenly—of baking fruit and pumpkin and sugar. But the delicious scent didn't have its usual, uplifting effect. Charlene and I could have been killed this morning by that stupid truck.

But I tied an apron around my waist and took orders, bussed tables. The dining area was a laughing, clattering madhouse. Charlene and Gordon were just wrong. Sure, my staff were amazing, but it wasn't right for me to ditch them when we had so many customers.

Three hours later, the feeding frenzy had died. A sedate line of customers queued at the register for pies to take away. Charlene and Takako had returned from their expedition and sipped coffee at the counter.

Exhausted, I handed the last customer in line her pie. I ambled to the pink counter. "Learn anything?"

Takako unzipped her hoodie and slung it over the back of the barstool. "Laurelynn's alibi is no good. Thursday afternoon, she was in and out of the barn, and sometimes for long periods of time. The staff assumed she was somewhere on the grounds, but you know how big that pumpkin patch is. No one can actually place her at the patch during the hour Dr. Cannon died. And the dog park is only a ten-minute drive from her patch. Laurelynn could have snuck away, killed Tristan, and returned with no one being the wiser."

"Same problem with Elon and Denise." Charlene blew on her coffee. "The woman at the cemetery said he arrived early for their two o'clock appointment. She doesn't remember when he left."

"And she just told you that?" I asked, surprised.

"Oh, we go way back. She buried—" Charlene coughed into her hand and looked quickly away. I guessed what she'd been about to say: the woman had helped bury Charlene's husband. "She's a friend," Charlene finished. Her face fell. "I didn't have to pretend to be a potential customer after all."

"And Kara's cousin, Denise?" I asked.

"Now, that's interesting." Charlene crossed her legs and smoothed one hand over her brown leggings. "Denise's receptionist verifies that she went into her office at two o'clock and didn't come out until five. Denise told her she didn't want to be disturbed."

"So, she's got an alibi," I said.

"Not quite. Denise's private office has a rear door to the outside. Denise could have left, and the receptionist never would have known."

I pressed one hand to the cool countertop. "But I don't see how Laurelynn could have been the driver of that truck today. She would have to be a track star to have gotten back to her barn that quickly. And she didn't look like she'd broken a sweat when I found her there."

"We're assuming whoever drove the truck was involved in the murder," Takako said. "But it's possible they were separate incidents."

I hesitated. "It's possible. But it's a huge coincidence, don't you think? We're there, asking about alibis, and then someone takes a truck for a joyride and runs us off the road?"

Charlene rubbed her chin. "We've irritated someone. There's no doubt about that."

Marla swaggered to the counter and sat, adjusting the folds of her elegant trench coat. "You've irritated someone, Charlene? Imagine." She angled her diamond rings for the brightest sparkles beneath the pendant lamps.

Grabbing a knife and fork off the counter, Charlene squared them into a cross. "Back off, creature of darkness!"

Marla turned to my stepmother. "Hello, Takako."

"Marla," Takako said, "you were right about there being more trouble."

I coughed. "Uh, Takako—"

Takako leaned closer. "A truck from Laurelynn's pumpkin patch ran Val and Charlene off the road. And several suspects—Elon, Denise, and Laurelynn—were nearby at the time. I don't think Mrs. Thistleblossom could have done it. She couldn't have reached the pedals. At any rate, we checked their alibis for Tristan's murder, and none of them have one."

Marla's mouth pinched into a straight line, her nostrils whitening. "My viewers will be thrilled to hear it. Takako, it's almost as if you're a full-fledged Baker Street Baker."

"It was a matter of expedience," Charlene said, gruff.

She rose. "I need to get Frederick. He's been alone at home for too long."

"Expedience?" Marla arched a brow. "When someone who lives in San Nicholas and knows all the people involved is right here, with a car, and an indoor movie theater, and a full video studio for filmed interrogations—"

"It was a spur-of-the-moment thing." Charlene shifted on the barstool.

"It was thoughtless," she said, her voice rising in pitch.

"Have some coffee." I poured a cup and set it on the counter in front of Marla.

"Your crummy coffee is a poor apology." Marla rose and stormed, trench coat flapping, from the restaurant.

"I'm getting my cat." Charlene followed her out the door.

"Did I say something wrong?" Takako asked.

"No," I said. But we'd hurt Marla's feelings by letting a noob join. Marla wanted to be a Baker Street Baker, even if she wasn't willing to admit it. It was long past time Charlene and Marla let bygones be bygones. True, Marla had a tendency to blab about our investigations on her video channel. But Charlene wasn't exactly innocent on that score either.

The phone rang in my apron. Pulling it out, I frowned at the unfamiliar number. "Hello, this is Val."

"Val? It's Alfreda Kuulik."

I moved away from the counter. "Oh, hi! What can I do for you?"

"Do you still have that job opening?"

"Yes," I said cautiously. "We have several applicants."

"I'd like to apply."

I smiled. "Are you available for an interview tonight?"

Chapter Twenty-Two

I wrung out the mop and glanced at the smiling, neon-rimmed clock. Charlene and Takako had broken three alibis for Tristan Cannon's murder in one day. Tonight was my chance to pull my own weight.

"Marla can't seriously want to join the Baker Street Bakers," Charlene grumped from the counter.

Coiled around the collar of her green, knit jacket, Frederick yawned. The cat burrowed deeper beneath her white curls.

"You *know* how she is," Charlene continued.

"Do we?" I leaned on my mop and arched my aching back. "She's made things difficult for us in the past, but nothing too disastrous." And unlike a certain piecrust maker, Marla hadn't waged a raid on San Adrian.

"Marla wants to make us look bad. Mark my words. She'll run to a reporter, or post a video on the Internet."

Frederick raised his head, his blue eyes widening with alarm.

"Maybe. But Marla really seemed hurt."

Charlene glowered. "She'd need a beating heart to get hurt, and vampires haven't got one."

"Charlene—"

"She'll ruin everything."

"Takako, Ray and Henrietta, my brother and Abril . . . All sorts of people have joined the Baker Street Bakers—"

"As associate members."

"And we've kept things under control." Back muscles protesting, I lugged the bucket into the kitchen.

"Do you really think you can control Marla?" she shouted after me.

"I think you can."

There was a long silence. I dumped the dirty water into the sink and gave the sink another scrubbing.

Charlene lounged in the open kitchen door. Her eyes narrowed. "I won't do it. There's too much at stake. Shaw thinks Petronella is a suspect. Her father and your detective are in the crosshairs. We're at a delicate stage."

"Agreed, but maybe—"

Someone rattled the front door in the dining area.

"That must be Alfreda." I hurried past Charlene and into the restaurant.

Alfreda peered through the glass, her broad face drawn in an anxious expression.

I crossed the black-and-white tiles and unlocked the door. "Hi. Come on in." The bell jangled above our heads.

She tucked strands of maple hair behind one ear. "Thanks." She shifted a leather portfolio beneath one arm of her long, brown coat.

"Have a seat." Motioning to a booth, I shut the door and hoped I hadn't just locked us in with a killer.

Stiffly, Dr. Levant's ex-office manager unbuttoned her blocky coat. She tossed it over the back of the booth, smoothed her neat white blouse, and slid into the booth.

I sat across from her. "I think you know Charlene. She's our piecrust specialist. We'll be interviewing you together."

"Plus Frederick." Charlene dropped beside me, jouncing our seat.

Alfreda flashed a warm smile. "Hi, Frederick."

The white cat purred.

"So, tell us about yourself," I said brightly. "Why do you want to work in a pie shop?"

"Well, I like pie."

"Good start," Charlene said.

"I have lots of experience dealing with customers, from my work as an office manager for Dr. Levant and Dr. Cannon. And I don't know if you have a bookkeeper, but I did that work for the doctors as well. Actually, the bookkeeping took up most of my time."

I *hated* accounting. Briefly, I indulged in the fantasy of foisting that job onto someone else. I scanned her résumé.

"And I did more than just the office finances." Alfreda checked her oversized watch. "I helped Dr. Levant with her personal income taxes too. I know all about how small businesses work. I'm experienced managing accounts for everything from sole proprietorships to close corporations."

I shifted, reaching behind me to grind my knuckles into the knot in my lower back. "I see you worked for a construction company," I said. "Did you get to drive the heavy equipment?"

"No. I worked as the accountant. Why?"

"We have a delivery van." Or at least we would once I got it back from the garage tonight. "I was only curious."

She pressed her large hands to the table and leaned forward, her forehead creasing. "Would you expect me to drive a van? I thought this was a cashier position."

"We all pitch in where we can," I said.

"What about hobbies?" Charlene asked, stroking the white cat's fur like a James Bond villain.

"Hobbies?" She rubbed the face of her silver watch with her thumb.

"Have you got any?" Charlene asked.

"I like to ski."

"Anything else?"

"Well, I write short stories, science fiction."

"Anything else?" Charlene leaned across the table. "Any . . . collections?"

Alfreda's face brightened. "I do collect glass paperweights."

Charlene leaned back. "You live in the right place then. Did you hit the post-pumpkin festival sale at the glass shop on Main?"

Alfreda's brow furrowed. "Yes, I did. Why?"

"I love those Halloween paperweights," Charlene said. "I wanted to get one with the bats, but they were all out."

"Those went fast."

"Did you buy one?" Charlene asked. "I'd love to see it."

"I did, but . . ." She shook her head and blinked rapidly. "I lost it somehow. I'm so angry at myself. I'd swear I brought it home from the shop, but I must have kept it in my purse and then it fell out at the White Lady."

"The White Lady?" I asked. Could Alfreda's paperweight have been stolen?

"On the restaurant's patio," she said. "I went back to the White Lady to look for the paperweight that night, but no one turned it in. I'm sure someone found it and kept it. People can be such jerks."

Frederick yawned and shook his head, his collar jingling.

"What do you mean, you'd swear you brought it home?" I asked.

"They're heavy, you know. So, after I bought it, I went home to drop it off before I went to the White Lady for lunch. But it was cold, so I changed into a heavier coat while I was at my apartment. I must have gotten so distracted picking out a coat, I forgot to take the paperweight from my purse."

"But wouldn't you have noticed it was still in your purse?" I asked. "Like you said, those paperweights are heavy."

"I don't know. Maybe."

"When did you realize the paperweight was missing?" I asked.

"When I got home from the White Lady." She crossed her arms, rumpling her white blouse, and frowned. "What does my lost paperweight have to do with the job?"

"Oh," I said. "Nothing. Sorry, I got distracted. You know how it is, Charlene and I love a good mystery."

Twin lines appeared between Alfreda's brows. "Why?"

"Because we're the Baker Street . . ." I trailed off. "Never mind. Tell us more about your job at the optometry office."

And she did, in excruciating detail. But when she'd finished, I still didn't know why someone might have wanted to kill its two owners.

"What happens to the office now that Dr. Levant and Dr. Cannon are, um, gone?" I asked.

"It's closed." Alfreda fidgeted, her slacks squeaking against the vinyl seat. "Didn't you know? I guess I got out just in time. Elon might try to sell his wife's share of the practice to another optometrist, but who knows what Tristan's heirs will do? If you ask me, by the time they get it sorted out, the clients will have found other doctors. The practice will be worthless."

"Tristan mentioned there was some sort of insurance?" I asked.

She shrugged. "I wouldn't know about that."

We ended the interview with promises to get back to her. I gave Alfreda a blackberry pie to-go. It was my guilt offering for dragging Alfreda here under false pretenses. Charlene and I ushered her out the door.

"What do you think?" Charlene asked.

I bolted the lock. "She didn't seem crazy. But her social media posts about Kara and Tristan were definitely threatening. I don't know. What do you think?"

"I think I need to sleep on it."

And I needed to talk this over with Gordon.

Charlene left, grumbling, and I called the detective.

"Gordon, how would you feel about an evening on the White Lady's patio?"

"It's a little cold tonight, isn't it?"

"They have fire pits and warm blankets."

"And I've got a fireplace at my condo," he said, his voice husky. "How would you feel about coming here? I could warm you up."

"Why, Detective Carmichael," I joked, "this is so sudden. I'll bring the wine."

"Forget wine. Bring pie."

I boxed a leftover cherry pie and speed walked toward Fred's garage. The fog dampened my cheeks. Muffled footsteps echoed through the mist. I stopped. The footsteps behind me stopped. An echo off the brick buildings?

I hurried onward.

The garage was off the Main Road, in a tiny industrial section near Highway One. I waited impatiently in the dingy office plastered with photos of WWII planes. After Fred was satisfied my payment was correct, I darted into the safety of my van and locked the doors.

Hey, you're not paranoid if someone really *is* out to get you.

At Gordon's, I hurried up the steps to his condo, glancing over my shoulder.

I knocked on his door and shifted the boxed pie in my arms.

He opened it and smiled. "Val."

My heart caught. His forest-green sweater deepened the color of his eyes. In that moment, I'd have gladly drowned in those emerald pools.

"At last." He pulled me against his muscular chest and kissed me, slowly, meticulously.

Pulse pounding, I passed him the pie. "Cherry."

He sniffed the box and closed his eyes. "Mmm."

I walked inside and shrugged out of my short, gray coat.

He hung it on a peg near the door. Setting the pink box on the counter of the open kitchen, he cut slices for us both and wandered to his murder board. "Did you hear anything new?"

"I interviewed Alfreda Kuulik for a job."

Gordon raised a brow.

I told him what we'd learned, about the alibis Charlene and Takako had broken, about the truck that had run us off the road.

"You should have led with the hit-and-run." One-handed, he stuck a sticky note on the whiteboard and turned to me. His gaze raked me from head to toes. "You and Charlene are okay?"

"We're fine. Even though it happened at Laurelynn's pumpkin farm, I don't see how she could have managed it. Elon, Denise . . . even Mrs. Thistleblossom could have stolen the key to that truck. Though she'd have had trouble reaching the pedals."

Gordon forked a bite of pie into his mouth. "Mrs. Thistleblossom? What's she have to do with this?"

"Nothing, probably." But she *had* been on the scene when Takako had found Tristan's body.

I glanced at his plate. It was empty. "Wow. You must have been hungry."

"What?" He looked at the plate. "I guess I was." He ambled to the kitchen for another slice. It vanished as quickly as the first, and I frowned.

I'd seen this behavior before. This was stress eating. "Gordon, are you all right?"

"I'm fine," he mumbled through another mouthful of pie. He pointed with his fork at the whiteboard. "What do you think?"

"About your murder board?"

"About any of it." He swallowed and set down the plate. "Shaw's on the wrong track. But I can't go behind his back this time and work the case. It would be the end of my career in San Nicholas."

My chest tightened. "Isn't going behind his back what you're doing now?"

"Semantics." Leaning against the back of the sofa, he pulled my back against his chest, so we both faced the whiteboard. "What do you *see*?" He motioned with his near-empty plate.

I studied the board. But if there was a clue in the mash-up of photos and maps and sticky notes, I didn't see it. "I'm sorry," I finally said. "I guess I'm not a visual learner. What do you see?"

"After we spoke on the phone, I got this idea I can't let go of."

"Oh?"

His phone vibrated in the pocket of his slacks, and I started. He pulled it out and checked the number. Gordon straightened, and I stepped away.

"Sorry," he said. "I've got to take this."

"The station?"

"My mom." He pressed the phone to his ear. "Mom? What's going on?"

I walked to the board and mentally blocked out the conversation. Gordon had shifted the photos, so Denise and Elon's were side by side. And he'd drawn a red line between Elon and Laurelynn. Alfreda was on the board as well, with lines to Dr. Levant and Dr. Cannon.

"Val."

I turned.

Gordon pocketed his phone, his green gaze somber. "I'm sorry, but I have to go."

"What's happened?"

"My father's had a fall."

My breath caught. "Oh, no. Is an ambulance there?"

"No." A muscle pulsed in his jaw. "My dad's refusing help. I could hear him bellowing over the phone. If he's shouting, then it's probably not life threatening, but my mom needs me."

"How can I help?"

"When my dad's like this, it's best if I just go."

"When he's like this? Did it happen often?"

Gordon gave me a long look, then tugged me against him and pressed his lips to my forehead. "We can't seem to catch a break, can we? Between your work and my work and my parents—"

"It's life. It's fine."

There wasn't much more difficult than watching a parent decline. I'd taken care of my mother at the end. And I remembered every awful moment.

What Gordon was going through with his parents wasn't the same. But that didn't make it easier. It did explain all the pie. And his obsession with the murder was about more than clearing his name. He needed the people he cared about to be okay. And his parents' health problems were making that impossible for two of the people he loved the most.

"Forgive me?" he asked.

I blinked away the heat in my eyes. "There's nothing to forgive." I brushed my lips across his. "Go. Help your parents."

"And what will you do?"

"I'm going to the corn maze to check out this vandalism that's got everyone up in arms. Follow every lead, right?"

He checked his watch. "Is the maze still open?"

"Until ten. I've got an hour or so."

Gordon saw me to the door. "Hold on." He lifted a navy-colored knit cap from a hook near the door and tugged it over my head. "I'd rather be the one keeping you warm, but until then . . ." He pulled me into another embrace. "Thank you for understanding," he rumbled.

I strode to my delivery van and drove away, sympathy twisting my heart. The fog thickened, swirling in front of my headlights. I turned onto Highway One and tried not to dwell on Gordon.

A rabbit darted across the highway.

I slammed on my brakes, heart thumping.

The animal disappeared into the fog.

I drove on, scanning the road for the sign to the corn maze. Finally, I spotted the simple wooden billboard, lit from below. I turned the van, bumping along a dirt drive and slowing to a stop on its shoulder.

Lowering my window, I craned my neck, studying the sign. Crude graffiti was spray-painted across it. I angled my head. Whoever had tagged my van had way better penmanship. And I was guessing the kids who'd wrecked the corn maze sign hadn't used chalk.

Since I was here, and the maze was open, I drove to the lot beside the black-painted barn and parked.

There was a thunk—the pumpkin cannon in action.

I strolled inside the barn.

A woman wrapped like a mummy in a thick gray scarf and matching sweater stood behind the counter. Her time stamp thump-clicked on a ticket.

With a start, I recognized her—it was my friend Joy.

She slid the ticket across the counter to a broad-shouldered brunette. The customer's maple hair was knotted in a bun beneath a black knit hat.

"Hi, Val," Joy said in her usual monotone.

The customer stiffened.

"Hey, Joy. And . . . Alfreda?" I asked.

The woman faced me and colored. "Val?"

"Running into you twice in one night?" I asked. "It must be fate. Are you going into the maze? I thought I'd give it another try myself. We can do it together."

"Oh. Um, no. I just remembered I have to . . ." She brushed past me and out the wide barn doors.

"Waste of a good time stamp." Joy picked up her comic book, caped superheroes winging across its cover.

"I'll take her ticket," I said.

"You'll have to pay for it. She never did." She looked up, expressionless. "What are you doing here alone?"

"Why wouldn't I be here alone? And what are you doing here?"

"I'm the volunteer night shift." She tilted her head, her black hair cascading over one shoulder. "And you're usually not. Alone, I mean. Besides, a corn maze isn't the sort of thing one does on one's own."

"Why not?" I adjusted the cap over my ears. The barn was cold enough I could see my own breath. I didn't know how Joy stood it.

"Because it's creepy." Her shoulder twitched—Joy's version of a shudder.

"I was relying on Charlene the first time. Tonight, I'd like to try and beat the maze myself. Was that the pumpkin cannon I heard?"

She rolled her eyes. "The damn thing's even more popular than the maze."

"How can anyone even see the pumpkins flying in this fog?"

Joy shrugged. "Beats me. The kids love it. Maybe I should get one for the comic book store." Her lips quirked. "Can you imagine me on the roof, lobbing pumpkins across Main Street?"

"I don't suppose you'd target Heidi's gym?" I laughed.

"Wrong angle." She glanced toward the door to the maze.

I paid for Alfreda's ticket. "Any leads on whoever vandalized the maze sign?"

"Please. Everyone knows who did it."

"Who?"

"San Adrian. This rivalry will lead to disaster."

That's what I was afraid of.

"You'll need to hurry if you plan to beat the maze," she continued. "We close at ten."

"Thanks. I will." I wandered through the door and into the maze.

Lamps on high poles made globes of light in the fog. I crunched along the dried, matted cornstalk floor.

Occasionally, I heard a murmur of distant voices, but I never saw anyone. The whomps of the cannon were the only reminder of life outside the maze.

My mother's cancer had been relatively quick—a matter of months rather than years. And there were times, God help me, when I'd thought that speed had been a blessing. The times I'd been up all night, listening to her groans. Flinching against the storm of her outbursts when the cancer had moved to her brain. When I'd had to slog to work the next morning, eyes burning, shaking with exhaustion. When I'd thought it wasn't possible for me to go on, my heart beaten and broken. The moments when I just wanted it to end, and in the next, the hard grip of remorse.

I hoped Gordon's father was okay.

I hoped Gordon was okay.

After twenty more minutes of wrong turns, I began to regret my impulse. Sure, battling the maze had mostly stopped me from thinking about Gordon and his parents.

Now I was thinking about getting murdered in a cornfield.

I veered left at a familiar-looking junction. But *every* corner looked familiar. There isn't much variety in a cornfield.

The stalks cast long, wavering shadows. Buttoning my coat to my chin, I hurried onward, invisible ants crawling up my spine.

I paused, my head cocked, listening. The cannon had fallen silent. Did that mean they were closing?

Breaking into a jog, I made random turns into dead ends and retraced my steps.

I checked the clock on my phone, and my throat tightened. It was a minute to ten. What happened when the corn maze closed? I imagined them turning off the lights and leaving me to stumble in the darkness until a mountain lion—

My grip tightened on my phone. Joy wouldn't abandon me. She knew I was in the maze.

I turned a corner. The cornfield opened up, revealing the puzzle's center.

My muscles loosened. I'd done it!

I stopped short in front of the empty gilt throne. Where

was the person to stamp my card and, more importantly, help me find my way out?

The pumpkin cannon whumped.

I oriented on the noise. Would I do any permanent damage to the maze if I just ran straight through—

A whoosh of air. The throne exploded in a hail of wood and gilt and pumpkin rinds.

Chapter Twenty-Three

My cheek burned, lacerating fire. Heedless of direction, I plunged into the cornstalks. Leaves thwacked my arms, face, legs. I stumbled forward, weaving, in the darkness.

The cannon whumped again, fell silent.

Heart hammering, I stopped, panting. I braced my hands on my thighs.

The cornstalks whispered, a menacing chorus. Shadows flickered between the crackling leaves.

I had to get out of here. But where? Moonlight silvered the fog, outlined the silhouette of the eastern hills.

I forged south, where I knew I'd eventually reach a road, the parking lot, the barn. Leaves slapped and scratched at my exposed hands and face.

I emerged in the parking lot.

A car roared off. Its tires kicked up a swirl of dirt in its wake. The taillights turned the dust to flame, and then the car vanished over the rise.

I stared after the car a moment, then shook myself and jogged to the black barn.

The door was shut. I tugged the handle, rattling a lock. There were still a few cars in the dirt and hay-strewn lot, so I wasn't alone. I banged on the rough, wooden door.

"Is that you, Val?" Joy shouted through the massive door.

My body trembled, the adrenaline rush collapsing. "Let me in!"

"Just a sec."

"Hurry," I shouted back. "Someone blew up your throne."

There was a rattling of locks. The door rumbled sideways, and Joy peered out. She shouldered into a long, black, wool coat. "What did you say?"

"The pumpkin cannon. Someone turned it on the maze. The throne's gone. Destroyed."

"That's impossible," she said flatly. "Petros would never fire a pumpkin in that direction. It could kill someone. What were you saying about the throne?"

"Petros? Petros Scala?" My heart deflated like a wronged soufflé. Petronella's father couldn't be involved in the murder, but why shoot a pumpkin at *me?*

"You said the throne was damaged?" She stepped from the barn.

"It's a total loss." But it must have been an accident. How, after all, had someone targeted me inside the maze?

Joy blinked. "That's—Petros?"

Petronella's father rounded the barn. Mr. Scala scrubbed his hands in a rag and stuffed it into the pocket of his thick vest. "Yeah?" He wiped his hands on the front of his plaid shirt.

"Val said the maze throne was hit with one of your pumpkins." Joy stepped past me into the parking lot.

"Impossible." He frowned. "Val? What happened to you?"

"Happened?" I asked.

"Your face is swollen." Impassive, Joy brushed a chunk of rind off my shoulder.

I touched my cheek and winced. "I was in the center of

the maze maybe five minutes ago when someone shot a pumpkin into it. It hit the throne."

Petros swore. "I thought I—" He turned and trotted back the way he'd come.

Joy and I followed.

"Thought you what?" I asked.

"Check the throne," he barked over his shoulder to Joy.

"There was no one at the throne to check my time when I arrived," I said. "Wasn't there supposed to be?"

My friend frowned and made a U-turn, toward the north side of the barn. "Not if you arrived around ten. Our time stamper had to leave a little early—there was a gym emergency."

"Gym emergency? You mean . . . Heidi? Heidi's working here?" I tamped down an irrational burst of anger. Heidi had every right to volunteer at the maze. But leaving me alone there seemed personal, even though logic told me it couldn't have been. Heidi hadn't known I was inside.

"I knew you'd react this way."

"I'm not reacting."

She pulled her silky hair from beneath her coat collar and flipped it forward. "Oh?"

"Well, it *is* suspicious," I sputtered. "She tried to get me disqualified as a pie judge. She put that SUGAR KILLS sign in the closest possible spot to Pie Town's window—"

"Nice haunted village, by the way."

"Thanks. But don't you think Heidi—?"

"Cut her a break. She's going through a rough patch."

"I'm sorry to hear that," I muttered insincerely.

"She and Mark Jeffreys broke up."

So, the rumors were true. I exhaled heavily. "That bites." And to my surprise, I meant it. "Okay, Heidi was here. How did I miss her leaving the maze?"

"There's a hidden path for the staff." Joy pointed to

where the cornfield covered the road and pressed against one side of the barn. "Never mind that. I'll be right back." She turned and strode through an almost invisible break in the corn.

Huh. Heidi and Mark were over. I'd had nothing to do with their breakup. So why did I feel . . . bad?

Pressing against the side of the barn, I slithered past the corn maze and to the winding road. Joy had obviously expected I'd wait, but I was curious about the cannon.

Mr. Scala's broad figure marched up the dirt road ahead of me.

I hurried after him, my chest heaving a little as the road stretched up a low hill. A mechanical hum grew, filling the air.

At the top of the hill, I slowed, astonished.

The pumpkin cannon was an actual cannon. A long orange barrel had been attached to what looked like a septic tank. The tank and barrel were mounted on the back of an old fire truck where the ladder should be. An American flag fluttered from a pole on top.

Petronella's father clambered onto the fire truck. He peered through a sighting mechanism. He cursed again and twisted toward me. "You said you were inside the maze when it happened?"

"In the center."

He turned a lever. The mechanical grumble silenced.

His shoulders slumped. "You could have been killed, Val. The throne was targeted deliberately." Petros motioned to the sight.

"But it was only a pumpkin."

"A pumpkin that flies nearly four hundred miles per hour."

I felt the blood drain from my face.

"There's a chance whoever targeted this didn't notice

you were in the center." He worked a hand crank, and the cannon rotated on the fire truck. "Maybe you walked in after they'd targeted the throne, and they fired without looking."

"Who knew how to work this?" I croaked.

His round face darkened. "Anyone who's watched me launch a pumpkin."

"But sighting properly? Turning the machine on? That must have taken some knowledge of the machinery."

He scratched his bristly cheek. "Maybe someone who worked here. But no one who works here would do that We've all busted our butts on this harvest festival and the corn maze." His jaw tightened. "San Adrian."

"No," I said. Heidi had better odds being the shooter, and those odds were win-the-lottery low. "I don't think—"

"They've got their own pumpkin cannon. They'd know how to work this one. It was bad luck you were in the center when they fired."

"When did you shut down the cannon tonight?" I asked.

"Nine-thirty. We close at ten, but that gives the spectators time to walk back to the barn, buy some souvenirs before they leave."

"And what were you doing after you shut it down?"

He seemed to crumple in on himself. "Val, you can't think I did this. Just because Chief Shaw . . ." His Adam's apple bobbed above the collar of his plaid shirt. "I'd never—"

"I know," I said. "Of course, you didn't. But if someone had gotten hurt inside the maze—"

"I'd be blamed," he said heavily.

"We need to figure this out. Tell me what you did after you left the cannon."

"I put the unused pumpkins away in the shed." He

motioned toward a small outbuilding near the black-painted barn.

"Did you notice anyone hanging around?"

He shook his head. "I never thought we'd need a lock and key for this cannon, but clearly we do."

"Okay, who was working here tonight?"

"Tomorrow's a school day," he said. "Business lightened up after eight or so. It's just the three of us. Joy, taking tickets and selling souvenirs, Heidi, in the center of the maze, and me."

"We need to talk to Heidi."

He pulled a phone from the pocket of his thick vest and made a call.

"Heidi? Where are you at . . . ? Okay . . . someone sabotaged our pumpkin cannon. . . ."

I frowned. It wasn't exactly sabotage of the *cannon,* but whatever.

"No?" he asked. "All right. Drive safe." He hung up. "She left a little before ten. Went straight to her car and didn't see anything suspicious."

"So, no one saw anything?"

"It must have been kids from San Adrian." He nodded, a hopeful expression on his face. "Who else could it be?"

"I don't know. There have been too many strange things going on, and I don't think we can blame San Adrian for them all."

A gust of mist drifted between us and as quickly vanished. He eyed me. "Now what? Are you going to call the cops?"

"It's not my cannon. Are you going to call them?"

His gaze shifted. "I'll have to talk to management."

In other words, *no.* I had to tell Gordon.

But I didn't want to, not now. He had his father to deal with, and I didn't want to pull him in another direction.

I drove home through the thickening fog. I didn't call Gordon.

I procrastibaked.

Though pie is my passion, woman cannot live on pie alone. There's also pumpkin bread.

I pulled a plastic container of recently baked pumpkin from my tiny refrigerator.

Soon my tiny house was filled with the smells of pumpkin and all its associated spices. There's no better smell for soothing the troubled soul. Unless you happen to hate pumpkin, in which case, we need to talk.

I *do* love pumpkin, but my thoughts remained unsettled. There'd been two attempts on me in one day. Unless sabotage of the maze really had been the goal?

But I suspected something worse.

Someone had been targeting me.

Chapter Twenty-Four

My tiny home's door shuddered, a fist rattling it in its metal frame.

I lifted my head from my pillow and squinted at the light streaming through the vertical blinds. Was it too much to hope I'd get to sleep in on Monday, my day off?

Apparently, yes. It was.

I staggered from my futon, hiked up the bottoms of my pie pajamas, and yanked open the door.

Charlene and Takako grinned up at me. They both carried paper coffee cups—Takako two. Around Charlene's neck, Frederick yawned, showing off needlelike teeth.

I took an involuntary step back.

"Good morning." Takako extended a cup to me. "Charlene told me you liked to wake up to soy chai." Takako wore all black: black jeans, black sweater, shiny quilted black jacket. She looked like she was about to knock over a liquor store.

"What are you doing still asleep?" Charlene asked.

"I'm not asleep anymore," I grumped. If only I *was* still tucked in bed. I glanced at my stepmother. "But there was an incident at the maze last night."

"Another?" Charlene asked.

They squeezed past me into my tiny house and settled themselves at the fold-down table. Since it was made for two at a pinch, I leaned against the kitchen counter and told them about the pumpkin cannon.

"Four hundred miles an hour?" Takako whistled. "Who knew pumpkins could be so dangerous?"

Charlene rubbed her chin. "Did someone follow you there?" She was dressed like a candy corn. Thick yellow tunic and jacket. Orange knit leggings. White socks and high tops.

I straightened off the counter. "I don't think so, but I wasn't checking for a tail."

"If you weren't followed," Charlene said, "then that cannon was fired by someone who had reason to be there and saw you. Someone who took advantage of an opportunity. Someone who worked there."

"Only Petros, Heidi, and Joy were working that night. None of them had reason to launch a pumpkin at me." Heidi might despise me, but she was no killer.

"Then you were followed," Charlene said.

"What about that Alfreda woman?" Takako asked. "You said she was there."

"If she wants a job at Pie Town, she'd better not have launched that pumpkin," Charlene growled.

"I didn't see Alfreda leave the parking lot," I said. "She could have stuck around to shoot the cannon. But it seems a stupid thing to do. She must have known it would make her look guilty of the murders."

"I hate to say it," Charlene said, "but this sounds more like another San Adrian prank gone wrong."

She laid Frederick on the table. Eyes closed, the white cat flicked his tail.

"Another?" I asked. "We don't know if someone from San Adrian was involved in any of the incidents so far."

"Whatever the case," Takako said, "these pranks are getting out of hand. Were the police called?"

"I don't know. It was late when I got home," I hedged, "so I didn't get a chance to call Gordon." I still didn't know how his father was, but I didn't want to disturb Gordon.

Charlene smacked her hand on the table, and the paper coffee cups jumped. "This is getting too complicated. We need to thin the herd."

"Who are we going to take out?" Takako asked.

Mug warming my hands, I looked askance at the two women. "You two sound like hitmen."

"Thistleblossom," Charlene said. "She's been lurking in the background, and she's up to no good. We need to remove her from the equation."

"See," I said, "there you go again with the language."

"Rub her off the list," Takako agreed.

"Neutralize her," Charlene said.

"Now you're just doing it on purpose," I said.

"Are you going to get dressed?" Charlene asked.

"So, we can iceberg the SS Thistleblossom?" I joked.

The two women stared blankly.

"Never mind." What harm could talking to Mrs. Thistleblossom do? She'd been at the pumpkin patch the morning we'd been attacked by the farm truck. She knew our main players. She might actually have some intel. And interviewing Thistleblossom would keep Charlene and Takako out of trouble.

I dressed quickly in a ribbed, white turtleneck sweater and sand-colored vest. Sucking in my gut, I buttoned my jeans. They must have shrunk in the wash. Because it couldn't possibly have anything to do with the holiday pies I'd been sampling.

We crowded into Charlene's yellow Jeep. I sat angled sideways, crushed in the back.

"Hold Frederick." Charlene twisted in her seat and dumped the cat in my lap.

"OK—"

The Jeep lurched forward. It zipped past the picnic table and made a sharp U-turn in my front yard. Rocketing through the eucalyptus trees and down the dirt trail, we exploded onto the main road. The Jeep darted between two semis and merged onto the highway.

I relaxed my grip on Takako's headrest. Who could blame Frederick for keeping his eyes closed? Valium and a blindfold were the sanest accessories when Charlene was driving. Sadly, I had neither.

Takako sniffed. "What's that smell?"

"I don't smell anything," Charlene said.

But I did. I twisted and peered into the storage space behind my seat. Charlene's pumpkin drone sat at an angle between a rolled-up sleeping bag and a hand ax. The jack-o'-lantern's face puckered, folding in on itself.

"Maybe it's time to retire the pumpkin drone," I said.

"Just because it's old," Charlene said, "doesn't mean it's no good. Besides, it looks scarier all wrinkled."

"Who do you want to scare?" I asked.

"Brinks." Charlene's knuckles whitened on the wheel. "He's not going to toilet paper my house *this* year."

"And your thirst for revenge has nothing to do with that kid winning the pumpkin race?" I asked.

She sniffed. "He didn't win. His father did."

All-righty then.

Trees and houses and ocean views blurred past us.

Charlene hit the brakes. The Jeep screeched to a halt in front of a crooked Victorian with peeling paint and an overgrown front yard.

"Here we are," she caroled.

"You're kidding me." Slap some candy on the front and

call us Hansel and Gretel. I hadn't seen anything this creepy since I'd helped Charlene clean out her attic. "No wonder people think she's a witch."

"Only you think she's a witch," Charlene said.

"*I* don't." I unlatched my seat belt. "I'm just saying—"

"Mrs. Thistleblossom wants you to believe she's got supernatural abilities," Takako said. "Her performance in your pie shop, the clothing, her odd gestures . . . all create fear, and that gives her power."

"Thank you!" At least someone got it. "I don't understand how you don't see it, Charlene."

"Because I grew up. I've learned better."

Ha. Charlene would never grow up. It was part of her charm. "Why are you being so rational about this? You think everything's supernatural."

"Do not." Charlene unsnapped her seat belt.

"You think Pastor Hiller is a werewolf," I said.

"He *is* a werewolf."

"Then when it comes to Thistleblossom, why are you acting like . . . me?"

"A better question," she said, "is why are you acting like me?"

"I'm—" Oh, damn. Was I?

Charlene unlocked her door. "Tell her Thistleblossom isn't a witch, Takako."

"Belief is a powerful thing," my stepmother said vaguely.

We stared at the small Victorian. Monterey cypresses and pines pressed against the crooked house. They created thick wells of shade, ideal for ambush by goblins. The picket fence had once been white. Now it was mainly the color of rotted wood.

"But I could be reading too much into her behavior," Takako admitted. "My PhD in anthropology had a specialization in witchcraft."

Charlene cocked her head. "You can specialize in that?"

"It was a useful combination with my specialization in ethnoarchaeology."

"Ethnoarchaeology?" I asked.

"Working with descendant communities to learn about traditional beliefs and rituals," Takako explained. "I have PhDs in archaeology and anthropology."

Wow. My stepmom was one smart cookie.

Which goes to show that even smart women can make dumb romantic decisions. I mean—my father?

"Are you sure Mrs. Thistleblossom's home?" Takako asked.

Charlene turned and removed Frederick from my lap. "Every Monday morning, she cooks her food for the rest of the week."

I scrunched my forehead. "Have you been surveilling Mrs. Thistleblossom?"

"She's had the same cooking routine for fifty years." She draped Frederick over one shoulder and stepped from the Jeep.

We followed her to the front gate. It stuck, and I had to give it a shove, scraping it across the concrete path.

A crow landed on a cypress branch and cawed. The branch swayed, dried leaves drifting to the ground.

I stepped through the gate. The temperature dropped in the shadows of the looming trees, and I rubbed my arms.

We crept down the path.

Something thudded softly, and I started, scanning the yard. A pine cone rolled to a shuddering halt on the overgrown lawn.

"Hold it." Charlene raised her fist.

We froze.

"She's in the kitchen," Charlene whispered, pointing at a curtained window on the left side of the porch.

"And?" I asked.

"And be quiet." Charlene tiptoed up the porch.

Takako shrugged and followed.

Shaking my head, I did the same.

Charlene ducked beneath the kitchen window and straightened on the opposite side. She peeked in and jerked away, flattening herself against the wall. Charlene motioned toward the window. Takako and I looked inside.

Cast-iron cauldrons steamed on the old-fashioned stove. Mrs. Thistleblossom plucked a dish towel looped through the refrigerator door. She slipped her arm through it to the elbow. The elderly woman leaned back, and the door creaked open.

She extricated herself from the towel. Reaching into the refrigerator, she drew out a bowl. It slipped from her hands and crashed to the tile floor. Liquid splattered the faded kitchen cabinets. She cursed and tottered to a narrow closet, fumbling with the knob.

I stepped from the window. "She has arthritis." I should have guessed from her gnarled fingers. No wonder she'd cheated in the pie contest. Rolling out piecrusts must be agony. And her spooky yard . . . Of *course,* she couldn't do yard work. "She needs help." I strode to the door and knocked. *A witch.* I'd been an idiot.

After a long two minutes, Mrs. Thistleblossom shouted, "No solicitors!"

"It's me, Mrs. Thistleblossom—Val Harris. I'm here with Charlene and my, uh, with Takako."

The knob started to turn, snapped back, and twisted open. Her wizened face glared out. "What do you want?" She jerked her head toward Charlene. "And why is she dressed like a candy corn?"

"We wanted to talk to you about the murders," I said. "We thought you might have some insight."

Her black eyes danced, her face creasing with glee. "You think I killed those eye doctors?"

"Absolutely not. Charlene and I have—and Takako—have been gathering evidence. We wanted to go over it with you and get your opinion."

She smoothed her twisted hands on her Christmas-tree apron. "My opinion?"

Charlene nudged me aside. "Everyone knows you've got your finger in every pie in this town."

"Is that a crack about me losing the bake-off?"

"No," I said.

Mrs. Thistleblossom sneered. "You're a fine one to talk, McCree, sticking your nose into murders and stolen surf-boards."

"We found that surfboard." Charlene jammed her hands on her hips. "And the moose head."

"Hmph! Come inside. I don't want riffraff cluttering up my porch. The neighbors will complain. And don't get cat hair on my sofa!"

We edged inside. Milo leapt from a dog bed near the door and emitted a rusty bark.

"Some watchdog," Charlene said.

"He can't help it if he's deaf," Mrs. Thistleblossom said.

"So's Frederick." Charlene pointed to the ball of white fur coiled around her neck.

Milo growled, spotting the cat.

I sniffed. Whatever was cooking smelled awful—like burning plastic and deep-fried death.

"That is the stupidest way to wear a cat I've ever seen," Mrs. Thistleblossom said.

Charlene bridled. "How—?"

"Did we interrupt your cooking?" I asked.

"Everyone knows I do the week's cooking on Mondays. My potions too."

I started.

Mrs. Thistleblossom cackled. "Heh. I had you going, didn't I?"

I crossed my arms. "Yeah, you got me."

Something hissed in the kitchen. "My stew!" Mrs. Thistleblossom hurried into the kitchen, and we followed.

A pot bubbled over on the stove. Orange liquid and broken bits of bowl spilled across the floor. Mrs. Thistleblossom swore.

Milo trotted after us, one crossed eye on Frederick.

"Where do you keep your mop?" I asked.

"I didn't ask for your help," the old lady snapped, "and I don't need it."

"Yes, but—"

"But you *should* clean it up," Mrs. Thistleblossom said. "It's your fault I dropped that bowl."

Charlene exhaled an outraged breath. "Our fault?"

I nudged her. "We'll clean it up."

"First cupboard on the right," Mrs. Thistleblossom said.

I pulled the mop from the tall cupboard and picked up the bigger pieces of broken bowl. Takako mopped the floor behind me. Soon we had the mess cleaned up.

Mrs. Thistleblossom braced her fists on her hips. "I suppose you want coffee now?"

Milo growled.

"We don't want to put you to any trouble," Takako said.

"But coffee wouldn't go amiss." Charlene cast a wary gaze at the dog and adjusted Frederick around her collar.

Mrs. Thistleblossom reached for an ancient-looking percolator. Her hands clenched.

"Let me." Hastily, I grabbed the pot.

She pointed to the cupboard with the cups, and I poured.

We settled ourselves in the breakfast nook on cracked

plastic chairs. Dried herbs lay piled in the center of the round table. Tall windows looked out on a trio of pines.

"You put that chalk graffiti on Val's van, didn't you?" Charlene asked.

"I was having a good day." She flexed her hands and winced. "And the crossing spell under your doormat."

"Crossing spell?" I yelped. What was that?

Mrs. Thistleblossom laughed, slapping her knees.

"I think," Takako said wryly, "that was a joke."

The old lady wiped her eyes. "I suppose you want me to apologize."

An apology would make a nice change, but Charlene never said she was sorry. Why mess with tradition? "Nah. But why did you do it?"

"To throw you off your game. I knew you'd sniff out my store-bought pie. You're a professional."

But I hadn't, I thought, rueful. "I'll bet you would have given me a run for my money before your arthritis."

"Oh." Her shoulders rounded. "You figured that out."

"Getting old is nothing to be ashamed of," said Charlene. "It will happen to us all, if we're lucky."

Takako and I carefully did not look at my piecrust specialist.

"And the graffiti on Pie Town's rear wall?" Takako turned her cup on the plastic tablecloth, a red and green poinsettia pattern.

Mrs. Thistleblossom hung her head. "I thought that was chalk-based as well. Sorry for the trouble."

"What about trying to run us off the road at Laurelynn's pumpkin patch?" Charlene asked.

"Drive you off the road?" She sneered. "What are you talking about?"

"We know you were there." Charlene jabbed a finger toward her. "You had access to the keys to the truck."

"I can't drive a truck! Look at my hands." She raised them for us to see. "I didn't do anything aside from what I told you. Well, there was that bit of hocus-pocus in your pie shop, but aside from that, nothing."

Milo worried at my shoelaces. I edged my foot away, and the tiny dog growled.

"All right." I set down my chipped teacup and gave the dog another nudge beneath the table. "I believe you. What about the pumpkin cannon last night?"

"What pumpkin cannon?" Mrs. Thistleblossom rubbed her temple. "What are you talking about?"

Charlene and I glanced at each other.

"Someone launched a pumpkin at Val from the cannon when she was in the maze," Takako said.

Mrs. Thistleblossom tilted her head. "Hmm. You could have been killed."

Milo sank his teeth into my ankle, and I gasped.

"Do you have any idea who might have been behind it?" I bent and detached the dog, depositing him in Mrs. Thistleblossom's lap.

"I don't know anyone who'd do something so foolish." She stroked Milo and made a shushing noise. "Must have been San Adrian. Revenge for our attack on their pumpkin festival."

"San Adrian had nothing to do with Dr. Levant's death," I said. "They may have been involved in other pranks, but not murder."

"Obviously, someone close to Dr. Levant and Dr. Cannon killed them," the old lady said.

Milo yipped an agreement.

"Which is why we've come to you," Charlene said.

"Is it why you were snooping around Laurelynn's pumpkin patch?" Mrs. Thistleblossom tapped her fingers on the plastic tablecloth.

One of Milo's eyes followed the motion.

"Laurelynn Lelli threatened to kill Kara the week before Kara died," I said.

Mrs. Thistleblossom nodded. "Well, sure she did. Kara was spreading rumors that Laurelynn was using prohibited pesticides on her pumpkins."

Whoa. Mrs. Thistleblossom really did have the low-down on San Nicholas. Why hadn't we used her as a source before? "But Laurelynn's pumpkin farm is organic." I raked my hands through my hair. "She'd lose her certification."

"Which is exactly why the rumor was so dangerous." Mrs. Thistleblossom scowled.

"Where did you hear this?" Takako set down her floral-patterned teacup.

"Kara told me about the pesticides, and I told Laurelynn."

"You old rabble-rouser," Charlene said. "You knew that would cause more trouble between them."

Mrs. Thistleblossom raised her chin. "Laurelynn had a right to know what was being said."

"Do you think Dr. Levant was telling the truth?" Takako leaned forward, her black jacket pressing into the table.

Mrs. Thistleblossom made a face. "How should I know? But Laurelynn sure reacted when I told her." She chuckled.

"Could it be true?" I asked. "About the pesticides, I mean."

Charlene adjusted Frederick on the shoulder of her yellow jacket, and Milo jerked forward in Mrs. Thistleblossom's lap. "We can send one of those pumpkins you bought in for testing to find out," Charlene said.

"Send it where?" I asked.

"I'll give it to Ray," she said. "He'll know some student somewhere."

That wasn't a bad idea. "Let's do that. Whether the

rumor was true or not, it sounds like Kara and Laurelynn's rivalry was more serious than Elon made out."

"Kara Levant was a troublemaker," Mrs. Thistleblossom said. "I'm not surprised someone knocked her off."

A draft of cool air crept between the windowpanes, and my grip tightened on the teacup. "What other trouble did she make?"

"She made Tristan's life miserable." She exhaled heavily. "He got me tickets for *Phantom of the Opera* last year. Good man. Bad end."

"But Tristan didn't kill her," I said. "What can you tell us about her husband?"

"Elon's a decent fellow, but Kara never gave him a rest. She controlled his life like one of those whatchamacallits, helicopter wives. I reckon that could make a man snap."

"Elon was in the haunted house the morning Kara died," I mused. "That's where the murder weapon came from. He could have slipped away and killed his wife."

Mrs. Thistleblossom sighed. "You never know about people."

Milo's stomach made a mournful whine.

"And then there's her ex-employee, Alfreda," I said. "She was angry about being fired. Dr. Tristan was killed with a glass paperweight a lot like one Alfreda had and claims she lost. She might have killed them both for revenge."

"Maybe," Mrs. Thistleblossom said. "Though I can't figure her for a cold-blooded killer. To kill in a fit of anger, sure. But to kill two people like that took planning. That's not Alfreda. That woman can't think more than two steps ahead. It's caused her no end of troubles."

That would explain her social media posts complaining about the optometry office. It was just the sort of thing that would scare off an Internet-savvy future employer.

A crow landed on the porch railing. The bird peered through the window, its inky eyes flat and fathomless.

"It sounds like you know her well," Takako said.

"I know everyone in this town." Mrs. Thistleblossom's voice sharpened. "Alfreda's got a head for numbers, that's for sure. But her math smarts don't translate to life smarts, if you know what I mean."

"I'm not sure I do," I said.

Mrs. Thistleblossom rested her hands on the round table. "Alfreda doesn't always understand how her desires might conflict with others'."

"And Kara's cousin, Denise?" Charlene asked.

"I don't trust that one," Mrs. Thistleblossom said. "Too slick by half."

Charlene crossed her arms. "We heard Kara pushed Denise's buttons too."

Mrs. Thistleblossom shrugged.

"Both Denise and Elon inherit pieces of Kara's estate," I said. "Denise and Elon also could have taken the keys to the truck and run us off the road by Laurelynn's pumpkin patch. Assuming the killer is the person who drove that truck, that leaves out Alfreda as well. I don't think she could have stolen that key. But why? None of the motives really add up."

"None of it does." Mrs. Thistleblossom's basalt eyes glinted with cunning. "And all of it does."

"How?" I asked.

Mrs. Thistleblossom sniffed. "That's for me to know."

"And none of our suspects have alibis for Tristan's or Kara's murders," Charlene said.

"So, you're nowhere," Mrs. Thistleblossom said.

"Pretty much," I admitted.

She folded her arms across her Christmas-tree apron. "Some detectives."

Chapter Twenty-Five

After lunch overlooking the bay, we zipped down the One, toward San Nicholas's downtown. The fog had lifted, the sky a flat, unyielding blue. But a line of white hovered on the horizon, fog threatening to sweep into town later.

"At least we can count old Thistleblossom out," Charlene said.

The heater's warmth swelled the odor of the rotting pumpkin drone in the Jeep's rear.

I tried not to inhale. "I'm a little worried for her, though." I checked my phone. Gordon hadn't called.

"Because she may know too much?" Charlene asked.

"Because she needs help around the house."

In the front seat, Takako twisted to face me. "She's going to let me help cook dinner tomorrow. I told her I was a terrible cook. She offered to teach me."

That would give Takako a chance to do the actual cooking. But this wasn't a long-term fix. "Would you ask if I can join in?"

"I'll try to set something up," Takako said, "so you can *learn* how to cook from her later."

"And when will you have time for cooking lessons you don't need?" Charlene asked.

I opened my mouth, closed it. Charlene was right. But I couldn't abandon Mrs. Thistleblossom. "I'll figure something out."

Coiled in my lap, Frederick flicked his ears.

"What next?" Takako asked.

I smoothed the white cat's fur. "We can't put off talking to Elon any longer. Mrs. Thistleblossom seemed to think he'd feel better off without his wife, and he does inherit the business."

"On it." Charlene turned sharply, tires screeching.

Frederick dug his claws into my thigh.

I bit back a yelp of pain.

We rocketed into downtown. The Jeep skidded to a halt in front of Pie Town.

"Well," Charlene said. "Get the man a pie. We can't come empty-handed."

"Right." I scuttled from the Jeep and unlocked the front door. There were always a few pies in the freezer for emergency purposes. Hurrying into the kitchen, I grabbed a frozen turkey pot pie.

I pulled my phone from my pocket and called Gordon. It went to voice mail.

"Gordon, it's Val." I tucked the phone against my shoulder and scribbled heating instructions on an order ticket. "I just wanted you to know I'm thinking about you. Let me know how you and your parents are doing."

I hung up and returned to the Jeep.

Charlene started the car. "What'd you get?"

We lurched forward. Takako grabbed the bar above her door.

I fastened my seat belt. "Comfort food."

Mindful of children and pets, Charlene drove more sedately into a residential neighborhood. Giant pumpkins filled the front yard of a mid-century modern home. I guessed it belonged to Petronella's parents.

Three houses down, Charlene cruised to a stop. Elon's home had what I'd come to recognize as a low-water garden. His front yard was dotted with spiky plants poking through the gravel. The look worked with his fifties-era house, with its gray and turquoise paint and metal trim.

Charlene draped Frederick around the shoulders of her yellow jacket. He burrowed closer, getting comfortable.

The three of us marched up the zigzag concrete walk. Charlene rang the bell.

Elon opened the door a minute or two later and adjusted his tortoiseshell glasses. A pair of comfy-looking gray sweats hung loosely on his lean frame. "Charlene, Val, and . . . ?"

"My stepmother, Takako. You met briefly at the haunted house."

"Of course. Forgive me for forgetting your name. But what are you three doing here?"

"Pot pie," Charlene said.

I extended it to him. "I hope you like turkey?"

His handsome face creased in a faint smile, and he took the pink box. "I love turkey pot pie. Come in." He pulled the door wider and stood aside. "I was supposed to go golfing today, but I couldn't muster the energy. I guess it worked out after all."

I tensed. Golfing? With Chief Shaw? Coming here might not have been the best idea after all.

We followed him through a wide hallway and into the open-plan kitchen. Clean plates were stacked pell-mell in the sink. Shoes and men's clothes lay scattered in the nearby family room as if they'd been thrown there.

"How have you been doing?" Charlene asked.

He studied the dishes in the sink. "I guess I'm at loose

ends. There are a lot of decisions to make, but Denise has been managing them all like a champion. She's even going to oversee the sale of Kara's share of the optometry office. I haven't had to lift a finger." He sounded a little wistful.

Sweat trickled down my back. I slipped off my sand-colored vest and looped it over one arm. "I imagine the sale's a tangle, since Tristan was a co-owner as well. Have any of his heirs come forward?"

"Kara was his heir."

I stared. "What?"

"He didn't have any family, so Tristan's share of the optometry business went to my wife."

"But she, er . . ."

"Predeceased him, yes." He tugged on his sweatshirt collar. "My understanding is the way the will was written, his share comes to me and Denise now. Not that there's much business left."

"I thought the two had some sort of insurance should one of them die?" I asked.

"Business interruption insurance," he said, "but it doesn't cover this situation. Denise thinks she can still get something for the business, but I don't know."

"Denise is sure helpful." Charlene stroked the cat around her neck.

He nodded glumly.

"You know how good deeds should be rewarded?" Charlene asked.

He shook his head.

"Pie," she said. "Good deeds should be rewarded with pie. Elon, what's Denise's favorite flavor?"

"Cherry, I think."

"Val, let's surprise Denise with a cherry pie. Elon, where do you think she's at today?"

"The optometry office, I believe. Kara kept all her personal files there—insurance and income taxes and such. But—"

"Great idea, Charlene." I might actually have a cherry pie in the freezer too. "Have the police come closer to making an arrest?"

He clutched the box more tightly, crinkling its edges. "Not that I know of."

"Do they have any leads?" Takako asked.

"Chief Shaw assures me they do. He said there's a pumpkin farmer . . ." He looked left, as if he could see through the walls to the Scalas' house, and frowned.

I handed him the order slip. "Here are the heating instructions."

His brows rose. "I have to bake it?"

"Don't worry." I gestured to the black, glass-topped range. "It's just a matter of reheating in the oven."

One corner of his mouth lifted, dropped. "I wasn't worried. I was excited. I haven't had much to do around here lately, and I'm feeling a bit useless." Elon walked to the sink and stared through the window at the succulent garden. His hands fisted. "Even my garden takes care of itself. It's on an automatic drip system. Kara made sure the neighbors trimmed their trees, so there was never much to rake. I wouldn't mind raking leaves."

"You wouldn't?" I asked. "Because Mrs. Thistleblossom is having trouble managing her yard."

"Does she need help?" he asked eagerly, and turned from the window. "I'd kill to mow a lawn."

"She needs help," I said, "but I'm not sure she'll take it."

"Old people can be proud." Charlene straightened off the tile counter. "You need to know how to handle them, like I do."

"Mrs. Thistleblossom would be doing *me* a favor," he said.

"Well," I said, "if you didn't mind us putting it to her that way, she might accept help."

"I'm not proud," he said. "Make me out to be as pathetic a widower as you like. Just get me out of this house."

"I'm seeing her later," Takako said. "I can put a word in her ear."

He wrung her hand. "Thank you. You have no idea . . ." He gulped.

"Oh," I said. "One more thing. Did you happen to stop by the corn maze last night around ten?"

"No, I was home last night. Why?"

"Nothing." But he had no alibi for the attack in the maze.

Charlene plucked a shiny plate from the sink and studied it. "You know, these usually go in the cupboard."

He winced. "It's my revolt against order."

"I'd think you'd be dirtying some dishes by now," Charlene said. "Have you been eating out all this time?"

"Not exactly. Like I said, people have been helping a little too much."

Charlene reached for the pink box. "If you don't want the pie—"

"No, no," he said. "I don't mean to sound ungrateful. Denise has been wonderful. I just wish she wouldn't take so much time off from her business on my behalf."

"Is she trying to make up for something?" Charlene asked shrewdly.

He blinked, the mild-mannered intellectual. "Like what?"

"I heard she and Kara could get competitive," Charlene said.

"Competitive?" He frowned. "They were both wildly

successful. They inspired each other. Denise especially—her software firm has put her on the map."

Charlene rested her elbow on the white-tile counter. "Then what's Denise trying to make up for?"

His cheeks reddened. "I don't think she or Laurelynn are trying to make up for anything."

"Laurelynn?" I asked.

He turned away quickly, dropping the pie box on the countertop, and I winced. That was no way to treat a pie. "I just meant Laurelynn's been a rock too."

"Is Laurelynn okay?" I asked. "We've, er, heard the rumors about the pesticides."

His expression darkened. "That farm is Laurelynn's life. She believes in organic food. She'd never use pesticides."

"Hmm." Charlene rubbed her chin. "Who do you think started the rumor that she was?"

He crossed his arms over his chest. "I get the feeling that's a question you already know the answer to."

My face warmed. And this was why I hadn't really wanted to come today. I hated this. I hated harassing a grieving widower. But I hated murder more.

"We heard it was your wife," Takako said into the silence.

His shoulders crumpled inward. "Do the police know?"

"I imagine they will soon if they don't already," I said.

"You don't understand." He looked out the square window over the sink. "Laurelynn wouldn't have killed Kara, not over that. It's not who she is."

But if the farm was her livelihood, if her heart and soul were wrapped up in it, would she kill for it?

We said uneasy good-byes to Elon. The three of us silently got into Charlene's Jeep and drove into town.

Charlene cornered sharply at a house with portholes for windows and revved the Jeep's engine. "Now that you've sorted out all the senior citizens in San Nicholas, do you think we can get back to investigating?"

"I thought that's what we were doing." I pushed off the door and righted myself.

"I shouldn't have accused his wife of starting that rumor," Takako said. "She's dead."

"No, I'm glad you did." Because I'd been losing my nerve. My hands dropped to Frederick, and I scratched behind the sleeping cat's ears. "I should have pushed harder to find out if anyone was seen at the maze last night, because Elon doesn't have much of an alibi."

"You'd just escaped death by pumpkin," Takako said. "Of course, you were rattled."

"She's right," Charlene said. "You screwed up, Val."

"Thanks!"

We wound through the outskirts of town, making a brief stop at Pie Town for a frozen cherry pie.

Ten minutes later, Charlene pulled into a shopping center parking lot and we escaped the Jeep.

The optometry office was located between a bookstore and a pizza parlor. A CLOSED sign hung in the glass front window.

Denise stood, red-faced, behind the glass. Her neck muscles strained in a muffled shout.

Another figure strode into view behind the glass—Alfreda Kuulik.

Interesting, I almost didn't want to interrupt, but I couldn't really hear their argument. I rapped on the door.

The two women jerked, whirling to face us.

Charlene and Takako waved.

Denise strode to the door and yanked it open. "I'm sorry, we're closed," she said briskly. Her hand tightened on the knob.

"Is everything all right?" I asked.

"Alfreda was just leaving." She threw a hostile look at the broad-shouldered woman.

Alfreda stomped to the door. "I want my money."

"Not *now*, Alfreda!"

The large woman pushed past us, jostling me.

"What was that about?" Charlene watched Alfreda storm down the brick sidewalk.

Denise tugged down the front of her black, company jacket. "She claims she's owed back pay. But I can't hand over what she wants right now. I need to verify what she's owed first. I have to account for every penny to the estate."

Denise wore her usual black slacks, and I felt a stab of pity. At least I got to wear jeans with my Pie Town gear. And I had more than one company jacket.

"Are you the executor?" I asked.

"Kara thought it would be easier on Elon if I managed things, just in case." Her expression softened. She shook herself. "Not that Kara ever really believed anything would happen. But we wanted to be organized and prepared. My father was an estate attorney. He used to say that being married without a will was spousal abuse. But you didn't come here to talk about that. What can I do for you? Have you learned anything?"

A customer opened the door to the pizza parlor and walked inside. The scent of tomatoes and melting cheese wafted down the sidewalk.

"It's what we can do for you," Charlene said. "Pie."

Denise blinked. "Excuse me?"

"We just came from Elon's," I said. "You both suffered a terrible loss. We wanted to bring you comfort food." I extended the pink box. This time, I'd written out reheating instructions and taped them to the top of the box.

"It's cherry," Charlene said.

Her eyes widened. "He told you it was my favorite?"

"Elon may have mentioned it," Charlene said.

She blinked rapidly. "He's so thoughtful."

"Technically," Charlene said, "we were the ones—"

I nudged her shoulder. This wasn't the time to get pedantic. "We're glad you like it. What are you working on?"

She glanced over her shoulder, into the office. "There's an optometry organization that will help sell the business. I have to act fast though, so the clients don't go elsewhere first."

"It's too bad Alfreda didn't work out," I said. "With her bookkeeping skills, it sounds like she would have been a big help."

Denise stiffened. "My cousin fired her for a reason."

"What was that reason, exactly?" Charlene asked.

Alfreda's charcoal Honda reversed from a parking spot at Charlene speed and missed a minivan by inches. The minivan honked. The Honda driver pounded on its horn, a staccato blare.

"It's not important now," Denise said.

"But Dr. Cannon brought her back," I said.

Denise shook her head. "Tristan was—"

The Honda roared past. Alfreda made a one-fingered gesture in our direction.

Denise snapped her mouth shut and briefly closed her eyes. "I'm sorry. The last week has been a roller coaster. The fact is, Tristan had a soft heart. It's why he had such a great bedside manner, but it didn't make him the greatest decision maker when it came to staffing." She shook her head. "If you must know, Alfreda was becoming too demanding. She wanted a raise, and when Kara couldn't give it to her, she became rude and aggressive with the patients. Kara had to fire her."

I nodded. That tracked with what I'd learned.

"Are the police any closer to figuring out who killed your cousin and Dr. Cannon?" Takako asked.

"The police?" Denise's lip curled. "You can't count on them. They don't know their collective asses from their elbows."

My midsection tightened, hardening. "There are good cops at the SNPD." Even if Chief Shaw made their work difficult.

One corner of her mouth wrinkled. "According to town gossip, if you want a crime solved, go to the Baker Street Bakers. Which is why I hired you. Is that why you're here, to investigate Alfreda?"

I shuffled my feet. "Uh . . ."

"If she killed my cousin, she needs to pay," Denise said fiercely. "I don't care how Kara gets justice, as long as justice is done."

"You're a sponsor of the corn maze," I said, "aren't you?"

She folded her arms over her logo jacket. "Yes. Why?"

"You didn't happen to stop by there last night, did you?"

"No," Denise said sharply. "Why would I? I'm a sponsor. I've funded it. I'm not going to repaint that sign myself. Why do you ask?"

"I thought I'd seen you there," I lied, "that's all. It's not important."

We said our good-byes. Denise locked the door behind us. Its window blinds rattled into place.

"Are you thinking what I'm thinking?" Charlene asked in a low tone.

"Probably not," Takako said cautiously.

But I was. "We need to return to the maze."

Chapter Twenty-Six

The afternoon sun had taken on a soft, misty quality as we whizzed down the One. Dried grasses along the side of the highway rippled at the Jeep's passage.

"I thought the maze was closed on Mondays?" Takako asked.

Charlene cackled. "So do the San Adrianites."

"What's that supposed to mean?" I asked, uneasy. I'd figured *someone* would be at the maze today—a guard or someone doing repairs to the sign or the shattered throne.

"It means if anyone tries anything today," she said, "they'll be in for a nasty surprise."

Uh-oh.

"Don't you think this rivalry between San Nicholas and San Adrian is getting out of hand?" Takako asked gently.

"Yes," I said.

"No," Charlene said.

"Maybe if everyone talked it out," Takako said, "you'd be able to resolve this peacefully."

"Maybe pigs will fly," Charlene said. "This is San Adrian we're talking about. They're pure evil."

"That sounds like demonization of the other," Takako said.

Charlene made a screeching right turn onto the dirt road leading to the maze. "That sounds like anthropology talk."

"I had to take a few psych classes for my degree," Takako admitted, clutching her seat belt. "And I can't help noticing that a lot of the plotting against San Adrian has happened in Pie Town."

"You heard that?" Charlene asked. "I hope no one from San Adrian did."

"What did you hear?" I asked. What were they up to now?

"And," Takako said, "that reflects badly on Pie Town and Val. She doesn't want to get drawn into a scandal. She may even be liable."

"Takako's not wrong," I said. "I mean, I don't know about liable, but we do need to get along."

"How?" Charlene asked. "This is San Adrian we're talking about."

"Their pumpkin festival isn't going away." I adjusted the collar on my turtleneck sweater.

The Jeep hit a pothole, and I jounced in my seat.

We pulled into the empty parking lot. Charlene whizzed around the black barn and parked behind an outbuilding.

My piecrust specialist stepped from the Jeep and waved her arms. "It's us, the Baker Street Bakers," Charlene shouted. She slid the cat from her shoulder and cradled it in her arms.

The cornstalks rustled.

"Are you sure there are guards out there?" I extricated myself from the car and laid Frederick on its warm hood.

"Guards? Oh, right. Yes," Charlene said, pressing a finger to her nose. "They're out there."

Takako eyed her askance.

"What's *that* supposed to mean?" I said slowly. "Are they hidden or something?"

Charlene studied the graying sky. "Well, guards wouldn't be much good if everyone could see them, would they?"

I gave up. "Let's try the barn."

"Hold on." Charlene adjusted Frederick around her neck. "You don't know the passcode."

"Passcode?" Takako raised a brow.

Charlene strode to the barn's rear door and rapped out a shave-and-a-haircut.

The wooden door cracked open.

Joy peered out. "Who goes there?" she said in her flat voice.

"Baker Street Bakers," Charlene said. "And associate members."

The door widened, and Joy let us inside. A comic book dangled from her hand. "You're not on duty yet," she said. "Is something up?"

"You tell me," Charlene said. "All quiet here?"

Joy nodded. "So far."

"Everyone's in place?" Charlene asked.

"Yes."

"And we're fully supplied?" Charlene asked.

"We are," Joy said.

"Supplied for what?" I looked around the cavernous barn. Orange twinkle lights provided the only illumination.

Heidi emerged from behind a bookcase filled with T-shirts and pumpkin knickknacks. "Is everything all right?" She caught my gaze, and her eyes narrowed to slits. Heidi folded her arms over her green yoga jacket.

"Oh. Hi, Heidi." I scuffed my feet on the straw-covered floor. "You look nice today."

"What's that supposed to mean?" Heidi flipped her blond ponytail over one shoulder. "You know, don't you?"

"Know what?" I asked.

Charlene nudged me. "Sweet-talking her isn't going to work," she whispered loudly enough for everyone in the barn to hear. "Not when she's just been dumped."

Embarrassment bubbled up from my chest. I remembered how it had felt when my engagement went kablooey. "Er . . . we're trying to figure out who shot the cannon at me last night."

Heidi's nostrils whitened. "And you assumed I did."

"No," I said.

"Why is everything always my fault?" she asked, shrill.

"I didn't say that, but if it wasn't one of the workers—"

"If!"

"Val could have been killed," Joy said flatly.

Heidi's jaw worked. "Ohmygawd, okay! What do you want to know?"

"You know Elon Levant," I said, "right?"

"He's a member of my gym."

"Did he stop by the maze last night?"

The two women shook their heads.

"What about Kara's cousin, Denise?"

"Our sponsor?" Heidi asked. "She knows she doesn't need a ticket."

"But was she here?" I persisted.

"I didn't see her," Joy said.

"And you were here," Charlene said, "inside the barn the whole time?"

"If by the *whole time*," Joy said, "you mean from six-thirty last night until past closing, yes. I came straight from my comic book store."

"What about you, Heidi?" I asked. "Did you see her?"

The gym owner's forehead wrinkled. "A car drove past

and around the other side of the barn as I was getting in my car. But I didn't get a good look. It had its high beams on, and I figured it was Mrs. Scala, coming to pick up her husband."

"Did you see its headlights go up the road to the cannon?" I asked.

Her eyebrows gathered inward. "No. It must have parked behind the barn. But why would she do that?"

Why, indeed, with a perfectly good parking lot nearby? Why, for that matter, had Charlene parked behind the barn? Who were we hiding from? "What time was this?" I asked, my heart rate speeding.

"Around a quarter to ten."

"What time were you fired on?" Charlene asked me.

"Ten o'clock, to the minute. What about Alfreda from the optometry office?"

Heidi shook her head. "Oh, it couldn't have been Alfreda."

"Why not?" I asked.

"Because her car was in front of mine." Heidi rolled her eyes. "We left the parking lot at the same time."

I frowned. My ticket had been time-stamped 9:32. Alfreda had left the barn right after that. She *could* have spent thirteen minutes futzing around in the parking lot at her car, but it seemed like a long time. But we were talking in generalities—Heidi wasn't sure exactly what time she'd left.

"And you're certain it was Alfreda's car?" Charlene asked.

The gym owner huffed. "I saw her get into it—a dark Honda Accord. I followed Alfreda onto the highway and into San Nicholas. She's a slow driver. I think she has night-vision problems. I've told her about the importance of vitamin A, but will she listen? It's like talking to you about poisoning the town with all that sugar."

For Pete's sake. "I am not poisoning—"

Something scuttled across the barn roof, and we glanced up.

"It's only raccoons." Joy grimaced. "The waiting is putting us all on edge."

"Waiting?" Takako asked.

"For the attack," Joy said. "San Adrian."

Charlene glared at Joy. "Loose lips sink ships."

"Aren't we all on the same side?" Joy asked.

I squinted at Charlene. "I'm starting to think we're not."

Gently, Charlene laid Frederick on the counter. "Best if we leave him here, until whatever happens, happens." She pointed at the white cat. "Stay."

His eyes didn't open.

Takako touched my arm. "I'm sure San Adrian won't do anything."

"I hope you're right." Heidi brushed a fleck of dust off her sleeve. "But people justify all sorts of atrocities."

"Sugar is not an atrocity," I said heatedly. "There is nothing wrong with an occasional slice of pie."

Heidi tossed her ponytail. "In *your* opinion."

"Is Mr. Scala here?" I asked.

"He's guarding the cannon," Heidi said.

"Thanks," I snapped.

"You're not welcome," Heidi said.

"Let's go find Mr. Scala." Takako steered Charlene and I from the barn.

We walked up the coiling, dirt road toward the cannon.

"At least you've cleared Alfreda," Takako said cheerfully.

"That leaves Elon and Denise," Charlene said. "Though there's always the X factor."

"The X factor?" Takako asked.

"The unknown element," Charlene said.

"Speaking of which . . ." Takako turned to me. "You've been quiet today. Is something bothering you?"

Charlene snorted. "Gotta be man trouble."

"Why do you say that?" Takako asked.

"At her age?" Charlene jerked a thumb toward me. "It's always man trouble."

"I guess I am a little concerned about Gordon," I admitted.

"Ha! Told you so," Charlene said.

"What's wrong?" Takako asked.

My stomach wriggled. "He's really frustrated that he's off the case. It helps that we've been feeding him the info we find. . . ." And he'd been feeding himself pie. . . .

"But what?" Takako prompted.

"Gordon keeps telling me it will be fine," I continued, "but I've never seen him so obsessed about a case. It worries me. Then I feel guilty for worrying about us, when Gordon has real problems." Like his parents. Why hadn't he called? Had something horrible happened?

"You worry a lot, don't you?" Takako asked.

"It's a hobby."

She looked down at her black boots. "I guess I can see why, after everything . . ." Her head came up. "Val, there's something I need to talk to you about."

"Sure. What's up?"

She opened her mouth and shut it. Bit her bottom lip. "What's really happening with you and Gordon?"

Okay, that wasn't what I'd expected. But it did feel better getting it out in the open. "Gordon made a comment about us not seeing each other often enough. His job has crazy hours."

"So does yours," she said.

"Yeah. I mean, our relationship seems to be working. *I* think it's working. But I thought things were working with my last boyfriend too."

"The one who dumped her at the altar," Charlene said.

Not helpful! "I wasn't at the— Will you stop saying that? I'm second-guessing myself enough."

"Hmm." Takako's brow furrowed. "There's something I should tell you about Frank—"

"Let's not talk about my dad. I'm aggravated enough today."

Takako's mouth crimped. She nodded.

We wandered past waving corn and rounded a bend to the cannon. The fire truck stood alone. Its cannon aimed toward the cornfield stretching to the highway.

Charlene cupped her hands around her mouth and hallooed. "Petros! You here?"

Mr. Scala, in jeans and a thick jacket, emerged from the cornfield. "Keep it down, will you?"

"You keep it down," Charlene muttered.

"We'll all keep it down." I rolled my eyes and asked if he'd seen any of our suspects at the maze that night.

"Nope," he said.

"Well, thanks anyway." I turned to go.

He grasped my arm. "Wait," he whispered. "Did you hear that?"

My scalp prickled. "Hear what?"

"I don't hear anything," Takako said.

Charlene scanned the empty road. "Petros is right. It's quiet." She lowered her chin. "*Too* quiet. Quick, into the corn."

I blinked rapidly. "What—"

Prodding us from behind, Charlene and Mr. Scala shuffled Takako and me into the cornfield.

"Get down," Mr. Petros hissed.

I squatted beside a straw basket of miniature pumpkins. And in spite of the ridiculousness of the situation, my heart was thumping, my breath loud in my ears.

Then I heard it too—stealthy footfalls, the gentle crunch of boots on dry earth.

Mr. Scala backed farther into the corn. He drew a red handkerchief from his jacket pocket.

On the road, a group of unfamiliar men and women crept toward the pumpkin cannon.

Mr. Scala threw his handkerchief high above the corn. "Now!"

Miniature pumpkins whizzed through the air. San Nicholas farmers stormed, shouting, from the field.

I grasped Charlene's hand.

She jerked free. "No time for that. Stay sharp!"

I glared at Charlene. "Couldn't you have armed yourselves with something less dangerous? Like, I don't know, throwing axes?"

"We could have," she said speculatively. "But we really needed to get rid of these extra pumpkins. Waste not, want not."

I looked helplessly to my stepmother.

"Val, there's something I need to tell you," Takako said.

A pumpkin whizzed over my head, and I ducked. "Now?"

"You need to know. This affects you. You, Gordon . . ."

"Did you learn something about the murder?"

"No, I did the math. It is my fault Frank left you."

My brain froze. "What?"

Charlene reached into the bin of pumpkins and hurled one into the melee.

"You said you were three when he left," Takako said. "You're twenty-eight, right?"

"Yes."

"Doran's twenty-six."

"Okay, what does that . . . Oh." Doran was two years younger than me, and that meant Frank had been seeing Takako while he'd been married to my mother.

I swayed, heat flushing from my chest to the top of my skull. Why hadn't I asked Doran how old he was? Or had he told me and I hadn't listened, because I hadn't wanted to know the truth?

Now I couldn't avoid it. Nausea spiraled up from my gut at my willful blindness.

It wasn't like I'd ever thought my father was exactly a good guy. He wasn't the devil, but he was more flawed than the average man.

A pumpkin thudded to the ground beside me, and I flinched.

The newcomers fell back beneath the barrage of mini-pumpkins. "Counterattack!" one shouted.

Minipumpkins pelted the cornfield. One slammed into my shoulder. Hot pain shot down my arm. I lurched backward, biting back a shout.

Takako caught me before I could fall.

"Take cover!" Charlene bellowed, grabbing pumpkins from the basket and piling them in her arms. Hooting, she raced into the road.

Takako flung herself on top of me. We tumbled to the soft earth.

"Oof." I gasped, the wind knocked from me. Takako didn't weigh much, but I hadn't been expecting the fall.

Tiny pumpkins thumped to the nearby ground. Shouts and curses echoed across the dirt road.

I couldn't think about Frank right now. "Someone's going to get hurt," I shouted. This was out of control.

I wriggled from beneath my stepmother.

She grasped my arms. "Val. Say something."

"It's okay." It had to be okay, because I couldn't deal with more revelations. "But now we need to stop this."

"I'll help."

Charlene stood atop the old fire engine. She pitched pumpkins like a baseball star, one leg raised in the windup.

"She'll fall and break a hip." I hurried from the corn.

A minipumpkin struck me in the lower back.

I staggered, grabbing the fire engine's brass railing. "Charlene, get down!"

She hooted, brandishing pumpkins. "I haven't had this much fun since our pie-tin UFO invasion!" A pumpkin whizzed past her left ear. Charlene ducked, wobbling on the fire truck.

My heart clenched. I grabbed for her and missed.

She straightened. "Whoa. Close one."

"Charlene," I said, "these are terrible battle tactics. You're exposed out in the open."

Pain exploded across one side of my face. I gasped, my knees striking the ground. Tears dampened my eyes.

"Val," Charlene shouted. "Woman down! Cease fire!"

One hand braced on the dirt, I touched the side of my head. I didn't feel blood, and I was still conscious. The pumpkin must have grazed me. But ow. *Ow!*

"Val?" Charlene touched my shoulder. "Are you okay?"

Experimentally, I wiggled my jaw. "It's all fun and games until someone gets hit with a pumpkin." I sat back on my heels.

"In fairness," Charlene said, "it was only a minipumpkin. But that must have smarted."

I took stock of the situation. The San Adrianites had

vanished. The defending farmers raised pumpkins in their fists and cheered.

I brushed at the dirt on my sweater and vest, but it was hopeless. I should have known to wear dark clothes when with Charlene. "Where's Takako?"

"Your stepmother?" Charlene scanned the area. "Still taking cover in the corn, I expect."

"I hope she wasn't hurt," I fretted. Bracing one hand on the cool metal side of the fire engine, I stood. "Takako?"

I walked to the edge of the cornfield and peered in. "Takako?" I brushed past the drying stalks. The basket of pumpkins lay overturned, tiny orange gourds scattered across the dirt. "This is where we were hiding," I muttered. "I'm sure of it." So, where was she?

Charlene followed as I pushed deeper into the field.

"Takako?" I called. "Are you all right?"

"Try her phone," Charlene said. "Maybe she ran deeper into the field and got lost."

I dialed. My call went to voice mail.

"She's not answering," I said.

"Reception's poor here," Charlene said. "It's probably nothing."

My mouth went dry. "But where *is* she?" I returned to the road and searched the charcoal horizon.

Petros ambled to my side and brushed off his hands. "You okay?"

"Have you seen my stepmother?" I asked.

"She was . . ." He turned in place and frowned. "She was next to me during the fight." He waved toward a gray-haired woman collecting miniature pumpkins in the road. "Hey! You see Val's stepmother? Asian woman about yea high?" He held one hand at chest level.

She shook her head. "I thought she was with San Adrian."

I sucked in a breath. "You didn't hit her with a pumpkin, did you?"

"No," she said, indignant. "She was unarmed, even if she was on the wrong side."

"She wasn't—"

Charlene clapped her hand on my shoulder. "We'll find her."

In the end, we organized a search party. The farmers walked through the cornfield shouting Takako's name.

But Takako was gone.

Chapter Twenty-Seven

The cornfield rustled in a bitter Pacific breeze. A door in the black barn creaked eerily in response. It slammed. Creaked. Slammed. Creaked.

My teeth clenched. I strode to the rear of the barn—the only spot I could find cell reception—and I leaned against the door. Charlene's Jeep sat parked beside an old tire. Hidden somewhere nearby, a generator rumbled.

I checked the glowing clock on my phone. Five-thirty. We'd spent over an hour combing the cornfields for Takako. Charlene had even brought out her rotting pumpkin drone for an aerial search.

Dread squeezing my lungs, I called my brother.

"Hey, Val. What's up?"

I looked skyward. Sunset had turned the western sky a magnificent tangerine streaked with blackberry clouds. "Um, have you heard from your mother?"

"No. Why? Has she done something? I told her to give you some space."

"No, she's . . . she's missing."

There was a long silence.

His voice rose. "What do you mean she's missing?"

"We were at the corn maze—"

"Isn't that closed today?"

I paced the dirt. "Yes, but we wanted to talk to some people—"

The door behind me banged.

"Talk?" Doran asked. "Don't tell me she got involved in one of your investigations."

I winced. "She might have tagged along. We were only talking to people!" But that was a lie. We'd been talking to murder suspects, and whatever had happened to Takako was my fault. I took a deep breath. "And then San Adrian attacked with pumpkins—"

"What?"

"Minipumpkins. There was a battle."

"Are you kidding me?"

"I think they'd come to sabotage the cannon or something. Anyway, when the dust cleared, your mother was gone. We searched the cornfield—"

"What do you mean 'gone'?" he asked, his tone ominous.

"We can't find her, and she's not answering her phone."

"Well, look again!"

The barn door banged, and I returned to lean against it.

"We are looking," I said. On the nearby hillside, lights bobbed in the cornfield. "I think—"

"Hold on." He paused. "A text just came through from Mom. . . . It says she'll return to the hotel late tonight."

My shoulders collapsed with relief. "Thank God. Where is she?"

"Wait a sec. I'll ask."

I waited.

"She's not responding. She never was one for texts though. So, thanks for panicking me over nothing."

"Sorry," I muttered.

He chuckled. "Don't feel bad. My mother makes me crazy too. I'll talk to you later."

The door bumped beneath my weight, and I jerked forward. Charlene emerged from the barn.

"Okay," I said to Doran. "Bye."

We hung up.

"What?" Charlene pulled Frederick to her chest. The purring cat hung limp over the arm of her yellow knit jacket, his eyes shut. "What did he say?"

"Takako texted him. She's okay. She'll be late returning to the hotel." *But how was she getting there?* I pursed my lips, doubt quivering in my gut. We'd come to the corn maze in Charlene's Jeep. It was a longish walk back to Takako's hotel and along a poorly lit highway with no sidewalks.

"That can't be right," Charlene said. "Takako doesn't text."

"How do you know?"

"We talked about modern technology over my special root beer. She says she hates texting. Only does it in emergencies."

We stared at each other.

"I'm going to try calling her again." I dialed my stepmother.

No answer. And since Takako's voice mail box was full, I couldn't leave a message.

Charlene's brow furrowed. "All right. I'm going to call off the search here. You keep dialing." She strode down the dirt road.

Bracing myself against the barn door, I phoned again. It was probably nothing. There had to be a reasonable explanation for her disappearance. So why did I feel so worried and . . . guilty?

The door shoved against me, and I leapt away.

Joy emerged from the barn. A faint line creased the spot between her brows, but I might have been imagining it in the dim light. "Any luck?"

I shook my head. "She sent a text to Doran saying she'd be back late, but I don't understand how. She came here in our car."

She nodded. "That leaves two possibilities. Uber or San Adrian."

"Yeah, if that crew hadn't come here to do whatever, this never would have happened—"

"No, I mean San Adrian might have her."

I blinked. "What?"

"Maybe I've been reading too many of my own comics, but think about it. They disappeared, and so did she. She might have sent that text under duress."

"But kidnapping?" I took a step backward and my thigh nudged the Jeep's fender. "That seems a little extreme." But one of the pumpkin cannon defenders *had* said she'd seen Takako with the San Adrian crew.

Charlene rounded the corner of the barn. "Kidnapping?"

"It's one explanation." Joy shifted her scarf.

Charlene adjusted Frederick in an unconscious imitation of Joy. "I'm afraid she may be right, Val. Something's off."

"This is—" I sputtered. "They have to know kidnapping's not a prank—it's a felony." But where *was* Takako?

The phone vibrated in my hand. I started and looked at the screen. "It's Takako." I sagged against the door, my muscles turning liquid. We'd—*I'd* been freaking myself out over nothing.

"Takako! Where are you?" I put the phone on speaker.

Charlene leaned closer, head cocked.

"I'm with some friends from San Adrian," Takako said carefully.

My stomach bottomed. *No.* Joy and Charlene had been right. She'd been taken. "Are you okay?" I whispered.

"Of course. They want me to tell you not to call the police. They're quite insistent on that."

My heart thudded in my ears. "Are they listening now?"

"You know my phone. I always have it turned to the loudest setting. I'm sure everyone can hear."

"What about my *boyfriend?*" I asked. The San Adrianites wouldn't know I was dating a cop.

She sighed. "Oh, Val. It's so obvious what's going on."

"It is?" I glanced at Charlene.

She shrugged and shook her head.

"Don't let your father do to you what he did to me," Takako said. "I haven't been able to trust myself or anyone else since he left. I buried myself in work, because I was on solid ground there. At work I could be confident and whole. But there's more to life than work. Don't make my mistake."

"My father?" My father was a criminal. Was this a code? Was Takako surrounded by the pumpkin mafia? I gripped the phone more tightly. "So, you think I *should* talk to Gordon?"

"Absolutely. Clear communication is critical in a relationship. If he's worth it, he'll understand where you're coming from. And if you're worth it, you'll be brave. I think you are worth it."

A bitter wind whipped across the highway from the Pacific, rippling the corn.

So . . . *be brave?* Did that mean it was up to me to rescue Takako? My stepmother won points for cryptic, that was for sure. "Okay," I said. "I'll talk to my *boyfriend.*"

"Good. You'll hear from me again soon." She hung up.

Charlene whistled. "She's good."

Joy frowned. "Sorry, but I didn't understand that bit about your father. I thought he wasn't around when you were growing up."

"Exactly," Charlene said. "He abandoned Val and her

mother, and Doran and Takako. That's what he did to them both."

"Oh," Joy said in a monotone. "That will do a number on a girl's confidence with men."

"My confidence is fine," I said. "We—"

"Sure, at Pie Town." Charlene arched a snowy brow. "But don't you wonder why you fill every waking hour with something or someone? You need to spend more time just *being*."

My gaze flicked skyward. Takako had been kidnapped, and they picked *now* to psychoanalyze me? "Charlene, we talked about this. You know you're not supposed to buy any more of those self-help books."

"I *didn't* buy any more," Charlene said. "I checked one out from the library."

"But she may have a point," Joy said. "Pie Town does sometimes seem like a shield for you. I mean, I don't work thirteen-hour days at my comic shop."

"You don't have to start baking at five," I snapped. "I'm calling Gordon."

Joy shook her head. "I'm not sure that's such a good idea."

"She said not to get the bacon involved," Charlene said.

Ignoring them, I called Gordon.

"Val." His voice rumbled through me. "What's going on?"

"Takako's been kidnapped. I think." I explained our conversation, leaving out the weird bit about my work-life issues.

Gordon was silent for a long time. A wisp of fog swept above us. It billowed toward the low hills.

"Are you sure that's what you heard?" he asked.

"No," Charlene shouted into the phone. "She left out the bit about turning into a workaholic."

"Workaholic?" he said.

"Over her daddy issues," she yelled.

"What daddy issues?" Gordon asked.

Biting back a curse, I told him the rest. "So?" I asked, anxious. "What do you think?"

"Well, I knew about your father," he said. "And then after what happened with your ex, it's little wonder if you're feeling self-doubt. That's why we've been taking things slow. I guess I didn't get that was why you've been burying yourself in work."

Unimportant! "Takako's being held hostage!"

"There's no real evidence of that," he said. "She texted Doran and said she'd be late. She told you she was fine—"

"She told us not to call the police."

"That is strange," he said, "but it could be innocent."

"How?" I asked. "How can it be innocent?"

"If she hasn't been kidnapped, there's no reason to call the cops. Look, I believe you, but the SNPD isn't going to mobilize without more evidence. Your stepmother's an adult, and she said she's safe. I can't believe any prankster from San Adrian would actually harm her. Can you?"

When he put it all rationally and everything . . . Heat suffused my face. "No," I said, a trifle sullenly.

"All right," he said. "I'm about an hour outside San Nicholas. Can you meet me at Charlene's?"

"Meet you at Charlene's," I said for her benefit.

She shook her head. "Tell him to meet us at Marla's."

"Er, can you meet us at Marla's instead?" I asked.

"No problem."

"Then what?" I asked.

"Then we solve your stepmother problem. Together."

Chapter Twenty-Eight

We sped down the darkening highway. Charlene whipped the Jeep left, into a neighborhood of Victorians and wind-swept cypresses.

For once, I didn't mind feeling like I was in a high-speed chase. I leaned forward in my seat, Frederick snoozing in my lap. "Charlene?" I said.

"Yes?"

"Takako told me something, right before she disappeared."

Charlene cut a quick glance at me.

"She said . . . she thinks she's the reason my father left us."

"Makes sense. Your brother's only two years younger than you, and your father left when you were three. I did the math."

Why was I the only person who hadn't bothered to do the math? I really needed to get over this fear and loathing of numbers.

"But," Charlene continued, "at least that explains what she wants. Forgiveness."

"There's nothing to forgive. It was years ago, and she said she didn't know about me."

The Jeep flew through a pothole, and we bounced in our seats.

"Val," she said kindly, "you're a good person, and that's exactly the right thing to say. So why don't I believe you?"

"I don't—" I blew out my breath. Okay. I *was* pissed. It wasn't fair. It wasn't rational. But there it was. And now I felt ashamed of my thoughts and grateful to Charlene all at the same time. It was really uncomfortable.

"It's okay to be upset. And we both know you'll feel better when you're able to let go of it."

Right. She was right.

Victorians blurred past the window, or maybe it was my vision that had blurred. Because I *would* get over it. Friends like Charlene, the people I loved, made dealing with life's craziness easier.

I changed the subject. "Why meet Gordon at Marla's?"

"After talking to Mrs. Thistleblossom, I've realized I need to be more patient with old people."

Uh-huh. Never mind that she and Marla had gone to school together.

"It's hard to believe," she continued, "but someday I'll get old like Marla. I know you've been resisting the idea, but it's time to make her an associate Baker Street Baker."

I swiveled my head to stare at her wrinkled profile. *I'd* been resisting? "Well, yes. But I didn't mean we should induct her on the night my stepmother's gone missing."

"Also, my computer's on the fritz, and yours is too slow."

"And you think Marla will let us use hers?"

"If she wants to be an associate Baker Street Baker, she will."

We flew past porch steps dotted with pumpkins. Turning on a cliffside road, the Jeep screeched to a halt at Marla's iron front gate.

Charlene rolled down her window and leaned out. She pushed the yellow intercom button.

The metal box crackled. Marla's voice floated through the aether. "Yes?"

"It's Charlene and Val. Let us in."

"Why on earth would I do that?"

"Adventure," Charlene shouted, pumping her fist in the air.

There was a lengthy silence.

I leaned across Charlene. "We'd like to make you an associate Baker Street Baker."

"In other words," Marla purred, "you need me."

Charlene bridled. "We didn't say—"

I nudged my friend. "Yes. May we come in?"

The iron gate creaked open.

"We don't *need* her," Charlene said. "We're doing Marla a favor."

"We can't let her know that, not if we need her computer."

We drove down the winding, flagstone drive. Charlene parked in front of Marla's storybook-style house, complete with turret. Its diamond-paned windows shone, warm with light. A pyramid of multihued pumpkins was stacked neatly on the doorstep.

Grumbling, Charlene followed me to the front door, carved in a peacock design.

A gust of wind swayed the nearby cypress trees.

I shivered, huddling beneath the eaves of the slate roof.

A shadow darkened the peephole, framed by an all-seeing eye. The door creaked open.

Marla braced her hand on the frame, blocking our entry. She looked us up and down and jerked her chin toward Charlene's living stole. "That cat makes a better detective than you two."

Turning on the heels of her elegant sandals, she strode into the high-ceilinged foyer. Marla's wide-legged white slacks swished in her wake. Her gold and diamond bling glittered against her blue-and-white striped shirt.

Feeling inelegant in my dust-covered turtleneck and beigey vest, I followed.

Charlene slammed shut the door.

Marla paused beside a bouquet of flowers atop a polished round table. She folded her arms. "So. You lost your stepmother."

My jaw slackened. "How did you know that?"

Gripping the gilt railing, Charlene sat on the curving staircase. "All of San Nicholas must know about the kidnapping by now." She scratched her ankle, wrinkling the fabric of her orange knit leggings.

Marla tapped a finger on her chin. "I suppose the kidnapping was inevitable. What do you expect when you let a rank amateur into your investigation?"

"You're saying this was our fault?" Charlene growled.

"Yes."

Charlene's shoulders dropped. "You're probably right."

"Probably?" Marla paced the foyer. "The question is, was she taken by the San Adrians, or by the killer?"

I started. "The killer? No. No way. Why would a killer take my stepmother?"

"I suppose it depends on how insane that receptionist, Alfreda, is."

"She's an office manager," Charlene said tartly. "Are you saying Alfreda kidnapped Takako? Why?"

Marla shot her a look that could have curdled milk. "Do you not know the meaning of the word *insane*?"

"Why do you think Alfreda's crazy?" I asked. Takako had said she was with people from San Adrian, but I wanted to know where Marla was heading with this.

Marla lifted a silvery brow. "Have you seen her nutty paperweight collection?"

"Have you?" I asked, suspicious.

"I was collecting for charity yesterday," Marla said loftily, "and she invited me inside."

Uh-huh. Marla had been amateur detecting. "Lots of people collect things," I said. "It might make them obsessive or quirky, but it doesn't make them nuts. Besides, Alfreda couldn't have kidnapped Takako."

Marla paced, her heels clicking on the foyer tiles. "Trust me, I know crazy. The way Alfreda looked, the way she talked. When I saw her last, Alfreda was . . . vibrating with some intense emotion."

"There was no way she could have lobbed a pumpkin bomb at me last night," I said.

"Pumpkin bomb?" Marla asked.

I explained about the attack in the maze. "It had to be someone else."

"Like Kara's poor husband, Elon?" Marla smiled, arch. "I should pay a condolence call on the bereaved widower."

"You can forget about vamping Elon," Charlene said. "That poor man's gone through enough. And he may be a killer. Plus, he's friends with Shaw."

Marla sniffed. "Shaw's not that bad. You just need to know how to handle him."

"Does Elon handle him?" I asked.

She sighed. "That's not Elon's style."

"And what is his style?" I asked.

"That will be interesting to see," Marla said. "Everyone knows he chafed under Kara's authoritarian rule. I wonder who he'll become now that she's gone?"

I shifted uneasily. "Elon has motive, means, and opportunity. If Shaw hasn't been ignoring him as a suspect out of friendship or obligation, then why?"

"Maybe because Elon didn't kill his wife and Tristan Cannon," Marla said. "Shaw knows Elon doesn't have it in him. It would be like Detective Carmichael arresting you."

"You're saying Shaw's instincts are *good?*" Charlene asked.

"Even a stopped clock is right twice a day," Marla said.

The two women laughed, sobered, glared at each other.

"What a day," Charlene grumbled. "First I have to make nice with Thistleblossom, and now this."

Marla straightened. "Thistleblossom?"

"Val's setting up a volunteer brigade to help her with housekeeping."

"That old witch?" Marla's face sagged. "Why?"

"Because she needs help," I said.

"She was putting the whammy on Val!"

"It was nothing," I said.

"Don't underestimate the woman. Once she caught me sneaking out with Reginald Philpott and told my parents." Marla's hands fisted. "I was grounded for a month. And then he started dating Rhonda Pratt. The two got married, and he became a millionaire. They've got a house in Malibu."

"But never mind," Charlene said, "because you've moved on."

"After I went to all that trouble at the pie—" Marla snapped her jaw shut.

"The pie what?" I asked. "Were *you* the one who told the judges she was cheating?"

Marla studied the chandelier. "If she'd lost because of you, Pie Town would have been over. The coffee might be terrible, but everyone who's anyone in San Nicholas knows that's the place to be on a weekday morning."

"How'd you—?" Charlene pointed. "You followed us that morning, didn't you?"

"I might have," Marla admitted. "I wanted to know what you were up to!"

"Mrs. Thistleblossom has arthritis," I said. "That's why she's been cheating. She can't bake anymore."

"Well. That's very sad," Marla said. "But how was I to know? And she ruined my eighteenth birthday."

"Reginald was a putz," Charlene said.

"You're right. Reginald is old news." Marla toyed with one of her gold necklaces. "I should get in there and rescue Elon before Denise swoops in."

I stared. "What?"

"Denise is in love with Elon," Marla said. "Didn't you know?"

"You're making that up," Charlene said.

Marla fluffed her platinum hair. "Hardly. I've seen the way she acts around him. She's got it bad."

There *had* been a few things Denise had said. . . . Could Marla be right?

"It's disappointing the way some women can be so smart in one area and so stupid when it comes to love." Marla fiddled with the table's massive bouquet. "That said, I wish I could have invested in Denise's software company. But my financial adviser said it was outside my risk tolerance. I need to stick with more diversified investments, like mutual and index funds." She beheaded a yellow mum.

"Also," Charlene said, "you're—"

"Fascinating," I said, before Charlene could remind her best frenemy she was also broke. "What else do you know about Denise's software company?"

"Only what she told us at her presentation at my Daughters of Western Pioneers chapter." Marla drew a yellow rose from the bouquet and inhaled. "Nearly everyone invested, we were so impressed."

"Daughters of Pioneers?" I asked. "That's a thing?"

"Western Pioneers," Marla corrected.

"A bunch of bored blue-hairs," Charlene said.

Frederick yawned his distaste.

"It's a networking group," Marla said. "There are thirty women in my Silicon Valley chapter alone."

"What do you need to network?" Charlene asked.

"As a businesswoman—"

"Ha!" Charlene sneered.

"Can we borrow your computer?" I asked. "There's something we'd like to look up."

"Fine," Marla said. "But everything is password protected, so don't even try to order off my accounts."

I followed her into a palatial kitchen. Tuscan floor tiles, marble counters, brushed-nickel fixtures. She pointed to a laptop at the wide bar beside a pink box from Pie Town. "Have at it."

"Thanks." I slid onto a cushioned barstool and stared at the glowing screen. I'd thought Charlene would follow me. After all, using Marla's computer had been her idea. My breath quickened. Charlene had rifled Marla's closets in the past. Was my piecrust maker using me as some sort of diversion?

Does Bigfoot live in the woods?

But I had to keep up appearances, so I opened up the Web site for Denise's company. It hadn't changed since the last time I'd looked. Ophthalmology software. Close corporation. Blah, blah blah.

I stared at the sliding glass doors. The ocean had deepened to cobalt, stars blotted out by the fog bank. I sneaked a peek inside the pink box. Mmm. Strawberry rhubarb.

Rising, I got a fork from a drawer and dug in. My stepmother had been kidnapped. I deserved comfort food. And stress eating gets a bad rap.

I had no idea what a close corporation was, and since Charlene and Marla still hadn't come to the kitchen, I looked that up.

As far as I could tell, it was a relaxed form of corporation, without all the rules of regular corporations. Designed for smaller businesses, it was limited to thirty-five stockholders. Maybe I could incorporate Pie Town someday to raise funds? Alfreda had said she'd had experience with—

Gordon strode into the kitchen. Grinning, he leaned one hip against the gold-flecked, stone counter. "So." He wore the navy suit that made him look like a sharp TV detective.

I leapt from my stool. "You're here. I've been going crazy."

"Never." Wrapping his arms around me, he pulled me against his chest and kissed me.

When we'd untangled ourselves and I'd gotten my breathing under control, he licked his lips. "Strawberry rhubarb?"

I angled my head toward the open box. "Marla's. I'll get her a new one."

"In that case . . ." He grabbed a fork and dug in.

"I'm worried about Takako," I said, "and about you."

"Me?" he mumbled through a mouthful of pie.

"Gordon, I know what it's like to watch your parents, the people you love the most, failing. I took care of my mother when she was sick. But"—I swallowed—"my mother's breast cancer was diagnosed too late. I only took care of her for a few months. This has been going on with your parents for much longer."

He grimaced, swallowed, put down the fork. "They're my parents," he said simply. "What am I going to do?"

"I don't know how or if it's appropriate for me to help.

But tell me. I'm here for you for whatever, even if it's just leaving you alone so you can get some sleep."

"I know you are. I don't know how . . . I don't know what I need right now. Or what my parents need. I can't help them the way they need. For the past week, it's felt like I can't help anyone."

His parents. The murder. His uncle. Shaw. It was a wonder Gordon had stayed as even-keeled as he had. "You are helping."

"Then let me do something for you." He pulled his phone from the inside pocket of his suit jacket.

"Hey, you're back in uniform."

He raised a brow. "I'm a detective. I don't wear uniforms."

"You know what I mean. The suit. Where were you?"

"I had to talk to a lawyer about the case." He dialed. "It's Detective Carmichael. Put her on the line." He handed me the phone.

"Hello?" I said.

"Val?" Takako said in an annoyed tone. "I told you not to call the police!"

Chapter Twenty-Nine

"Hey!" Takako shouted.

A crash, a scuffle on the other end of the line.

I gripped the edge of Marla's marble counter. "Takako? Are you okay? Takako!"

Outside the sliding glass doors, the waning moon slipped between a gap in the oncoming fog. Its reflection glinted, bright, on the ocean, and vanished.

Marla and Charlene hurried into the kitchen.

"For God's sake," a man's voice graveled over the phone. "You didn't call the cops, did you? We didn't take her! We don't want her!"

"Who is this?" I asked.

"Farmer John. Who's this?"

Farmer John? He really called himself that? I glanced at Gordon. "Val Harris."

"She jumped into one of our cars," the farmer said rapidly. "In the chaos, we didn't even realize . . . Look, take her back, will you?"

"Take her?" I shook myself. Why was I arguing? It had all been a mistake. This was wonderful news.

Suspiciously wonderful.

I raised my voice. "What do you mean take her back?"

"She's driving us nuts. We'll stop harassing your festival if you stop interfering with ours. It's what you want, isn't it?"

"We don't negotiate with terrorists," Charlene hollered into the phone.

Marla folded her arms over her striped top. "I hate to agree with Charlene, but I agree."

"I heard that," he shouted back. "That *woman's* the terrorist! She won't leave us alone."

I stuck a finger in my ear and walked to the glass doors. Somewhere beyond them the ocean crashed, but all I could see was my bemused reflection in the dark glass. "Okay, what do you want?"

"Weren't you listening? We want you to take her away."

"Fine," I said. "But where? Where are you?"

"Wherever you want us to be, lady."

"Can you bring her back to the corn maze?"

"We're on our way now. You'll be there, right?" he asked, his voice strained. "You'll take her off our hands?"

"I'll be there. How far away are you?"

"Forty minutes."

"We'll see you then." I hung up.

Gordon's mouth twitched.

I pointed an accusing finger at him. "You knew." Drat his sexy cop smarts.

"I made some calls after I got off the phone with you," he admitted.

"You did?" I asked, my heart swelling. He'd taken it seriously. He'd taken *me* seriously.

"You didn't think I'd ignore a possible kidnapping?"

"*Possible* kidnapping?" Charlene asked. "What do you know?"

"Takako went with the San Adrianites of her own accord," Gordon said.

I gaped. Why the heck would she do that?

"They didn't even realize she was in one of their cars at first," he continued.

"So why didn't she return?" Marla asked.

"Because Val's stepmother is determined to make peace between San Adrian and San Nicholas." Gordon paused and met my gaze. "I'm not sure why she cares so much."

But I thought I knew why. The same reason she'd come here. The same reason she'd stayed so long to get to know me. Atonement. She wanted to make up to me for her role in Frank's departure. And since she couldn't help at Pie Town, and I hadn't really let her help with the investigation, she'd tackled the San Adrian problem. She'd said I might be liable for the plotting that had gone there. Takako must have really believed it. I rubbed the hollow between my collarbones and nodded for him to go on.

"Your stepmother wouldn't leave until the folks from San Adrian would agree to a deal," he finished.

"A deal?" Charlene's brows lowered with suspicion. "What sort of deal?"

He shrugged. "No idea. But my guess is she's succeeded if she's returning now." His emerald eyes twinkled. "So, the hostage release is at the corn maze?"

"It seemed only right they return her from where they took her," I said. "Though I guess they didn't actually *take* her." I checked my watch. "They said they'd be there in forty minutes or so, but—"

"We should get there early," Charlene said, "in case it's an ambush."

"Good thinking." Gordon's lips pressed into a quivering line. He checked his watch. "But there's one thing I've got to do first. I'll meet you there." He bent and kissed my cheek. "*Numquam taediosum,*" he murmured and strode from the kitchen.

The front door snicked open and shut.

"*Numquam taediosum?*" Marla asked. "Are you two speaking in code now? What does that mean?"

"It's Latin for *never boring,*" I said, smiling. As a motto, it wasn't half-bad.

Marla sniffed. "Show-offs." She glanced at the open box. "And who ate my pie?"

"We'll get you another pie." Charlene walked to the arched doorway and turned. "Are you two coming?"

Marla started. "Me?"

"You're an associate Baker Street Baker, aren't you?" Charlene asked, tart as a key lime pie.

"Hmm. What does one wear to a handoff?" Marla puttered from the kitchen.

Charlene folded her arms and leaned against the door frame. "This'll take a while." Around her shoulders, Frederick yawned in agreement.

Twenty anxiety-inducing minutes later, Marla swanned down the spiral staircase. She'd changed into black yoga pants and a sleek, matching jacket. Marla turned in place beside the round table laden with flowers. "What do you think?"

"We've wasted enough time," Charlene growled. "Let's move."

We shuffled out of Marla's beach palace and into the Jeep.

"What is that smell?" Marla asked.

"Victory," Charlene said, handing Frederick over the seat to me.

"No," Marla said, "it definitely doesn't smell like that."

I glanced over my shoulder at the drone in the rear compartment. The pumpkin was molding. Tonight, I swore to myself, Charlene was either getting a new pumpkin, or retiring the drone.

We roared up the drive, lurching to a halt while we

waited for Marla's iron gate to swing open. Then we were off, bulleting down narrow roads and onto the One.

"Don't take this the wrong way," Marla said, "but it's a little disappointing the killer doesn't have Takako. Then we might have wrapped up this case."

"I don't see how," I muttered, annoyed, and tapped my phone's screen.

"The hostage handoff is a distraction from the murder," Marla said. "It may be unintentional, but it's a distraction nonetheless."

"This case has been full of distractions," Charlene said. "The pumpkin war with San Adrian, old lady Thistle-blossom . . ."

I pressed the phone to my ear. The phone rang once, twice.

Alfreda picked up. "Hello?"

"Hi, this is Val Harris."

"Oh! Are you calling about the job?"

I blanked for a moment. *Job?* Oh, right, the job we'd supposedly interviewed her for. "We've got one more question. You mentioned you knew about closed corporations. I checked the companies you worked for, and none were that form. Where did you learn about them?"

There was a long pause. "Why? Are you thinking about incorporating?"

"It's a definite possibility." Because anything's possible, right?

"That's the sort of thing you should talk to a lawyer about," she said.

"Yes, but where—?"

"I really can't talk now." Alfreda hung up.

I frowned at the phone. There was no reason for Alfreda to be cagey about this. Unless . . .

"What was that about?" Charlene asked. "Pull over,

you idiot!" She banged her fist on the horn and swerved around a slow-moving Corvette.

"You were talking to Alfreda," Marla said, "weren't you? I told you she's crazy."

I bit the inside of my cheek. "You know, I think she might be." *Dangerously crazy.*

Chapter Thirty

The Jeep's headlights painted blurry circles on the black barn. Three empty and unfamiliar cars parked in the maze lot. A generator rumbled nearby. The San Adrians had said to meet here. Where were they? Where was Takako?

At the Jeep, I started to hand Frederick to Charlene.

She shook her head. "You keep him for now." She opened its rear door and reached into the compartment.

Marla wrinkled her nose. "Are you sure that cat's still alive? Perhaps that's what I've been smelling."

"You've been smelling my drone." Charlene pulled the wilted jack-o'-lantern drone from the car and sighed. "You should have seen it with a candle inside, flying through the air."

Marla pinched her nose shut. "It's rotting!"

"I don't care what Gordon said." Charlene fiddled with the drone's controls. It buzzed up and into the night. "I don't trust those San Adrianites. This will give us a bird's-eye view of the action."

Cold, damp air rippled the corn, and Marla's head jerked nervously.

I shivered, rubbing the arms of my sweater. Maybe I

should have gone wild and worn a jacket with actual sleeves instead of this vest.

"Where is everybody?" I asked.

The barn's main door rolled open, and Joy emerged.

"Joy!" I hurried to the comic store owner. "Have you seen my stepmother?"

She nodded. "She's fine. They asked me to tell you they're in the corn maze. Take the shortcut." Joy nodded toward the other side of the barn.

"For Pete's sake," I said. "Why the cloak and dagger?"

Joy frowned. "You do remember we live in San Nicholas." She scanned the parking lot. "Where's that other woman?"

"What other woman?" I asked.

"The tall brunette with the big shoulders."

"Alfreda?" I looked toward the highway, my gaze clouding. Ribbons of fog blacked out the stars, a waning moon gliding in and out of the mist and casting eerie shadows. Why would she be here?

"Yeah," Joy said, "that receptionist."

"Office manager," Charlene corrected.

"What's going on?" I asked.

"Alfreda was here earlier," Joy said. "I thought she'd joined your gang."

"It's not a gang," Charlene said. "We're the—"

Marla elbowed Charlene's side. "It's a gang."

The Jeep's headlights flicked off, plunging us into darkness. An uneasy silence fell.

Takako was okay. Joy had seen her, and there was no reason to worry about what the darkness held. But I pressed my arms to my sides.

Charlene coughed. "No worries." She worked the drone's controls on her phone. "This baby's got night vision."

"Let's get a move on," Marla said. "I'm freezing."

"What do you expect wearing that cat suit?" Charlene sniped.

Marla struck a pose. "Everything," she purred.

"Blech." Charlene returned to fiddling with the drone app. "Got 'em."

"Do you see Takako?" I draped Frederick around my neck for warmth and peered over her shoulder.

The phone screen displayed the greenish figures of four people, pacing in the center of the maze. One might have been Takako, but it was impossible to tell from this angle.

"All right," I said. "Let's go."

"It could be a trap." Marla bit her bottom lip. "Maybe I should wait here."

My shoulders tightened. She was leaving us to rescue Takako on our own. "Marla—"

"It's fine," Charlene said, surprising me. "If something goes wrong, it's good to have backup. But we keep the drone. And Frederick."

Marla rolled her eyes and motioned to Joy. "Are there any adult beverages in the barn?"

"There's coffee," Joy said. "And brandy."

"That will do."

"And vodka," Joy said. "I think there's cinnamon whiskey."

Marla linked arms with Joy. "I do like the way you work."

The two women strolled into the black-painted barn and rolled shut the wooden door.

"You knew Marla was going to chicken out," I said.

"A vampire doesn't change its spots." She buttoned the top of her jacket. "Let's rescue your stepmother."

We walked into the corn and down the staff's secret path, straight and narrow as a knife. Dry stalks brushed against our clothes and whispered warnings. Ahead, flashlight beams danced and shifted eerily through the stalks.

"We're getting close," Charlene said in a low voice. "Are you ready?"

"Yes," I said. "We'll be fine."

We emerged in the center of the maze. A folding metal chair had replaced the gilt throne. It sat empty. There was no one here.

"I don't understand. I saw them in the maze." Charlene checked her phone and hissed. "Val, it's a trap. Run! They're—"

A bulky figure emerged from the corn. "About time." A short, middle-aged man aimed his flashlight into my face.

"J—Farmer John?" I raised my hand and squinted. "Do you mind?"

"Whoops." Looking abashed, he lowered the beam. "Sorry. I didn't realize. And yeah, I'm Farmer John." He squinted at me. "Why are you wearing a cat?"

"I'm not wearing—" *Ugh!* I was turning into Charlene. "He's Frederick," I said, as if that explained everything.

His head turtled backward. "Whatever, weirdos."

"You're calling *me* a weirdo?" What was *wrong* with these people? "You kidnapped my stepmother!"

"I told you, we didn't kidnap her." Farmer John rubbed a hand over his square jaw. "This isn't usually how we operate."

"But it has been lately." Takako stepped from the shadows of the corn. "Everyone's been reacting instead of thinking. It isn't healthy."

Rushing to her, I pulled her into a hug. "Are you okay?"

She patted my cheek. "I told you I was."

"Yes, but . . ." I stepped away. "I wish you would have told me what you were up to before you'd left. We were worried."

"It was an accident," she said. "I sort of got swept into a van. And since I was there, I started talking with the people from San Adrian. It was obvious they're not happy with the situation either."

"We're not happy with San Nicholas hogging all the Halloween glory." An older, weatherbeaten man with faded red hair twisted his face in a scowl. "You don't own the pumpkin festival idea, you know."

"At least we grow our own pumpkins," Charlene said, "unlike *some* towns."

"You don't grow as much as you used to though, do you?" Farmer John asked. "Most of your pumpkins are imports."

Charlene bridled. "How *dare* you."

"Okay, okay," I said. "He actually hasn't said anything that wasn't true."

Charlene harrumphed.

"Have your towns considered working together?" Takako asked.

No one spoke.

I cleared my throat. "It's not a bad idea. Since our festivals run right after the other, we could promote them as a moving festival. Maybe do joint promotions and get more marketing bang for our buck?" And it hadn't escaped my notice that San Adrian didn't have its own pie shop. Pie Town might be able to chisel in on the San Adrian action.

Charlene and the men shuffled their feet.

"Or," Takako said, "I could go back with you to San Adrian, and we can work on alternate solutions."

"Fine," the redhead said quickly. "We'll do it." He pointed at Charlene and me. "But how do we know you two have the authority to stop the pranks or promote the festivals together?"

Charlene's mouth twisted.

"They'll listen to Charlene," I said before she could argue. "She's a respected member of the community."

"And?" Charlene prompted.

"And the best piecrust maker on the Northern California coast," I said.

Charlene sniffed. "That is true."

My muscles loosened. Was this actually going to work? Since I suspected Charlene was really one of the driving forces behind the pranks, I thought it might.

"Unless one of you jokers dropped a pumpkin on our ophthalmologist," Charlene said. "Then the deal's off."

"Why would we do that?" Red Hair asked.

"I didn't even know her," Farmer John said.

"What about the graffiti on the maze sign?" she asked.

Farmer John's mouth puckered. "That might have been a kid from our town. We'll take care of it."

"Then okay," she said. "It's a deal."

He and Charlene clasped hands.

Farmer John turned to Takako. "So, are we good?"

She nodded. "We're good."

Gordon stepped into the center of the maze. "What did I miss?"

"We're leaving." Red Hair jerked his head at the hidden exit, and the two men fled.

Gordon raised his brows. "Success?"

"I think so," I said.

"Good." He pulled me against his chest and kissed me. Frederick didn't like that, so Frederick went on the ground. The cat curled into a ball on the flattened corn leaves.

"Congratulations are in order for us both," he murmured.

Someone coughed nearby.

"Takako," Charlene said, "have I shown you this interesting feature of our corn maze . . ."

Their voices faded, and Gordon and I kissed some more.

I came up for air, weak-kneed and gasping. Gordon knew how to kiss. "From now on," I said, my hands on his broad shoulders, "I'm taking more time off. I'm also telling you everything. Even if it does make me look neurotic."

"You're not neurotic. You've worked hard to build Pie Town. And you've built a team to support you."

"And I'll let them," I said ruefully. It was time to cowgirl up and talk to Petronella. "From now on, I'm taking Tuesdays off and trusting my brilliant assistant manager to manage."

"Petronella will be thrilled. And I won't mind more quality time with you either."

"You won't?" I teased, then blinked. "Hold up. You said congratulations for us *both*. Did you catch the killer?"

"Not caught. Not yet. But I have a good idea who was responsible, and after a long conversation with the chief, he seems to agree. We've got an APB out."

"That's great, but . . ." I gnawed my bottom lip. "Alfreda may be in danger."

"The office manager? Why?"

"She may have been blackmailing the killer."

He stepped away from me. "You know who the killer is."

I glanced down at the flattened corn leaves. "Maybe. The point is, Alfreda was here, at the maze, the night I got pumpkin bombed. We were both wearing dark caps. From above, from a distance, we probably looked a lot alike. And if the person she was blackmailing—"

"The person? You're not going to say who it is, are you?"

"—if the person she was blackmailing expected her to be there, they meant to kill her." And no, I wasn't going to tell him whom I suspected. What if I was wrong?

"Alfreda was nervous," I said. "She kept looking at her watch like she had somewhere to be. What if I scared her off, and then when I went into the maze, the killer fired the cannon meaning to target Alfreda?"

"You think she's in danger."

"Worse," I said. "I think Alfreda's here."

Chapter Thirty-One

The corn maze darkened. Involuntarily, Gordon and I glanced at the sky. The moon disappeared behind a thick wave of fog.

He rubbed his temple. "If Alfreda came here to meet the killer once . . ."

"Exactly." I scanned the corn behind him. "Joy saw Alfreda and assumed she was part of our rescue party. But she's not. So what is she doing here? And where is she?"

"All right, I'm going to look for her." He pointed at Charlene and Takako, pretending to examine an ear of corn. "You three stay together." Gordon strode down the narrow shortcut leading to the barn.

Charlene cocked her head, her phone gripped in her hands. "Of course, you realize, he didn't tell us to stay *here,* only to stay together."

"If what you said is correct," Takako said, "Alfreda could be in danger."

I retrieved a sleeping Frederick from the corn leaves and clutched his limp form to my chest. "If I'm right, we all could be. Come on."

We hurried down the straight passage and into the black-painted barn.

Its high-ceilinged interior blazed with orange twinkle lights. They swagged the rafters, the wooden posts, the ticket counter.

Behind the counter, Joy looked up from her comic book. "Everything okay?" She raised her voice over the roar of the generator.

"Where exactly did you see Alfreda?" I adjusted Frederick over my shoulder. I might be morphing into a seventy-something conspiracy theorist, but at least I was warm.

"Your boyfriend asked me the same thing." Joy nodded toward the rear of the barn. "She was headed toward the pumpkin cannon."

"Then that's where Carmichael went," Charlene said, staring at her phone. "We should check somewhere else instead of covering the same ground."

"Agreed." Going in the opposite direction also meant we were less likely to run into trouble. I'd seen enough of it in the past to be okay with letting the pros handle any danger.

"Where's Marla?" Charlene glanced up from her phone's screen.

Joy laid her comic book beside the cash register. "She went with Gordon," Joy said.

"And he let her?" Charlene asked.

"Well," Joy amended, "it was more like she went *after* Gordon."

"That vamp's after him, Val." Charlene's brows skewered downward. "He's not safe."

"I'm not worried about Gordon," I said.

Takako patted my arm. "You shouldn't be. He's a keeper." She smiled bitterly. "Though I suppose you've no reason to trust my judgment. Not after . . ." She clamped her mouth shut, but I knew what she'd meant to say.

After my father.

"He's handsome and charming and fun. None of this was your fault. *None*." We'd talk later, in private, about guilt and forgiveness. But for now . . . I shook my head, fighting back a wave of raw grief. How do emotions and memories get so tangled? I'd thought I'd been busting my butt at Pie Town to honor my mother's memory. But in part, I'd been doing it to escape memories of my father.

I swallowed and turned to Joy. "If someone wanted to meet privately here, where could they go?"

"We've got some outbuildings," Joy said, "where we keep supplies, but we keep them locked. There's also the corn maze, since we're closed, but I don't know what idiot would go in there."

"Let's assume the locks on the outbuildings aren't a problem," I said, "and check there."

Joy rolled the comic book into a tube. "Suit yourself. Do you want company?"

"Maybe it's best if you stay here." Charlene didn't look up from her phone. "Man the fort."

Joy saluted with the comic book. "Will do."

We exited the barn. Fog drifted like smoke across the tops of the corn.

"Where to?" Charlene asked.

"Is the drone still flying?" I asked.

She peered at her phone screen. "I thought it might be useful, but I don't see Alfreda anywhere."

I pointed. "The sheds Joy mentioned are behind the barn, I think." And they were roughly in the direction of the pumpkin cannon. "Why don't you and Takako stay here and watch the drone?"

"Gordon told us to stay together," Takako said.

Charlene kept her gaze glued to her phone. "I'm not going to miss the action. Just steer me in the right direction."

We circled the barn, and I pointed out hazards before Charlene could trip over them. Behind the barn, three ramshackle wooden sheds tilted on the uneven ground.

"I'm flying over the cannon now," she said over the growl of the generator. "I see your detective but not Alfreda."

Takako grasped Charlene's elbow and steered her around an abandoned tire. "What about the cornfield?"

"I'm looking," she muttered, "I'm looking. It's this blasted fog. I think it's messing with the night-vision sensor."

I rattled the padlock on one of the buildings. "She's not in here."

We walked to the next. A generator grumbled inside, cables snaking to the barn. The door hung ajar. I pulled it wider and peered inside. A generator. Red, plastic gas cans. No Alfreda.

I exhaled. "Empty. Maybe third time's a charm." Or maybe Alfreda was long gone.

Takako came to walk beside me. "I overheard what you were saying to Detective Carmichael. Do you actually know who killed those optometrists?"

"I'm not sure." But in my heart, I knew. I knew because I *understood* the reason behind it all, and that understanding sickened me. I opened the door, and Charlene bumped into me from behind.

"Isn't it obvious?" Charlene asked.

"Not to me," Takako said.

"Dr. Levant's cousin," I said, "Denise Tatari."

Alfreda stared from the shadows of the ramshackle wooden shed, her oval face pale. "You shouldn't have come."

Denise stepped from the shadows. "No, you really shouldn't have." She aimed a gun at Alfreda's back.

I sucked in my breath. "Denise." Slowly, I raised my hands. I'd been right, and I hated myself for it.

Denise clucked her tongue. "Alfreda, look at all the trouble you've caused."

"It wasn't Alfreda." I tried not to stare at the gun. The gun. But the idea of it was overwhelming, all consuming. My heart thumped against my ribs, filled my ears with sound. "The police know too. They're looking for you."

"I don't believe you." She nudged Alfreda with the barrel. "Move."

Alfreda edged toward the open door.

I backed from the shed, Charlene clinging to my vest with one hand.

"Come on." I hoped Denise didn't notice my trembling hands. "You had to know it was only a matter of time before you got found out. A closed corporation only allows for thirty-five shareholders. You had way more than that. You were running a sort of pyramid scheme like in that play *The Producers*. That's what Dr. Cannon meant when I overheard him on the phone in the grocery store. You'd sold more than thirty-five shares or partnerships or whatever. You used the money from the excess shares to pay the older investors' dividends."

The skin bunched around Denise's eyes. "I had to save my company. This wasn't about greed. The software development was taking longer than I expected. If I didn't get more money to pay the engineers, everything would have fallen apart. You know what it's like, all those people depending on you."

"I . . ." I *did* know what it was like. Pie Town was more than a business, more than a livelihood. It was part of me. But to kill someone over it? Acid burned my throat. "How did Dr. Cannon figure it out?" *Stall, stall, stall.* At some point, Gordon would realize Alfreda wasn't where he'd thought she was and return to the barn.

"Tristan wasn't smart enough to realize I was talking to him from a couple aisles over."

"So," I said shakily, "you pushed the rack on top of me?"

"It was a bad decision. I'd hoped to crush him."

"You nearly killed me instead."

We stood in the open now. The fog had thickened, hugging the top of the barn.

"But you did attack me at the haunted house," I said. "And you tried to run Charlene and I off the road at Laurelynn's barn." *Gordon, see us.* "Why?"

"When I saw you in the haunted house, I panicked. I thought you were after Elon. I had to stop you."

"It just made Elon look guilty," Charlene said.

Denise's face creased in a pained look. "That's why I went after you at the pumpkin patch. I thought it would make Laurelynn look guilty. Everyone knew she hated my cousin."

Denise had been pinballing, panicked, reacting irrationally. She still was. "But Laurelynn didn't hate Kara as much as you did," I said. "What happened?"

"She had to always be so perfect," she spat. "And she never let me forget it. Things came so easily to her. She never understood what it took to build a real company."

"Then, when things started to go wrong at your company, you couldn't let it fail." Charlene tried to edge in front of me.

I blocked Charlene with my arm.

"Of course, I couldn't," Denise said. "How could I? It's my business."

Takako glided in front of me. "It's over," my stepmother said. "The police have an APB out for you."

"Then I guess I'd better buy some time," Denise said. "Into the maze, all of you."

She nudged Alfreda with the gun.

The tall woman stumbled forward with a faint cry.

We walked behind the barn toward the cornfield. "But why the pumpkin?" I asked. "Why drop one on Kara?"

"I went to the haunted house that morning to see Elon. I just wanted to see him, that's all. But Kara was there, on the street. She accused me of trying to steal her husband. I never did. Never! But she wouldn't listen. She told me she knew all about the extra shareholders and was going to expose me. There was a pitchfork nearby. I didn't think. I just used it. And then I realized what I'd done."

"That you'd murdered your cousin?" Charlene said.

"No, that I'd accidentally framed Elon. The pitchfork was from his haunted house. I couldn't let him take the blame. So, I moved her body. I put her in my pickup, but I had to get rid of her quickly. When I saw the giant pumpkins and the forklift, I realized it was the perfect spot."

"But the police found the pitchfork," I said. "They know where it came from."

"It doesn't matter." Denise's gun wobbled. "You said they know I did it. He won't be blamed. Now hurry. Get inside."

We walked into the maze.

"Keep going," she said.

"You know," I said, "that's not a bad idea. Run!"

We sprinted around a corner, taking random turns through the rustling corn. I didn't care if we got lost. I didn't care if Denise got away—Gordon would catch up with her eventually. I just didn't want to be found.

The sound of the generator faded. I stumbled to a halt, panting.

Alfreda slammed into my back, knocking me to my

hands and knees. Frederick's claws dug into my chest, and I whimpered.

"Sorry, Val." Alfreda winced and gave me a hand up. "Sorry, Frederick. I'm sorry about all of this."

Charlene snorted. "What did you think would happen when you tried to blackmail a killer?"

"Where's Takako?" I asked, anxious.

"Here." She stepped around a corner of the maze. "Who's got a phone?"

"Phone! Right!" I fumbled in my vest pocket and pulled out my phone, dialed Gordon. And for once, I got a signal.

"She's not here," he said.

"We found Denise in one of the sheds behind the barn." My words tumbled over each other. "She knows the cops are on to her. She's running, and she has a gun."

He cursed. "And Alfreda?"

"She's safe with us."

"Okay. Stay put." He hung up.

"He said to stay here, out of the way." We were safe, but nausea swam up my throat. "She killed two people for a business." I thought of all the mad things I'd done for Pie Town. About my mother's insurance money, her recipes that had gone into the pie shop. If someone tried to take it from me . . .

Charlene gripped my shoulder. "You and Denise are not the same."

"I know," I lied. But I could become her, if I wasn't careful.

So, I couldn't let that happen. I'd relax my grip on control. I'd give myself and Pie Town some breathing room. And I'd already taken the first step, telling Gordon I was handing over more management to Petronella. "I'm just worried about Gordon. She's got a gun."

Her hand squeezed. "And he knows it now."

"Right." Gordon knew what he was doing, but Denise had a gun. Anything could happen. Anything could go wrong, and my blood pulsed erratically.

"Alfreda," I said, "when I ran into you here the other night, you were waiting to meet Denise, weren't you? At ten o'clock?"

"Yes. When you showed up"—Alfreda shrugged—"I chickened out."

"You were lucky you did," I said. "She thought I was you. We were both wearing knit caps that night, and through a scope, in the dark, from a high angle, we must have looked the same."

"Through a scope?" Alfreda asked, wan.

"I was in the center of the maze, where you were supposed to be. Denise tried to kill me with the pumpkin cannon. I'm only surprised she didn't finish the job when you came to her cousin's office earlier today."

She pressed her hand to her throat. "But you turned up there too. You saved me."

Takako sniffed and frowned.

"Blackmailers rarely come to a good end," Charlene said. "And how long are we going to hide in here? Frederick's going to get cold."

"Oh. Right." I reached to lift the cat off my shoulders.

"Keep him. I've got my hands full watching the drone action." She dug into the pocket of her yellow jacket.

"Do you smell smoke?" Takako asked.

I sniffed.

Charlene pulled out her phone and fiddled with the screen. "Let's see how fast this baby . . . Oh." Her voice dropped.

"Oh, what?" I asked, alarmed.

"We need to go back."

"Not likely," Alfreda said. "Even if I wanted to, which I don't, do you have any idea where we are in this stupid maze?"

"Out of the frying pan and into the stew," Charlene said. "The cornfield's on fire."

Chapter Thirty-Two

Fire.

The acrid scent was unmistakable now, carried on a breeze that rattled the cornstalks.

"Where is it?" I pivoted, searching for a landmark and unable to get my bearings. High walls of corn hemmed us in and obscured the eastern hills, wherever they were.

Charlene studied her phone. "The flames are on the south side, by the parking lot, and moving north, toward us. We can't take the shortcut out or the regular cut for that matter."

"We need to move," Takako said.

Alfreda whimpered. "Why did I come here?"

I patted Frederick to calm the limp cat. "Okay, let's head northwest, toward the highway and away from the flames." There was another field due north of this one, and I didn't trust the fire to stick with burning corn. "Er, which way is northwest?"

Charlene bit her bottom lip. "Hold on. I need to give the drone more height . . . Too high—stupid fog. There!" She pointed. "That way."

Wordless, Takako switched on her phone's flashlight and plunged into the corn.

We followed. Stalks slapped at our faces, stinging our bare skin. We cut across the maze's paths, but we never stayed on them long.

The smell of smoke grew stronger.

Charlene paused to reorient the drone. She cursed under her breath.

"What?" I asked. "What's wrong?"

"There's another fire now," she said, "along the highway."

I swallowed, throat dry. "You mean it spread?"

"No," she said, "it looks like a second fire."

"Maybe it jumped." Alfreda's breath came in short, high-pitched gasps. "Fires can jump, can't they?"

"It doesn't matter," Takako said. "We can't go west anymore."

"There's a dirt road to the east," I said, "where the cannon is. The road forms a crescent, curving to the barn and parking lot. On the other side of the cannon it drops along the field to the north. If we hit that road, we can decide which is the best route from there."

Takako nodded. "It's as good a direction as any. Which way?"

Charlene pointed.

We jogged through the field, the corn whispering *disaster* at our panicked passage.

Alfreda stumbled and cried out.

Charlene whirled. "If you've turned your ankle, so help me we're leaving you. We've got no time for damsels in distress, especially when they're blackmailers."

Alfreda straightened, wincing. "No, I can go on."

"Good," Charlene said.

We huffed forward.

I tried to ignore the thickening smoke. "How did you

find out about Denise's scam?" I asked Alfreda. A cornstalk whacked me in the face, and I rubbed my cheek.

"I was helping Kara with all sorts of financial issues, including her taxes." Alfreda panted. "She was a big investor in Denise's company. Kara was unhappy with what she thought were low returns. I tried to explain the returns were actually pretty good for a new business, but she wouldn't believe me. Kara was insulting, so I decided to prove her wrong."

We emerged on another path in the maze.

Charlene wheezed and braced her hands on her knees.

My gut clenched with worry. "How are you doing?" Eyes streaming, I laid my hand on her back.

Charlene coughed. "It could be worse."

"How?" I pressed a hand to the stitch in my side and tried not to inhale the burning smoke.

"Marla could be here." She straightened and examined her phone. "We're off target. We've got to head that way." She pointed.

Charlene was tiring, her steps slowing. I kept a hand near her elbow, in case she stumbled. Charlene was tough, but I didn't think she'd be able to take much more of this.

"So, you decided to learn more about Denise's company," I said to Alfreda. "Then what?"

"It's a small town," she said. "The more people I talked to, the more people I realized were investors. The numbers were easily over thirty-five, the maximum for that type of corporation."

Covering my nose with my sweater sleeve, I shoved through the corn. "And you knew there was a con."

"No," Alfreda said, "not right away. Just because she's got more investors than the state allows doesn't mean she was conning the investors. It might have been an administrative error. But I told Kara. That's when she fired me."

"For what?" Takako asked. "Giving her bad news?"

"She was furious I'd been investigating her cousin. She told me I was nosy and untrustworthy, and she'd never asked me to do it. It wasn't fair! I was only telling her the truth. I deserved a reward, not to be fired."

"But why didn't you come forward when Dr. Levant was killed?" Takako asked.

"For all I knew," Alfreda said, "Elon had done it. I mean, it's always the spouse, right? And I *did* tell someone."

I groaned. "Tristan Cannon." A sudden burst of anger dizzied me. If only she'd told the police, hadn't been so damned greedy, he might have survived.

"Tristan deserved to know. He was an investor too."

"And then he was murdered," Charlene rasped, "and you still didn't tell the police."

"Denise tried to frame me with that paperweight!"

"How did she get it?" I asked, thrusting a cornstalk aside.

"I'm not sure. I keep a key under my front mat. She might have found it."

A gust of smoke rolled through the corn.

"So, she tries to frame you," I said, coughing, "and instead of telling the cops, you tried blackmail." I shoved a cornstalk aside and let it go too quickly. It struck Alfreda.

"Ow!"

I looked over my shoulder. "Sorry," I said, insincere.

"I'd been fired." She pushed forward. "This was all Kara and Denise's fault. I deserved—" Her expression shifted. "I . . . deserved to know the truth. It wasn't really blackmail. It was just a ruse. I thought I could flush her out."

"Liar!" Charlene shook her finger.

"You can't prove anything," Alfreda said.

"When Denise is caught," I ground out, "and Gordon

will catch her, she'll tell the police about your attempted blackmail."

"She's a killer." Alfreda shrugged. "Who'll believe her?"

Sirens wailed in the distance.

"We should leave you in this field." Charlene's bellow twisted into a cough.

Alfreda's eyes widened and teared up. She blinked rapidly. "You can't!"

"We should leave you," Charlene said, hurrying onward, "but we won't, because we have a code." She checked her phone and pointed. "That way."

We jogged through the corn.

My lungs strained. Was the snapping and crackling of the cornstalks fire or the sound of our passage?

The four of us burst onto a curved road.

Charlene bent, one hand to her chest.

On my shoulder, Frederick stirred and emitted a concerned meow.

I felt the blood drain from my face. "Charlene!"

Takako and I hurried to the older woman.

"What's going on?" I asked. "What are you feeling?"

"I'm fine, dammit." She swatted our hands away. "Just a little winded. I knew I should have taken up martial arts instead of yoga." She drew a long breath, coughed, and stood. "Gimme Frederick."

I handed her the cat.

She coiled him around her neck. "Where's Alfreda?"

We looked around.

Aside from the three of us, the road was empty.

Takako paled. "Did we leave her in the field?"

"No," I said. "She was here, on the road. I'm sure of it."

"She's running," Charlene said. "But she won't go

far." She skimmed her fingers across the phone's screen. "Got her."

My insides knotted. "Where is she?"

"Around that bend." Charlene motioned down the road. "She's heading northwest."

"Okay," I said. "She's an adult, and she's safe for now. As far as I'm concerned, the police can deal with her. What's our best exit?" I asked Charlene.

"The fire's by the barn. But there are fire trucks there, in the parking lot. I say we follow the road back toward them. Oh. The barn's smoking."

"Smoking? The barn was damaged?" I'd completely forgotten about Joy, and I pulled my phone from my pocket. There were three missed calls from Gordon. I called him, got voice mail, and rang Joy.

"Yes," she said, unflappable as ever.

"Joy, it's Val. Are you okay?"

"I'm fine. The barn needs a new roof."

"Thank God. Not about the barn. About you." I covered the phone with one hand. "She's okay."

Charlene gave me two thumbs-up.

"Where are you?" Joy asked.

All I saw was dark and smoke and fog. "We're on the road to . . ."

"The pumpkin cannon," Charlene said. "Tell her Alfreda's done a runner."

"Right," I said. "Joy, is Gordon there?"

"He looks busy."

Gordon was okay. Weak with relief, I pressed one hand to my eyes. "Can you tell him Alfreda took off? She's on the same road we are, but headed in the opposite direction."

A glimmer of orange limned the fog like an outraged sunset. Then the glow faded to black.

"The firemen have everything under control," Joy said. "I'm sure she'll be fine."

"That's not what I'm worried about. Gordon will understand."

"Roger." She hung up.

"Well?" Charlene asked.

"The barn roof took some damage, but Joy is fine, and the fire is under control."

Takako's shoulders slumped. "What a relief."

We walked at a more relaxed pace down the road.

"You didn't have to make yourself a hostage," I said. "It wasn't your fault Frank left."

"Intellectually, I know it was Frank's fault. But the signs were all there that something wasn't right, that he wasn't being honest about something. I just didn't want to see them. And because of me, your family was destroyed."

But a new one had been created. I had a brother. "My mother threw him out because of his involvement with certain, um, criminals. He didn't leave. He was pushed."

Takako stopped in the road. Soot smeared her face. "She did?"

"She kicked him to the curb. She didn't know about you." I wasn't a hundred percent sure of the last bit. But I was sure enough, and Takako needed to hear it.

"Then I didn't break up their marriage?"

"No."

She threw her arms around me. "Oh, thank God. This has been . . . You have no idea how much this has . . . I haven't talked to Doran about this yet."

"I won't say anything."

Charlene clapped her shoulder. "Don't you worry. Val's good people. She can keep a secret, and so can I."

I called Gordon again.

"Val!" Anxiety roughened his voice. "Where are you?"

"Safe. We're on the road by the pumpkin cannon."

"Thank God. When I saw the fire, I thought you might have been—"

"In it?" I loosed a quavering laugh. "Not quite. But we lost Alfreda. Not in the field. She knows she's in trouble for trying to blackmail Denise. As soon as we reached the road, she headed in the other direction."

"Don't worry about Alfreda."

"Did you—?"

"We have Denise."

We passed the unmanned cannon and headed toward the barn. Coils of smoke twined from its peaked roof.

The three of us made our way through the outbuildings and to the parking lot.

Gordon paced beside his gray sedan. He gestured roughly at Chief Shaw.

It was a moment I probably shouldn't interrupt, but pent-up adrenaline flooded my system. I raced to him on wobbly legs. "Gordon!"

He looked up, said something to Shaw, and in two strides he was gripping my shoulders. Laughing unevenly, Gordon hauled me into a rough embrace. "You had to be in that damned field. Where else would you be?"

"You got Denise?"

"I caught her setting a fire by the highway. She was using gas from the generator." His face darkened. "Why were you still in the field? I was sure you wouldn't stay after I'd left you."

"Denise drove us in there. I thought she was just buying time for a clean getaway. And she had a gun."

Gordon's jaw hardened. "She tried to kill you. I never should have—"

"Oh, Detective!" Marla waved and swanned over to us. "I hate to break up this little reunion—"

"I told you to go home." He frowned.

Charlene stormed to our group. "For Pete's sake, they're having a moment. Leave the kids alone!"

"I *tried* to go home." Marla braced her hands on her hips. "But then that *stupid* receptionist ran out in front of me—"

"Office manager!" Charlene said.

I gasped. "Alfreda?"

Marla rolled her eyes. "Alfreda's fine. But you wouldn't *believe* the caterwauling. I had to put her in the back of my Mercedes and promise to take her to the hospital. But the road's blocked and there are all those lovely firefighters and paramedics *here*." She laid a hand on Gordon's broad chest and batted her eyelashes. "Can you be a dear and take care of her for me?"

"Do you mean to say, you've just captured a fugitive blackmailer?" Gordon asked. "With your car?"

Charlene brushed a fleck of ash off her sleeve. "She's an associate Baker Street Baker, you know."

Chapter Thirty-Three

Charlene's doorbell trilled. She peered through a gap in the drapes and cackled. "Remember the drill—"

"Yeah, yeah," I said. "Distract them with candy while you scare them from behind." Normally, I was against terrifying children. But tonight was Halloween, and all bets were off.

Bowl of candy in hand, I opened the door.

A half-dozen ghosts and goblins raised plastic pumpkins and pillowcases. "Trick or treat!"

"Happy Halloween! You all look great." I dumped candy into the sacks. One thing I'd say about Charlene, she was generous when it came to Halloween treats. I handed out full-sized candy bars plus smaller candies as accessories.

Silent as a vampire, the pumpkin drone lowered behind the children. Candlelight flickered from the villainous jack-o'-lantern. Because the drone itself was black, the jack-o'-lantern appeared to be floating in midair.

It was seriously creepy.

"Thank you," the kids caroled.

So sweet. So innocent.

They turned and shrieked at the drone.

I chuckled. "It's only a—"

An unholy groan emerged from the jack-o'-lantern's mouth.

The children's squeals turned to genuine screams of terror.

Escape blocked by drone and porch railing, the trick-or-treaters stormed through the doorway, knocking me flat.

Candy flew across Charlene's faded carpet. A panicked ghoul stepped on my midsection.

"Wheeeeee!" Charlene cackled, dipping and bobbing the drone. "Happy Halloween, jerks!"

I wheezed. "Eeep."

Charlene strolled to the entryway, phone in hand, and chuckled. "Haven't you ever seen a pumpkin drone?"

She demonstrated how to work the device. Soon they were happily buzzing other trick-or-treaters. Superheroes and villains screamed down the sidewalks.

We only removed the kids from Charlene's house when the next gang of candy hunters arrived. By this point, the entire street was aware of the drone, so their reaction wasn't quite so hysterical.

I handed out candy and shut the door. "Small flaw in your plan."

"Where? I haven't got this much screaming since my husband built that haunted house in our yard. Now *that* was a Halloween."

And my getting trampled was a small price to pay. I sighted a stray candy bar beneath an end table and dropped it into the bowl. "I guess all's well that ends well."

My phone rang. I whipped it from my pocket and checked the number. It wasn't Gordon.

"Ray?" I asked. "What's up?"

"Hey," the engineer said, "I had that pumpkin Charlene gave me tested. It's pesticide-free."

"It is? Thanks!" I didn't really think he'd be able to pull that off. It looked like Kara really had started that rumor out of nothing.

People are nuts. Some delightfully nuts, like Charlene. But others . . .

"Need anything else?" he asked. "I need to keep my associate membership with the Baker Street Bakers active."

"Don't worry. You're good through at least next year. I'll talk to you later."

We signed off.

"Laurelynn's pumpkins are organic," I said.

"Kara was lying about the pesticides," Charlene said. "I'm guessing that's because she knew about Elon's feelings for Laurelynn."

"You're probably right."

The doorbell rang.

"Hurry," Charlene whispered. "Get in place, get in place!"

I gave her a minute to fly her drone into position, then opened the door.

Gordon stood on the porch, a flat, rectangular package beneath one arm. "Happy Halloween, you two." He stepped inside and drew me in for a kiss.

Charlene's drone let out a ghastly wail.

Gordon cocked a brow and glanced over my shoulder. "Flying a pumpkin without a license?"

"It's a jack-o'-lantern," Charlene said loftily. "And licenses are for suckers."

"I'm just glad she hasn't lured you into another Bigfoot hunt," he murmured into my hair.

"There's always Christmas," I whispered back. We'd probably be staking out Santa Claus.

"What's the word on Alfreda?" Charlene asked.

"Alfreda?" he asked. "I thought you'd be more concerned with Denise."

"Well," Charlene said, "I assumed you'd be prosecuting Denise for murder."

"The DA is. Forensics found one of Denise's hairs in Alfreda's apartment. Alfreda's neighbor says he saw Denise lurking the day Tristan was killed. We're assuming that's when Denise stole the paperweight. The pieces are coming together, but we have a lot of work to do collecting evidence."

"What about all the people who invested in her company?" I perched on the arm of the leather couch.

"The forensic accountants are figuring that out," he said. "I don't know what's going to happen."

"At least Marla didn't invest," I said. She didn't have the money to lose. But who in San Nicholas did? The investors I'd met hadn't exactly been wealthy, and I worried about the aftermath.

"Marla will land on her feet." Charlene peered through the curtains at the street. "She always does. I wish Alfreda *had* sued."

Alfreda had threatened a lawsuit after Marla had hit her with the Mercedes. Luckily for Marla, the crash-scene investigators had pinned the blame on Alfreda. With the threat of the suit hanging over her head, Marla had been surprisingly quiet about her role in "apprehending" the blackmailer.

"Have you heard if the prosecutor is going after Alfreda for blackmail?" Charlene asked.

"They're still arguing over whether they can make it stick," he said. "They're also looking at charges for interfering in an investigation. Alfreda withheld evidence from the police and lied about it during her interview."

Charlene nodded wisely. "Interfering in an investigation is a serious offense."

And one we regularly skated on the wrong side of. I smothered a guilty smile.

"So, what's in the package?" Charlene asked.

He handed it to me. "For surviving your first pumpkin festival."

Perplexed, I tore the brown paper wrapping. Cat. Barn. Pumpkins. It was the painting I'd coveted, and I gasped. "How did you know?"

"Know what?"

"That I wanted this painting?"

His cheeks reddened. "I didn't. I just figured . . . I mean your house is so small, but I thought there might be room for something on the wall."

"It's perfect," I said. "You're perfect. Thank you."

"Should have got her the T-shirt," Charlene said. "It would have been cheaper."

"I hear Petronella's going to be managing Pie Town on Tuesdays," Gordon said. "And by coincidence, I've got next Tuesday off."

I slid my arms around his waist. "Do you now? I can think of a few things we might do."

"Cool it, lovebirds. Or get a—" Charlene hissed. Dropping the curtains, she drew away from the window. "Brinks, I've got you now," she growled softly. "Scuffing my fence. Scaring my cat. Egging my house."

Gordon and I glanced at each other.

"Charlene," I said, "he's a kid."

"That's no excuse."

"If he runs into the street," Gordon says, "and gets hit by a car—"

"That's not the plan." She stared out the window, her shoulders hunched. "Come on . . . a *little* closer."

"What are you doing?" I strode to the window and yanked back the curtains.

"Now!" she shouted.

Something round and white bulleted downward. It slapped atop the head of a freckled kid in a THIS IS MY COSTUME T-shirt. There was an explosion of water, and he shrieked.

"Ooooh." I dropped the curtain shut. She'd water-ballooned him. Via drone strike.

"Gotcha!" Charlene raced to the door and threw it open. "It's karma! You're lucky I didn't egg you, you little—"

I tugged her inside and slammed the door. "Charlene, that's—that's—" I looked helplessly at Gordon.

He bent over an end table and studied the sleeping Frederick. "Didn't see it," he muttered. "I didn't see a thing. It didn't happen. There are all sorts of things flying around tonight. A water balloon could have come from anywhere. Teenagers. Birds."

"I think he's snapped," Charlene said in a low voice.

"I'd better take him home," I said and led him onto the porch. "I'm sorry about Charlene. I had no idea—"

"I've been trying to nail that kid for vandalism all year, and she just . . ." He shook himself and braced his hands on my shoulders. "I just realized something."

"Oh?"

"In forty years, that will be you."

"Possibly." If I was lucky. "It wouldn't be such a bad thing, would it?"

He smiled. "I'm counting on it."

VAL'S PUMPKIN BREAD

Ingredients

   1⅓ cup flour
   ¾ tsp. baking powder
   1 tsp. baking soda
   ⅛ tsp. salt
   1 tsp. cinnamon
   ½ tsp. nutmeg
   ⅓ cup shortening
   1⅓ cup sugar
   ½ tsp. vanilla
   2 eggs
   1 cup cooked and mashed pumpkin (or canned)
   ⅓ cup cooking sherry
   1 cup chopped walnuts

Preheat oven to 350 degrees.

Stir together flour, baking powder, baking soda, salt, cinnamon, and nutmeg. In a medium mixing bowl, cream shortening, sugar, and vanilla. Add two eggs to the mixing bowl, one at a time, beating thoroughly after each addition. Stir in pumpkin. Add dry ingredients and then cooking sherry. Fold in nuts.

Pour into 9 x 5 loaf pan.

Bake uncovered in preheated oven for 60 minutes. Use a toothpick to test for doneness.

Can't get enough of the antics of
Val, Charlene, and the Pie Town Crew?

Don't miss the rest of the series,
available now from

Kirsten Weiss and
Kensington Books,

wherever books are sold!

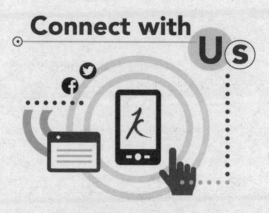